For my mother.

About the Author

Catriona King trained as a doctor and a police Forensic Medical Examiner in London, where she worked for many years. She worked closely with the Metropolitan Police on several occasions. In recent years, she has returned to live in Belfast.

She has written since childhood; fiction, fact and reporting.

'*The Coercion Key*' is the seventh novel in the Craig Crime Series. It follows Superintendent Marc Craig and his team through the streets of Northern Ireland investigating a series of apparent suicides.

Book eight in the Craig Crime Series, 'The Careless Word' will be released soon. Book nine is currently in edits.

Acknowledgements

My thanks to Northern Ireland for providing the inspiration for my books.

I would like to thank Crooked Cat Publishing for being so unfailingly supportive and cheerful.

My thanks also to Andrew Angel for beta-reading this book.

And I would like to thank all of the police officers that I have ever worked with, anywhere, for their unfailing professionalism, wit and compassion.

Catriona King
Belfast, August 2014

Also by Catriona King

The Craig Crime Series

A Limited Justice
The Grass Tattoo
The Visitor
The Waiting Room
The Broken Shore
The Slowest Cut
The Coercion Key
The Careless Word

Discover more at: **www.catrionakingbooks.com**
Engage with the author: **catriona_books@yahoo.co.uk**

The Coercion Key

Chapter One

Belfast. Wednesday, 2nd April 2014. 10 p.m.

It was a long way to fall and it was going to hurt; hurt like hell. But the fall that wasn't at his feet would be even greater and take longer than he could bear. Drawn out for months of computer seizures and looks of disgust, then court hearings, prison rape and his name on a register for the rest of his life.

Nelson Warner shook his head and gazed down at the River Lagan, wondering how cold it was and if the tales of it being haunted by sailors who'd drowned there would prove true. It looked forbidding; the April wind whipping its waves into tall peaks that warned off even the gulls overhead. He gripped the balcony railing hard, whitening his knuckles until they hurt, and marvelled at the flock of starlings swooping above the Albert Bridge. They did it every evening, performing their perfectly synchronised dance. A natural wonder, like so much else in the world. Such a pity that he'd always focused on other, less savoury things.

He cautiously mounted the frail wicker chair, part of a set that his sister had bought him, so that he could sit out on his balcony and admire the view. He teetered inelegantly for a moment, laughing at his poor balance; it had never been very good, no career in gymnastics ahead for him. Glancing back towards the living room, at the thing that had forced him to this point, Warner nodded in acknowledgement, accepting that they'd won.

Then he jumped.

The Lab. Friday, 5 p.m.

"Of course, you realise it's out of your hands now, don't you?"

John Winter didn't answer, so Craig continued, on a roll.

"It'll be endless hotel brochures, colour schemes and wedding lists from now until the big day."

Craig laughed, seeing his friend's terrified expression. "There's no escape and nothing you suggest will ever be right. So just smile and say 'yes dear' to whatever you're asked; that's my advice."

John tapped his computer screen into sleep mode and glared at his friend. They were sitting in his small office in the pathology lab having a rare relaxing drink after work. Rare in the sense that it normally occurred in Bar Red in the centre of town; there was nothing rare about the amount of whisky they were knocking back. His own consumption had dropped slightly since his engagement to Natalie. He wasn't sure why. She drank like a fish, so it wasn't as if he was marrying Sister Mary of the Abstentionists who expected him to take the pledge. It was more a sense that he didn't need to get drunk to have a good time anymore, when he could have it just by being with her. Craig's drinking, on the other hand, was becoming an issue.

John gazed through doctor's eyes at his unfeasibly handsome friend and wondered what was going through his head. He rarely looked at Craig, really looked that was, in the way that you look at someone when you don't know them at all. But now he did and what he saw would have made any sane woman happy. Six feet plus of tanned, muscled male with a handsome face and navy eyes so blue that they almost looked unnatural. Craig also had brains, a loving family and a job that he excelled at, so why did John feel unhappiness oozing from his every pore?

Craig smiled broadly, making a lie of John's assessment. If he'd been able to read his friend's mind he mightn't have been grinning.

"What are you staring at me like that for? You know I'm right. You proposed marriage and now Natalie's planning her wedding, not yours. All that'll be required of you for the next however long is to nod, say 'yes dear', and turn up on the day. So you'd better set a date. The sooner you do the sooner your torture will be over."

"Mmm…"

"I hope that was an mmm… of agreement. Because you know that I'm right."

John realised that he was still staring at his friend and changed the subject to other things. "I might have a case for you."

Craig leaned forward eagerly. "Might have? You mean you have a body but you're not sure that it's dead." He laughed at the ridiculousness of the idea. "Or it's definitely dead but you're not sure it's murder."

"The latter."

John puffed out his cheeks and frowned as he realised something. He mightn't just have one body for Craig, he might have several. He crossed to a cabinet in one corner of the office and started rifling through the top drawer. After a moment he tutted loudly and closed it, yanking out the one underneath. He repeated his search several times until he had three files in his hand, then he sat back down and tapped the cover of the top file triumphantly.

Craig had watched the performance hopefully. They'd been quiet since the Carragher case in February, apart from a couple of domestic murders. He hadn't really minded. The Carragher case had opened a huge can of worms, with the discovery of bodies buried at two different sites in Newcastle and Bangor. Twenty-five bodies in all; one adult female and twenty-four children. They already had Ryan Carragher, their only living suspect, in custody, so the past eight weeks had just been hard graft, wrapping it all up for court. But they were almost there now. Time for a new case.

Craig set his whisky glass on the desk and waited for John to start. When he didn't he prompted him encouragingly.

"OK. Let me guess. This case that you weren't sure was a murder has now turned into three that might be. Yes?"

John startled, wondering how Craig had landed on the exact number, then he realised that he had three files on his desk. He nodded thoughtfully as Craig continued.

"And you're not sure why you think they might be murder, except that your gut instinct is saying so."

"Scientists don't believe in gut instinct."

"You do, because you've seen it in action so many times." Craig held out his hand for the files. "If I'm right, not only do you think you may have three murders on your hands, but you think that they might be linked in some way?"

John nodded again, but instead of handing the files to his friend, he left them firmly on his desk.

"I want to go through them one by one. OK?"

Craig shrugged and reached for the whisky bottle to top himself up. He caught John's disapproving glance and smiled. "OK. Get it over with, John."

John's eyes widened innocently. "What?"

"You know what. The lecture. No, wait, I'll give it myself." Craig turned to the side as if he was talking to someone else.

"Marc, you're drinking too much." He turned his head again, replying. "Yes, I know." He swapped sides again. "Well why? And what are you going to do about it?"

He was just about to turn his head again when John banged the desk in irritation. "You can take the piss all you like, Marc, but it's true. You are drinking too much and I am worried about you."

The expression on Craig's face changed from amusement to

hostility, and then to defiance. John sat back, astounded.

"I haven't seen that face since you were sixteen and one of the masters at school tried to tell you what to do."

Craig realised how he must have looked and laughed so hard that it washed all his attempts at anger away. John joined in. When their laughter tailed off he stared at his friend again.

"It's true and you know it."

Craig nodded grudgingly and screwed the top back on the bottle, setting it to one side. He walked to the percolator against the wall and poured a coffee instead, saying something so softly that John strained to hear. John could only make out one word: alone.

"You're spending too much time alone? Or carrying too much responsibility alone?"

Craig smiled at how well John knew him, but then thirty-odd year's acquaintance will do that. He sat down again and said one more word. "Time." Then he reached over and tapped the top of John's files. John knew the conversation had gone as far as Craig would allow, but he had all the information he needed. Craig was lonely and he was going to do something about it.

John opened the top file and scanned the summary sheet then he shot Craig a puzzled look.

"These three cases came over my desk in the last six weeks and at first glance, actually even at second glance, they all seemed like suicides. The scenes fitted, the methods were the usual…"

"How did they kill themselves?"

"All differently. One was a hanging, one an overdose and the latest jumped off his balcony into the Lagan two nights ago and drowned."

Craig nodded. They were all common methods of suicide. About the only ones missing were slashing your wrists or a bullet to the head.

"Who did the investigations?"

"I post-mortemed the last two and Mike Augustus did the first. There was nothing to suggest foul play in any of them. I spoke to the coroner and the first couple were declared suicide. But..."

Craig leaned forward eagerly. "You're not sure. Why?"

John screwed up his face for a moment and then shook his head. "I don't know. I can't put my finger on it. It's just..."

"Gut instinct?"

John laughed loudly then shrugged. "OK. Maybe. Even though I definitely don't believe in it. I'm sure there's something odd going on here though. Would you..."

"In a heartbeat. We've pretty much finished preparing the Carragher prosecution; we can't do anything more until we get a court date. And Liam's bored."

"Which means he's disrupting the whole squad?"

"Yup."

Liam Cullen was the squad's Detective Chief Inspector and Craig's right-hand-man. He was a brilliant street detective with a true copper's nose. He was also known throughout the force for his sense of humour and tendency to say outrageous things. Both made him a familiar target for the political correctness brigade. When Liam was on form he made the worst case easier to bear, but when he was bored he behaved like a recalcitrant teenager. Right now Liam was bored.

Craig had been about to suggest that he took a holiday, but a new case would be even better. He grinned, feeling his own enthusiasm grow. He poured them both fresh coffees and propped his feet up on John's desk.

"OK, John. Let's take it from the top. Tell me about the first death."

Chapter Two

"Everyone drop whatever you're doing. We have a case."

Craig scanned the Murder Squad's open-plan floor, expecting a flurry of activity. Instead he was greeted by two empty chairs where Annette and Jake, his Inspector and Sergeant, should have been, and a paper plane flying between Liam and Davy Walsh, their analyst. He was just about to start shouting when the silence was broken by the huskiest voice in the thirteen-floor Coordinated Crime Unit.

"Easter fever. You'll have to shout louder than that if you want to get through to them."

Craig turned to face Nicky Morris, his P.A., and his eyes were quickly drawn to her feet. She was wearing over-the-knee silver boots that looked like they were made of tin-foil! His gaze travelled to her face, registering a purple cat-suit on the way. To say that Nicky's fashion sense was 'out there' would be an understatement, but Craig knew better than to comment, even with a pointed glance.

"Easter's not for another ten days. Where are Annette and Jake?"

Nicky stared at the ceiling, as if she was trying to remember something, then she nodded. "Annette's taking a few hours' personal time, remember? You signed it off weeks ago. And Jake, well I don't know where Jake is, but it's not even nine o'clock yet."

Just as she said his name Jake McLean appeared through the floor's glass double-doors. He caught Craig's eye and strolled over to him innocently. "Did you want me, sir?"

"Yes. I want all of you." Craig waved towards the improvised flight-path that Davy and Liam were making of the floor. "Grab those two and come into my office. We have a case."

Two minutes later they were crammed into Craig's small corner office and the coffee was being poured. Liam leaned his six-feet-six frame against the back wall and folded his arms. His pose was bored and his expression matched.

"What sort of case, boss? Only if it's not urgent I was going to ask for a couple of weeks off, seeing as it's Easter next weekend."

Craig tapped the files in front of him, looking thoughtful. He couldn't say that it wasn't urgent; after all three people were dead. But then again, was it really urgent, when they weren't even sure that it was murder? His gut instantly dismissed the question. It was murder all right; they just had to prove it. He turned to Liam.

"We're not on call next weekend so you'll all get Good Friday and the Monday off. I've no objection if you want to tag on some holiday either side, Liam."

Liam squinted at him. 'No objection'? That sounded suspiciously like he'd be missing something if he did. He broke with the habit of a lifetime and pulled up a chair to sit down. Davy did the same, following his lead. Davy was still at the stage of hero-worshipping detectives and mimicking their every move. Someday soon he'd stop doing it, but for now it amused them all.

Craig took a sip of coffee and started. "Right. John brought three cases to my attention on Friday because he felt uneasy about them. In a moment I'll tell you why. But first, you need to know that this isn't a straightforward murder case."

Liam interrupted. "What is it then, boss? 'Cos it's not like we need to go looking for work."

The others nodded, thinking of the twenty-five buried bodies they'd discovered two months before, not to mention the quadruple murder that had led to them. Craig stilled their growing murmur with a glance and turned back to the files. He tapped the top folder.

"These are three cases of death, the first two apparently by suicide. At least that's what the pathology and forensics showed and what the coroner was quick to agree."

Liam leaned forward to interrupt again but Craig shook his head and carried on. "John got the third case last Wednesday. On first impressions it seemed like another suicide, except that he doesn't think it was and neither do I."

Davy signalled to interrupt. "Even if they killed themselves and there's nothing to s...say otherwise?"

Davy was a brilliant analyst. Far too brilliant for what he was paid, but he loved the work, especially the detecting side. He was also shy, but not as shy as he'd been when he'd joined the squad two years before. As his confidence had grown so had his dry sense of humour, and his stutter, once so strong on 's' and 'w', had diminished; until now it had almost disappeared.

"It's a valid question, Davy. I'll answer it once I've outlined the cases." Craig spread the files across the desk and opened the first.

"OK. Jonathan McCafferty. Forty-five years old, divorced, father of three small children. He was the manager of the Malone Road branch of NIBank, earning over one hundred and fifty thousand pounds per year. He hanged himself at the beginning of March and left a note saying that he was depressed and had nothing to live for."

He opened the second file. "Diana Rogan. A thirty-three-year-old married mother of two, aged eight and four years old. She worked as a middle manager at a company in town. Mrs Rogan killed herself eight weeks ago with an overdose of Paracetamol, leaving a note saying she was depressed and had nothing to live for."

Craig turned to the third. "This Wednesday evening fifty-six-year-old Nelson Warner's body was fished out of the Lagan. He drowned after he apparently jumped from the balcony of his apartment overlooking the river. When the police arrived they found a chair pulled up to the balcony's edge and a note saying that he was depressed and had nothing to live for. He was a retired stockbroker who had been married for thirty-five years. And he'd just booked a cruise with his wife to celebrate their wedding anniversary in June."

Liam removed the pen he'd been chewing from his mouth and shrugged. "People kill themselves every day, boss. And none of them ever look as if they have enough reason to do it."

Craig nodded. "That's true. But when people are lonely, in debt or a hundred other situations, we accept that it might have felt that bad to them. But not these people. These people have nothing in their lives to explain their actions and their families are devastated. So 'why?' would be my first question. The second is the wording of their suicide notes. It's identical for each one. Not an apostrophe out of place. 'I am depressed and have nothing to live for.'"

Jake interjected. "But isn't that pretty standard? I mean no-one suicidal writes a note that says they're happy, do they?"

Craig shook his head. "No they don't. But unfortunately Liam and I have both seen too many suicide notes and they're rarely as neat and logical as this."

Liam nodded grudgingly, conceding the point. "That's true, lad. They're usually messy or rambling, and there's almost always something personal in them. Something that they wanted to tell someone but never did; like, I'm sorry I cheated on you, or I love you." He turned to Craig. "Was there anything like that?"

Craig slipped three photocopied notes from the files and everyone leaned forward for a closer look. Nicky had entered a moment before with fresh coffee. Now she stood behind Craig, peeping over his shoulder and teetering on her five-inch heels.

On the desk in front of Craig were three sheets of A4 paper, each bearing the hand-printed words 'I am depressed and have nothing to live for'. Nothing else. Not a kiss or a name. Nicky gasped. It was wrong. More wrong than suicide normally was.

Even Liam's eyes widened. It was like nothing he'd ever seen before. He gestured at the notes.

"Is that definitely their handwriting?

Craig nodded. "Des says yes. He checked handwriting samples for all three. The victims definitely wrote the notes."

"You want us to look at possible connections, backgrounds, phones and computers, boss? The works?"

Craig scanned their faces and saw that everyone agreed. They definitely had a case.

Chapter Three

Victoria Linton prided herself on being precise in everything she did. Precise and logical. If she'd had a hero, it would probably have been Mr Spock. The Star Trek box sets had been her guilty pleasure for years. Except that she didn't believe in hero worship. It was juvenile, self-indulgent and worse of all, illogical.

She brushed down her navy suit and assessed her appearance in the long mirror she'd purchased just for that purpose. Shoes polished; check. Skirt a sensible length; check. Long curly hair swept back in a tight chignon and pinned into submission at the nape of her neck; check. Make-up discreet and up to the standard that market research showed optimised a woman's earning power in the workplace; check, check, check. She was ready.

Ready for another day spent shuffling paper and working out the best way to prosecute her case. Another day sitting in her plush air-conditioned office and lunching in the club with the rest of the boys. Ready in fact for another day spent being one of them, all semblance of her female softness and compassion stripped away. There was no place in the law for emotion. She'd heard it every day at law school and every day since she'd become a barrister. Now she actually believed it. That would be her mistake.

***

Docklands C.C.U. Monday, 1 p.m.

Craig gazed out the window of his tenth floor office and wondered what to do about his problem. John was right, he was drinking too much. He knew why; he was lonely. What he didn't know was what to do about it.

He stared out at the bright spring day, watching how the sun lit up the Harland and Wolff cranes up-river. It made them embody their nicknames, Samson and Goliath, and become two yellow giants instead of just bits of steel. He knew it was fanciful but that had never stopped his day-dreams before.

Craig tried to imagine them having a conversation; what would they say? They should have plenty to talk about after presiding over their small river kingdom for forty years; watching ships being built and launched and bombs detonating in the streets below. They'd seen bad fashion and even worse haircuts, watched couples courting on the river bank and buildings rising around them, their architecture echoing Belfast's sea-faring past. With nautical names, and chimneys and roofs shaped like parts of a ship.

Samson and Goliath had seen it all. The rowers on a Sunday morning and the drunken youths at night. The starlings swooping over the Albert Bridge at sunset and the swans and seals that swam their way to parts of the river where they shouldn't have been. Craig smiled to himself. What a chat they could have; him and the Lagan's two old men. Maybe they'd tell him to stop drinking so much as well.

He was still imagining the exchange when his desk phone rang, disrupting his fantasy. He reached back over his shoulder for the receiver.

"Craig."

Normally that one word would have been sufficient to start a conversation about work. His team knew who he was, as did anyone in the force who was calling the Murder Squad. He'd bargained without it being an outside call.

"Pay attention, Superintendent Craig."

The man's voice was strong and local with an undertone that Craig couldn't nail down. But Craig recognised its intent and it wasn't good. He spun his chair round and strode, still holding the phone, to his office door, yanking it open and signalling Nicky to trace the call. The voice chuckled quietly, sending a shiver down his spine. He knew exactly what Craig had just done.

"Trace away, Mr Craig. It will dead-end somewhere in the United States. Now listen."

"What do you want?"

Not 'who are you?' or 'where are you calling from?' Those questions would have been a waste of breath. Anyone who was calling through a re-routed line was never going to give his name. But the man had called for a reason, so Craig cut straight to the point. The voice laughed again, admiringly this time.

"Very good. I'd heard you were clever. Well, be clever now and listen. You have three cases in front of you and you think that you have a puzzle to solve."

The voice paused as if waiting for a reply, but Craig hadn't heard a question, not one he was going to answer anyway. After a moment's silence the man carried on. As he spoke Craig heard his words, but he was listening for so much more. An accent, a background noise, some quirk that would give him away. Craig listened hard and heard it all.

"I won't insult you by saying that there's no puzzle here, Craig. And I won't say I expect you to stop investigating and back off. You would see both those things as a challenge and I don't have time for games. What I will say is simply this. Hunt me and I will hunt you, Mr Craig. Your team, your family and everyone you love. I have nothing to lose. You've already seen what I can do, be careful that I don't do it to you."

Then there was silence. No sound of the call being cut and no dialling tone, but the man had gone, Craig was sure of that. He dropped the receiver and was at Nicky's desk in a second, lifting her back-up phone.

"Switchboard? It's Marc Craig from the Murder Squad. I want to know who just came through on my line."

He listened for a second, tapping his pen irritatingly against Nicky's computer screen.

"No, they weren't put through by my secretary. The main switchboard is already running a location trace, I want you to get onto the provider and find the caller's name. It can't have come from thin air."

He listened for another moment then nodded and cut the line, turning to face a very curious P.A.

"You didn't put that call through, Nicky, did you?"

She gave him a look that said 'as if'. Nicky had been his P.A. for more than three years now and she was one of the best in the force. She would never have made such a rookie mistake. If Nicky had answered the call and she hadn't recognised the voice, she would have subjected the caller to name, rank, serial number, birthdate, star-sign and favourite colour before she would have transferred the call to him.

Craig smiled sheepishly, knowing that he'd been stupid to ask.

"I take it they didn't give you their name?"

Craig shook his head and pulled a chair up to her desk. Liam had been watching nosily from halfway down the room, now he voted with his feet, joining them in two giant steps. Craig nodded as he approached.

"Grab a seat, Liam. I want to run something past you."

Craig took the fresh coffee Nicky held out to him and screwed up his face, puzzled. "I've just had a phone call."

"So? You get plenty of calls."

Craig shook his head slowly. "Not like this one."

He repeated what the voice had said and Liam whistled. "It's like something out of a spy movie."

"Isn't it just. But at least we know we're on the right track."

Liam stared blankly at him.

17

"The three cases John gave us are obviously worth following up, if someone wants us to stop looking at them this badly."

"Oh aye, I see."

Liam scanned Nicky's desk for biscuits. She read his mind and handed him a pack, gazing pointedly at his growing girth. Liam sucked-in his stomach huffily and bit defiantly into a chocolate crunch. He carried on talking. "Did you notice anything about the voice, boss?"

"Yes. A lot. Definitely from here; Belfast or the surrounds. Polished. Middle-class vocabulary."

"What do you mean?"

"His sentence construction. He said 'I won't insult you by saying that there's no puzzle here'. That's a complex sentence formation..."

Craig stopped mid-phrase and turned urgently to Nicky, unsurprised that she was already holding her notepad and pen. She'd probably been waiting for him to ask his next question since he'd sat down. He recited the phone call verbatim as she scribbled quickly in shorthand then turned back to her keyboard to type it up. A minute later he and Liam had printed copies in their hands.

Liam gawped at Craig and then at the sheet. "How the hell did you remember it word for word?"

Liam's 'I'm astonished' face was hard to miss and within seconds they were joined by the rest of the team, milling curiously around Nicky's desk. Craig saw her warning glance and lifted his chair, moving the conversation further down the room. Craig passed round his sheet and started talking.

"OK. A middle-class Northern Irish man, probably from the east of the province, has just managed to get through to my line without going through either Nicky or the switchboard. The conversation we had is on that page. He was educated and I'd say in his twenties or thirties somewhere. So what has he told us?"

Just at that moment Annette walked onto the floor. She

18

joined the small group, staring quizzically at Craig. As he brought her up to speed Annette scanned the page. She volunteered her thoughts.

"He's telling us that we have a case and that he's responsible for it in some way. Obviously he doesn't want us to solve it."

Craig nodded eagerly. "Yes, and why?"

"Because if we do, it will lead to him."

"OK, what else? Anyone?"

Davy pushed back his long dark hair and smiled. He liked puzzles and he was good at them.

"The w…way he said; 'you've already seen what I can do, be careful that I don't do it to you' means he's taking responsibility for the suicides in some way."

Liam interrupted and Davy shot him an irritated look.

"Aye. And he's threatening to do it to anyone who tries to catch him."

Davy interrupted back. "Yes, but particularly the boss. He knows w…who you are, chief. He came right through to you and he called you by name."

Craig nodded. The fact hadn't escaped him. "OK. So how did he know?"

Annette smiled. "That's obvious. You head up the Belfast Murder Squad. If the cases are being treated as murder then who else would be leading the case?"

Craig smiled. God bless Annette's common sense. While the rest of them were looking for Machiavellian plots and surveillance techniques she'd go straight to the simplest answer and be right.

"You're right, Annette. Thanks for the reality check. OK. But how did he even know the squad was looking at the cases? The only person who knows about this other than us is John. The rest of the world would believe the coroner's verdict on the first two cases was the final word."

Jake had been quiet throughout the discussion, now he spoke.

"Doctor Winter wasn't the only person who knew, sir."

Craig swung round to face him. "Who else?"

"You mentioned the coroner this morning so he'd obviously spoken to them too, and he's bound to have discussed it with the other people at the lab."

"Aye, the lad's right. And the Doc might have called the families of the first two victims as well, asking questions."

Craig raked his thick hair. They were all correct. The list of people who knew John was looking into the cases was long. It would get even longer if they didn't plug any leaks, fast.

"OK, Jake. I'll speak to Dr Winter and find out who knows he's looking at the cases. I'll make sure he doesn't discuss them with anyone else. Meanwhile you plot any possible connections between the victims." He turned to Nicky. "Nick. Can you get that transcript over to linguistics please? Explain the context and ask them to see if there are any clues in the sentence construction, speech patterns etc."

Craig turned back to Liam. "Liam, where are we with the backgrounds of the deceased?"

"At the beginning, basically. Davy's looking into the obvious; finances, health, families. Anything that might give them a reason to commit suicide. But our hands are a bit tied."

"How so?"

"These people's families believe they committed suicide. How do we go digging for murder motives without letting them know what's up?"

Liam was right. For all his bluntness even Liam had been more sensitive on this one than him. Craig thought for a moment then sighed.

"You're right. Sorry. I should have approached the families straight away but I wanted to see if we actually had a case before upsetting them. I'll find out how much they already know from John and then tell them what we suspect before we go any further."

Annette could tell from Craig's face that it wasn't a task he was looking forward to. She interjected kindly. "I'll come with you, sir, if that's all right? I did a stint in psychiatric nursing during my training and dealt with a few suicide cases."

Annette had been a nurse for years before she'd joined the force and it had proved useful on several occasions. Craig smiled gratefully.

"Thanks, Annette. Relatives aren't my favourite thing." He glanced at the clock. It was one-thirty. "If we start this afternoon we should get through all the relatives by tomorrow. The rest of you do what you can behind the scenes until all the families are on board." He paused meaningfully. "And while it's easy to dismiss our caller as a nutter, remember what he said and watch your backs." He took his car keys from his pocket, readying to go. "Nicky, which family lives nearest?"

"Diana Rogan's. They're in Andersonstown."

"OK. Call them and say we'd like to drop round this afternoon. If that doesn't suit then contact the next family." Craig headed for the door, signalling Annette to follow. "Nicky, we're going to the lab first to update John, then on to the coroner's office to check out some things. We'll head to the Rogan's after that. Call me on the mobile with the times."

***

John was sitting in front of his computer screen wearing a stunned expression when Craig and Annette entered. He hit the screensaver quickly and greeted them both as if he hadn't seen them for months. Craig knew immediately what John had been doing and walked round the desk, tapping the PC back to life. As the screen filled with images he chuckled and beckoned Annette over to take a look. In front of them was a photograph of a large banqueting room filled with circular tables and chairs covered in satin bows. Craig tapped the screen again and images of stationery and flowers appeared. He turned to see a blushing John.

21

"I told you, mate. This will be your life for years unless you set a date. It's Natalie's equivalent of the Chinese water torture."

Annette gave a mock frown. "It's not that bad. They're lovely pictures and she just wants your opinion before she starts looking."

She grinned and John slumped in his chair and waved them towards the coffee, shaking his head.

"No. Marc's right. Nat's been on at me to set a date for weeks and I've been less than enthusiastic, so she's bombarding me with pictures and wedding websites. She sets me tests at night to make sure I've looked at them." He dropped his head into his hands and adopted a dramatic voice. "Will no-one rid me of this troublesome woman?"

Craig's slow handclap made him look up. "To paraphrase Henry the Second. The answer's no and you'd miss her if we did. Just bite the bullet and set the date, for God's sake. She'll stop spamming you and you can get on with your work." He took the coffee Annette was holding out and grabbed a chair.

"Anyway, that's enough of that. We're here to warn you."

"So now it's the Ides of March?"

"Something like that."

Annette stared at them quizzically. She pictured them thirty-odd years earlier as schoolboys, talking in some obscure private short-hand. Nothing had changed. Craig was still talking.

"Your false suicides have rattled someone's cage. We had a threatening phone-call to the squad."

Annette interjected. "They came straight through to the chief's phone."

John's stared at them in turn, confused. "What? They managed to bypass Iron Nicky and the switchboard?"

"Iron Nicky... that's not bad, but don't let her hear you saying it."

Nicky guarded Craig like his Italian mother Mirella, except Mirella was even scarier.

"They routed the call from overseas. They told me the trace

would show America but I've put switchboard on it anyway."

John leaned forward, interested. "So? What was the warning?"

Craig pulled Nicky's printed sheet from his jacket and laid it on the desk for him to see. After a few seconds John glanced up, slightly paler.

"Was he serious?"

"He wasn't laughing."

John grinned and punched the air. "I was right! They were murdered and this proves it."

Craig shook his head. "It proves nothing yet, except that our caller was involved with your three suicide victims in some way. Anyone can claim things, and you said it yourself; we have no forensics to suggest murder and no sign of foul play. All we have is three dead bodies and a threatening phone-call."

John sat back, deflated. "Then why are you here?"

"To warn you and to see if you know how this leaked. Only your team, the squad, the coroner and the relatives presumably know that you had any suspicions about the deaths."

John shook his head. "All I told the families was that I was re-examining the files for research purposes. I didn't want to upset them until I knew if we had something to investigate."

Annette cut in. "I meant to say this earlier, sir, but the victims' family doctors might know by now. If the coroner got in touch."

John's eyes widened in realisation. "Not to mention the coroner's office staff. Remember that I had just asked for the files. If you're trying to locate your man by who knew that I had suspicions, I would give up now, Marc."

Craig said nothing. There was nothing to say; they were right.

"OK. But whoever called had enough knowledge to suggest he was close to the case, and he obviously knew that you'd handed the cases off to me. Who knew we met about them last Friday?"

John thought for a moment then tapped the sheet in front of him. "Was the voice disguised in any way? Like someone messing about?"

"It didn't sound like it."

"Well then, it doesn't make any sense. Only you, Des and I knew we were meeting on Friday and if none of us made that call that means..."

"That someone was watching the lab and saw me leave here last Friday afternoon with the files."

John's voice was firm. "No. Even if they'd seen you leaving it could have been any three files that you were carrying. They didn't say 'suicide' on the front!"

Craig shook his head and fell silent, thinking. Annette went to pour another coffee and John joined her, whispering under his breath.

"If I set a date for the wedding do you really think Natalie would stop sending me all this stuff?"

"Definitely. In fact you'll probably never be asked your opinion again. Natalie and her mother will take over and you won't see another flower arrangement until your wedding day."

"But it's my wedding as well as hers!"

Annette gave his arm a sympathetic pat. "You keep on believing that if you like. Women know different."

They turned back to the desk to see Craig scribbling something.

"OK. Whoever phoned me has something to do with our three deaths. If not forensically then they at least knew about them. Enough to know that they weren't suicides, no matter what the coroner's verdict said. That implies that they had a hand in the deaths somehow. Yes?"

The others nodded dumbly.

"OK. The threatening tone of the phone call implies culpability, so either they caused the deaths somehow, or they feel that they did. Their approach was too aggressive to suggest remorse, so I'd rule out this being someone who feels guilty for not doing more to prevent the suicides. This is someone who feels they actually did something to cause them." He glanced up and saw their blank expressions. "They actually caused the suicides; as opposed to feeling that they should have stopped them. OK?"

John nodded. "Ah, right. I get you now."

"Right. So we have someone who managed to cause three people's suicides, which suggests that they're clever and manipulative."

Annette cut in. "Or they threatened them."

"OK. Good. So did they threaten them physically or in some other way? And why these three people? Were they random sadistic killings, or was there some link between them and some logic to the choice?"

Annette smiled in realisation. "Which is why Jake's busy trying to find links between the victims. Like the Adams' murders in 2012, where the victims were all linked because they were on the jury in a court case."

"Yes. So what links these three people? OK, it's our job to suss that out so let's leave that for now. But how did the caller know that John had passed his concerns on to me?" Craig turned to John. "John, when did you first start feeling uncomfortable about these verdicts?"

John tapped idly at his PC screen as he thought, jerking back suddenly as a large wedding cake appeared. He shuddered and tapped the screen to sleep again then turned back to Craig.

"Mike Augustus did the first post-mortem, Jonathan McCafferty's, in late February, when we were up to our necks in the Carragher case. I didn't even see the file until after Diana Rogan's death three weeks ago. I remember thinking then that two suicides so close together was slightly unusual."

Craig looked sceptical. "What about the high rate amongst young men?"

John nodded, conceding that Craig was right. There was a high level of teenage suicide, especially among the boys.

25

"OK, it was unusual to see two suicides in middle-aged adults then. Maybe that's what made me take a second look; the fact that the victims were older. Something made me notice them anyway. I remember mentioning it to Des after Diana Rogan's death, but it was last Wednesday's case, Nelson Warner, that really made me sit up and take notice."

Craig tapped the desk as he thought.

"OK. So let's say we have someone guilty of 'causing' three people to commit suicide. The first two deaths get past the coroner and after a gap of three weeks they cause the third. If I were them I'd be beginning to get anxious, wondering if my luck was going to hold out. I'd be keeping a very close eye on the third case until it got safely past the coroner. So where's the most logical place to set up surveillance?"

John's jaw dropped. "Here? Do you mean they've been watching us since Warner's body came in?"

Craig nodded. "Perhaps even before that, on the others as well. It's what I would do until there was a coroner's verdict on each case."

Annette shuddered. This was part of the reason Craig was such a good detective; his ability to think like a perp. But sometimes his ability to think like a killer worried her. Craig was still talking.

"This would be the logical place to observe, and the pathologist would be the most logical person, until the body left."

"But they would have to have waited at the lab for days."

"Not really. Nelson Warner's suicide was on Wednesday evening, wasn't it?"

John nodded.

"OK. So they waited to see Warner's body being pulled from the river, or perhaps they didn't even bother. They already knew he was going to end up here. Every unusual death in Belfast ends up here. It wouldn't have been difficult to find out who the pathologist on-call was. Then all they had to do was stake-out the lab until they saw Warner being shipped to the undertakers. Probably on Friday sometime. That would signal the end of the P.M. and the cause of death would become public knowledge soon after."

John rubbed his chin and nodded. "Except instead, they saw you entering the path lab on Friday afternoon."

"Yep. Of course that could have just been a social call, except that I left carrying three files. When Warner's body didn't leave here by Friday night they must have known something was up. They probably hoped the body would leave this morning at the latest, and when it didn't..."

"They phoned you. They realised I'd passed the files to you on Friday and you were taking them seriously because Nelson Warner's body was still here today." John shuddered. "They've been watching me for days."

Craig shook his head. "Not you, the building. You only became a problem because you weren't prepared to sign off the body, and because of your contact with me." Craig paused, his face sombre. "But he's made threats now, John. I don't know how serious they are and they're more likely to be aimed at my team, but just watch your back."

John nodded. "Well at least the suicides will stop now."

It was Annette who asked the question first. "Why would they?"

John blustered, searching for an answer. "Well...I mean...he must know that any future suicides will be treated with suspicion."

Craig shrugged. "So what?"

"Well... because you might catch him then."

Craig shook his head. "If the trail is going to lead to him from the first three killings anyway, he might want to kill as many as he can before the net closes in. And if the trail is really hard to pick up then he can go on killing with impunity. It all depends how clever he's been in his choice of victims and whether they were chosen at random or for a specific reason."

Annette shuddered again. "If it's random we might never catch him."

Craig smiled at her reassuringly. "My gut tells me there's some warped logic behind his choice of victims and we'll find a connection between them. But that doesn't mean that he'll stop killing while we're looking."

John took off his black-wire glasses and wiped them on the sleeve of his white coat. "So when you find him, Marc, what will you charge him with? These people killed themselves, there's no forensic ambiguity about that. So what is he actually guilty of?"

Craig raked his hair for a moment then shook his head. "I don't know yet. Blackmail, threatening behaviour, whatever we can find evidence of. At the moment we don't even have a link between the victims, never mind know how he made them do it."

Craig slipped the sheet of paper back into his pocket then stood up and smiled at his friend.

"Watch your back and let me know the minute you get another suspicious death or suicide in."

He leaned forward and tapped John's screen, guffawing at the new image of lilac bridesmaids' dresses that popped up. John retreated several feet, horrified.

"And for God's sake set a date or Natalie will have you wearing one of these very soon."

Chapter Four

Bedford Street, Belfast. 3.30 p.m.

Natasha Nunes' phone buzzed angrily and she dropped the file she was carrying and rushed back to her desk. She stared at the handset for a moment, reluctant to lift it, knowing from its ring-tone that it was an internal call. She was a grown woman with a daughter for God's sake, so why should the mere buzz of a phone reduce her to a quivering mess? She already knew the answer and it was confirmed as soon as she picked up the phone.

"Where is the Girton file? I told you I needed it ten minutes ago."

The woman's voice at the other end was cool and its aggression was as controlled as a tightly clenched fist. Even so, in any other context such a voice wouldn't have frightened Natasha half as much, but this wasn't any other context. This was the chambers of Linton and Roche, Barrister's at Law, and Victoria Linton wasn't a woman to be trifled with.

Natasha grabbed the file hastily, knocking her coffee cup off the desk in the rush. She swore quietly and reached for a cloth to stem the flow of liquid before it reached the pink-ribboned briefs resting on her desk. As she turned she caught sight of the morning post. The mail-room had left it there without her noticing. The young P.A. quickly sifted the ones addressed to Ms Linton and carried them into the room with the Girton file.

Victoria Linton regarded her secretary icily. "How many times have I told you to knock?"

"L…Lots of times, Ms Linton."

"Many times. Not 'lots of', Natasha. Now, where's Girton?"

Natasha rushed forward and placed the file on Linton's desk then stood holding the mail in her hand. Victoria Linton had already dismissed her secretary in her mind so she was surprised when the girl didn't leave. Girl. It was a strange word for a twenty-four-year-old mother, particularly as Linton had been a qualified lawyer at that age. It just went to show that infantilising someone was rarely an age-based approach. Class, intellect and power were just as useful.

"Well? Was there something else?"

"Y…Yes, Ms Linton."

Natasha stepped forward and placed a white padded envelope on Linton's dark-wood desk. The other post she'd recognised as letters from solicitors and chamber's bills, but the envelope was marked private.

"I thought I should bring it in. It's marked private."

Linton arched an eyebrow at her statement of the obvious then stared curiously at the small jiffy bag. She was a naturally suspicious person and it had served her very well in life, so she lifted the envelope and turned it over then held it up to the light. It felt heavy, heavier than a letter but not as heavy as a gift. In the glow of her newly-purchased green-glass lamp, one she'd copied from a law drama she'd seen on TV, she could just make out the outlines of a small object and a note. There were no wires and nothing else that suggested it might be some dissident terrorist's game. Besides, she never prosecuted terrorist cases – she valued her life too much.

Linton glanced up from the envelope and saw her P.A.'s curious gaze. She glared at her and Natasha stepped quickly back.

"That will be all."

Natasha nodded hurriedly and headed for the door, glad of her escape. She only had one more month left in the office, although Victoria Linton didn't know that. She'd got a job offer nearer home, with better hours for her daughter. She'd tell Linton tomorrow when she put her notice in and then she'd pack her bags and vote with her feet. She was owed four week's holiday and what with Easter as well, she'd never have to darken Linton and Roche's doors again.

As the door closed Victoria Linton reached for her paper knife and slit the bag open. She widened the opening and peered in. Nothing suspicious so far. Just a sheet of white paper and what look like a curiously shaped metal object. As she tipped it out she saw that the object was a key, cut in a gothic design. As Linton turned it over, examining its delicate scrollwork, her eyes widened. It was made of platinum! She would recognise the metal anywhere; Julian had given her a necklace made of it for Christmas. The key weighed at least three ounces, worth a couple of thousand pounds.

Linton scrutinised the key closely and saw that there was something lodged inside its wide, engraved shaft. It was a memory stick. She slid it out and examined it curiously, tempted to put it straight into her PC. It would never accept it of course. Every computer in chambers was locked against the theft of files, so no USBs but chamber's issue would work. Never mind. She would see what was on it when she went home.

Linton turned her attention to the note, expecting it to be a love-letter from some admirer. After all, who else would possibly send her something worth so much? The words she read left her even more puzzled than before. 'I am from the past.' Nothing else. She turned the paper over repeatedly then held it up to the light, certain that there must be something more; but there was nothing.

'I am from the past.' What the hell did that mean? That it was from an old lover? She thought back to her exes and dismissed the idea at once; none of them had the imagination to think up something like this, never mind have been willing to spend the money. So, what was it? An old case? She doubted it. She was a prosecutor and the people she put away didn't tend to send presents. Linton peered hard at the note's font and the paper it was typed on, as if they would yield some clues, but they were common and available everywhere.

Her thoughts were interrupted by her office line ringing. Linton seized the receiver irritably.

"What?"

"S...Sorry, Ms Linton, but the High Court's on the phone. Can I put them through?"

Victoria Linton sighed and packed away her curiosity. She pushed the cryptic note and key into her handbag and returned to the mundane business of her day.

***

By the time Craig and Annette arrived at Diana Rogan's home on Belfast's Glen Road, the long road's backdrop of the Black Mountain was lit by a reddening sky. It made the urban landscape strangely beautiful and made sense of the road's name. They drove past the tall spire of a church and its companion school and into a prosperous, suburban housing estate, whose modern houses were made older looking by their nods to the Tudors long ago.

The cul-de-sac that held the Rogan's house was still and quiet, apart from the occasional child's squeal splitting the air, as they played in some nearby back garden, and the echo of car doors slamming, punctuating the close of the working day.

Craig checked the number that Nicky had texted through then he took a deep breath and walked up a short, tarmacked drive, readying himself to knock on the half-glass front door. He didn't need to. Before Craig's hand fell the door sprang open and a small figure stood in front of them. A boy of around eight year's old. Exactly eight year's old in fact; Nicky had texted that the boy's birthday had been the day before. Craig smiled down at the child sadly, knowing that his birthday celebrations had lacked one extremely important thing – his mother.

The boy gazed up at them with solemn brown eyes then he pulled the door wide, almost falling backwards under its weight. Craig slipped out his badge and held it out for the boy to take a look.

"Is your father...Daddy home? I'm..." He hesitated at the use of rank when he was talking to a bereaved child and instead changed the word to Marc. "Marc Craig and this is Annette. Could you tell your Daddy that we'd like to speak to him, please? He knows we're coming."

The boy frowned seriously as befitted his important role. He scanned Craig's badge exaggeratedly then reached out a small hand to Annette, gripping hers. Just then a slim young man with a shock of blond hair came rushing into the hall. A small girl was clinging to his leg, giggling and hindering his approach. The man extended his hand to Craig and smiled, his face a grown-up version of his daughter's.

"I'm Conor Rogan. Thank you for coming."

Rogan stepped back, taking his daughter with him, and waved them into a bright kitchen-dining room. As they took their seats he detached his small daughter gently and she hovered in the doorway beside her brother, watching everything. Annette smiled warmly at them and gave a small wave, tempting the pair to move cautiously into the room as their father carried a ready-prepared tray of refreshments to a table.

"Tea or coffee?"

Craig nodded Annette to answer first and smiled down at the boy, who had taken up residence beside his chair.

"Coffee please." She glanced at Craig. "Two cups would be great."

After the drinks were poured and biscuits offered round, Rogan shooed the children to play in another room.

"I'm sorry. David's fascinated by the police. It's all cops and robbers at that age, isn't it?"

Craig nodded, remembering his own childhood games. He'd never grown out of them. After a moment's silence Craig started to speak, introducing himself and Annette again and broaching the reason why they'd come. Conor Rogan halted him with an outstretched palm.

"I appreciate your diplomacy, Superintendent, but you don't need to tiptoe around my wife's death. In fact I'd rather that you didn't. I've never believed that Diana committed suicide; she had everything to live for and she certainly wasn't depressed. Quite the opposite in fact. We were planning a trip to Disneyland this summer with the kids and she was more excited than either of them." He paused and Craig could see tears brightening his eyes. "When a verdict of suicide was handed down I was devastated. No, more than that, I was furious."

Craig leaned forward. "Did you ask for the inquest to be re-opened?"

Rogan nodded then rubbed his face in frustration. "For months. I tried everything, but the coroner's office was adamant. They said the forensics were indisputable. I even asked my senior partner to intervene. He tried but it made no difference."

Craig could only imagine the anger Rogan felt.

"You're a solicitor, Mr Rogan. Is that correct?"

Rogan nodded and sipped his coffee. "I deal mainly with employment law."

"And what exactly did Mrs Rogan do for a living?"

Craig already had the information that Nicky had sent through, but it was generic. Diana Rogan had been a middle manager in a firm of brokers in town. That could have meant anything.

"For a living... that sounds so strange now." Rogan gazed into space for a moment then asked a question of no-one in particular. "Why do we get so obsessed with money and material things? Can you tell me that?" He carried on, not waiting for an answer. "We both worked so hard to give our children the things we thought they needed, the latest toys and games, but they won't touch them now. All they want is their mum; they don't care about anything else."

His voice broke suddenly and he dropped his face into his hands, sitting in silence for a moment as the two officers looked on, powerless to help. Eventually he looked up and gave a weak smile.

"What was your question? Ah, yes, for a living. Diana was a manager at a small brokerage firm in the city centre; Murphy Johnson Limited. She trained as an accountant originally then moved sideways into stocks and shares; mostly for small investors." Rogan laughed. "She used to try to explain it to me; swaps and futures and hedge-funds, but I never understood a word of it. Numbers aren't my strong point I'm afraid."

Annette smiled in agreement. "Nor mine. Not when they get to that level."

Craig asked another question. "Had your wife complained about any problems at work? Any disagreements with colleagues – anything at all?"

Rogan shook his head. "No. Quite the contrary, she loved her job. It's a very small office, only her, an actuary and her boss Jacob Johnson. They were all on good terms as far as I know. Apart from that they had a couple of secretaries and the occasional student attached from Queens, or from one of the local accounting firms. In fact they had a student there last month as far as I know."

He shook his head vaguely and stared into space again. Craig could hear the children chattering in the other room but Rogan seemed oblivious to the noise. Finally he shook himself from his reverie and turned to Craig with a defiant look on his face.

"There was no reason for Diana to take her life and I will never believe that she did."

Twenty minutes of routine questioning later, Craig completely agreed with him.

***

It was almost six o'clock by the time they left Diana and Conor Rogan's warm family home so Craig dropped Annette home, instead of back to the office to collect her car. He offered to collect her the next morning but she shook her head.

"Don't worry, sir. Pete can drop me in tomorrow morning on his way to school."

Pete McElroy was a P.E. teacher and Head of Sport at a secondary school near Newtownards. It was rare that the team ever saw him, even rarer since his and Annette's marital problems the year before. Craig drove the twenty minutes to Annette's house and parked. As she went to open the door he placed a hand on her arm.

"How is everything?"

Annette smiled thinly, knowing he was referring to Pete's affair the previous year. It had almost ended their marriage and it had definitely ended her willingness to take second place in it. Pete had cited her job and working hours as his excuse for infidelity and she'd gone along to marriage guidance, willing to do anything to make things work. But it had had the opposite effect. She was more ambitious than ever now and more determined that she wouldn't let Pete or his petty insecurities stand in her way. She would go for Chief Inspector in a few years, when Craig said she was ready, and Pete could bloody well lump it.

Craig watched the thoughts running through Annette's mind, knowing that she was composing the answer that she thought would fit, and sanitising the facts for her boss. He'd watched her change and grow since the affair and he'd wanted to cheer her on. She was a good detective and she'd get better. Pete's attempt to control her had backfired badly and if anyone had the upper hand in their marriage now it was Annette.

Annette smiled and gave the answer that Craig knew she would. "Everything's fine, sir. Would you like to come in for a coffee?"

Craig smiled at her polite invitation and shook his head, so Annette climbed out of the car and waved him away. As Craig drove to the junction and turned right towards town, he completely missed the car following three car lengths behind.

***

Jenna Graham really wanted to hear Victoria Linton's exclamation when she inserted the key, and see the horrified look on her face. But she couldn't. She wouldn't be in the room with her when it happened so she could only wait for the inevitable effect. And it was inevitable, just like Linton's two weeks of skiing in the winter and her weekends spent sailing out of Cultra.

Graham smiled at how easy it had all been so far. She wanted it to continue until the end, needed it to, but the Murder Squad were getting nosy and she had to make them stop. Everyone had a weakness that could be used against them; she just needed to find out what Superintendent Marc Craig's was.

***

9 p.m.

Craig threw his jacket on an armchair and loosened his tie. He slumped on the settee and flicked idly through the channels as he thought. Diana Rogan had no more wanted to kill herself than Cleopatra had. She had a loving husband, two cuter-than-hell kids and a job that she seemed to love. She was going to Disneyland for God's sake; people who were going to Disneyland didn't take their own lives!

Craig paused his thoughts like a DVD and skipped back several frames. Her job. Her husband had said that she'd loved it but her death had to be linked with her job in some way;

there was no other possible source of stress in her life. He'd searched Conor Rogan's face for signs of lies about their marriage. So had Annette and she said that Rogan was telling the truth, so he must be. He trusted Annette's judgement of people even more than his own. They'd speak to the neighbours and Diana Rogan's family about the marriage of course, but it would be a dead end, he was sure of it. But Diana Rogan's job... now that was something else.

Craig made a note to get onto it in the morning then he wandered to the fridge to grab a bottle of beer, ignoring John's medical lecture earlier that day. He sat back down on the settee and gazed around his small living room. It felt empty. It was empty. He was alone in life apart from his parents and sister, and pretty soon John would be married and living in domestic bliss. He rubbed his face in irritation, not at John but at himself. Why couldn't he settle down like everyone else?

He took a swig of beer and gave himself a pass. He and Camille had split up because of her ambition. She was in New York now, acting on Broadway; she still sent him occasional postcards with tales of her exciting life. Good luck to her, he wished her well in the States, but it wasn't the place for him. His parents needed him as they grew older and he loved his job. The job. Was that it? Was the job the reason he was still alone?

Craig shrugged and then realised he was sitting in total darkness. He reached over to turn on the light and an image of Julia filled his mind. He pictured her lying beside him on the couch with her red hair spread out and her blue eyes smiling. Why had it all gone wrong between them? He already knew the answer. Stubbornness and geography, just like with Camille. If it had just been his stubbornness he could have done something about that, but theirs he had no control over. And geography? Well New York or Limavady, there was no way to shorten miles, regardless of whether they were land or sea.

Career had been the reason he was still single, not just his but theirs. Neither of them had been ready to drop everything to be with him and he'd had no right to expect it. The same was true in reverse. What was interesting was why he was attracted to such career-driven women in the first place. And he definitely was; John was the same. Was it their intelligence or their ambition? No, it wasn't ambition in any formal sense. He didn't care if they didn't have big titles or earn a lot. It was their drive. Intelligence and drive; it was a very sexy combination. He just wished he could find a woman with those qualities who wanted to live in Belfast, like John had managed to with Natalie.

Craig wallowed in self-pity for a moment longer then kicked himself up the ass and surfed the channels until he found a football match to watch. As he stared at the screen half-dozing, the image of a woman's face floated into his mind and he smiled, realising that he might already know the answer to his prayers.

Chapter Five

Victoria Linton threw her briefcase in the corner of her large open-plan living room then rifled through her handbag for the padded envelope she'd opened earlier that day. She poured a large glass of Merlot and sat down on a leather couch with her laptop on her knee, turning the key over in her hand. She stared at it for a moment, wondering again who it was from. 'I am from the past', that was what the note had said. She snorted with laughter thinking of her exes throughout the years.

It was far too cryptic for Nathan; he'd been a concrete thinker. Correction, a leaden thinker. Nathan had thought creativity was something that should be vaccinated against. And as far as Robin was concerned, the idea of doing something as romantic as sending a key would have brought him out in hives. She reached up and loosened her chignon, letting her dark curls fall down her back. What about Julian? She imagined her impoverished partner being able to afford a platinum key and dismissed the idea instantly. And Julian wasn't in her past yet. As soon as the idea occurred to her she shuddered, pushing it away. Julian Mooney was staying in her life regardless of what her family would think.

Victoria stopped speculating and took another gulp of wine. Whoever had sent it, the key would reveal them once she inserted the USB. She deposited her wine glass carefully on a side table, ensuring that she placed a coaster underneath, and pulled off the memory stick's valuable outer casing, inserting it into her laptop. She watched while the computer scanned for viruses and when it was sure there were no contaminants she clicked to open the USB and reveal what lay inside.

Her eyes fell on a file with the title 'Your future' and she felt a bubble of excitement rise. This was it. Someone who had worshipped her from a distance was about to declare their love and whisk her away from her mundane life. She'd daydreamed about it of course, just as every woman had, but it was actually happening to her because she was special. She had no idea just how special. As Victoria Linton clicked open the file she had no idea that her life was about to change for good.

***

Tuesday, 4 a.m.

Craig was woken by the sound of a mobile phone ringing somewhere in his dream. As his dream was set in Rome during July he wasn't amused to wake up and find he was actually in a freezing spring in Belfast. He grabbed the handset grumpily and banged it on.

"Yes?"

Craig's voice was hoarse and if he sounded angry it was because he was. He'd glimpsed the time on the screen as he'd answered. Four a.m. someone had better have a damn good reason for phoning him in the middle of the night. It was John Winter and he had.

"There's been another one, Marc. In the next block along the river to yours."

Craig was confused. One minute ago he'd been in Rome, strolling through the Piazza Navona with an attractive blonde on his arm, and now this. Either the booze had finally got to him or there'd been another death. He sat up quickly, throwing his feet onto his bedroom's wooden floor, then he raked his hair ruthlessly, trying to wake himself up.

"OK. Give me that again, John. What, who and where?"

"Another death; apparently suicide. A barrister called

Victoria Linton. She lives in Stranmillis Quay."

He was right. It was the next block along. Craig dragged a jumper and his jeans from a nearby chair and pulled them on as John continued talking.

"She was found in her car in the communal garage."

"Carbon Monoxide poisoning?"

"Yes." John paused and Craig knew what was coming next. He wouldn't have woken him up at four a.m. for a suicide case, no matter how lonely he felt. "She left exactly the same note, Marc... I'll see you there in ten."

The line went dead and Craig slipped his mobile into his pocket and went to freshen up. He looked a shambles but he didn't care, neither would Victoria Linton. He brushed his teeth sleepily as her name turned over in his head. He knew that name, he was certain he did. Then he remembered where from. She'd prosecuted a case of his six years before, when he'd first come back to Belfast. She'd been a snippy piece of work, but attractive. Craig wondered idly what she looked like nowadays then he remembered she was dead and chastised himself.

Ten minutes later he was staring down at her corpse, the familiar cherry-red discolouration of her skin confirming John's diagnosis of a Carbon Monoxide death. Craig gazed at the woman's face, remembering her from the courtroom. He could almost hear her voice. Cool but not unpleasant, like a BBC Newsreader in a vaguely pissed-off mood. It was her stare that had really wilted her opponents; fierce and unblinking, as if she could make them tell the truth by her sheer force of will. A tap on his shoulder told Craig that Linton's apartment was ready to view and he nodded John to cover her face with the sheet.

"Pity. She was young."

Craig nodded in agreement.

"Did you know her, Marc?"

"I came up against her in court once. She was a criminal prosecutor. Pretty good as well. I don't know if she was still doing it."

"Her apartment will tell us."

"Who found her, John?"

"A neighbour who was coming home late. He heard the car engine running and went into the garage to take a look. He pulled her out and tried to resuscitate her, but no joy. Uniform at Stranmillis caught the call." John pointed at a young man who was leaning against a police car, holding a cup of coffee in his hand. He was shaking so much that he was spilling it all over the ground.

Craig walked over to him and extended his hand. "I'm Superintendent Craig, Mr...?"

"W...Wallace. James Wallace."

Wallace's voice was shaking as much as his hands and Craig smiled kindly at him. "It must have been a shock."

The man nodded vaguely. "I knew her. Vicky. She used to come to the boat club the odd time and we'd all go to Cutter's Wharf together."

Cutter's was a popular riverside bar in Stranmillis that Craig had been to many times. Wallace was still speaking.

"Why would she do this to herself? She had everything. Her job, Julian, her..."

Craig interrupted gently. "Who is Julian?"

Wallace stared at Craig as if he was looking through him, searching for something. It was probably his peace of mind.

"He's her boyfriend. They've been together for a while. It was quite serious I think." His mouth dropped open. "Oh God, maybe he dumped her? Maybe that's why she did it?"

Craig shook his head. "There's no point speculating, Mr Wallace. We'll sort all that out later."

Craig thought about going over the events with the young man again but a glance at his pale skin and reddening eyes said that he'd had quite enough for tonight.

"Thank you for being so helpful, Mr Wallace. I think you should go home now and get some sleep. A constable will contact you in the morning." Craig turned to enter the apartment block then thought of something and turned swiftly back again. "Just one more question. How do people gain access to the development?"

Wallace stared at the high gates that separated the exclusive apartments from the road and then back at Craig. "Electronic gate opener." He reached into his pocket and withdrew a fob, holding it out to Craig. "We get them from the managing agents. Only apartment owners have them, although several people have rented their apartments out now, so I suppose…"

Craig finished the sentence. "Any tenant would have one."

Craig smiled again and nodded Wallace to continue on his way. He walked back to where John was standing with a C.S.I.

"Ready?"

John nodded and they headed for Victoria Linton's fifth-floor apartment. Penthouse would have been a better name for it. As they walked through the heavy front door Craig gasped. He'd seen some amazing homes in his time, especially during his years in London, but this was up there with the best. The door opened directly into an open-plan living area of over one thousand square metres. The back wall held a modern kitchen, with steel appliances and every gadget known to man. The front was made of ceiling-to-floor glass and gave a view over the river at Stranmillis that Craig could only dream he had. He smiled, thinking of his small two-bedroomed place. Quaint was how Julia had always described it, scruffy would have been nearer the truth. He was hardly ever there so it hadn't seemed to matter, but…

John watched Craig's face as he scanned the room and hoped he was doing more than admiring the drapes. He was, and something was niggling at him. Without preamble Craig crossed to a wide black desk by the window and scanned the items neatly arranged on top. Pens, in and out trays, a docking station and a computer mat. So far so ordinary for a professional of any sort. There was nothing out of place on the desk; in fact there was nothing out of place anywhere in the room. Victoria Linton must have had O.C.D. Then he saw what was wrong. Where was the computer that went with the docking station? Craig scanned the room and then turned to John.

"Has anyone taken her computer?"

"Yes. It was a laptop. Forensics are taking it back for examination."

"Where is it now?"

John waved towards a white-suited C.S.I. in the corner and Craig crossed the room to her in three strides.

"Have you got the laptop from that desk?"

The girl looked up at him, her small face almost enveloped by the hood of her white jump-suit. "Yes, sir. But it wasn't on the desk; it was on the settee when we arrived. Did you want to have a look at it?"

She stared pointedly at Craig's un-gloved hands and handed him a pair, then she extricated a sleek laptop from its sterile wrapping and opened it towards him, pressing the 'on' key. As it booted-up, Craig thought quickly. Forensics would work with Davy to dig into the deeper files, but it wasn't something deep that he was looking for. Whatever had made Victoria Linton kill herself was either going to be obvious or it wasn't going to be on her computer at all.

A moment later the computer's desktop screen appeared, devoid of personal images. The only images on it were shortcuts to documents archived elsewhere. Craig stared at it for a moment then he shook his head and looked at the C.S.I.

"Was there anything else near where you found this? Anything at all?"

The girl went to say no then she stopped, remembering something. She placed the laptop carefully on one side and rifled through a pile of evidence bags. After a moment's search she beckoned another C.S.I. across.

"Damien, you cleared this room, didn't you?"

The middle-aged man nodded. "Yes. Why?"

45

"Did you find anything near the laptop?"

"Aye, loads of stuff." He pointed to a plastic crate set in one corner then lifted a clipboard and ran his finger down a page. "It's all in there; bags marked twenty-three to ninety-six." He turned over the sheet and tapped the one beneath. "That's the list."

"Thanks."

The girl turned towards the crate and Craig followed. John stood with his arms folded, watching the pair. Craig was like a dog after a bone and that usually meant that there was a bone to find. Two minutes later four evidence bags were spread out on the floor.

Their contents were curious. A white jiffy bag addressed to their victim at an office called Linton and Roche. So Victoria Linton had her own chambers now, well done her. A wine glass with a residue of red wine in it, waiting to be tested for contaminants. An open felt-tipped pen and a hair clasp. Anything that the C.S.I.s thought Linton might have touched immediately before her death.

Craig pictured the deceased woman's evening. She'd come home from work and dumped her coat and briefcase beside the front door, then she'd poured a class of wine and sat down with her computer, loosening her hair. Was she at her desk or on the settee at that point? She didn't strike him as the sort to drink at her desk.

He turned back to the C.S.I. "Where was the wine found?"

The girl turned to ask Damien the question but he was nowhere to be seen. She walked into another room and returned a minute later with an exasperated shrug. "Damien's disappeared. I'll check later and let you know for sure, but we cluster items by location and these are listed as being together, so I'd say the wineglass was found near the laptop. By the settee."

Craig frowned, unconvinced by her conjecture. "OK, thanks."

He returned to the story of Victoria Linton's evening. If Linton had poured herself a glass of wine to drink while she sat on the settee looking at her laptop, it's unlikely that she was working. The whole act implied relaxation. Was she going to surf the Net? Perhaps. But then why was something posted to her at work sitting nearby?

Craig seized the jiffy bag urgently and held it under a light. The postmark was April 4th; the Friday before, which meant that the envelope would have been delivered to Linton's chambers on Saturday or Monday. So whatever it contained had been delivered to her office and she'd brought it home, then sat down at the computer with a glass of wine to look at it? Why would she have done that with something related to work? And then there was the hairpin. Victoria Linton had long thick hair that she tortured into submission for work, removing the pin said she was relaxing, or that someone else had wanted her to relax.

Craig turned to John. "John, was there any sign of a boyfriend here this evening?"

"None. There were no male clothes or shaving gear either, so maybe the neighbour was right and he'd dumped her."

Craig frowned. Victoria Linton hadn't struck him as the sort to kill herself over a man, but you never knew.

"OK."

Just then Liam loped in, looking as if he'd been dragged through a hedge. Craig laughed at how they must both have appeared.

"Hi, boss. What's up Doc?"

John rolled his eyes. "You love saying that, don't you?"

"Yep."

Craig's voice was urgent. "Liam, I'm glad you're here. Go and find out where Julian, the victim's boyfriend, was this evening."

"And hello to you too."

"Hello. Now go and do it."

Liam raised an eyebrow quizzically at John. John shrugged

and shook his head. Universal shorthand for 'God knows what he's up to'.

"Aye well, does this Julian have a second name?"

"You're a detective. Detect."

Craig turned back to his puzzle as John and Liam filtered out of the room. When they were on the stairs Liam asked the question. "Who rattled his cage?"

"Four deaths will do that to a man. Uniform should have the boyfriend's name; let's find them."

Craig returned to his evidence bags and ran through them one by one, adding detail to Vicky Linton's story. She'd finished work that evening, they could check the time with her office, then she'd come home, poured herself some wine, loosened her hair and removed the jiffy bag from her briefcase. Or removed the bag then poured the wine, etc. The order didn't matter, what mattered was that she was treating post that she'd received at work in a personal way. Why?

Craig scrutinised the jiffy bag again and wanted to kick himself. In one corner, almost obscured by fingerprint powder, was a word that confirmed his thought process: 'Private'. He'd been right.

Craig shook his head again. OK, so the envelope was marked 'private', but he got private things at work every day; they usually turned out to be someone offering him an ISA and went straight in the bin. This envelope had to have contained something personally important for Linton to bring it home. But if the envelope had contained something personal and it had been sent to her at work then again, why? Why not simply post it to her home?

Craig parked the question behind the much bigger one that still needed an answer. What had been in the jiffy bag? He grabbed the clipboard and ran his finger quickly down the list, there was something missing. Craig turned to the young C.S.I. who had been staring at him curiously the whole time.

"Where's the fifth exhibit?"

"What?"

"You said the exhibits were numbered. Forty-two to forty-six are listed as being found together on the settee; that makes five exhibits. I only found four. Number forty-six is missing."

She stared at Craig blankly for a moment then nodded and rifled through the crate, pulling out the final bag. "Sorry. It was mis-filed."

As the girl held out the small plastic bag a smile lit up Craig's face. This was it. This was what he'd been looking for. If he was right it would solve all four of their murders, not just this one.

Chapter Six

By the time they'd finished at the scene it was six a.m. so the three men decamped to Craig's flat for breakfast, such as it was. Craig took a shower first while Liam rifled through the fridge, searching for something edible amongst the cans of beer.

"You could open a pub with this lot, but there's no food."

Craig couldn't hear him so Liam yelled louder, eliciting a reply from the depths of the shower. "Well, nip down to the deli on the corner then, it opens early. I'll have a ham croissant."

Liam made a face and turned to John. "What do you fancy, Doc?"

"I'll just have coffee, thanks. I'll put it on while you're out."

Twenty minutes later they were fed and watered and it was Liam's turn to get clean. Craig dressed in his suit and poured himself a fresh espresso then he turned to John with an eager look.

"How quickly can I get my hands on that exhibit, John?"

John smiled. Even his curiosity had been piqued by Craig's discovery. The fifth exhibit had been a silver-coloured computer memory stick.

"Ask Des, forensics is his domain. They'll have to print it, check it for viruses and download the contents before they'll let you see it. Why not just get him to e-mail you a copy of the files?"

Craig shook his head. "No. I want to take a look at the memory stick itself. I'm positive there's something significant about it. More than just the contents of its files." He glanced at his watch and made a decision. "I'll come to the lab with you now and see Des. Liam can start things back at the ranch."

As Craig said his name, Liam wandered into the living room draped in a minuscule towel. It looked ridiculous against his six-feet-six of blue-white flesh. John burst out laughing and Craig shook his head.

"That's a hand towel, Liam! There were two bath sheets sitting on the stool." He made a face and pushed his coffee away. "I never thought anything could put me off my coffee but you've just managed it." Liam turned to one side and posed like Rodin's 'Thinker'.

"Ah now, you're just jealous. Sure you'd love muscles like this." John smiled and shook his head.

"You look like a giant milk bottle, Liam. Hurry up and get dressed."

Craig laughed. "I'm heading into the lab with John. You can take my car to the C.C.U."

Liam's towel looked perilously close to giving way under the strain of his paunch so Craig headed for the door and threw his car-keys on top of his clothes.

"Just pull the door behind you when you leave."

Craig pulled the front door behind them and they wandered down to John's car. John drove slowly up the Stranmillis Road towards its junction with the Malone. After a few minutes silence he spoke, in a confiding voice.

"I did it."

Craig responded distractedly. "Did what?"

"Set a date. Last night."

"You got married last night?"

John sighed and explained himself slowly, as if he was talking to a child. He might as well have been for the length of Craig's attention span. Until Craig had that memory stick in his hand he wouldn't listen to anything.

"We set the date for the wedding last night. The second of August. It's a Saturday."

Craig turned in his seat. "This August? You're kidding!"

51

"No, I'm not kidding. There's no point hanging about and I wanted to get married on the same day my parents did."

Craig laughed incredulously. "Have you any idea how long it takes to plan a wedding, John?"

"Ah, well now, that's where you're wrong. It takes years if it's one of those frothy Northern Irish jobs, where you have to invite the world and his wife, but we're not having that."

Craig smiled, knowing exactly what was coming next.

"We're getting married abroad. We haven't decided where yet. And instead of paying twenty grand for a bunch of bridesmaids and a mediocre meal, we're going to fly a select few guests out for the ceremony."

Craig smiled. It was exactly what he would do, in his case the venue would have to be Italy somewhere, otherwise he'd never hear the end of it from his mum, but his money was on John choosing somewhere much farther afield.

"Where are you thinking of?"

"We've a shortlist of the Caribbean, the Azores and the Seychelles. Somewhere with great weather and lots to drink."

"Good for you. At least now Natalie will stop sending you pictures of flower arrangements."

John nodded, looking relieved. "Book the time off now, will you? And the rest of your team."

Craig smiled. John didn't have any relatives except an elderly aunt in Carryduff, so Craig's family and team were pretty much it.

"They'll love it. Give me the list of people you want to go as soon as possible and I'll organise their leave."

"Don't tell them why though. Natalie wants it to be a surprise when the invitations arrive."

Craig laughed at the image of Liam in a sarong. After this morning's exhibition the image made him shudder. John turned off the Saintfield Road and they parked at the lab. Craig jumped out first.

"I'm heading up to see Des. I'll be with you in ten minutes."

"Victoria Linton's body has arrived so I'll be in the dissection room. Join me there."

Craig took the lift to the third floor and knocked on a white door embellished 'Dr Desmond Marsham. Head of Forensic Science.'

He smiled, he'd never thought of Des as a Desmond before and he was certain that Liam didn't know that was his name, otherwise he would have been slagging him about it for years and playing Desmond Dekker songs whenever he got a chance. Des and John worked well as a team, pretty much like Liam and him. John with his bodies and Des finding whatever nasty implement had killed them.

After a few seconds knocking a cheerful voice yelled, "Come in."

Craig pushed open the door and went to say hello just as Des turned around from his microscope. Craig stopped mid-word, shocked. In place of Des' normal bushy beard he was sporting a Che Guevara moustache. Craig gawped at him for a moment, not certain what to say, then he told him the truth.

"My God, Des. You look ten years younger. When did that happen?"

Des grinned cheerfully and it made him look younger still. "Do you like it?" He stroked his moustache proudly. "Annie made me shave the beard off. She was fed up with people thinking I was her dad." He smiled confidingly. "To be honest, even I was getting fed up with it. It was bloody itchy."

"And it made you look like something out of ZZ Top."

Des waved Craig to a chair, talking quickly. "Before you ask, Marc, no, you can't have the memory stick yet."

"How…?"

"I have my spies." He tried to look mysterious then caved in. "OK it was Jenny, the C.S.I. at the scene. She told me you stared at it like you'd fallen in love."

"I need it, Des, it's important to the case."

"You mean the file on it is?"

Craig shook his head vehemently. "No. Not just the file, the USB itself is important, I'm sure of it." Craig realised what Des had said and did a double take. "There was only one file on it?"

"Yes and a very short one it was. I'll tell you about it once I've explained a few things." He leaned over and opened a drawer, withdrawing the USB still in its evidence bag. "When we get items of electronic equipment we have to do a number of additional checks on them. It's not just the usual finger-printing and what have you. We have to test them for booby-traps, explosives, radiation, poisonous deposits, the works. If they pass all of that then we scan them for viruses on a special machine. We can't just put them in one of our PCs and open them; they could crash the whole system."

He turned the evidence bag over in his hand. "Victoria Linton worked in a barrister's chambers and they would have a closed system as well. So that no USBs but those issued by the chambers could have been used in their computers; they would have been automatically locked out. Yes?"

Craig nodded. He hadn't thought about it, but Des was right. That could have been why Linton had brought the USB home from work.

"That means she couldn't have viewed it at work, even though it was delivered there."

Des nodded. "Correct. Plus the fact that the envelope was marked private would likely have made her want to look at the USB's contents away from prying eyes. That was clever of whoever sent it, considering what it contained."

Des reached into the drawer again and withdrew two more evidence bags. One of them held the jiffy bag that Craig had seen the night before.

"This is the jiffy bag that the USB probably came in. I say probably because we're assuming she got this at work yesterday and took it home to view last night. That might not be the case. She might have had this USB for weeks and there could have been something completely different delivered in the jiffy bag."

Craig shook his head. "The USB was in it and it was delivered yesterday."

"Probably."

Craig's voice was firm. "Definitely, but we'll check with her office to make sure."

Des smiled wryly then handed Craig the other evidence bag. It contained a sheet of crumpled paper. Craig turned it over in his hand, puzzled.

"I haven't seen this before. It wasn't listed."

"Ah yes it was, but not amongst the things found around her settee. It was listed under the contents of her wastepaper bin. That's where it was found, screwed up in a ball. There's nothing unusual about the paper. No prints, standard A4 and Times Roman font. But read what it says."

Craig peered through the plastic and made out five neatly printed words. 'I am from the past.' Nothing else to say where it was from or who'd sent it. He glanced at Des.

"She would have thought it was something romantic. A personal letter sent with the USB."

Des nodded. "Yes, especially given the shape of the USB."

Craig screwed up his face quizzically. What did he mean, shape? It was just a memory stick. Des removed another plastic bag from the drawer and handed it to Craig. It held a silver-grey metal key in a gothic design. Craig examined it carefully. The key's head was ornate and there was intricate scrolling down its wide shank. The end was hollow, as if there had been something hidden inside. Of course...

Des gestured at the key. "That was found on the floor. It's a cover for the memory stick. The stick slips neatly inside."

"Very romantic, especially when she read the note. Key to my heart and that sort of thing."

"Even more romantic given the fact that the key's made of platinum."

Craig felt the key's weight and gave a low whistle. It was worth a small fortune. His dad had bought his mum a platinum ring for their fortieth wedding anniversary and it had cost him well over a grand. This was worth at least twice that. Craig said nothing for a moment then he smiled slowly.

"Everything here is telling us something about our killer, Des. The note, the shape of the key, the use of platinum and whatever was on the file. What was on the file?"

Des shook his head. "You're not going to like it. Whoever is doing all this isn't going to make it easy for you."

Craig was insistent. "What was it?"

"Just the number '111012' and a few words."

Craig's eyes widened in surprise. He'd expected more. "You're certain that was everything?"

"Positive."

Craig frowned. "What were the words?"

"'I am depressed and I have nothing to live for.' Exactly what was written on the suicide note left beside her body in the car."

"And at every one of the other scenes."

Des nodded. "All four suicide notes were identical: a six-digit number written on the back and ten handwritten words on the other side. The handwriting matched the victims and the only prints on the paper belonged to the victims themselves."

Craig frowned again. "The suicide note's had numbers on them?"

"Yes. Didn't John tell you?"

Craig shook his head. It wasn't like John to be sloppy. Maybe Natalie's wedding spam had been getting to him. Des' sudden look of realisation said that it might not have been John's mistake after all.

Des rushed over to a cabinet and withdrew a file, spreading out the four pieces of paper inside. Three were photocopies of identically worded suicide notes from Diana Rogan's, Jonathan McCafferty's and Nelson Warner's scenes, without any numbers to be seen. The fourth piece of paper held three sets of numbers.

Des set his jaw. "I'm going to bloody kill Jim."

"He only copied the text to John?"

Des nodded. "The original notes go into our reports, ready to be sent to the coroner or court, and we keep photocopies of them in the files. Jim must have thought the numbers weren't important for John to see so he didn't put them on the copies he sent John and copied them together on a separate sheet." He shook his head. "I'll have a word."

He handed the page holding the list of numbers to Craig. They made no sense at all. Craig shook his head.

"I'd have said they were dates, except that there aren't seventeen months in any year or fifty days in any month as far as I know. Linton's and Rogan's numbers look like dates, but not the other two. They could be the combinations of safes for all we know." He shrugged, knowing Davy would enjoy cracking the puzzle. "There were no other files on the memory stick at all?"

Des shook his head. "Nothing." Craig was incredulous.

"Then whatever those numbers meant to our victims, they were enough to make each of them copy the text into a suicide note and kill themselves?"

"It seems so."

Craig shook his head. "No. There's something more here. There has to be. No-one's that easily intimidated!"

"Well, good luck with finding it."

They sat in silence for a moment, Des doodling the key's design over and over again on a page and Craig trying to make things fit inside his head. After a minute Craig leaned forward.

"Each victim's note was identical, and they knew to copy it out in their own handwriting. That means they got instructions from somewhere. Were USBs found at the other scenes?"

Des rubbed his face. "The problem is that the first two scenes weren't preserved, Marc. Diana Rogan was found dead at home from a Paracetamol overdose and Jonathan McCafferty hanged himself, again at home. They looked like open and shut suicides. It was only with Nelson Warner that John thought there might be foul play. His scene was preserved; in fact his apartment is still taped off."

They smiled simultaneously and stood up.

"Have you got your car, Des? I lent Liam mine."

"Yes. But remember that John's expecting you downstairs. We'll give him a yell as we pass."

Five minutes later they were in Des' car, leaving John preparing to start Victoria Linton's P.M. After ten minutes they were standing inside Nelson Warner's apartment overlooking Belfast's Albert Bridge. As they'd driven into the development the title on the name plate had rung a bell with Craig. 'St John's Harbour'. Where did he know the name from? He hadn't visited there before, he was certain of that.

Craig wandered onto the balcony that Nelson Warner had taken a swan-dive from and stared into the Lagan five storeys below. The small balcony was empty, apart from a circular metal table and the wicker chair that their victim had jumped off. There was nothing else to see so Craig turned back towards the living room. It was long and wide, laid out in an L-shape, with a pale wood kitchen arranged along the shorter arm. He paced the room several times, from the outsized flat-screen television at one end to the wide settee and long pine table at the other, then he turned to Des.

"Where was Warner's computer?"

"On the table, there." Des pointed at the rough pine slab.

"Have all the contents of the apartment been taken back to the lab?"

"You've already seen the suicide note. His laptop, papers etc. are still being examined." Des paused for a moment before he spoke again. "We wouldn't have specifically noted a USB amongst his effects because we weren't looking for anything like that. Give me a minute."

He pulled out his mobile and made a call while Craig wandered around the rest of the large flat. It was nice; almost as nice as Victoria Linton's apartment and it was only Nelson Warner's weekday Pied à Terre. Linton and Warner had both been wealthy and that was already too much coincidence for him. But then… Diana Rogan hadn't been, so where did she fit in?

Des found Craig in the bedroom, staring down at the oversized bed. Craig doubted that Nelson Warner had been sleeping in it alone every night. He turned to Des eagerly.

"Well?"

Des nodded. "Jenny was just filing Warner's effects to bring them to me. There's a memory stick with a cover identical to the key that Victoria Linton had."

Craig grinned. Now they were getting somewhere. They cast a final look around the apartment and then headed for the lift. As he pressed the button Craig had a fleeting thought about phoning the squad. He dismissed it immediately. Liam and Annette would get on with things, although he'd better phone in at some point or Nicky would send out a search party. As they stepped out of the lift at ground level a woman went to get in. Craig recognised her instantly. It was Katy Stevens! He smiled broadly.

"Hello."

Katy stared at him confused, in the way you are when you see someone somewhere you least expect.

"Mr Craig. What are you doing here?"

Craig glanced upwards in reflex and she nodded.

"Ah… Mr Warner on the fifth floor. Very sad. He was such a nice man."

Craig smiled at her kindness. "Do you live here?"

"Yes. I have done for years."

Craig nodded. That was where he'd recognised the name of the development from. She'd been a witness in the Murray-Hill case the year before. He would've seen her address when he'd interviewed her.

Des watched the exchange with a focus that made Craig blush and he said goodbye hastily. They walked to the car in silence and as they fastened their seat-belts Des shot Craig a knowing smile.

"Old flame of yours, Marc?"

Craig gave him a look that had made grown men quake.

"That look doesn't have any effect on me, you know. I take it that's a yes."

"It's a no."

"Well, then I'll lay odds on that it won't be long before you give her a call…"

***

By the time Craig returned to the C.C.U. it was time for lunch, so he gathered everyone together and they headed to The James bar, the C.C.U.'s local watering hole. As they were walking down Princes Dock Street Liam fell back beside Craig and dropped his voice.

"We've done a search on the boyfriend, boss. Linton must have fancied a bit of rough."

"In what way?"

"Well he doesn't live in BT9 for one thing. He has an address somewhere out near Sydenham."

BT9 was the postcode of an expensive area of Belfast that nestled between University Road and Balmoral Avenue. It was home to Queen's University, Belfast's academic jewel, houses worth millions of pounds, and restaurants and shops with prices that would make the average Belfeirstian's eyes water. It was just known as BT9 to the rest of Belfast. Shorthand for Northern Irish prosperity.

"When are you seeing him?"

Liam shot him a surprised look at the 'you'. "This afternoon. Don't you want to be there?"

Craig shook his head. He needed some time to make sense of the past few hours.

"He's not a suspect yet, Liam. Remember we have four cases so it's unlikely that whoever did this was just linked to Victoria

Linton. We're beginning to find things that tie the cases together."

Liam went to ask the question but Craig shook his head. "Give me a few hours. We'll have a briefing at four o'clock and I'll tell you everything then."

Craig glanced at the group walking slowly ahead. Nicky and Annette were deep in conversation and Craig watched as Nicky balanced perfectly on her five-inch heels, despite the street's surface being broken by tram lines and the remnants of builders' waste. Davy and Jake were walking together. Davy hunched over, with his hands pushed deep into his jean pockets, his six-foot plus gangly frame still towering over Jake's much more compact five-feet-eight. Craig smiled; glad to see Davy back in his dark jeans after a few months trying out his girlfriend Maggie's suggestion of wearing a suit. He'd never really looked comfortable and it hadn't been necessary when he didn't work with the public face-to-face. But Craig was glad to see that some remnants of the style change had survived in the shirts he now wore instead of his old, ripped T-shirts.

They reached the pub and ordered and while they were waiting for the food to come Craig brought them up to speed on his thoughts.

"We definitely have four cases that were made to look like suicide but are effectively murder. They killed themselves, but only after they were coerced into it."

Jake went to ask a question but Craig nodded him into silence while the waitress put down their plates then he picked up the file he'd brought with him and explained. "Each of them left a suicide note using exactly the same words."

Jake interrupted, more confident now that his secondment to the team had become permanent.

"How did Victoria Linton kill herself, sir?"

"Car exhaust. She was found this morning by a neighbour coming home after a late night."

Annette made a face at the image. She'd seen Carbon

61

Monoxide poisoning once when she'd worked in A&E and it wasn't pretty.

Nicky scanned Craig's face, looking concerned. "Were you up half the night?"

Craig nodded and Liam chipped in, looking for sympathy. "And me."

Nicky came back at him, quick as a whip. "You'll soon catch up. You're always half asleep."

Liam objected loudly, starting a moment of banter. As it died down Jake spoke again.

"But if they all killed themselves, even if they were coerced into it, where's the chargeable crime? If I tell you to kill yourself otherwise I'm going to... kill your budgie, say, what crime can you charge me with?"

"Here, son. What did budgies ever do to you?"

Craig smiled and raised his hand, stilling the next round of jokes. "John made that point to me yesterday, Jake. They killed themselves, we're sure of that, but I think they were blackmailed into it. So that's one crime for a start. We're also pretty sure that John was being stalked."

"And you got a threatening phone-call, sir, don't forget that." Craig turned to Nicky just in time to see a chip disappearing through her indignantly pursed lips.

"If we ever catch them there'll be plenty to charge them with, Nicky, don't worry about that. I'm more concerned with finding them before someone else dies."

Annette gave him a smile that said 'come on now, tell the truth'. Craig laughed, acknowledging that she was right.

"OK. Yes, I want to solve the puzzle too."

They reverted to normal chatter while the meals were eaten and the teas and coffees came. As he sipped his espresso Craig remembered something.

"Has anyone seen Des recently?"

There was a series of 'no's'.

Liam caught on first. "Why? Is there something we should

know?"

"Annie made him shave off his beard. He looks ten years younger."

Nicky screwed up her face. "I'm not surprised. It must have been like kissing a Brillo-pad."

Davy interjected. "Do married people still s…snog then? I thought you were all too old."

"You cheeky young…"

Annette smiled and shook her head. "It's hard to imagine Des without his facial hair."

Craig smiled. "Ah now, I didn't say that. He's grown a moustache."

"Hitler or Stalin?"

"More revolutionary Guevara. It looks good."

Liam took a gulp of tea and then laughed. "Sure, whether it does or not it'll give us something to slag him about."

***

Jenna Graham watched the team as they strolled back from lunch, past the Rotterdam Bar and on towards the high-rise building that housed the C.C.U. Craig had ignored the warning; he was still on the hunt. That meant he needed a reminder. Craig was a stubborn bastard; normally one threat was all it took to scare people off. She shrugged and turned away, walking down Corporation Street until she reached her car. It didn't matter what Craig did, the list was almost complete. Then they could disappear for good. Craig might think he was getting somewhere but she defied him to join the dots in time. In fact she defied him to join them at all. Only she and the others knew what this was really about and soon there would be nothing left to give the game away.

Chapter Seven

St Mary's Healthcare Trust. 1 p.m.

"Guess who I saw today?"

Natalie Ingrams picked at her sandwich trying to work out what the pink lumps inside it were, and nodded absentmindedly at her friend. They might be prawns but she couldn't see their normal pale coat beneath the sauce, or they might be chicken, but who would cover chicken with pink paste? Finally she pushed her plate away and glanced across the canteen table at Katy. She was giving Natalie an amused look.

"Are you going to eat that or dissect it?"

"I was trying to work out what it was but I've given up. Sorry, you said something. What was it?"

"I said, guess who I saw today?"

"I give up, who?"

"God, you don't make much of an effort, do you?"

Katy paused huffily until Natalie urged her on with a threatening look.

"Oh, OK. Marc Craig. He was at my apartment block with another man with a moustache."

Natalie leaned forward, excited. "That's Des Marsham. He works with John. They must have a case there."

Katy screwed up her face. "I don't think so. We had a death last week, but it was a suicide. My upstairs neighbour Mr Warner jumped into the Lagan from his balcony and drowned."

Natalie's face lit up. "Can you reach the river from your place then?"

Katy gave her a horrified look. "Yes, you can, if you jump far enough. But that's not the point. A man's dead, Natalie!"

Natalie sniffed, ever practical. "The mortuary's full of dead people but most of them didn't die in such an interesting way." She warmed to her theme. "John told me about this one case where…"

Katy stood up and Natalie stared at her in surprise. "I don't want to hear it, Nat, at least not over lunch."

Natalie waved her down. "OK, OK, keep your hair on. What's eating you?"

"I was trying to talk to you about Marc Craig and you turned it into a diatribe about dead people!"

Natalie thought back over the conversation then laughed aloud. Katy was right; she had. She leaned in with a mock-attentive look on her face.

"OK, then, tell me all about Mr Wonderful."

"Don't you like Marc?"

"I like Marc fine. In fact I'd go as far as saying I like him a lot. He's kind and he's funny, when he's not being anal about his work."

"But?"

Natalie sat back and threw her hands up in the air. "But nothing. God, Katy, you can read something into nothing better than anyone I know. I wasn't damning him with faint praise, I was telling the truth. I really like him." She smiled knowingly. "Although not half as much as you obviously do." She glanced around the canteen then leaned in like a conspirator. "I thought that you and Rowan…"

Katy set her jaw. "Rowan and I are just friends."

"That's not what I saw at the radiologists' party last week. I'm sure I saw you slow dancing with him and there wasn't much space between your lips."

"Natalie!"

"I'm just saying. If you like Marc Craig then you should do something about it, before Rowan gets the wrong idea."

Katy shook her head shyly. Her long blonde waves fell across her face hiding her expression. Natalie reached across and pushed them back like a mother.

"If I ever have a daughter I'm going to make her shave her head, or at least tie her hair back. I can't stand people hiding behind their hair."

Katy smiled at Natalie's long dark curls, they were pulled into a low ponytail down her back and Katy knew they wouldn't dare try to escape. She returned to the subject of Craig.

"I can't ask him out."

"Why not? I practically did with John. He might like to think he did it, but really I made it impossible for him not to."

Katy gawped at her. "I wouldn't have a clue what to do, and anyway…" She turned away and said something that Natalie couldn't hear. She didn't need to hear it, she already knew what it was. "I'm shy."

And she was. Terminally shy. She was worse than a teenage girl. Katy was still speaking. "He knows where I live and I gave him my card when we met last year at that art gallery, but he didn't call. He didn't even ask me to dance at your engagement party. So…"

Natalie wasn't listening, she was already making plans. If Mohammed wouldn't come to the mountain then it would have to be vice versa, and two weeks in a hot country while she got married would give Craig no chance to escape. She interrupted Katy rudely.

"What are you doing in August?"

"What? I don't know. It's too far away to think."

"Well I do. You're being my bridesmaid on an island. Somewhere that even Marc Craig, John's best man won't be able to escape from."

***

The C.C.U. 2 p.m.

Craig swung his chair around to face the window, certain that he wouldn't be disturbed for an hour. He'd promised Nicky one whole hour from three to four p.m. to go through her list of things for him to do. In exchange she wasn't to allow anybody through his door until then and she had his permission to bite anyone who tried. He pictured her sinking her teeth into Liam's leg and laughed. They flirted mercilessly with each other but so far it hadn't gone further than that, leaving both their hearts intact. If it ever progressed Craig hoped he was long gone; he wouldn't have a clue whose side to take.

He turned his mind back to the case. Four deaths, four apparent suicides. Four identical notes written in the victims' hands and four obscure six-digit numbers. So far they had two identical platinum keys from Linton and Warner's scenes and he was still waiting to see the second one. He didn't even know how Nelson Warner had received it. Victoria Linton's had been posted to her office but Warner didn't work now that he'd retired. So where had his come to? His home?

That left the two earlier deaths of Diana Rogan and Jonathan McCafferty. Had they received keys as well? They must have, so where were they? Annette was visiting the McCafferty family this afternoon so they would know more when she came back, but Diana Rogan's husband hadn't mentioned anything to him about a key. Rogan definitely hadn't had any reason to kill herself – quite the opposite. Craig thought back to her children's faces and the obvious love of her husband. She'd had everything to live for, so why?

And what did the four victims have in common? Linton and Warner were obviously wealthy. A barrister and a retired stockbroker who could afford the best. But the Rogan family was just comfortable, and most of their income would have come from Conor Rogan's job. Was he part of the equation?

And what about Julian Mooney, Victoria Linton's partner? Craig made a mental note to check into him and the other's spouses then he turned his mind back to their victims' occupations. Diana Rogan had been a middle manager in a firm of brokers, Nelson Warner had been a broker too, but he'd been retired for years. Victoria Linton was a prosecuting barrister and Jonathan McCafferty was the manager of a high street bank. What was the connection between them? Money? Their own or other people's? Money might tie three of the four together; they'd all worked with it in different ways. But not Victoria Linton. And NIBank wasn't a merchant bank, it didn't deal in stocks and shares like Rogan's and Warner's brokers firms would have done, it was just a bog-standard 'go in and cash your wages' type of place.

Even if he could establish a connection between them, like they had with the victims in the Jessica Adams' case eighteen months earlier, what was the significance of the key? Its design was too expensive and elaborate for it to mean nothing. It definitely meant something, but what?

Craig stared out at the river, looking for inspiration and caught sight of some small sailing boats set against the opposite bank. Their sails were fluttering in the light April breeze and they had flags hanging from their masts with something written on them. He walked to the window and peered out, straining to see the words. He could only read one. 'Northern'. The boats were obviously part of some company-sponsored publicity event. Craig watched them for a moment longer, wishing that he was out on the water as well. He'd sailed a lot when he was younger and Julia had bought him some refresher lessons at the Abercorn Marina for his birthday in June. He hadn't got round to taking them yet; work always seemed to get in his way.

Craig let himself think about Julia for a moment, smiling as he remembered her long red curls and freckles, then he remembered her moodiness and shuddered. They hadn't spoken since November and fortunately work hadn't made their paths cross. He'd been worried about hurting her so he hadn't had another relationship since they'd split, but it was time to move on. Craig was just about to make a phone-call to start that process when his desk-phone started to buzz.

He glanced at the clock. Two-thirty. He'd asked Nicky not to bother him until three. He lifted the phone, expecting to hear her voice saying it was important, then he froze; it was the male voice from the day before.

"I warned you not to hunt me, Craig, and now you're making me warn you again. I don't like having to repeat myself, so I think your team needs a little lesson. You'll get it when you least expect."

As soon as the line went dead Craig was out of his chair and at the door. He yanked it open. "Nicky, get a trace on the call to my line five seconds ago."

Nicky stared at him aghast and grabbed the phone. Craig knew a trace would give them nothing but they had to try. It wasn't just a threat now, it was a promise and it was time for all of them to watch their backs.

Craig lifted the line to High Street and Jack Harris answered it in one.

"Jack, is Liam there?"

"Ach, and hello to you too, sir."

"Sorry, Jack. I haven't got time for the niceties today. Get Liam on the line please."

Twenty seconds later Craig heard Liam's booming voice in the background. "What do they want? Tell the eejits that I'm busy…" Craig heard Jack mutter something then Liam's voice again, less booming this time. "Oh, right. I'll be there now."

Craig imagined the faces that Liam was pulling. He would have laughed if his message hadn't been so serious. He heard the phone being fumbled then Liam came on the line.

"What's up, boss?"

Craig's voice was urgent. "I've had another call. They've said they're going to teach the team a lesson for not dropping the case. I want you to watch your back, Liam."

"Ach now, calm down. They're all talk, that's all."

Craig's voice grew harder. "Take me seriously on this, Liam, or I'll take you off the case. Do you understand?"

Liam stared at the phone, making a face, then he acquiesced. "Aye, aye, OK. But we've no idea where or when, so all we can do is keep our eyes peeled."

"Do that. At least it's something. I need to phone Annette now. I'll see you at four. Bye."

Craig dropped the phone and called Annette, repeating the message. She was still at Jonathan McCafferty's parents and as she put down the phone she grimaced. Angela McCafferty gazed at her anxiously.

"What's the matter, Inspector? Is everything all right?"

"Yes, please don't worry, Mrs McCafferty. Now, let's go back to what you were telling me about your son."

Angela McCafferty glanced at her husband and he gave a heavy sigh. They were an elderly couple. Older than Annette had imagined from the age of their son. She'd expected a spritely pair of sixty-somethings like her own parents, but she'd been taken aback when Niall McCafferty had opened the door of their small apartment. Taken aback by two things. At the straitened circumstances they were living in, given their son's important job, and by their age. They were both in their eighties and forty-five-year-old Jonathan had been their only child. A late baby perhaps?

Angela McCafferty had corrected her obvious assumption. "Jonathan was adopted. Unfortunately we couldn't have children of our own. .Jonathan always knew. He was a good son."

Not as good as he should have been, given the shabbiness of their clothes. The elderly woman saw Annette's glance and smiled. "Jonathan offered to buy us things all the time but we wouldn't allow it. Material things aren't important to us, Inspector. We place much more importance on the love of

God."

Annette glanced round the room, noticing a cross and bible. She wondered if Jonathan McCafferty had been as religious as his parents. Not if his lifestyle and divorce were anything to go by. She changed the subject hastily; religion really wasn't her thing.

"Did his divorce affect your son a great deal?"

Niall McCafferty shook his head. "Not half as much as it should have done. Amelia was a good girl and they were happy, until he met that whore."

Angela McCafferty frowned at her husband. "Niall! That's terrible language to be using. The Inspector doesn't need to hear about all that."

Annette stilled her with a smile. "I'm afraid I do, Mrs McCafferty. I need to hear about anything that might have been important in your son's life." Annette turned back to her husband, Niall. "Do you think the divorce could have been a reason for your son's suicide, sir?"

Niall McCafferty snorted. "Not a bit of it. He didn't care. What did he have to kill himself about? He was off flying his kite all over the world. France, America, you name it. Anywhere he fancied a holiday he took one, never mind about Amelia and the kids. Well at least they'll inherit all his money. They'll be OK now."

Annette startled. She hadn't thought about his wife having a motive to see McCafferty dead. Did the same apply to the other victims? She made a note to raise the point at the briefing and carried on asking questions. Thirty minutes later she had a true picture of Jonathan McCafferty and it wasn't the image of a loving son that his mother had wanted to portray.

She said her farewells and headed back to the car, checking her mobile. She'd missed two messages. Craig saying something about being careful, and Nicky telling her to call the ranch urgently. She slotted the phone into speaker mode and dialled the squad as she drove.

Nicky answered in one ring. "Annette!"

"Yes. What's up?"

"The boss wants a word."

She transferred the call immediately and Craig barked at her down the phone. When he stopped Annette backtracked gently on his words.

"So we've been threatened and you think he was serious, sir?"

"Yes. That's what I just said."

"No. With all due respect you've just told me to be careful or I'll be sacked from the case."

Craig stared at the phone aghast. She was right. He was letting his fear for them make him threaten fire and brimstone. Annette was still talking.

"We can't protect ourselves completely, short of never leaving the C.C.U."

"I'm sorry. I know I'm barking at everyone but…"

She laughed. "It's nice to know you care. I'll see you in five minutes and you can bark at me some more."

Annette cut the call gently and drove to the C.C.U., parking in the basement garage and thinking how exposed they all were. If someone wanted to kill one of them they only had to lie in wait and put a bullet between their eyes. It was a risk, but not one they could avoid. By the time she reached the tenth floor the other teams on the floor were buzzing with rumours.

"Did you hear? Someone's been named as a target?"

"No. I heard that a contract had been taken out on Superintendent Craig."

Annette walked straight past them to her desk and started to type up her notes. Everyone on the Murder Squad had their heads down, trying to ignore the murmurs. At four o'clock Craig emerged from his office and beckoned the whole squad in. It was a squeeze once Nicky joined them but better than the other teams overhearing and speculating even more. Annette was certain they'd have declared one of them dead by the end of the day!

Craig poured them all a fresh coffee and then sat down behind his desk. His face took on a sheepish expression and he glanced at them each in turn.

"Nicky says I've been behaving like a pillock for the past hour."

Nicky's jaw dropped. "I did not. I never said the words."

"Well you should have, you've been thinking them."

She went to protest just as Craig said. "And you were right. I've been overreacting to a threat against the team and playing straight into our stalker's hands." He turned to Annette and Liam in turn. "I owe you two an apology for barking at you."

Annette waved him away with a smile, but Liam sat back and stared at the ceiling as if he was thinking weighty thoughts. When he spoke it was in a solemn tone.

"Nicky's right. You have been acting like a pillock. You threatened to sack me if I didn't do as I was told."

Nicky squinted at him in warning. "Liam..."

Craig winced. "I only meant sack you from the case, not completely."

Liam sniffed in mock hurt. "I had visions of being on the breadline, out on the street with a wife and two small children."

Davy interrupted in a dry tone. "Cut to the chase, Liam. This isn't the Oscars."

"You cheeky pup. I was just working up to my finale." He turned to Craig who was struggling to stop laughing. "I think compensation is in order, boss."

"Three pints?"

"Done."

"OK. Now, can we get on with the briefing? Good. The reason I overreacted is that the same man who called yesterday called again today at two-thirty and told me that he was going to teach the team a lesson for not dropping the case. I took it that he was going to harm someone in the team. I'm hoping that it's me that he comes for, so that I can have the pleasure of taking him down, but it may be one of you."

He stared pointedly at Davy and Nicky. "And that doesn't just mean officers. You two need to be careful as well. In fact even more careful than us because we can arm ourselves." He turned to Annette and Jake, who rarely carried guns. "I want both of you to carry your personal weapons until further notice."

Annette objected first. "Ah, sir, do I have to? You know that I hate guns."

"Yes, you have to. You too, Jake. Old Wyatt Earp here and I are always armed, but you and Annette need to be as well, just until we tie up this case."

Davy leaned in eagerly. "Can I have a gun as w...well? I've messed about on the firing range."

Craig shook his head, smiling. "Sorry, but no, Davy. You would probably shoot yourself. You and Nicky are pretty safe during the day because you're here, but I'll assign close protection officers to escort you to work and home at night, until further notice. If you're going out in the evening they'll go with you as well."

Davy made a face. "Maggie won't like that." Maggie Clarke, Davy's girlfriend, was a journalist for a local tabloid, the Belfast Chronicle and she wasn't a woman to be trifled with.

Craig smiled. "Don't worry; I'm sure she'll get a few column inches out of the case at some point."

Davy gave him a hopeful look. "Can I tell her she'll get an exclusive w...when it's cracked?"

"I'll think about it. Right, now let's get on with the case. Liam first on Julian Mooney, then Annette on the McCaffertys, Davy and Jake on their side and I'll bring you up to speed on everything else. Liam?"

Liam grinned and Craig knew he was still thinking of his three pints of beer. "Well now. Mr Mooney. I didn't get to see him but I spoke to him on the blower; he's in the Republic on business and can't get back for a few days. He was pretty cut-up about the girlfriend, Vicky Linton, there was no mistaking that.

He said that he'd no idea who would have sent her such an expensive gift. She's a criminal prosecutor so it wasn't likely to have been a grateful client."

"Expensive gift?"

Craig nodded at Jake. "Something I told Liam. We'll get to it later. That's a good point about her being a prosecutor, Liam. Her only client would have been The Crown. That means, depending how successful she was at her job, that she must have put hundreds of people away over the years. Plenty of angry cons and their relatives to consider." He raked his thick hair. "Though that wouldn't really fit with the other victims."

Davy interjected. "S...She specialised in cooperate law for years, chief, not criminal cases. She only joined the court system in 2007."

Craig gave him a puzzled look. "That's an unusual career shift. She was defending corporate clients then?"

Davy nodded. "Yes. I'm only s...starting to get the details, but I'll know more tomorrow."

"OK. Thanks. Sorry, carry on, Liam."

"Julian Mooney and Vicky Linton had been dating for nigh on a year and he said he was working up to proposing, but then we all say that, don't we?"

Craig winced, remembering his own moment down on one knee many years before. The engagement hadn't ended well.

"And Mooney must know it would make him look less of a suspect in her death if he seemed loved–up."

Craig interrupted. "What does your gut say?"

Liam shook his head. "Not guilty. He sounds a bit smooth for my liking. Like the sort you wouldn't trust near any woman you cared about, but not guilty of this. Like I said, he was pretty cut-up."

"OK, that's Mooney out of the way until we can meet with him. Davy, run all the usual checks on him anyway, please." Craig turned to Annette. "Right, Annette, the McCaffertys. Anything?"

Annette was rummaging in her handbag for something and Craig waited until she pulled it out. It was a photograph of Jonathan McCafferty on a beach, and judging by the sunshine and the exotic looking brunette by his side, it wasn't Portstewart Strand. She passed the picture round and started reporting, ignoring Liam's noisy "Phoaw."

"Jonathan McCafferty wasn't the paragon of virtue that his job and press clippings might have suggested. He was the only son of two elderly parents. They adopted him when they were in their forties; they're in their eighties now. Nice people, very religious."

Jake interrupted with a wary look on his face. "Like the Fosters?"

Craig recalled the case Jake was referring to; a murder on the North Coast the winter before. The Fosters had been a couple who'd adopted a child late in life and they'd been religious as well, expressing their love of God by beating their son half to death. He sincerely hoped that the McCafferty's approach to worship was more benign.

Annette shook her head at Jake's question. "No, nothing like the Fosters, thank God."

Craig smiled at her choice of words.

"The McCaffertys seem like genuinely devout people. They live very simply and there's definitely no money to spare. They disapproved strongly of their son's fast lifestyle. The father in particular was very vocal about it."

"What about his lifestyle? What was he doing that was so bad?"

She pursed her lips, gesturing at the circulating picture. "That wasn't his wife and she wasn't the first. Apparently he had several affairs. He was very good at spending money on himself too; took off to exotic places whenever he felt like it. Eventually his wife, Amelia, took the kids and left. The McCaffertys took her side. The father said he thought Jonathan was into cocaine as well."

Liam squinted suspiciously. "How would an eighty-year-old know about coke?"

Annette arched an eyebrow. "You'll know about more than that when you're eighty, I bet. Anyway, he didn't call it cocaine." She flicked open her notebook and read aloud. "That white stuff they put up their noses." She gave Liam a sarcastic smile. "OK now?"

"Aye, well. I like accuracy."

"It's your middle name, isn't it?"

Craig intervened before their barbed exchange took over the meeting. "Grow up you two. Keep going, Annette."

"Well, the rest of the conversation was basically the mother singing Jonathan's praises, along the lines of 'don't you remember that tie he bought you for Father's Day when he was ten?' and the father calling him all the worthless whatevers of the day. It was clear they'll never agree on the subject."

Nicky smiled. "Motherly love."

Annette nodded. "There was one interesting thing, sir. Neither of them believed that Jonathan had committed suicide, but the father said that at least his wife and kids would get all his money now. Motive?"

Craig frowned. He doubted that Amelia McCafferty had managed to drive her husband to suicide, the other way about sounded more likely. But they had to rule it out. He smiled ruefully. She wouldn't be the first black-widow spider in the world.

"OK, that's interesting, Annette. I'm not sure it will take us anywhere, but go ahead and interview the widow." He turned to Davy. He was whispering something to Jake, making him laugh. "Care to share it, lads?"

Craig had asked the question pleasantly but Davy blushed anyway. He decided to brazen it out.

"I was just s…saying that if Maggie killed me all she'd inherit would be my PlayStation games and a pile of black T-shirts."

A quick laugh went round the group and Craig could see

77

them all thinking about what they would leave behind.

Davy was on a roll. "At least if I s...snuffed it now, I'd be a good looking corpse."

Jake chipped in. "Like James Dean. Live fast, die young and be a good looking corpse."

Nicky had had enough of the conversation and tutted loudly. "And leave your poor mothers crying their eyes out too. There's nothing glamorous about dying, at any age."

Craig stifled a smile at her serious face and folded arms. They didn't quite go with today's outfit of black and white cat suit and false eyelashes. He didn't know who Nicky's fashion icons were because she changed them every week, but today's looked like Siouxsie and the Banshees.

"OK, let's get back to work. Annette, interview Amelia McCafferty. Take Jake with you please. Davy, check her out in depth and Julian Mooney as well, in addition to the checks you're running on everyone else."

"Will do."

"Right, what have you found on our victims, Davy?"

Davy uncrossed his gangly legs and leaned forward with a solemn look on his face.

"Jake's been helping me and between us w...we've looked at all but the most recent victim, Victoria Linton. I'll get to her today. S...So far there's nothing obvious on any of them. No criminal records, no obvious debts, no nasty little secrets. W... Well, none that are illegal anyway."

"Did Jonathan McCafferty's affairs show up on your searches?"

Davy nodded. "Yes." He turned to Annette apologetically. "Sorry, Annette, I s...should have told you about him. It came up when I was doing his financial checks. Hotels and meals for two all the way through his marriage, even w...while his wife was in hospital giving birth, so it obviously wasn't her he was eating them with."

Annette smiled ruefully and Craig nodded Davy on.

"There's nothing obvious that connects the three victims, chief. I've run the combinations between them in pairs and all three of them together. They didn't go to s...school or college together, they didn't w...work together anywhere at any time, not even student attachments. They didn't even like the same things."

Liam interrupted. "In what way, lad?"

"McCafferty was into s...sailing, exotic holidays and he played five-a-side football up at the Olympia playing fields once a week, with a bunch of other suits. W...Warner was into ballroom dancing and the theatre, and Diana Rogan never left the house without her kids."

Craig stopped him. "Not even the odd night out with her friends, Davy?"

Davy shook his head hard, making his long hair fall over his face. He pushed it back, irritated. Craig predicted he'd cut it soon and he wondered what style would appear next. As long as he didn't take fashion tips from Nicky he should be all right.

"Nothing. She was a real home bird."

Craig turned to Liam. "Check that out, Liam. I want to know if Diana Rogan and Nelson Warner had any skeletons in their closets, they both sound a little bit too perfect to me."

Annette and Nicky exchanged an indignant look and Craig sighed. "OK, tell me off. What have I said now?"

Nicky answered first, in her husky voice. "Well, I know everything has to be looked at, sir, but some people just have normal lives. Lots of women never go out without their husband or kids; I don't. And lots of people lead quiet lives and go dancing or to the movies."

Craig smiled, enjoying her challenge. "That's perfectly true, Nicky, and I agree with you. But lots of people don't end up being killed in such a strange way. I know you and Annette have said before that we look as if we're blaming the victims, but we're not. We're looking into the darkest recesses of their lives hoping that we'll find nothing there and can rule things out. If their killers escaped because we didn't bother looking, how would you feel then?"

Nicky folded her arms defiantly and Annette gave a sceptical, "Mmm…"

Craig laughed and turned back to Davy. "What about the suicide notes, Davy? Anything there?"

"No, s…sorry. Des says there are no prints but the victims' on any of them. Hand-written on s…standard paper." His face lit up. "But the phone-call you got was a bit tasty. The report came back from linguistics this morning."

He rushed to his desk and came back with a piece of paper, while Annette prised the beach photograph she'd passed around out of Liam's reluctant hand.

"OK. The report says that the caller w…was male."

"That was pretty obvious!"

Davy gave Liam a triumphant look. "No, it w…wasn't actually. I only gave linguistics the w…written text; I didn't tell them that it was a man who'd phoned."

"How'd they know then?"

Craig intervened. "Speech patterns. Now shut-up and let Davy report, Liam."

Liam snorted. "You mean men's speech patterns are different from women's? I could have told you that years ago. Men only talk when we've something worth saying."

Nicky and Annette rounded on him together. "Shut-up."

Liam shrugged and Davy carried on. "The phrasing and vocabulary indicates s…someone educated, like you said, chief. University or college."

"They're sure, Davy?"

"Certain. More than that. The w…wording in the phone call, 'You would see both those things as a challenge' indicates a particular use of English. I know you said he had a local accent but the language indicates that the caller spent some time in England, probably in London or the south-east."

"Anything on their age?"

"No. They said that it was more likely that they were older than thirty, but if younger they could have s…spent time around older people."

"He was somewhere in his twenties or thirties, I'm sure of that." Craig paused then turned to Nicky. "Nick, get permanent recording and traces on my mobile and desk-phone until I say stop. I want his voice on tape next time." He turned back to Davy. "Anything else on that, Davy?"

"Nope. S…Shall I go on to the USB now?"

Craig saw the other's blank faces and shook his head. "I'll update everyone first then we'll come back to that."

Over the next five minutes he brought them up to date on Victoria Linton's suicide scene and his and Des' findings. The padded envelope marked 'private' that she'd received at work, and the note that had accompanied it, mysteriously inviting her to look at her past. When Craig reached the description of the USB, Annette gasped.

"What is it, Annette?"

"I'm not sure, sir, just something you said rang a bell. Let me think about it and I'll get back to you."

Craig updated them on his road trip with Des. "We were sure that we'd find something and we did. An identical USB was found in Nelson Warner's effects."

"With the key cover, sir?"

"Yes, Jake. Why? Is that significant in some way?"

Jake frowned in concentration then nodded his head hesitantly. "It's probably just me being ridiculous, but when I was a kid there was a computer game we used to play a lot."

Something occurred to Craig and he interrupted. "How old were you when you played it?"

"About fourteen or fifteen. It was all the rage at school."

"And you're twenty-eight now, is that right?"

"Twenty–nine next month."

Nicky mentally added the fact to her team birthday list as Craig continued. "So this game might have been popular with anyone who's around their late twenties or early thirties now?"

"Yes. It was rated 16 so it was mainly played by A Level students. Parents wouldn't have bought it for anyone younger, that's why we played it at school."

"That fits with the age of the man who called me. OK, Jake, sorry for interrupting. Carry on."

"Well, the game had several levels of difficulty, like they usually have, and when you reached the top level you got a key that allowed you to open a door. Behind it was a great treasure and you had to fight your way through a series of opponents to reach it."

Davy cut in. "Sounds like a cool game. What was it called?"

"Justification."

Craig's ears perked up. "Justification as in it was OK to kill your opponents to get to the treasure?"

"Basically, yes. But also, you had to kill to get through the levels as well. You could do whatever it took to get to your goal, including killing anyone who tried to prevent you, in any way that you fancied. The ends justified the means, hence the title."

Davy nodded. "I remember it now. My mum wouldn't buy it for me 'cos I w…was too young and she said it was immoral. The older boys at s…school played it all the time."

Annette sniffed. "It certainly sounds immoral, giving children permission to behave as badly as they want and rewarding them for it. I never let Jordan and Amy play computer games. You never know what goes on in there."

Jake shrugged. "I turned out all right."

Liam tapped the side of his nose. "We only have your word for that, son."

Craig waved them into silence and turned back to Jake. "What about the key, Jake?"

"Let me draw it then you can tell me if it looks anything like your USB."

He grabbed a sheet of paper from Nicky's printer and sketched quickly with his pen. When he was satisfied Jake turned the page round. The grin that covered Craig's face said it all. The gothic design on Jake's page exactly matched the key-shaped cover they'd found on Victoria Linton's and Nelson Warner's memory sticks, down to the ornate scrollwork down its shank. Craig seized the page urgently.

"What was the key made of, Jake?"

"Sir?"

"In your game. What metal?"

"Oh, right. It was anything you fancied it being. You could choose. Why?"

Craig smiled, realising that they were on to something. "Not specifically platinum?"

Jake shook his head. "Why platinum?"

"That's what Linton's and Warner's keys were made of."

"You could have chosen platinum I suppose, but most people I knew chose gold."

Annette interjected. "That's what most kids would think of as the most valuable metal, even nowadays. The choice of platinum might mean something specific to our killer."

Jake continued. "I think the whole game was really supposed to signify the corrupting influence of greed, or the dangers of desire or something like that, but the message was totally lost on kids." He smiled, remembering. "I used to play it for hours on end unless my mum took it off me."

Liam rubbed his chin thoughtfully. "Wasn't that the game that was banned in the States?"

Jake nodded excitedly. "In the Bible belt, yes. They said it was the Devil's work."

They chatted about the game for a moment until Liam realised that Craig wasn't joining in. He was sitting quietly with a thoughtful look on his face.

"Penny for them, boss?"

Craig started talking slowly, as if he was working things out as he spoke.

"Jake's drawing of the key matches the cover of Warner's and

Linton's USBs exactly... down to the scroll work on its shaft. The key's design was copied directly from Jake's game. That means our perp played it and... the deaths are probably being justified as a means to an end as well... again, like in the game."

Annette cut in. "So what's their treasure at the end?"

"I don't know. It could be money, power, anything, but I'm pretty sure that in their mind our four victims had to be killed so that they could reach it." He glanced at Jake urgently. "How many opponents were behind the locked door in the game, Jake?"

"I can't... no, hold on, I can remember. There was no number put on them. As soon as one was killed another one sprang up."

"So how did you ever reach the treasure?"

"You just had to keep killing more brutally until you got close enough to touch it, then your enemies suddenly disappeared into thin air."

"Do you still have a copy of 'Justification', Jake?"

Jake blushed to the roots of his hair and Liam caught on instantly.

"He still plays it! You big kid, McLean."

Craig gazed at him hopefully. "Do you, Jake?"

Jake nodded.

"Can you go home and collect it now? I want to look at it ASAP."

"It'll take me about an hour, if that's OK?"

Craig glanced at the clock. It was almost five p.m. "Would you mind? I think it's best if we view it tonight."

"No problem. Aaron's away in London for work so I'd only be sitting at home alone. I'll be back by six."

It was the first time Jake had mentioned his partner in front of everyone and Craig was pleased that he had.

"OK. I need to go to the lab to see John and Des, so I'll be back by then."

Suddenly there was a loud gasp. "Oh my God!"

Everyone turned towards the source of the exclamation. It was Nicky. She looked horrified.

"You realise what this means, don't you?"

Everyone looked blank.

"It means they'll keep killing anyone who gets in their way, and we've all just been added to their list."

Chapter Eight

John stared at the key in front of him and then slid it back across the desk to Des, grinning at his moustache.

"You really need to put wax on it for the best effect, Des."

Des screwed up his face in disgust. "Candle wax! Why the hell would I do that? It would make it stick out."

John laughed loudly. "Not candle wax, you Muppet. Hair wax. You know, like that stuff Marc puts on his hair to make it stick up."

"Does he? I thought it stuck up like that all by itself."

John thought for a moment and then shrugged, conceding that he was right. Craig's thick black hair had been like that since school, especially when he raked it with his hands. If anything wax would have smoothed it down.

"Well anyway, it's some sort of wax. You can buy it in hair salons."

Des stared at him sceptically. "Do I look like I go to hair salons, John?"

John gazed at his bushy hair and smiled, conceding. "Anyway, what about this key then?"

"It's platinum and it was the cover of a USB found at Victoria Linton's home. It had the suicide note on it in a document file. We found a second one in Nelson Warner's effects. Exactly the same but with a different number."

"Number?"

"Yes, Victoria Linton's file had a number on it: 111012. Warner's was 740150. The others had numbers as well."

"I didn't see any numbers."

Des shook his head. "Long story. Anyway, I've no idea what they mean. I've sent them over for Davy to take a look."

"They're probably some sort of code." John paused for a moment. "Keys and codes, this is turning into some sort of kid's game."

Just then Craig pushed open John's office door and overheard the remark.

"A kid's game. You're exactly right."

He stared pointedly at the coffee machine and John took the hint, brewing a fresh pot.

"I wasn't expecting you, Marc. Something up?"

Craig glanced at their faces in turn, trying to work out how best to tell them about the threat. He'd made a mess of it with Liam and Annette, so he decided to try a gentler approach. He led off with Jake's computer game and meandered round to the transcript of the phone call.

"So we think we're looking at a man, late twenties or early thirties who's masterminding the suicides somehow. The design of the key seems to be linked with this 'Justification' game that Jake played in his teens."

Des interrupted. "You think our killer played it?"

"It fits with the caller's age."

It was as good a lead-in as any to the threat on all their lives. Craig took a deep draught of his coffee then set it down and gave them a solemn look.

"He called again. Today at about two-thirty."

John leaned forward eagerly. "And? Was he annoyed that you hadn't backed off?"

Craig gave him a rueful look. "You could say that. He basically promised he was going to harm one of the team next."

John laughed automatically, certain that Craig was joking, until he saw the solemn expression on his face. "Oh crap, you think he's serious, don't you?"

Craig nodded imperceptibly and took another sip of his drink. Des watched the exchange with a puzzled look.

"Are you telling me that this bastard's going to kill one of your team, Marc?"

Craig nodded. "That's about the size of it. And that means both of you as well. Anyone who's helping on this case is in danger now."

John's jaw dropped and Craig was certain that he saw Des' moustache begin to droop.

"You're probably safe enough during the day while you're here, although I would stay away from any windows that are overlooked, just in case he has a gun. But you'll both need close protection officers."

Des went to protest but Craig stilled him with a glance. "Remember what happened to the nurse who ignored her protection officer last year, Des?"

Des nodded slowly. Craig was talking about the Murray-Hill case twelve months before. A nursing sister involved in the case, Laurie Johns, had slipped away from her protection officer and ended up dead.

"I'm sorry, both of you, but this sort of threat is always a risk in a serial case. Thankfully it doesn't happen often. Nicky and Davy have protection details as well and the rest of us are tooled up. Your protection officers are waiting outside. OK if I call them in?"

John said nothing just nodded and Craig wondered what was going through his mind. He made a call to the liveried car outside then put on some fresh coffee and waited for the knock on the door. It came a moment later. Craig opened the door, beckoning two people in. They both had the healthy glow and lean fitness typical of protection officers, but that was where their resemblance to police officers ended. They looked so unlike the average peeler that Des burst out laughing. He stopped himself abruptly, realising that it must have sounded rude. Craig made the introductions.

"John, this is your protection officer. Marlene Carey."

He beckoned the officer forward and saw a smile cover John's face. Marlene Carey was a highly skilled undercover officer, so deep undercover that she could have passed for a page three girl. Her curvy figure and long blonde hair belied a third Dan black belt in Karate and firearms skills up to wazoo. She extended a slim hand and shook John's. "Nice to meet you, Dr Winter."

Des wasn't as fortunate. The officer who stepped up to protect him looked young enough to be his teenage son. Joseph Cohen was tall and tanned, with a shock of jet black hair. He looked more Italian than Craig did, although his family hailed from the middle-East. His accent however hailed from somewhere much closer to home.

"Shore and it's grand to meet you, Dr Marsham. I'm shore we'll get on foine and dandy."

Cohen's Dublin burr was so strong that Des only caught the gist of his words. He eyed the young man's lean muscles and sucked in his stomach instantly. Des' heart sank; with him in the house Annie was going to give him hell about eating too much. Craig waved the two C.P.O.s towards some chairs.

"Grab a seat and have a coffee."

"Sarry, sor, I niver tuch the stuff."

"I'll have one, sir, thank you."

Marlene Carey beamed at John and Craig knew that John was going to enjoy her company a bit too much. Natalie would soon put paid to that.

"Right. Officers Carey and Cohen will collect you in the mornings, stay here all day and escort you home in the evenings. They'll hand over to the night shift who'll keep watch outside your homes overnight." He stared at John and Des pointedly. "I know you may find this restrictive but please cooperate with the officers and do exactly as they ask. They're here to protect you, remember that."

Craig handed Marlene her coffee and then headed for the door. "I'll leave you to get acquainted. I'm heading back to the ranch to play a computer game."

The pathologist was the weak link, even better now that they'd paired him with a girl for protection. Jenna normally persuaded people to commit suicide, loath to get her hands dirty, but she would make an exception this time. Craig needed to be distracted, enough so that he took his eye off the ball while she completed her 'suicide' list. Killing his best friend should do the trick.

Jenna turned her attention back to the computer screen in front of her and watched as the pile of dead bodies grew on the dungeon's dark stone floor. Ten points for each one until she'd earned enough to get a stone tablet and progress to the next level. She flicked to the small Skype window set in the top right-hand corner of her screen and smiled coldly at the man who was her opponent for the day. They were anonymous people in a fantasy world, playing a game as if it was real life. The man had no idea that it was real-life for her. The game mattered more than anything in the world outside and it had done for almost twenty years.

***

7.30 p.m.

Craig and Jake played 'Justification' for an hour, until Craig was familiar with all the rules, which were basically zero. He could see why Jake was so keen on it; it was addictive. The concept of destroying anything that got in your way and justifying it as necessary, so that you were freed of guilt, was seductive.

They would examine the game again tomorrow but before Craig called it a night he had one last visit to make so that he could have peace of mind. He headed down the M3 motorway towards Holywood and his parents' old-fashioned home. He'd already called Lucia, his younger sister, and asked her to meet him there. She'd been curious why but there was no way he was discussing things over the phone; if it had been easy for their perp to access his office phone a mobile would be a no-brainer.

Craig pulled his Audi into the wide suburban driveway and parked behind Lucia's scrapheap of a car. Before he could even open his driver's door he was greeted by a cacophony of noise. The two sounds he could distinguish clearly were his elderly Labrador Murphy barking, and his mother's voice gabbling something in Italian. The rest would have to wait until he was inside the house.

Opening the front door didn't enlighten Craig much but it shocked him a lot. Instead of his father Tom sitting as usual in his comfortable chair, he was standing in the hall waving something at his mother. His face was redder than Craig had ever seen it but the most shocking thing was that he was yelling, actually yelling, at his mum!

Tom Craig was a man who'd sat placidly for the whole of his married life in the eye of the storm created by his extrovert wife. Craig had never seen the positions reversed, but they were now. Mirella was standing, head bowed, meekly twisting a dishcloth in her hand, while Lucia tried to calm their ranting father down. It would have been almost amusing if Tom Craig hadn't had a heart attack twelve months before.

Craig strode over and faced his father, blocking Craig Senior's view of his wife. He placed his hands on his shoulders then glanced down at what was he was holding in his hand. It was a computer tablet, a high-end one that had probably cost a couple of grand. Craig wondered where he'd got it from then he remembered his father's part-time job. Tom Craig had lectured in physics at a local University until he'd retired and since then he'd written freelance science articles for a local rag. It was the perfect job for him. It gave him permission to sit and read the scientific journals that he loved reading anyway, and the perfect excuse to avoid doing any housework for his wife. Mirella didn't mind; she was just happy to have him there while she flitted around the house tidying, or practiced her piano for the many recitals she gave. It was an arrangement that suited them both and helped generate the gentle banter that kept their marriage alive.

Craig stood nose-to-nose with his father, staring at his bright red face. This was no banter; his father was genuinely angry. For a moment Craig wondered whether he'd really inherited his temper from his mother, as he'd always thought. Tom Craig kept on yelling as Mirella gabbled pathetically until finally Craig had had enough and he shouted so loudly that Lucia burst out laughing, ruining the effect.

"Be quiet, both of you!"

The voices stopped abruptly and the only noise to be heard was Murphy barking, until Craig shot the dog a look that silenced him as well. When the room was finally quiet Craig removed his hands from his father's shoulders and stood back, scanning everyone's faces for answers. Lucia was stifling a giggle, his mother was close to tears and his father was glancing down at the device in his hand with a furious expression on his face.

"Now. Dad. Will you please tell me what this is all about?"

Before Tom Craig had time to speak Mirella leapt into the gap.

"He blame me, but I not know why." She waved her dishcloth at the device. "Stupid machine. Good for nothing."

Craig shot her a warning glance but softened it with a smile. She smiled back and clammed up. He turned back to his father.

"Dad?"

Tom Craig squinted at his wife. "Your mother took it into her head to be helpful."

Mirella started again and Craig could see that she was close to tears. "I try to help. It was dirty."

"Mirella! Let me speak."

She clammed up again and Craig's father continued. "She thought that my brand new, eighteen-hundred-pound touch-screen, wireless computer pad was dirty. So instead of wiping it with a cloth like any normal person would, your mother..."

The emphasis on 'your' made both Craig and Lucia smile. Mirella had always referred to them as 'your' children when they'd done something wrong, now their father was using the tactic in reverse.

Tom Craig was still speaking. "...decided, in her infinite wisdom, to put it in the dishwasher. The dishwasher, for God's sake! Of all the idiotic..."

So that was it. His father never lost his temper over anything; in fact Craig could hardly recall another occasion. But Mirella had destroyed the most precious thing he possessed; his shiny computer pad. Tom Craig turned to his son for agreement that Mirella had committed the most heinous crime, but he was sadly disappointed. Craig laughed and then Lucia laughed. When Mirella saw her children laughing she knew that she'd won, so she laughed as well and then stuck her tongue out at their father behind his back. Tom Craig looked fit to be tied, but Craig nodded him to a seat and took the pad from his hand.

"Dad, calm down. It might work when it dries out, but if not it'll be covered by the insurance. If it isn't I'll buy you another one. Chill out, will you. Mum meant it kindly."

Craig Senior shot him a look of disgust that he'd sided with the enemy, then he conceded grudgingly. "I suppose it is funny... in a way."

Lucia interjected helpfully "It'll make a great column for you next week, Dad. You can talk about repairs and insurance policies or something."

Tom Craig perked up and smiled at his younger child. "That's a good idea." Then he gazed at his wife with a sheepish look and beckoned her over. "I'm sorry, Mirella. I shouldn't have got so angry."

She kissed his forehead affectionately. "You can have temper once in life, but never again." She turned and flicked her dishcloth at her son. "Now it is Tuesday and we see Marco and Lucia for change, so I cook wonderful dinner and we talk."

Craig smiled ruefully, knowing that she wasn't going to like the topic of after-dinner conversation.

Chapter Nine

Wednesday, 8.30 a.m.

"Right. Until this case is wrapped up we'll be meeting every morning at eight-thirty, and every day at twelve and four for mini-briefings. Just so I can check that you're all still alive."

Craig noticed Nicky's nervous expression and smiled apologetically.

"Sorry, Nicky. I realise that you and Davy didn't sign up for this."

Liam cut in. "If you're talking about being killed, I didn't sign up for that either, boss!"

"It's an occupational hazard for us, Liam."

Liam shrugged then nodded grudgingly. "Aye, OK. I suppose you're right."

"If it's any comfort I got hell from my folks last night, when I told them they had to restrict their movements."

Nicky giggled huskily. "I can just imagine your mum's face."

"Her language was worse, trust me. The only thing that calmed her down was telling her that John and Natalie had set a wedding date. She was talking about new hats a minute later."

"Have they, sir?"

"What?"

"Set a date?"

Craig suddenly remembered that John had told him not to mention it and realised that he'd let the cat out of the bag. He shrugged. The team would've had to know soon anyway, to get themselves organised.

"OK, yes, he has. It's Saturday the second of August and I've been asked to book you all off on holiday for two weeks."

Liam boomed "Two weeks!" so loudly that Craig jerked away from him, rubbing his ear. "Even I can't drink for that long!"

"You won't be drinking the whole time, Liam. They're getting married abroad, somewhere exotic. Instead of spending money on cakes and whatnot in a hotel here, John wants to fly everyone out for a fortnight's holiday."

Davy had been sitting quietly, resting his head on his hand, still half-asleep. He woke up with a bang.

"A holiday! And the Doc's paying for everything?"

Craig nodded.

"Happy Days. That's awesome, boss."

"The only way it will be awesome is if you all pretend to be surprised when Natalie invites you. I'll be a dead man if she finds out that I've given it away."

Annette winced at Craig's choice of words and stared at him thoughtfully until the chatter died down, then she brought them all back to earth. "Are they getting protection officers, sir?"

"Who?"

"Our families."

Craig's face became serious and he shook his head. "Not at the moment, Annette. They aren't directly under threat in the way that you all are. I've restricted my family's movements to the house and I'll have to take care of them as best I can, just as you're doing with yours." He paused for a moment then restarted. "John and Des have protection details as well."

Liam leaned forward, catching Craig's eye. "Who's with the Doc?"

"Marlene Carey. Do you know her?"

Liam whistled then he grinned. "Marlene the Darlin'."

Annette snorted. "That doesn't even rhyme."

"It suits her though, doesn't it, boss?"

Craig tried not to grin. John's eyes had certainly lit up when he'd seen who was guarding him, but Natalie was staying with him tonight and there'd be fireworks when she met Marlene.

"No comment. OK, let's move on. There's a lot to get on with today. Annette and Jake are visiting Amelia McCafferty, I'm going back over Diana Rogan's case and Liam's taking a good look at Nelson Warner." He turned to Liam with a warning look. "Liam, we don't know if Warner had a mistress he stayed with at his Belfast apartment, but if he had then please be careful around his wife. She may not know, and if she does I'm damn sure she won't want it rubbed in her face. So, a bit of diplomacy, OK?"

Liam feigned innocence. "I'm the soul of discretion."

Craig gave him a sceptical look and continued. "Jake, have you booted up the game?"

"Yes. It's ready on my screen so that you can all have a look."

Two minutes later they were huddled around Jake's computer, watching as he worked quickly though Justification's increasing levels of difficulty. On each level he had to kill anyone who got between him and a stone tablet. When he had enough tablets he gained entry to the final level where the tablets were exchanged for the key which opened the door to the ultimate trial and the treasure.

Davy leaned in curiously. "W...What's the treasure?"

Jake grinned. "Like I said yesterday, that's the thing that makes it cool. The player chooses what their treasure is at the very start of the game. Money, power, love, whatever you fancy. You set it at the beginning of the game and work towards achieving it by killing anyone who gets in your way."

Craig said what they were all thinking. "Apart from teaching hand-eye coordination, all it teaches is how to kill."

Jake glanced at him defensively. "It teaches different methods of killing as well, sir. You can choose to have weapons or use unarmed combat: bare-knuckle fighting, wresting, martial arts, anything you like. It requires skill."

Craig smiled sceptically. "In the hands of a well-balanced

individual like you I'm sure that's possible, Jake, and it may have improved your fighting skills. But if someone is even slightly disturbed this is going to make them worse. It's essentially rewarding them for destroying anyone or anything in their path."

"And giving them a serotonin buzz."

Craig turned to face Annette. "Go on."

"Serotonin is the brain's 'feel-good' chemical. There's a theory that some behaviours or situations that cause repeated pleasure can elevate its levels in the brain and create psychological dependency. I'd be very surprised if this game didn't do that pretty quickly."

Craig nodded. He could feel it happening to him when they'd played the evening before.

"So an already vulnerable individual could become dependent on the game."

"Yes. And the morality it encourages."

Nicky tutted loudly. "It's a playground for psychopaths and addicts."

Liam rubbed his chin. "Aye, this is all fine and dandy, but what's it got to do with our killer? The key's the only connection and they might just have liked the key's design and copied it."

Craig smiled. Liam hated anything abstract or theoretical. "Don't forget our caller's age, Liam – that fits as well. This game was in vogue in the late 1990s, early 2000s, when our caller would have been in their teens, and it was a game used predominantly by teenagers."

"So you're saying that our killer became addicted to this game all those years ago and decides now to make it the basis for a killing spree? That's a stretch, boss, but OK. But where's the connection with suicide? The people in the game are killed directly, they don't kill themselves."

Craig thought for a moment, Liam was making valid points, but he still knew that he was right.

"OK. Let's say our killer was a vulnerable or shy teenager

who sought refuge from the world in this game. He played it all the time and basically became addicted. Yes?"

There was a series of nods.

"But that doesn't turn him into a killer on its own. Let's say that something traumatic happens to him in real life, perhaps something involving suicide. Something inside him breaks and he descends even further into the fantasy world of the game."

Annette nodded enthusiastically. "So he tried to commit suicide?"

"Or someone else he cared about did and they succeeded. Whatever happened suicide is part of it, I'm sure of that, and the experience skewed him somehow."

Davy shook his head, making his hair fall into his mouth. He pulled it out quickly as Craig nodded him on. "That w... wouldn't explain why he didn't start killing years ago. W... When things first went wrong in his life."

"Good point, Davy. Let's look at that. He's a teenager and something traumatic twists him, so that the game he was already playing too often suddenly becomes his whole world. He retreats into it. So why start killing years later? One idea might be that he was a child when he was traumatised, with no access to the means to kill."

Liam shook his head. "Nah. That would only work until he was an adult, maybe late teens. Why wait another ten years?"

"OK then, anyone else?"

Nicky chipped in. "What about if he'd been in therapy or locked away? If he'd been in a psychiatric unit or prison, he couldn't get out to kill anyone."

Craig nodded. "Very good. So far we've got no capability because he was too young, or no access because he was incarcerated. Anyone else?"

Jake tapped his computer screen thoughtfully. "How about... how about if he was looking for justice for something criminal that had happened in his life, and he tried the legal route but it failed. It might have taken him years to go through the courts. It might only have been when that failed that he decided to take the law into his own hands?"

Craig barely breathed for a moment. All of the theories made sense. Something had happened to their killer in his teens and he was taking delayed revenge for it now. It might have been delayed for all sorts of reasons. But what was it that had traumatised him so much originally? Craig didn't know why but the idea of something criminal didn't ring true.

"I think you're almost there Jake, but I don't think this was something criminal. What happened to him was something emotional, something to do with suicide."

Davy turned to Craig, excited. "Maybe it's an insurance case, chief? That would combine the court and emotional things. W...What if someone connected to him committed s...suicide and his family were denied their life insurance money? It could have taken years for the courts to say no?"

Craig raked his hair, thinking hard. It was almost right but he knew there was still something missing, he just couldn't work out what it was. He sighed and nodded. It was as good a place to start as any.

"Good work, everyone. OK. Davy. Start looking at suicides in Northern Ireland between the mid-1990s and early 2000s, if our killer was a teenager that would put him between his late twenties to early thirties now. Look for any and all suicides where the surviving family contained a teenage son. Also, find out if there are any online forums for this particular computer game. If he's so obsessed with it then it's odds on that he'll still be playing it."

Liam's voice boomed across the room. "He might just play it alone, boss. Lurking in some darkened room."

Jake shook his head. "No, there are gaming forums for everything. Everyone uses them when they get bored playing alone."

Craig nodded. "OK. Davy, Jake can help you on that when he gets back from Amelia McCafferty's. You've all got other checks to work on as well, so there's plenty for everyone to do before we meet again at twelve o'clock."

Craig strode across the floor towards his office and then turned back with a grim look.

"Remember that we're all under threat so don't forget that, please. You need to watch your backs."

***

The Rogan's. 10 a.m.

"You never saw your wife with anything that resembled a key cut in a gothic design?"

Conor Rogan thought hard for a moment then shook his head despairingly at Craig.

"There seems to have been so much about Diana that I didn't know. She never even told me that she was feeling sad. I must have been making her miserable and I never realised."

Craig really felt for the man. His young wife had killed herself and he had no idea why; it was natural to blame himself. Craig wanted to tell Rogan where their investigation was pointing but he couldn't, in case it turned out to be smoke and mirrors and Jake's computer game turned out to be just that: a game. He decided to take a different tack.

"Your wife worked in a firm of brokers in town, you said?"

Rogan nodded vaguely. The shadows under his eyes were so deep that Craig wondered if he'd slept at all since they'd last met. Davy would rule him in or out as his wife's killer with his computer checks. They had to do them to be sure, but Craig already knew the man in front of him had had nothing to do with Diana Rogan's death.

"Did they specialise in any particular area of broking?"

Craig's knowledge of the stock market could have been written on the back of a stamp but he knew enough to know that brokers often specialised in different markets, some in commodities like coffee, others in telecommunications etc.

Rogan shook his head. "I honestly don't know. Diana didn't talk much about her work. I know she was good at it and that she worked hard, but it was such a small part of her life. The kids..." He sobbed suddenly and tears began to trickle down his face. "They were everything to her. She would never have left them voluntarily." His voice dropped. "Except she obviously did, didn't she...?"

Craig couldn't stand it any longer. He had to give the man something to hold on to or he might be the next death. Craig said the words quietly, as if less volume somehow meant that he was giving less away.

"You don't know why she did it, Mr Rogan, and neither do we. But I can tell you that if we thought this was a straightforward suicide we wouldn't be investigating it like a murder."

Rogan's eyes widened. "But the post-mortem..."

Craig nodded. "Yes I know. The post-mortem was conclusive that she died by her own hand, but that doesn't mean it was by her own choice."

Rogan gawped at him. "You think she was forced into it?"

Craig raised a hand to prevent more questions. "I've already said too much, Mr Rogan, and I must ask you to keep it to yourself. Please."

Rogan nodded reluctantly.

"But I honestly don't believe that your wife chose to leave you or your children. I can't say any more than that right now."

Just then the children giggled in the next room. Rogan glanced towards the door in case they'd overheard then he nodded again. "Thank you for telling me, Superintendent. It helps to know in one way, but in another..."

Craig knew that he was picturing his wife being pressured to end her life and feeling unable to discuss it with him. Hopefully they'd find the metal key that Craig was sure Diana Rogan had been sent, but until then, they could only speculate as to why she'd been chosen to die.

"When your wife... Did you tidy up the room?"

Rogan shook his head sorrowfully. "I couldn't... The police had a look around and then my mother-in-law cleared up. I haven't been in the bedroom since. I've...I've been sleeping downstairs."

Craig set his coffee down and rose to his feet, glancing towards the hall. "Can we take a look now?"

Rogan hesitated for a moment and Craig read his mind.

"If you show me which room it is, I'm happy to go in by myself."

A look of relief covered the younger man's face and Craig wondered how long it would be before he sold the house. Rogan would never sleep in that bedroom again without thinking of his wife.

They climbed the stairs slowly and Rogan pointed Craig towards a room at one end of the landing. Craig turned the door handle hesitantly as Rogan raced back downstairs. Poor sod. He knew he would be the same if someone he loved killed themselves. He shuddered, trying not to imagine it.

When Craig entered the small bedroom he was surprised by its everyday ordinariness, as he often was at the place where someone had died. Somehow death belonged in dingy alleyways and abandoned barns, but not in the neat suburban houses where most people really met their end.

It was all so normal looking. A king-sized bed, with a small table on either side. One covered with bits of screwed-up paper and a spy novel. The other heavy with pictures and jewellery, the difference between the sexes captured in the small tableau. Craig turned his head and saw fitted wardrobes at the other end of the room. He slid the doors open. One side was completely empty and the other was full of a woman's clothes. He glanced down and saw Diana Rogan's shoes; high heels and trainers to match the suits and tracksuits above, the wardrobe of every working mum. It was so poignant it made Craig catch his breath. He couldn't imagine how he would feel if they belonged to a woman he loved.

After a moment he turned back towards the bed, his eyes drawn towards the right-hand side. That was where the police report said Diana Rogan had been found, at four-thirty in the afternoon. She'd been found by her mother when the school had phoned her to ask why no-one had collected the kids. Poor woman, finding her only daughter in such a way. It must have nearly killed her; he knew it would kill his mother if she found Lucia like that.

Diana Rogan had been wearing her suit when they'd found her, but she hadn't gone into work that day. The post-mortem estimated her time of death at one o'clock. Five hours since she'd kissed her husband and children goodbye, letting them believe that she was leaving for work soon after. Five hours of plucking up the nerve to swallow the Paracetamol tablets, and then swallow more to replace the ones that she'd vomited up.

Craig gazed at a framed photograph on her bedside table then walked over and peered at it. It was a group shot at a family gathering, showing everyone that she loved. Her parents and children, and in the middle Conor and her. Her husband's statement had said it normally sat in the living room. She'd brought it upstairs specially. For comfort or for courage? What could possibly have persuaded her to take her own life when she had so much? What was the hold that their killer had over Diana Rogan, or any of the people who had died? Was it the same for all four suicides or different for each one?

Craig stayed in the room for so long that finally Conor Rogan climbed the stairs and knocked the door. He retreated quickly, in case he glimpsed the room's interior when Craig emerged. As Craig approached Rogan he turned his face away, his message clear: don't tell me what you found because I don't want to hear the words. Craig said nothing, merely nodded and thanked him, then he left the small, ruined, family home and drove swiftly away.

***

Jake and Annette walked away from Amelia McCafferty's elegant home certain that she wouldn't be mourning her ex-husband at all. To say there'd been no love lost between them would have been an understatement; Jake thought the ice age had probably been warmer than their marriage.

"Well, she hated him for sure."

"Was that a statement or a question, Jake?"

"A fact."

Annette nodded, conceding that he was right but understanding better than he did how a marriage could foster hate. She and Pete were trying to make a go of it after his affair the June before, but there were days that she still wished him dead.

"She may have hated her husband but she didn't kill him."

"How do you know, Ma'am?"

Annette smiled at the old-fashioned term. She kept telling him to call her Annette. He'd remember for a while, then lapse back to her default title again.

"Because our killer's clever, and to be blunt, that woman was as thick as two short planks!"

Jake burst out laughing at the most un-Annette-like phrase; it was something he'd have expected Liam to say. Nevertheless it was true. When beauty had been handed out Amelia McCafferty had been at the top of the queue, but when brains were being distributed she must have been doing her nails. Annette continued.

"She would never have thought up something like that key. Besides, she's female and too young."

She wrinkled her nose in disgust. Jonathan McCafferty had been fair, fat and forty-five. His bride of seven years was twenty years younger.

"He must have met her at the school gates, Ma'am."

"Yes, when he was kerb-crawling!"

They both laughed this time and Jake made a note to tell Liam Annette's joke. They climbed into the car and Annette turned over the engine, doing a U-turn towards the Belmont road.

Jake pointed back over his shoulder.

"Aren't we going the wrong way? The C.C.U.s back there."

"We're not going back yet. We're going to his parents' place. I think I saw something there yesterday and I want to check."

Ten minutes later they were knocking on Niall McCafferty's apartment door. He opened it with an unwelcoming look on his face.

"What now, Inspector? Didn't you upset my wife enough yesterday?"

Annette gazed at him apologetically. "I'm sorry, Mr McCafferty. I only have one more question, I promise. This is my colleague Sergeant McLean. May we come in for a moment?"

The old man sighed heavily and waved them into the small living room, then took up position behind his wife's chair. Angela McCafferty looked even more fatigued than she had the day before and it was hard not to see the tell-tale signs of tears. Annette vowed to make the visit quick.

"Mr and Mrs McCafferty, when I was here yesterday I couldn't help but notice something."

"What?"

Niall McCafferty's voice was flat and its undertone said 'hurry up and get out'.

Annette walked over to a small bookcase set on one side of the room, where they'd erected a make-shift shrine to their son. It had photographs of Jonathan growing up arranged in a semi-circle, with a young boy's knick-knacks sitting in front. The photos stopped at the age of around twenty. Annette presumed that was the point where McCafferty senior had lost control of his son.

Annette withdrew a plastic glove from her handbag and put

it on then she lifted the small object she'd noticed there the day before. As she held it up Jake gasped. It was a key made in a gothic design.

"Could I ask you, Mr McCafferty, did your son give you this?"

Angela McCafferty struggled to her feet and reached out to retrieve the key. Annette held onto it tightly.

"Did he, Mrs McCafferty?"

"No. It was found amongst his effects. Amelia didn't want it so I asked for it as a little reminder of him."

Annette turned the key over, inspecting it, then she withdrew the USB that lay inside. Angela McCafferty gawped at it.

"What's that?"

Annette smiled, certain that the woman wouldn't have a clue what to do with a memory stick.

"It's a computer stick that contains information. With your permission I'd like our forensic lab to take a look at it. It will be returned to you."

"You promise? Only I want it to remember Jonathan by."

Annette nodded firmly. "I promise. But we must examine it. It might be important in explaining why your son died."

The elderly woman nodded and Annette saw that she was close to tears. She put the key quickly into an evidence bag, ready to be dropped off at the lab on their way back to the squad.

***

Liam left the Warner's slim, modern house wearing a faux-grave expression, by the time he'd reached his aging Ford it had changed to one of incredulity. He let out a long whistle. There wasn't much that shocked a hoary old cop like him but Erica Warner had just managed it. Maybe he was getting old, like Davy and Jake were always joking or maybe even he had more morals than modern society possessed.

He was turning the car engine over and wondering how the others would react to his newly acquired information when his mobile rang. It was Craig.

"What's up?"

Craig smiled at Liam's lack of preamble. Good. He didn't have time to waste on 'how's the weather?' Niceties were reserved for conversations with girlfriends, and not even that in his life nowadays.

"Meet me at the offices of Linton and Roche, Liam. We're interviewing Victoria Linton's P.A. in half an hour."

"Fine. I'll see you there."

The line clicked off and that was it. No bye-bye or cheerio, no 'what's it about?' or 'what's her name?' Just the Vulcanesque shorthand that had developed between them over the years. Logical and efficient. All that was missing was the 'live long and prosper' hand gesture and they would be the perfect Kirk and politically incorrect Spock.

Twenty minutes later Spock and Kirk were sitting in a café opposite Victoria Linton's elegant chambers, drinking coffee. They were early and even if they hadn't been, Natasha Nunes had extended her coffee-break to run some errands, leaving them with twenty minutes to kill.

Craig finished his scone and went to the counter to order a fresh round of drinks, scanning the room carefully on his way back. Any man in the café could be their mystery caller and try to end one of their lives. Or would he? Would killing first hand be as easy as coercing someone to kill themselves, or pressing a button on a computer game and watching a monster fall to the ground? Killing by proxy was easy: distant, clean and quick, without any of the blood-letting, air-gasping reality of death. Killing close-up was quite another thing.

The waitress brought their fresh coffees just as Craig sat down again. Liam dropped the last corner of a pastry into his mouth and took a slurp, starting to talk before he swallowed as he always did.

"I was going to keep this for the briefing but it's no good, I have to tell you what I found out about Nelson Warner."

Craig could see Liam was bursting to impart whatever juicy titbit he'd learned. He was tempted to torture him by changing the subject, but his curiosity kicked in and he waved him on.

"Aye well, you know those pervs who were killed in February?"

He was referring to a headmistress called Eileen Carragher and her husband, who they met on their last multiple murder case. They fully deserved Liam's lack of sympathy; they'd both been child killers. Craig nodded him on.

"Well, if you think they were pervy you want to hear what old Warner was up to."

Craig wasn't certain that he did while he was eating, but Liam was on a roll.

"He only had a girlfriend he lived with during the week in the Belfast flat and a wife at home in Randalstown! And the wife knew all about the mistress!"

Craig barely blinked. It wasn't the first time he'd heard of wives being more tolerant than they ought to be. He wondered if that was all Liam was going to say.

"But here's the best bit. He had a second family as well."

"With the mistress?"

"NO! That's it. With a third woman in Antrim. They had three small kids together. His kids with the wife are grown-up and gone."

Craig gave a wry smile. "Perhaps he liked children."

"Liked children, my ass. He just didn't believe in contraception."

"How do you know that?"

"The wife told me, open as you like. Says they belong to some weird church."

Craig laughed. "St Polygamy's, presumably."

Liam missed the joke completely. "I don't know what you call it, but the thing is, they all know about each other! And the wife was fine with all the other women, just as long as Warner paid the bills."

"At least he kept the petrol costs down."

Liam screwed up his face in confusion. "What?"

Craig took out a pen and drew a map on his napkin to show Belfast, Antrim and Randalstown, joining the dots.

"They live within twenty odd miles of each other."

Liam grinned down at the napkin. "The Bermuda Triangle."

"The lust triangle you mean."

They were still laughing a minute later when Craig's phone rang. He glanced at it quickly. The number was withheld. He gestured Liam into silence and answered it warily. Five seconds later he smiled and said 'fine' then he stood up to leave.

"The P.A.?"

"Yes. She's waiting for us."

Spock and Kirk headed back to work, more enlightened about Nelson Warner's mating habits than they'd ever wanted to be.

***

The C.C.U. 11.50 a.m.

Davy stared at his screen, exasperated, trying to make sense of the numbers in front of him. They had four numbers from the suicide notes and Des had three keys now, out of what they had to assume would be four. Victoria Linton's, Nelson Warner's and Jonathan McCafferty's, spotted in his parent's shrine to their son by Annette's eagle eye. That only left Diana Rogan's key to find.

The keys were identical in every way, including the fact that they each concealed a USB within. Each USB so far had held the same thing: a single file containing the words 'I am depressed and have nothing to live for' and a number. The numbers were all different and Davy was staring at them now, trying to work out how they were linked. They had to link in some way because the deaths did, but how?

He read the numbers over again; 111012, 740150, 501760 and 070645. He ran them through the computer for important dates in their victims' lives: passport and national insurance numbers, weddings, anniversaries, birthdays, even the dates that they'd first started work, but there was nothing. Social and world events, anniversaries of national significance, even the phases of the moon didn't yield anything useful. He was down to trying star signs when the others trudged in for the briefing.

Craig wandered over to Nicky's desk and deposited a box of cakes then he saw Davy beckoning him across.

"What have you found, Davy?"

Davy scratched his head and then the fresh stubble on his chin. It looked like he was attempting to grow a goatee without much success.

"Not a lot. Annette found the third key, but I'll let her tell you about that. Des gave me the four s...sets of numbers, but there's no link between them that I can find. I'm running them for a Fibonacci s...sequence but I'm not holding out much hope."

Craig smiled, wondering what Liam would do when Davy tried to explain that.

"OK. Leave it until after the briefing. There are some cakes there if you'd like one."

Craig grabbed a chair and sat down beckoning the others to join him. Jake and Annette were deep in discussion at their desks and Liam was rifling through the cakes even though he'd eaten one less than an hour before. When they were all seated Craig started.

"OK. We're going to begin with Liam on Nelson Warner, then Annette and Jake, then I'll take Victoria Linton's P.A. and Davy will bring us up to speed on the search side."

He nodded Liam on and listened while he recounted the scandalous lifestyle of Nelson Warner, pillar of the community.

The team's expressions ranged from shock from Jake and Nicky, through Davy's amusement and finally to boredom with Annette. Craig smiled at her questioningly.

"When you've heard about one pervy middle-aged man, you've heard about them all, sir. Frankly I'm starting to be shocked when a Northern Irish man isn't up to something shady."

Liam was indignant. "Here, do you mind! I'm not pervy and neither is the boss."

Annette sniffed. "We've only your word for that, Liam." Then she realised what she'd said and grimaced at Craig. "Sorry, sir."

Craig laughed. "Don't worry; I've been called a lot worse. The interesting thing about Nelson Warner isn't his lifestyle but why his wife put up with it."

Annette sniffed again. "Because she's weird as well."

"Maybe. She's certainly religious and it seems to be part of their church's doctrine. The next question is, for a man who never seemed to be without a woman, how come Warner was alone on the evening of his suicide?"

Liam answered him. "That's my next port of call, boss. I'm going to see the mistress this afternoon."

"Good. Annette can go with you."

"Aw, hell. I was hoping for a laugh."

Annette arched an eyebrow. "And the rest, I bet."

Craig cut short their exchange. "Annette, tell me about the third key please."

Davy chuckled. "What a cool name for a computer game. 'The Third Key'. I must design one."

Craig smiled. "I want royalties for the name when you do. Annette?"

"Jake and I went to see Jonathan McCafferty's wife Amelia this morning, and I can tell you there was no love lost there. There was a big age gap between them." She wrinkled her nose in distaste. "She's twenty-five to his forty-five, but that still didn't stop him having affairs."

"Some men are like dogs in heat."

Everyone turned towards Nicky's husky voice and she suddenly realised that she'd said her thoughts out loud. She blushed furiously. "I'm only saying... I didn't mean any of you..." Finally she gave up and folded her arms defiantly. "Well, they are!"

Everyone gave her deadpan looks, just long enough to make her squirm. Craig was the first to laugh.

"You're right, Nicky, some men are, but we couldn't let that one pass." He waved Annette on.

"Amelia McCafferty was very pretty but not very bright. That was my opinion anyway. Jake, what did you think?"

Jake was flicking through his notebook and he answered without looking up. "A pretty plank. As in 'thick as two short ones'."

Craig laughed again, not sure whether to rein them all in or not. Their off-hand humour was worse than usual today. It was probably a way of letting off steam, given that they were all under threat, but if anyone from outside heard it wouldn't go down well. He decided to say something.

"Listen, everyone. While all the comments are very amusing, can I ask you not to say them in front of outside teams, please? They'll think we're running a comedy club in here."

Liam nodded sagely. "Aye. Me and the boss are the only ones allowed to make cracks from now on. Rank has to have some privileges."

At that Craig gave up trying to control them and Annette continued her report. "Amelia McCafferty hated her husband and she was quite open about it. She said she really doesn't care that he's dead, just as long as she gets his money."

"Did she give you his key or did you find it there?"

Annette widened her eyes questioningly then glared at Davy. He shrugged apologetically, knowing that he'd stolen her thunder.

"She gave it to her in-laws. She didn't realise what it was."

"Or that it was made of platinum, I suspect."

"No. Anyway, I thought I'd seen it at his parents' the day before, sitting beside some pictures of Jonathan when he was a boy, so I went back and retrieved it as evidence."

Craig nodded. "Good. I know Des has looked at it and Davy has the files now. We'll come back to that in a minute. First I'm going to update you on Diana Rogan. I went back to the house and her husband let me look in the bedroom." He shook his head sadly. "That's where she killed herself. Her husband hasn't set foot in the room since. He's been sleeping on the couch."

He paused for a moment remembering Conor Rogan's pain then went on. "There was nothing significant in the bedroom but Diana Rogan was found wearing her suit, even though she hadn't gone in to work that day."

Annette gave a weak smile. "She wanted them to think that everything was normal as they left that morning, when she was really planning to kill herself. She didn't want to spoil their day... It's what I would do."

Craig stared at her gravely, remembering her despair the summer before. "She must also have known her husband would have tried to stop her and she didn't want to be stopped."

Jake interrupted "Why not, sir? What was so bad about her life that she wanted to kill herself? She had everything; a loving family, two gorgeous kids, no debts as far as we know, so why? Do you think it was the same reason in all four cases?"

Craig nodded. "That's exactly the question I asked myself, Jake. Was it the same reason? We know that our victims have to be linked in some way, but that could be more to do with the killer than anything between them. If they were being coerced into killing themselves would the reason they did it have been different for all of them, or the same?"

Liam's loud voice rang through the room. "Here now, this is getting complicated. If I'm right you're saying that all four of them had a link to their killer but it might not have been the same link? And whatever trigger he used to get them to kill themselves might have been different for every one of them?"

Craig nodded. "That's almost right, Liam. The triggers that made them commit suicide might have been different, but I think what linked each of them to the killer was the same. I think Rogan, Linton, Warner and McCafferty were all involved in something to do with our killer and the clue to their involvement lies in the numbers on the USBs. As far as what made them commit suicide, my guess is that he blackmailed each of them with something different."

"Like?"

"Something they didn't want anyone else to know, the lives of their family and friends, the prospect of prison, anything like that. But it was something that our killer knew about each of them that was enough to make them kill themselves rather than let it happen."

Craig stopped abruptly and scanned the five faces in front of them. He turned to Liam first.

"What would make you kill yourself?"

Liam blustered then decided to make a joke out of it. "Danni's mother's Irish Stew. It's foul."

He started to laugh then realised that no-one else was taking Craig's question as a joke. Craig stared at him until he caved in.

"Nothing anyone could do to me would make me do it, but if they were going to hurt Danni and the kids, then would I kill myself if I could be sure it would protect them? Yes, probably. But I'd have to be certain."

Craig nodded and turned to the others. "Anyone else?"

Annette spoke up. "I'd do it to protect my children, but no-one else."

Liam and Craig glanced at each other, noticing how firmly she'd excluded Pete.

"Anyone else?"

Jake blushed and nodded. "The same as the others, but I'd also kill myself if I ever thought I had to go to prison."

Davy jumped in. "Me too. I couldn't s…stand it. Or if I was completely paralysed. I couldn't stand that either."

Nicky was the last to speak. Her voice was uncharacteristically soft and she looked more embarrassed than Craig had seen her before. Her words explained why. "Shame or hurt. If I did something to make my family ashamed of me, or if I'd hurt one of them so badly that I couldn't repair it. I couldn't live with that."

Craig nodded. "My reasons would be the same as Liam's, but for my family and close friends." He paused for a moment, giving them each a moment to think, then restarted in a more upbeat tone. "OK. So that tells us that every individual has a different trigger that might force them into suicide. Natural suicides might be depressed, lonely, homeless or something else, but for seemingly healthy, solvent people…" He stopped abruptly and turned to Davy. "Davy, we did check that all our victims were healthy, didn't we?"

Davy nodded. "Yes. No s…serious illness of any kind."

"Good. OK, so for people with everything to live for to commit suicide there has to be a bloody good reason. Somehow our killer found out which button to press for each of our four victims and he pressed it hard. Agreed?"

He was answered by a series of nods, each of them still thinking of the worst thing that could happen to them in life. Craig carried on.

"But that doesn't explain why these four people were chosen in the first place. What did they have in common with each other or the killer? Whatever that is we need to find it because it will give us our killer's name." He waved Davy on.

Davy scratched his chin hard before starting and Nicky winced. The black hairs peppering his jawline were sparse and blunt. They looked nothing like a beard, they just made his face look dirty and she wanted to give it a good scrub. Davy saw her look and scratched again very deliberately.

"I've been running every possible connection between our

victims and s...so far there's nothing that links all four. For example, two of them bank at NIBank and two don't, three had dark hair and one didn't, and so on. On their own there's nothing nasty lurking in any of their backgrounds..."

Liam interjected. "Unless you count casual polygamy and affairs."

Davy shrugged. "True, but they w...wouldn't show up as crimes."

Nicky muttered. "Even though they ought to."

"S...So I've found no links between the four of them yet."

Craig interrupted. "Have you looked at their professional lives?"

"Not in depth yet. That's next. But on first look there's nothing obvious. OK, w...we now have three of the USBs and the four numbers from the s...suicide notes are on the pages that Nicky's handing out."

Nicky passed around a pile of pages and they each took one. The numbers 111012, 740150, 501760 and 070645 were printed on each sheet. Davy restarted.

"We know the w...wording for the suicide notes was exactly the s...same but the numbers on the notes were all different. I've searched under everything general that I can think of and the numbers don't fit. S...Same with any important dates in the victims' lives." He paused and turned to Craig. "Can the families be asked about these numbers, chief?"

"We'll get onto it tomorrow. I don't want us going back to annoy them again today."

"OK. The other thing I'm trying is a Fibonacci sequence to see if that makes any sense."

Davy paused, waiting for the inevitable roar from Liam. He wasn't disappointed.

"A fibber what? Have you been messing about learning Italian again, son?"

Craig chipped in. "Actually you're right. Leonardo Fibonacci was a thirteenth Century Italian mathematician."

"His s…sequence is made up of integers…."

Liam mimicked being hanged, implying that it was preferable to a discussion on thirteenth Century mathematics. Davy sniffed haughtily.

"If you don't understand you only have to ask."

Nicky slapped Liam hard on the arm. "And it's very bad taste to pretend to hang yourself during a suicide case."

Craig laughed. "Not only then. Go on, Davy."

"Anyway. I'm not holding my breath. I don't think it is a s… sequence, although I've got The Met's code-breaking team looking at it as well. So that leaves us with the numbers being relevant to the victims, or something I haven't thought of yet that links them. If it wasn't for the numbers showing s… seventeen months and fifty days, I'd say they were dates over the years that refer to some event."

"An event that ended in the suicide of someone linked with our killer, sir?"

Craig nodded. "That's possible, Jake. But the event could have been anything, and unless we find out what links our victims and what these numbers mean then we could be here all year. Davy, how are you getting on with the list of suicides?"

"S…Slowly. I've extended the search to include s…suicides up to the current day, just in case."

Craig nodded. "OK, good work. Jake, any joy on the online game forums?"

"Davy and I are getting onto that this afternoon."

"Right. Good work everyone. You all know what you're supposed to be doing."

Craig paused and swallowed hard, not wanting to remind them they were under threat, but needing to ask the question nonetheless.

"Has anyone noticed anything strange? Anybody following them or any odd phone-calls for instance?"

He was answered by a chorus of 'no's'.

"OK. Nicky and Davy, how are you getting on with your

close protection officers?"

Nicky smiled. She'd invited her C.P.O. in for a Chinese meal the night before and he'd ended up playing scrabble with Jonny, her son. Davy looked less amused.

"Couldn't you have given me an ugly one, boss? Mine looks like Brad Pitt. Maggie s…spent all last night flirting with him!"

Craig fought a smile. "Sorry. I'll write 'ugly' on the request form next time." Something occurred to him. "Does he have a goatee beard by any chance?"

Davy blushed to the roots of his hair and then disappeared off the floor to shave.

***

John peeked through the door of his corner office and watched Marlene Carey strolling around the room outside. She was staring curiously at his deep-rose coloured walls covered in renaissance prints and lifting his collection of antique medical instruments one-by-one. She snapped them open and closed briskly, as if she was imagining herself as a Civil War surgeon, operating on Stonewall Jackson. John smiled as he watched her trying to work out what each item was for. The collection was his pride and joy, gathered from all over the globe in his travels. He was considered an expert in his field and that meant he was invited to every war zone, natural disaster and psychopath's playground to advise, no matter where in the world it might be. He was living proof that tragedy was universal. His collection of antiques was proof that it had ever been thus.

He'd developed an interest in history when he was a student and started his collection then. At first he collected whatever he could find in local junk shops, but now he had medical memorabilia from Japan, America and elsewhere, stretching back as far as the fifth Century. John wondered what Marlene was thinking as she examined the pieces. This man's a nutter? Or worse? Or perhaps she was as curious as he was about what had happened in the past.

John opened his office door quietly and coughed so that she wouldn't be surprised. Surprising a protection officer could get you shot. Marlene swung round and her hand flew automatically to her gun. John raised his hands in peace and she laughed. Her soft smile made her look more Charlize Theron than Arnold Schwarzenegger and he couldn't help thinking that she made an unlikely looking bodyguard. He blushed and held up an empty mug.

"Coffee?"

"That would be lovely, Dr Winter."

"John. Please. There's no-one here to be official with."

She smiled again, sending his heart soaring towards Des' lab and John wondered fleetingly how he was getting on with Joseph Cohen. He'd definitely got the best of the bargain, although he couldn't imagine Natalie being impressed when she met Marlene that night. John was just heading back into his office to make the coffee when a loud noise in the corridor made him turn. It sounded like one of the waste bins tipping over and he was about to go outside to check when Marlene signalled him to stand back.

She backed John into his small office and closed the door then moved quietly across the lab. John peered through the door's frosted glass, tracking her outline and kicking himself for not being fire-arms trained. He'd meant to do it years before, when Craig had returned from London. It made sense given the number of Craig's cases he ended up working on, and how personal they often got. But something had made him reluctant; perhaps it was the thought that he could never take the shot. Still, at least if he had a gun he wouldn't be hiding in his office now, letting a girl do all the work. He didn't care how well-trained Marlene was. It just felt wrong somehow.

As John berated himself for his inadequacies Marlene Carey was moving stealthily through the lab, viewing each object and creak as a potential source of pain. She pressed her back against the wall and listened for noises. There'd been nothing since the single crash they'd heard. It had been a bin, she could see the dark-green outline on the corridor floor outside, but she couldn't afford to take chances. She pushed the PVC double-doors open cautiously and scanned the corridor's deserted length. The only movement came from the bin's contents fluttering in the breeze from the outside world, and the only sound from their flapping to and fro. Marlene glanced quickly back towards John's office, satisfied that his door remained firmly shut then she stepped out into the corridor to do her job.

John had just sat down behind his oversized desk when he heard the noise behind him. It wasn't familiar and yet he knew exactly what it was; it had been in every movie he'd ever watched. A slide pulling back, a bullet clicking into the chamber and the slight creak as a killer's finger tightened on the trigger, releasing their gun's charge.

Time was a strange thing. Einstein said that it was relative; my time isn't yours and the earth's time isn't the same as the sun's. Faster, slower, a road-runner's dust or a snail's slow progress across the floor. Movies loved time as a device; it gave them the chance to display special effects, like a bullet skewering quickly through the skin. Yes, time was relative and John Winter's time had never felt shorter in his whole life, yet in another way it was longer than it had ever been.

John didn't know where he'd learned to move so fast, throwing himself to one side just as the bullet left the gun. He watched himself move like it was a film clip. Slowed down, frame by frame, turning first to his right, his dominant side, and hurling himself across the desk, trying frantically to avoid the bullet that would end his life. Natalie was there and he leapt out to touch her, so many words left to say that he'd thought were yet to come. No time left; all gone. Then the moment of impact and John Winter's world went dark.

Chapter Ten

The C.C.U. 2 p.m.

Craig was gazing out of his office window searching for inspiration when someone hammered furiously on his door. He kept staring at the river and threw 'come in' over his shoulder, then he heard the click of Nicky's heels. The sound stopped suddenly, signalling that she needed him to turn; when Craig did the tears in her eyes said that something awful had happened. The appearance of Annette behind her said it was something that would affect him more than most.

He leapt to his feet urgently. "What happened?"

Nicky shook her head, incapable of speech, so Annette stepped forward and moved her to one side. Her tone was calm and Craig knew that she was using it just for him.

"It's Dr Winter, sir. He's been shot."

Craig froze behind his desk. He couldn't move or speak; only his eyes answered her, saying 'tell me the worst'. Annette reached over and touched his hand.

"He's still alive, but it's bad. One shot through the back of his chest, close to the pulmonary artery. He's in theatre now."

Craig was out of the office and across the floor before Annette could say anything more. She gave Nicky a look that said 'get Liam' then she flew after him, catching up at the lift. They descended in silence, the only sound Craig's rapid breathing. Annette watched his fists clench and unclench slowly as he struggled to regain some control. When they reached his car she held out her hand for the keys. Craig ignored her, raking the gears into reverse and screeching his Audi onto Pilot Street then towards the motorway and St Mary's Healthcare Trust.

In the ten minutes it took them to blue light and park, Craig didn't utter a word, but Annette could hear his thoughts. John Winter was a civilian, an innocent bystander. A scientist whose job it was to give them facts and clues, not risk his life. He hadn't signed up for this, not in the way they had. Where the hell was John's protection officer while he was getting shot? He'd have her sacked. Worse, he'd shoot her himself if John died. Even as Craig had the thoughts he knew that it hadn't been Marlene Carey's fault. If someone really wanted to kill you there were pretty good odds that they would. John would have been an obedient charge and done whatever she'd told him to do. Carey had done her job, he was certain of it. These were just the breaks.

Craig tried to focus his anger onto something neutral as they raced towards the theatre block; Marlene's job, John's job, anything but let himself think about what he really felt. This was his friend, a man he'd known since he was twelve-years old. They'd kicked footballs together and chatted-up girls. They'd got drunk in town more times than he could count. He would be John's best man at his wedding in August and godparent to his first child. John was more than his friend; he was the brother he'd never had. As he thought it Craig stopped dead in the corridor. People walked past him on either side and Annette stared up at him, saying something that he couldn't hear, then tears filled her eyes and Craig realised that he'd thudded to his knees on the floor. John couldn't die, he wouldn't let him. But what if he did? What if his sheer force of will wasn't enough to make him breathe? Craig wanted to howl and rip the place apart and kill the man who'd done this to his friend with his bare hands. Instead he wept – right there in the hospital's main corridor with Annette gripping hard on his hand, until finally he had no tears left and unrestrained fury took their place.

It had been nicely done although Jenna did say so herself. Tip over the bin as a diversion to get the guard-dog out of the way then one shot and bye-bye John Winter. She'd nothing against the man in particular but Marc Craig had been warned. Hunt me and I will hunt you. Perhaps he'd take her warning seriously now.

Jenna turned the Browning HP over in her hands, admiring its lines. Very elegant and very effective; it was probably why police forces around the world liked it so much. She'd never taken a shot before outside the internet and she'd been surprised at how pleasant it felt. Perhaps she'd made things overly complex for herself with the suicide game? She could have just shot them all. As soon as she thought it she shook her head. No. They'd had to suffer much more than a single shot would allow and the game had needed to be played.

Jenna gazed down at the gun for a moment and then reluctantly wiped the handle down. She checked there was no-one around then held it over the fast-flowing Lagan as it tumbled over the Belfast weir, and dropped it silently into the foaming waves. She watched for a moment as the gun sank then she straightened her hair, brushed down her suit and strolled casually away.

***

The C.C.U.

"How's the boss?"

Liam's face was grim and it grew even grimmer when he saw Nicky's swollen eyes. Why the fuck didn't people think before they acted? They didn't just hurt the person they shot, they hurt everyone around them as well. Or maybe they had thought and that was exactly what they'd wanted to achieve.

Liam pulled up a chair and sat down beside Nicky's desk, smiling at her in sympathy. They were all fond of John Winter but he knew that Nicky was mostly crying for Craig. He was losing his friend and there wasn't a thing any of them could do to help.

After a moment's silent sympathy Liam's need for action kicked it. He dragged his chair into the centre of the floor, beckoning Davy and Jake across. Annette was at the hospital with Craig so they would both be out of commission for a while. It was up to him to push forward with the case.

"Right. You've all heard about the Doc and I've a few things to say on that before we start. He's still alive, so can everyone please stop burying him, OK?"

He scanned their blank faces then raised his voice. "OK?"

A staggered 'yes' echoed feebly around the room.

"Good. The second thing is this fucker obviously means business." He turned to Nicky with a sheepish grin. "Sorry about the language."

Nicky gave a weak smile. "Carry on. That's just how I feel."

"OK. He means business and we're all at risk until he's caught, so let's catch him. The boss is going to be at St Mary's until he isn't, so we need to get on with things here." He turned to Davy. "Davy, call Annette at the hospital and find out what sort of bullet the Doc was shot with and then work with Des on that. Find out who purchased the gun and where. I'm going back to Diana Rogan's house. If three of them had USBs then she did too and I'm going to turn the place upside down until I find it. Jake, I want you to go to Rogan's office and search for the key there. Call me ASAP, then get back here and check every online forum you can by four o'clock. I need the name of every geek who plays 'Justification' then I want you to get onto the internet provider and get their real names and addresses. If you need warrants come back to me. Meanwhile, Davy, keep going with those numbers and anything else Des can give you, and hurry up and find out what ties our Vics together, for God's sake. Like the boss said this is the link to everything."

Liam rose and gazed down at them from his six-feet-six inch height, then he nodded once and was out the door, leaving the others staring at each other incredulously. They liked and respected Liam, but sometimes his affable clown act made them forget he had nearly thirty years of policing under his belt and was a Chief Inspector for a reason. Now he was taking the lead he was impressive, and he was going to crush anything that stood in the way of him catching their perp.

***

4 p.m.

Annette walked into the waiting area carrying a coffee and a sandwich for Craig. He'd been keeping guard outside the operating theatre like a centurion for two hours. Time he had a break.

Craig was sitting bolt upright on a leather banquette as Annette approached. His stillness was unsettling. The only sign of movement was an occasional blink of his eyelids and even that had slowed to an almost Zen-like rate. Annette went to sit six feet away, loath to disturb his thoughts, but Craig turned towards her with a thin smile, beckoning her to approach.

"Is that coffee for me, Annette?"

"The sandwich as well, sir."

Craig shook his head and she placed the sandwich down. She watched the calm way he sipped the coffee, wondering where his peace had come from; it contrasted starkly with his reaction a few hours before. John was still in theatre so it definitely hadn't come from good news.

Craig read her thoughts and smiled again. "It's a technique I learned during combat training."

"I didn't know you did that."

"We all have secrets, Annette."

Just then the automatic door to theatres hissed open and a middle-aged woman approached them, dressed in scrubs. She was tall and almost regal looking and around her neck she wore a half-tied paper mask. As she walked towards them Craig sprang to his feet, so quickly that Annette was taken aback.

"Superintendent Craig?"

Craig nodded once and Annette willed him to vocalise the question on both their minds. She'd studied the surgeon's face as she'd walked towards them, searching for some hint that John was alive with her experienced nursing eye. But she couldn't read the woman; there was only steely concentration and fatigue written on her face.

"Dr Winter came through the operation, but he still has a long way to go. You understand?"

Craig exhaled so quietly that only someone standing beside him would have heard the sound. Annette knew it contained the same violent emotion that he'd displayed a few hours before, but so well controlled now it made her shiver. Craig's lips moved to speak but no words emerged so Annette leapt into the gap.

"I'm Inspector McElroy."

Annette extended her hand for the woman to shake. The surgeon took it distractedly, still watching Craig's face as if she was uncertain what he would do next. Annette knew that Craig needed breathing space so she carried on.

"Dr Winter. What injuries did he sustain?"

"The bullet nicked the pulmonary artery and lodged in his left lung. We had to resect part of the lung and he's lost a lot of blood, but we managed to repair the tear. Now it's just watch and wait."

The woman glanced at Craig again and then back at Annette. "He doesn't look good."

Annette shook her head. "He's OK, just thinking about how to get the man who did this."

"I understand. The bullet's gone straight to the Forensics

laboratory as you requested. Can I leave it to you to follow up on that?"

"Yes. Thank you. And Dr Winter?"

The surgeon nodded towards the lift. "He's in the Intensive Care Unit. Sixth floor." She turned to go and then hesitated. "Do you know which next of kin to notify? The only contact information we had was for you."

Natalie! Oh God, Natalie didn't know that John had been shot! Craig's warm voice cut across Annette's panic.

"Thank you, I'll notify them." He reached out to shake the surgeon's hand. "Thank you, Ms…"

"Smyth. Catherine Smyth. You're welcome, Superintendent. Inspector."

And with that she disappeared back through the automatic doors to save someone else's life. As soon as she'd gone Annette's face lit up.

"He's alive, he's OK! I have to let the others know."

Craig nodded. "You do that and I'll go and find Natalie and bring her up to I.C.U. I might need the car so can you get back all right?"

Annette didn't ask Craig where he might be driving to; somehow she thought it was better that she didn't know.

Chapter Eleven

Liam was knocking the Rogan's front door too hard and he knew it, but he didn't care. The game had changed now and anyone who might have information was in his sights. The net curtain that covered the top of the half-glass door twitched slightly and he expected to hear the click of a lock. Instead, a small face appeared at waist height and a pair of curious brown eyes stared up into his. Liam hunkered down and came face-to-face with a little boy. He smiled through the glass in a way he hoped wouldn't scare him to death.

"Is your daddy in, son?"

The boy stepped back, startled, whether because of his smile or the loud volume of even his softest voice Liam didn't know, but he didn't want him disappearing so Liam smiled again and held his gaze. He withdrew his badge slowly from his pocket and held it against the glass. The boy stepped forward again and pressed his nose on the pane, flattening the tip, then he smiled and turned, running down the hall and shouting, "Granny, Granny, there's a giant at the door."

Liam straightened-up, expecting to see a benevolent old lady approaching; instead he was shocked by the vision that walked towards him down the hall. Granny was all of fifty and a stunning fifty at that. She had curves exactly where they should have been and flowing dark hair. Liam didn't know whether to be pleased or affronted. Grandmothers weren't supposed to be his age! It made him feel old.

His trivial thoughts were squashed by the thought of John Winter's torn body and by the time the woman had opened the door Liam had remembered again why he'd come. She pulled the door open wide and smiled up at him, threatening to discomfort him again. Liam flashed his badge in an attempt at officialdom. He saw the brown eyes peeping from behind a door jamb and dropped his voice.

"I'm sorry to bother you, but we're investigating Diana Rogan's death."

"Hello, officer. I'm Madeleine Dodds. My son's not here I'm afraid. He had to go into work. Conor said you were re-opening the case."

"It's one of a number that we think might be linked. There's been a bit of an escalation today so we urgently need to see if there was a particular item in Mrs Rogan's effects that we've missed."

Liam glanced down the hallway meaningfully and Madeleine Dodds stepped back, realising that she should invite him in.

"I'm so sorry. Keeping you here on the doorstep; what was I thinking of?"

She waved Liam towards a small front room and offered him some tea. He shook his head.

"No tea, thank you. But I wonder if you would mind if I took another look around." He had a sudden thought that she could help him with the search. "We're looking for a key-shaped object that was found at all of the other scenes."

The glamorous grandmother wrinkled her nose in thought. "A key? I think we've only got the usual: car, house, that sort of thing."

Liam shook his head. "Sorry, no. It isn't actually a key, it just looks like one." He reached into his pocket and withdrew the photograph Davy had provided, pointing at the ornate Gothic shape. "It looks like this. It's a bit unusual so you might have noticed it."

Madeleine Dodds took the page and stared at it as Liam watched hopefully. His heart sank as she started to shake her head.

"I don't think… it…"

She paused for a moment and Liam felt his heart lift. The key had to be somewhere in the house that they hadn't looked. Diana Rogan must have had it close to hand while she'd written the note; she'd had to copy the text verbatim and her mind would have been too disturbed with thoughts of suicide to think to hide the key. But Craig had been all through the Rogan's bedroom and found nothing, and Jake had called him on the way there and said that it wasn't in Rogan's office either; her work computer only took their own USBs. Liam had a brief thought that every office in Belfast must be run by paranoids then Madeleine Dodds spoke again.

"Just a moment…"

Her words lost definition as she disappeared down the hall. Liam held his breath, afraid to think positively. Two minutes later he heard her call his name and he followed the sound into a large, bright kitchen. She was standing in one corner of the room, smiling down at something. As Liam got closer he saw that there was a little girl playing at her feet. He remembered that the Rogan's had two children; the eight-year-old boy who had greeted him and a little girl of four. The girl was kneeling in front of a doll's house glaring up at her grandmother defiantly. Her expression was so like his daughter Erin's when she was in a snit that Liam almost laughed.

"No!"

The word was shouted and accompanied by the girl folding her arms in a way she'd obviously seen an adult do at some point.

"Yes, Molly. You have to. It's not a toy."

"It's mine!"

The volume of her shout was so impressive that Liam had to stifle a grin. Her grandmother was having none of it and she bent down and reached inside the doll's house, taking something out and placing it in Liam's hand. She waved him back into the hall, shutting the door firmly behind them to block out the oncoming storm. Liam stared down at the object and his jaw dropped. It was the fourth key! The little girl must have found it and thought it was a toy. Madeleine Dodds shrugged.

"I noticed it last week, but I thought it was a toy that Conor had bought her. She was pretending it locked the doors in her doll's house." She smiled proudly. "She's a bright little thing."

Liam thanked God she wasn't bright enough to use a computer yet.

***

Craig walked down the long corridor from the I.C.U. bracing himself for his next task. He could see John clearly in his head, not the bandaged pale body that he'd just left, hooked up to drips, but John sitting cheerfully surrounded by Chinese carry-out, in the same corridor one evening eighteen months before. It had been Liam's turn to be targeted by a killer then and they'd been standing vigil for him. Thankfully he'd recovered quickly but taking risks was part of Liam's job description; John hadn't signed up for any of this. Craig remembered them bantering and laughing so loudly that evening that a young constable had given them a disapproving glance. They'd always had the same sense of humour, even the darkest bits. It was probably why they'd been friends since they were twelve. That and their love of playing cops and robbers.

Craig pushed through the doors into the surgical corridor and headed to where the nurse had said the consultants' offices were. He had to find Natalie and tell her about John before she heard it through the grapevine. Hospitals were like the police force, one big village, and every village had its gossips.

Craig reached the end of the corridor and stopped outside a door marked 'Admin'. He hesitated before knocking then entered without waiting for a reply. In front of him sat a low wooden desk and behind it twenty more. The room was filled with the usual office symphony: keyboards clicking, phones ringing and a kettle on the boil. Craig was dragged from his reverie by a female voice enquiring, "Can I help you, sir?"

A small, slim woman of pensionable age stood in front of him with a vague smile on her face. Craig stared at her for so long that she repeated her question. Her voice was kinder this time and he knew that she'd seen him instantly for what he was; someone with a friend who was ill. He went to speak and realised that his mouth was bone dry – adrenaline was a funny old thing.

"Yes, please. I hope you can. I'm looking for Dr Ingrams." He corrected it immediately to 'Miss' remembering that surgeons dropped their doctor title on the way through. It was considered rude to hand it back to them.

The small face smiled. "May I ask why? She's very busy, I'm afraid."

Craig recognised the filtering questions needed to sift the necessary enquiries from the rest. People always thought they needed to speak to a consultant and no-one less would do. He smiled.

"I'm a personal friend of hers, Marc Craig. If you tell her I'm here I'm certain she'll want to see me."

The woman smiled again and then frowned, working out the implication of his words quickly. Craig looked distressed which meant that someone close was ill; either someone he loved or someone Miss Ingrams did. The woman rushed quickly to the telephone and made a sotto voce call. One minute later Natalie came flying out from an inner room. She bounced towards Craig with her usual verve and a wide smile on her face.

"Hi, Marc. What's the occasion?" She didn't wait for his reply just shouted over her shoulder at a younger girl, "Louise, you can bleep me if you need me." Then she linked Craig's arm and drew him out the door, oblivious to the concerned glance of the woman who'd called. Natalie babbled away without pausing until they reached the end of the corridor and were alone, then Craig stopped and turned towards her. His eyes said the words before they hit the air. Natalie's face dropped then she spoke as if she was in a dream.

"John?"

Craig nodded and she screamed the words that followed. "Is he dead, Marc? Tell me now, is he dead?"

Craig placed his hands on her shoulders and tears sprang to his eyes. He shook his head firmly. "No. He's alive, but he's in I.C.U., Nat…"

Before Craig could finish his sentence Natalie was running down the surgical corridor. He ran after her, catching her up just as they reached the door of the I.C.U. He pulled her to him, hugging her against his chest as Natalie struggled furiously to break his hold.

"Let me go, Marc. I have to see him."

Craig gazed down at her in silence until her struggling stopped and she let him draw her to a seat. He took her hand and outlined the past few days.

"They got into his office, somehow. They distracted his protection officer, I don't know how yet, but I'll find out. They shot him once in the back and they must have thought that would be enough." He smiled tightly. "But you know John, stubborn as hell, thank God."

Natalie said nothing, just nodded. Craig carried on.

"Miss Smyth, his surgeon, said they'd managed to repair the artery and removed part of one lung, so he's going to be OK, Natalie. With care he'll be OK." Craig repeated the words firmly until Natalie gave a nod and he was certain that she'd heard. After a long pause she spoke calmly.

"Why didn't you tell me when he was in theatre, Marc?"

Craig took a deep breath. He'd known that she was going to ask the question and he'd been searching hard for the reason why he hadn't. Why hadn't he told her earlier? She'd had a right to know, to be there. Had he been trying to protect her? Yes, that was part of it certainly, but not all. Did he think that because they weren't married yet she had fewer rights? Craig shook his head as soon as he thought it. No. That definitely wasn't it. Natalie was John's world and he was hers; no-one had a bigger right to know than her. Why then? The conclusion that he'd come to was the answer that he gave her now.

"I was afraid, Nat. Afraid that if I said the words out loud then somehow they would come true and he would die. I'm sorry. I'm really sorry."

She smiled at him and nodded, then she leaned over and kissed him on the cheek and Craig knew that she understood. He'd known John for thirty years and he was almost Mirella's adopted son. Craig had been John's only family since his parents had died and he'd been afraid he was going to lose the brother he loved. Natalie stood up slowly and turned towards the sliding door of the I.C.U. with a faint smile on her lips, then she disappeared and Craig sat back to wait again.

***

The C.C.U. 5.10 p.m.

Liam strode across the squad-room floor, booming his return.

"OK, the boss is incommunicado and we've got work to do."

He threw the small evidence bag on Davy's desk in a way that said 'what do you think of that?'

"The fourth key? W…Where did you get it?"

Liam tapped his nose and sniffed. "Copper's nose. I've told you before, never underestimate it."

Just then Craig's voice cut across the floor. "Never underestimate what? The strength of Jake's hair gel?"

Liam's eyes widened. Not at the fact that Craig looked like crap, with his tie awry and his jacket as crumpled as if he'd slept in it. He just wondered why he was there at all.

"What are you doing here?"

"Now there's a welcome. It's lovely to see you too, Liam. You didn't answer my question. Never underestimate what?"

Davy waved the evidence bag. Craig snatched it out of his hand and held it up to the light.

"Is this…?"

Liam grinned and nodded. "It is. The Rogan's youngest was using it as a key for her doll's house. She must have found it."

"Did you ask where?"

Liam stared at him blankly for a moment and then swore. "Oh hell, I forgot. Give me a minute."

Craig waved him to a seat and grabbed a chair. "You can call later." He scanned the room. Everyone was there and they were all staring at him. "OK. Get a drink and a seat and let's get on with this." Once they were settled he took a deep breath and said. "John's all right."

A chorus of 'thank Gods' and 'that's brilliants' erupted. Craig silenced it with a raised hand.

"He's not out of the woods yet. The bullet…" He stopped abruptly and turned to Davy. "Do you have anything on it yet?"

Davy nodded. "It's a 9 by 19 millimetre Parabellum. Full metal jacket. They're used in a lot of handguns, mostly s…semi-automatics, and they're lethal at close quarters. W…Whoever fired at Dr Winter definitely meant to kill him."

Craig's eyes darkened. "Thanks, Davy. The bullet nicked John's pulmonary artery and entered his left lung. He's a very lucky man; two inches lower down and he might have been dead. As it is he's lost part of his lung and a lot of blood. He's in the I.C.U. Natalie's with him."

Annette interrupted. "You found her then, sir? How is she?"

Craig nodded. "She's doing OK. Like all of us but with a surgeon's knowledge, which is good and bad. She's planning on staying in the I.C.U. tonight."

"Is he awake yet?"

Craig shook his head. "Not yet, he lost a lot of blood." He paused for a moment picturing John, then shook himself and carried on. "OK. I'd like to hear from each of you in a minute, but first Davy, what's on the USB?"

"I w…wasn't sure if I s…should look. What with forensics and things."

Liam interjected. "I didn't send it to forensics, boss. I reckoned the kid had been handling it so much that Davy could sneak a look without doing too much harm."

Craig thought for a minute. "You're probably right, but get it over to Des anyway, after Davy's checked it."

He waved Davy on and they all gathered round his desk. A moment later the USB's solitary file opened on the screen displaying the same suicide note they'd seen hand-copied by every victim. Accompanying it was the number they already had from Diana Rogan's suicide note; 070645

"Are the numbers making any sense yet?"

Davy shook his head. "A watched computer never dings, chief. W…We'd be better leaving it to run and getting on with something else."

Craig motioned them back to their seats and gave a wide yawn. "Good find on the USB, Liam. Take over; you seem to have everything under control."

"Aye, well. I had a hunch about the USB, but I forgot to ask the girl where she found it, so I'll do that after we break. Jake checked Rogan's office in town. Tell us about that."

Jake went to run his hands through his hair then he remembered Craig's crack about hair gel and bit his nails instead.

"I went to Murphy Johnson Limited, the offices where Diana Rogan worked. They were happy enough to let me look in her office."

"What sort of firm are they?"

"They specialise in hedge funds. Very exciting... not. She was a middle manager. She'd been there since 2007."

Craig stopped him for a moment and turned to Davy. "Davy, what was that number again?"

"On her USB?"

"Yes."

"070645."

Craig concentrated for a moment, reaching for something that kept slipping away. Eventually he gave up.

"Davy, find out where Rogan worked before her current post. In fact find out where all of our victims have worked in the past twenty years please. Sorry, Jake, carry on."

"Well, there was nothing much in her office. Just odds and ends and a photo of her kids."

"I would have thought they'd have sent that back to the family by now. After all, she died weeks ago."

Jake shook his head slowly. "That's what I thought, sir, but I asked one of the girls in the office and she said that no-one wanted to clear the office out. She said they were like a family there and Diana was very well liked."

Craig nodded. He wondered fleetingly how long it would take them to clear his desk if he died. An image of John's cluttered desk popped into his mind and he turned hastily back to Jake. "Go on."

"I phoned Liam when I couldn't find the key then came back to the office to look at the chat-rooms."

Liam cut in. "I asked him to hunt for frequent players of that crappy game." He turned to Jake. "Did you find your own name on there, son?"

Jake blushed and Nicky smiled, thinking it made him look like the Milky Bar Kid. All he needed were the round glasses.

"Yes, I did, but I've eliminated myself from the enquiry."

"Now, lad, don't be so hasty. I think you should bring yourself in for questioning."

Liam guffawed and Craig laughed for the first time in hours. Jake smiled thinly and carried on.

"There are several solid users of the game online, so I thought the best way to narrow it down was by geography. To rule out any who weren't in Northern Ireland first of all. I've phoned the online provider and I'm waiting for them to call back."

"You can also eliminate anyone who was online at lunchtime today."

Jake stared blankly at Craig. "Why, sir?"

"Because that's when they were shooting John. Unless they've got three hands it's unlikely they were playing the game at the same time."

Liam rubbed his chin thoughtfully. "Maybe not, boss. But they could be logged on permanently, just not playing."

Jake and Davy gawped at him simultaneously. "Blimey, Liam, that's technical. W…When did you join the 21st Century?"

"Cheeky pups."

Davy carried on. "It's a good point though, boss. Our man could s…stay logged on permanently. Unfortunately if he's really clever he could also be re-routing his server so that he w…wouldn't show up as playing from Northern Ireland."

Craig sighed, knowing that they were right. "Try anyway and keep your fingers crossed that he got too cocky to think of it. Is there anything else we could use to narrow the pool, Davy?"

"I w…would say only pick out the male players because your caller was male, but most gamers are male anyway."

"Try it anyway. Jake, was there anything else?"

"You said his accent was local, sir, didn't you?"

"Yes."

"Then couldn't we run an English language filter on all the chat-room posts, and find out who uses English as a first language? If we're lucky we might get some Northern Irish phrases as well."

"Brilliant idea, Jake. They were from Belfast or round about."

Davy interjected. "W…We can programme it for Belfast dialects and third level education, that's what the caller's words s…suggested."

Craig nodded eagerly. Male, local, English speaking with a

Northern Ireland dialect and with a third-level education. Even if they'd been clever enough to re-route their posts that should narrow the things down.

"Don't forget his age range, Davy. Allow for that in your filters as well. And computer literacy perhaps?"

Davy shook his head and gave Liam a sly glance. "Every Muppet in Northern Ireland is computer literate nowadays."

Liam roared indignantly. "Here, I saw that. Did you see the way he looked at me?"

Craig ignored him and turned back to Jake. "Finished, Jake?"

Jake nodded and Craig waved Davy on. "Have you got anything else for us, Davy?"

"Only w…what I've already said, chief. The gun and bullet are working through the s…system and we should have the gamers' names from the providers by tomorrow. Linguistics is coming back on your phone conversation as well."

Craig picked at some fluff on his trousers as he spoke, hesitantly, as if he was working out more pieces as he went along.

"OK… Male, late twenties to early thirties… college educated, computer literate, local… targeting victims with apparently no links in exactly the same way. He sends them a platinum key…"

Jake interjected. "So he's wealthy. And if he has time to arrange all of this, perhaps he doesn't work?"

Craig smiled. The team always came up with something that he hadn't thought of, especially when he was preoccupied.

"OK, good. He's independently wealthy perhaps, or at least not on the bread line if he can afford the platinum to make the keys. So he's unlikely to be in the benefits system."

"But he might have investments, sir."

Everyone turned towards Annette and Craig waved her on.

"Well, I thought that when I saw the platinum. It's not the first choice of metal in most people's minds, is it?" She turned towards Jake. "And, keep me right, Jake, but you said that the key in the game wasn't platinum, didn't you?"

Jake nodded. "It's never specified what it's made of. Most people seemed to choose gold."

Annette nodded. "So that means platinum means something specific to our killer."

Craig finished her thoughts. "So investments… or he worked or had family associations with platinum."

"Especially when he was a teenager playing the game? That's where the whole thing seems to stem from."

"Yes, good Annette. Perhaps…" Craig paused for so long that they stared at him. He was trying to follow the thought that had eluded him earlier, but it slipped away again. He shook his head and continued speaking. "OK, so we need to look at the world of platinum. Anyone know anything about it?"

There was a series of 'no's' and Liam grimaced. "Danni wanted me to get her a platinum bracelet once, 'cos she liked the design. I nearly had a coronary when I saw the price. Two grand for a hoop of metal!"

Craig smiled. "I think that's everyone's experience of platinum. Except our killer's. Annette, can you and Jake take that side of things, please? Search for anything you can find on the platinum markets, now and up to twenty years ago. Mining, investments, people who work with it, stocks, shares…" He paused as something occurred to him. "Diana Rogan worked with shares, so did Nelson Warner, and Jonathan McCafferty was a bank manager. There's a trend emerging here."

"Dosh."

"Yes, as Liam so delicately put it; dosh. Money and the handling of money seems to play a big part in this case. Except…"

"Victoria Linton. She was a barrister but she did work in the corporate world for a while."

Craig turned eagerly to Davy. "Davy, you've been looking for connections in their backgrounds. Exactly what sort of work did Victoria Linton do?"

Davy tapped some keys and pulled up her biography on his central screen. They gathered around and started to read.

Victoria Jane Linton. Forty-four years of age. Daughter of Henry, a law graduate and Maeve, a housewife. One brother, Noah – a doctor working in the Christian missions in Africa.

Liam let out a low whistle and Craig knew that a joke was about to follow. "Religious family, eh! There wasn't much religion about her luxury flat. Looks like Vicky was the black sheep."

Craig had to agree. Linton's life had been about conspicuous consumption, from the Porsche in the car-park to the Armani suits in her wardrobe. And there hadn't been a single religious symbol anywhere in her flat. He read on. Law school at Queen's University where she'd graduated near the top of her class. She went straight into pupillage and was called to the Bar in 1998. So far so normal, so what did Victoria Linton do next that got her killed?

Davy scrolled quickly down her list of jobs. She'd moved from criminal defence to corporate law and then back to criminal cases, in prosecution this time. She'd obviously found her niche because in 2005 she'd set up Linton and Roche with Stephen Roche, a slightly older barrister, and the Crown's work had started rolling in. Craig turned to Jake.

"Jake, get me a list of every case Victoria Linton was involved in from the day she left law school. She may not have worked directly with money but she was very close to it in the commercial world."

"Will do. You think the deaths are connected to a commercial case?"

"Perhaps. Although…"

Annette chipped in enthusiastically. "Although what did a high street bank manager like McCafferty have to do with stocks and shares or commercial litigation?"

Craig nodded. There were a lot of what-ifs and leaps of logic here, but his gut told him they were on the right track.

"OK. The answer is, I don't know, but I'm sure we're on the right path, so everyone start digging."

A husky voice from the edge of the group interrupted him. Nicky had been watching, listening and noting everything down for almost an hour, now she was having her say.

"No."

Five pairs of eyes turned towards her. They widened as she went on.

"It's almost six o'clock and there's been a near tragedy today; it's a miracle that we don't have a funeral to plan. Once it's clear that you aren't backing off the case then whoever shot Dr Winter will try again, and if you're all exhausted you'll get careless and then we will have a death."

She stood up and folded her arms defiantly, glaring at Craig. "I look terrible in black so I've no intention of wearing it. That means no dead friends. Go home and rest all of you, and then start afresh tomorrow." She pointed an orange-tipped finger at Craig. "And that means you too, sir. In fact, it means you most of all."

There was silence for a moment while everyone held their breath and stared at Craig, wondering what he would do. Jake was stunned. In his other jobs the idea of a secretary telling everyone what to do was unheard of. But this was Nicky's kingdom and at times like this they lived by Nicky's rules.

Craig's gaze narrowed into a crinkled smile and his navy eyes shone as he started to laugh, so hard that Liam thought he was going to choke. They all followed his lead, even Jake, although his laughter was more hesitant than the rest. He hadn't learned yet that Nicky's role wasn't just to be the best P.A. the force had, but to be everyone's office mum as well. Craig nodded at her then turned to the others.

"Nicky's absolutely right. The last thing we need is someone else getting shot because we're all half-asleep. Everyone go home and come in at ten o'clock tomorrow morning ready to work. We'll pick it up then."

Liam winked at Nicky, making her blush, and Annette smiled, adding. "And please don't anyone try to visit Dr Winter tonight. He's in the I.C.U. and Natalie's with him. They won't thank you for visitors. Calls or whatever you want to send him will be enough."

Craig nodded. "Everyone, listen to Annette, please. Stay away from St Mary's. There's an armed guard on the I.C.U. and John needs his rest."

He turned towards his office, intent on spending an hour staring at the river in peace, but Nicky blocked his way.

"No, sir. Home and bed."

He was about to object then he shrugged instead. She was right, just as she always was.

Chapter Twelve

Jenna Graham gazed out of the window at the river and sighed with frustration. Craig's friend was still alive. She'd shot through vital organs so he would probably die eventually, but it was frustrating that it was taking this long; she'd really wanted Craig to learn his lesson and stop his hunt. Still, it was keeping them all busy so that would have to do for now. It would give her the time to finish off her list.

That was the problem with the police, or rather not a problem, but a plus for her. They saw a crime and got so absorbed in trying to solve it that they missed the next. It was almost as if they had some touching belief in the rules of fair play. 'Any decent criminal will wait until we've solved this crime before they commit another; after all it's the gentlemanly thing to do'. Well, Mr Craig, I've news for you, I'm no gentleman and neither were the people that I killed.

Killed? That wasn't strictly true; they'd very obligingly killed themselves. All she'd done was present them with a choice and they'd done the rest. But John Winter was all her own work and he was preoccupying them all now. The fog of war was useful and she intended to use its camouflage quickly, before they could work out where she was heading next.

***

Thursday, 8 a.m.

Craig knew that Nicky was right. He should have stayed in

bed until nine o'clock and then headed into work after a leisurely breakfast. And when you knew something was right you should do it, that was the rule. But criminals didn't play by the rules and neither did he, that's why he was sitting outside St Mary's Intensive Care Unit at eight in the morning.

He'd arrived an hour earlier, waiting in the corridor until Natalie emerged, looking as wrecked as he felt. She sat down heavily on the banquette and yawned, stretching her small arms out as far as they reached, then she slumped against him with a tired grin.

"It nicked the pulmonary artery then lodged in the parenchyma of the left lung's upper lobe. They didn't have to remove the whole lobe, just a small portion of it. Once I've got him out jogging for a month he won't notice any problems at all."

Craig gave a weak laugh. "Does John know you're already planning his rehab?"

She shook her dark head. "Not yet. He's barely conscious. He opened his eyes a couple of times at around five a.m. then went back to sleep. He's weak from loss of blood but he recognised me OK, thank God. If it had been a head shot I mightn't even have that."

Craig said nothing. They both knew that if it had been a head shot John would be dead.

"OK if I go in for a minute, Nat?"

She smiled kindly. "Marc, you don't need to ask permission from me. You're the only family John has; you've more right than I have to be in there."

Craig shook his head and stood up, gazing down at her.

"I'm so sorry this happened, Nat. It's this bloody case."

She stilled him with a touch. "If it wasn't this case it would be another one. John loves his work and he loves helping you catch the bad guys." She laughed. "I think he's a frustrated detective; he never stops watching those stupid cop shows."

Craig nodded. Every forty-something in the UK had been

weaned on 'Hill Street Blues' and 'The Professionals', playing cops and robbers in the street.

"John will get better and he'll take the same risks again, Marc, so there's no use beating yourself up about it." She turned to go. "Now, go in and visit him. I'm going to my on-call room to change then I'll do a bit of work and come back." She grinned. "I never thought there'd be perks working in a hospital, but unlimited access to I.C.U. is one."

She walked off down the corridor as Craig watched, marvelling at her strength. She was five feet of steel, and just what John needed to drag him kicking and screaming from his lab into the real world. Craig walked past the armed guard flashing his badge and a nurse showed him into the small, relative's room. It was familiar, too familiar. They'd gathered there eighteen months earlier when Liam had been poisoned. It was somewhere he'd rather not have seen again.

Ten minutes later he was allowed onto the unit. Craig braced himself before he pushed open the I.C.U.'s inner door, but no amount of bracing would have prepared him for what he saw next. It was even worse than the night before. John was barely visible amidst the metal stands feeding fluid and blood into his veins, and the machines bleeping and clicking his life signs on either side. With Liam it had been much less crowded around the bed, but then poison didn't necessitate a major operation.

Craig walked slowly towards one side of the bed, thinking that Davy would probably know what all these things did. He didn't care as long as they kept John alive. In the centre of the extra-wide I.C.U. bed John was barely visible against the white sheets, he was so pale. It occurred to Craig that he'd never actually seen John with a tan, but he'd never seen him as pale as this either. He'd always been an indoor creature, busy staring down a microscope while Craig was tearing around some sports pitch or pool. Although John had always come to watch him compete so he could chat up the prettiest girl in the group.

Craig stared down at the bed, seeing the twelve-year-old

John that he'd first met; shy and thoughtful, the total opposite to his sporty, moody self. They made an unlikely pair but they'd bonded over a common sense of humour and they'd been friends ever since. All through his fifteen years in London and his five years of wall-offed defensiveness after he'd split with Camille, John had always been there, no matter which women came and went. Craig sat down by the bed absorbed in his thoughts, as if he was watching a movie of the last thirty years. His thoughts were interrupted by a croaking voice.

"Hopeless shot."

Craig jerked to attention at the sound and was shocked to see a smile in John's eyes.

"You're awake!"

"Of course I'm awake. You don't think I was going to miss hearing Natalie telling me how great I was."

"She'll kill you if she knows you heard her."

"Too late, someone else got there first."

Craig stifled a laugh and saw that John was trying to as well.

"Ow! Bugger, that hurts."

"Stop laughing then."

Craig's face became solemn and he was preparing to say something when John spoke again.

"If you're going to say all sorts of deep Italian things, give me a break and don't. My head hurts enough. I know you care and I know you're beating yourself up about this. So don't. OK?"

"But…"

John winced and Craig looked around for a nurse.

"I don't have the energy to argue, Marc, so listen. I saw the shooter."

Craig leaned in urgently. "Can you I.D. him?"

"Her."

Craig's eyes widened. "What? But it was definitely a man who called me."

John shook his head weakly. "It was a woman, Marc. She must have a male partner. My shooter was a woman."

He gestured towards the water at the side of the bed and Craig helped him take a sip.

"She was white. She looked local; you know that bone structure you see sometimes that could only come from here?"

John was right. There were some faces that looked typically Northern Irish. He was still speaking.

"Blue eyes. She was wearing one of those beanie hats pulled down, but I saw some of her hair. It was auburn and wavy. It looked natural but it might have been dyed, I don't know. Slim, tall for a woman, about five-ten. Late twenties or early thirties. Freckles too." He smiled wryly. "For one minute I thought it was Julia."

He started to laugh then winced at the pain in his back. Craig smiled. John would make a brilliant witness. He'd seen more in a split second than most people did in an hour.

"No. Julia would have shot me, mate, not you. And she'd have finished the job."

John smiled and closed his eyes. Craig could see his energy seeping away. It was time to go. He stood up to leave and John raised a weak hand to stop him.

"If I don't make it, tell Natalie that I've written her a letter. It's in my desk. There's one for you as well."

"What! What the hell did you do that for? When?"

John waved him away. "Ages ago. Best to be prepared."

'DYB DYB DYB'. John had been a scout at primary school and it had never left him.

Craig shook his head. "You'll make it. Now rest, and thanks for the I.D., it will help."

Just then a middle-aged nurse appeared at the end of the bed and squinted at Craig suspiciously. "Did I hear you say 'thanks for the I.D.'?"

"Yes."

She folded her arms and Craig grimaced at the universal sign that he was in trouble.

"I didn't give you permission to question my patient,

Superintendent."

Craig found himself stammering like a kid. "I didn't...he...it was him who wanted to tell me."

She grabbed quickly at a chart hanging from the end of the bed. "When did he start speaking?"

"As soon as I came in. He's been talking for five minutes."

She walked to the side of the bed and leaned in close to John. "Dr Winter." There was no answer. "Dr Winter, there's no point you pretending you can't hear me. Mr Craig's given you away."

John opened one eye and glared at Craig. "God, Marc, now they'll start asking me questions about my bowel habits. I'm going to get you for this."

Craig grinned and got out while the going was good, certain that John was on the way to recovery and armed with information that would help steer their case. He walked into the corridor, still thinking about John's revelation that his attacker had been female, and got another surprise. Katy Stevens was standing outside the I.C.U. talking to the guard. Craig swallowed nervously, unsure why he always felt like that when he saw her, and walked over to say hello. She greeted him with a question.

"How is he?"

"John? On the mend. Why don't you go in and say hello?"

Even as Craig said the words he wanted to bite them back; he wanted to talk to her. He hurried past the suggestion and said the first thing that popped into his mind. "Are you coming on or going off?" Doctors worked such strange hours that you never knew. She smiled and his heart flipped over, just as it had done the first time he'd seen her a year before.

"Going off. I just met Natalie in the office and she told me what happened. She was very upset."

Natalie? The mini-Boadicea who'd walked away cheerfully twenty minutes before? Craig kicked himself for not seeing behind her bravado.

"John's fine. He's talking now. He's just given me an I.D."

Her large eyes widened incredulously. "On the person who shot him?"

Craig nodded and glanced at the clock behind her head. It was only eight-forty. He decided to take a chance.

"I don't suppose you've time for coffee? We're not briefing until ten and..."

She smiled and nodded. "I have actually. I'm off today so I've no patients to see. Where were you thinking? The coffee shop in reception is quite decent. Well, the coffee tastes like coffee anyway."

She laughed and its high tinkling sound cheered Craig up instantly. He glanced back at the door of I.C.U. with a momentary pang of guilt. John had a hole in his back and he was busy chatting up a pretty woman. Then he smiled, knowing that John would be cheering him on if he knew, and be doing exactly the same thing if the positions were reversed. They wandered down the corridor together talking about the case. When John was out of danger perhaps they would chat about other, more personal things, but right now this was as much fun as Craig's guilt would allow him to have.

**

Damn, damn, damn. The pathologist wasn't going to die after all, judging by the expression on Craig's face when he'd arrived at the hospital. There was something hopeful there that hinted at survival. Jenna didn't care whether John Winter lived or not, she'd just wanted grief to overwhelm Craig's team long enough to let her finish her work. Now they'd be hunting her even harder.

She pulled a cigarette from her pocket and lit it up, blowing the smoke out in a stream into the cold morning air. She loved smoking at the best of times but smoking in a hospital's grounds felt like a real 'fuck-you'. She hated the places. She'd seen the inside of too many of them in the past decade.

Jenna Graham thought about the man lying in bed six floors above. Her best hope was that he hadn't seen her for long enough to make an I.D. If he had then they might start to put things together and stop her before she'd achieved her goal.

She took one last drag of her cigarette then dropped the butt on the tarmac and ground it in with her heel, sighing out the last of its fumes as she walked to her car. Time was getting short and she needed to shift; the last one on her list was still walking around Belfast without a care in the world. He was keeping her from her treasure and that would never do.

Chapter Thirteen

The hospital coffee shop was cosy and warm, with twists and turns that revealed more tables each time Craig expected to see a wall. It was almost nine o'clock by the time they reached it, just emptied of people heading to work but too early for elevenses, leaving no-one there but them. It was a double-edged sword; on one hand they had no-one else to look at but each other, on the other, at least they could hear what the other person had to say.

Craig carried a tray of coffees and Danish pastries to the small alcove that Katy had chosen, wondering if she was aware what signals her choice was sending out. It was probably where she sat all the time, chatting to workmates and sipping at a cappuccino. In that context it would feel fun and exclusive, its banquette seats forcing each person to huddle close, making them all feel like part of some special gang. To Craig its dim intimacy felt romantic, even in the early morning, although he was certain that wasn't her intent.

They sat down across the sturdy wooden table from each other, hiding behind their drinks' ritual milking and sugaring until there was nothing left to add. They reached for the tray simultaneously to place it on one side and laughed as it locked mid-air between their grips. Craig broke the silence first.

"Natalie's very strong, isn't she?"

Katy smiled at the incongruity of his comment, wondering for a second whether he meant that Natalie could have wrestled the tray from his grasp, before she realised that he was referring to Natalie's emotional strength. She went to nod then paused and shook her head.

"Yes and no. She puts up a good front, but inside she's terrified. John is her world."

Craig nodded and glanced around the café, trying not to meet Katy's gaze for too long. It had a curious effect on him, making him feel like a man and a boy all at once. Katy smiled shyly, as if she'd read his thoughts.

"How is the case going?"

He shook his head thoughtfully, feeling on surer ground. "It's moving slowly. But John's just remembered something very useful about his shooting."

She leaned forward as if she was fascinated by what he was going to say and Craig shook his head in apology. "I can't, I'm afraid."

She laughed unexpectedly. "Don't tell me. Confidentiality? The story of my life. OK, let's change the subject. Any holiday's planned?"

Craig laughed loudly at her attempt at a hairdresser's opening gambit in the middle of a hospital café and picked up the casual chat, following her lead. It was surreal talking about trivia when John was in I.C.U., but then, so was everything that had happened in the past two days.

***

The C.C.U.

Liam was at his desk at eight o'clock and Davy and Jake were there at five past. Craig had plenty on his plate so the least they could do was help by getting a head start. After twenty minutes Jake's smooth tenor cut through the sound of everyone tapping on their PCs.

"Anyone interested in what I've found?"

Liam set down the file that was annoying him and gave a loud yawn. "Go on then, I need a laugh."

"Five people currently play the game in Northern Ireland, out of over one hundred gamers."

Davy interrupted. "Five that you know of."

"That I know of. That doesn't count the ones who might be routing their play through servers elsewhere. Although..."

Davy leaned forward eagerly. "Yes?"

"I went back twenty years for each of the players, all of them, not just the local ones, and none of them suddenly changed their location."

Liam frowned in concentration. "So that means twenty years ago they were all playing from the same place they are now? Where was that exactly?"

Jake lifted a folder and walked towards him. They met halfway at Davy's desk, each grabbing a seat. Jake withdrew three sheets from the folder.

"On the first page are the screen names of the players nowadays and their locations. OK?"

"OK."

"On the second and third are the same things twenty and then ten years ago. If you check you'll see that a new player was added ten years ago in New York and there are three more now, in China, Spain and London."

Liam shrugged. "So?"

"Wait."

Liam pulled a face that Jake ignored. He pointed to the list from twenty years before.

"Anyone in their late twenties or early thirties who started playing the game when it was really popular back in the day is unlikely to be on this list unless they started playing pre-teen." He tapped the ten-year page. "But they should definitely be on this one if they'd kept playing. Everyone with me so far?"

The others nodded him on.

"All right. The odds are that when they first started playing the game, twenty or even ten years back, they wouldn't have had the wit to re-route their location through other servers."

He glanced at Davy for confirmation. Davy nodded.

"The w...web was pretty basic back in the nineties and early two thousands. A kid in their teens back then wouldn't have had a clue how to re-route." He grinned. "I only found out how to do it in 2000, w...when I was thirteen, and I was a boy genius."

Liam snorted. "And modest with it."

"The truth hurts."

Liam waved Jake on.

"OK. So if they started playing the game twenty years ago when they were pre-teen, which is unlikely unless their parents were very liberal, or between then and ten years ago when they were somewhere in their teens, then they're very unlikely to have re-routed to an overseas server. Agreed?"

"Agreed."

"And even ten years ago, that was unlikely."

"Unless you w...were me."

Liam raised his eyes to heaven. "Unless you were Davy."

Jake nodded. "Good. So that means that the places listed here on the ten and twenty year pages, are likely to be their true locations." He gathered the sheets together then withdrew a fourth page from the folder. "OK. This page has all the names that were playing either twenty or ten years ago and are still playing now. The ones marked in yellow are the ones in Northern Ireland. Like I said there are five of them now. There were seven in 1994, then six in 2004 and now five."

They stared at the list intently. The screen names made Liam smile: 'Central Perk', 'Beavis' and 'Blur'. They all referred to things that had been popular in the '90s.

"Those take me back a bit."

Davy cut in. "Back to when you were young."

Liam shook his head and grinned. "No. Back to when I was your age."

Jake stifled a laugh. "He got you there, Davy." He tapped the paper. "Focus, you two. I want us on top of this when the Super arrives."

Liam arched an eyebrow but said nothing. Ambition wasn't a bad thing in moderation, although he'd never suffered from the complaint himself. But they had two ambitious squad members now, Jake and Annette. It could make for sparks soon.

"OK. W…We're focusing. What you're saying is that our killer is definitely on this list of five. That makes s…sense. But we'll need a warrant to get past their screen names."

Liam stood up. "Aye, Davy's right, lad. There's no way the internet providers will cough up real names and addresses without legal encouragement; we've locked horns with them too many times before. They'll want warrants, although feel free to have a go if you've nothing better to do."

Liam turned to leave the floor and Jake called after him.

"Are you off to apply for the warrants?"

"Aye well, I'm off to start the ball rolling. Give the providers a call and if they're willing to help out without them, then call me and let me know before I do any unnecessary toil. Otherwise I'll be back at ten for the briefing."

He stopped at the double glass-doors and gave Jake a small salute. "Well done, lad. Good work."

***

9.50 a.m.

Craig walked onto the floor and straight past Nicky's desk, wearing a small smile. Her yell told him that he wasn't getting away that easily.

"Sir!"

Craig turned to face her, the picture of wide-eyed innocence. "Yes, Nicky."

"Don't you 'yes Nicky' me. How's Dr Winter?" She squinted at him suspiciously. "And what's making you so cheerful this morning?"

"John's coming on leaps and bounds and that's cheered me up no end."

Nicky's squint grew deeper and she looked like a mother inspecting her teenage son for contraband. She knew Craig wasn't telling her everything. There was something else going on and it was making him smile. She would get to the bottom of it, but there was more than one way to skin the proverbial so she relaxed her squint and tried a different tack.

"Coffee, sir?"

"Yes, please."

Craig scanned the squad-room curiously. They were briefing in ten minutes and neither Liam nor Annette was there. He was just about to ask the question when Annette bustled in, out of breath.

"Am I late?"

"Not yet. Any sign of Liam?"

"He's coming. He was talking to someone in reception when I walked past." She glanced hopefully in Nicky's direction. "Is that coffee fresh? I'm dying for a cup."

Nicky shooed them away from her desk. "You're cluttering the place up. Start your briefing and I'll bring over a tray."

She glanced at Craig again, narrowing the cause of his cheerfulness down to one thing – a woman. No, surely not. He couldn't possibly have met someone new between leaving the office last night and this morning. Unless…

"By the way, sir. That nice Dr Stevens phoned just before you arrived."

Craig swung round and his smile told Nicky everything that she needed to know.

"What did she say?"

"Nothing. She got cut off."

Craig knew immediately that he'd been had. He was stuck for words for a second then the moment was lost in Liam's loud entrance.

"Morning, boss. Good sleep? How's the Doc?"

Craig gave Nicky a warning smile and pulled a chair into the centre of the floor, beckoning them all to sit.

"He's much better this morning, thanks. Very weak, but that's to be expected with a big hole in your back. He's on blood and pain relief and they're keeping a close eye on him."

Annette interrupted. "Was Natalie there all night?"

"Most of it. I saw her briefly this morning. John's lost part of one lung, which will affect his breathing for a while, but he should be fine with time. He's sore from the operation but you know John, he's finding being shot a fascinating experience."

"Fascinating's one word for it. Bloody and sore are two more."

Liam winced, remembering when he'd been shot back in'89 and rushed in an ambulance to St Mary's with a young doctor pummelling at his chest. There was bugger all fascinating about it but he had managed to get a date with a pretty nurse from intensive care. Craig's voice broke through his thoughts.

"John's remembered some information about his shooter, but I'll come onto that later. For now, let's go round everyone and see what you've got. Davy?"

Davy crossed his long legs and stared down at the sheets in his hand, frowning. He didn't know which to start with – the gun or the other stuff. He decided on the gun. As John Winter hadn't died it seemed safe enough.

"Dr Winter was s…shot with a Parabellum full metal jacket cartridge, most likely fired from a s…semi-automatic weapon. There are too many to speculate which one."

"Any markings that match?"

Davy shook his head. "Not on any of the known databases. The gun w…was probably an unlicensed import."

Liam shrugged. "It'll be a dead end. There are so many guns coming in on the lorries that we'd be chasing our tails for weeks."

Craig nodded. "Liam's right. We'll match it when we catch our perp. Carry on, Davy."

"That sounds like a film title."

Nicky arrived with the coffee just at that moment. She sniffed. "Yes, a rude one. Typical of Liam to think of it."

Davy ignored them both and turned to his next page. "OK. Connections between our victims. There might be s...some light there. Diana Rogan had a significant previous relationship."

Annette was surprised. "But she was only thirty-three and she had an eight-year-old son with Conor Rogan."

Davy shook his head. "The boy isn't Rogan's child. He's his s...step-father."

Craig interrupted, knowing there was something relevant there. "Who's the boy's father, Davy?"

Davy smiled and its smugness suddenly irritated the hell out of Jake. Jake realised immediately that he was jealous and that he needed to nip it in the bud fast. He'd always been competitive but Davy wasn't a cop; there was no mileage in competing with him.

"Nelson W...Warner."

"Nelson Warner! But he was old enough to be her father. Dirty old man."

Craig burst out laughing at Annette's outraged tone. She had a real thing about age-gap relationships.

"When did they marry and divorce, Davy?"

Davy smiled at Craig kindly and Craig knew at once that he'd just betrayed his age and traditional approach to life.

"Never. S...She interned at a firm of brokers Warner w... worked in, back in 2005. They must have met then."

Annette interjected. "Oh, let me guess. He was her boss and it was 'take a letter Ms Jones and let's see what comes up'."

Liam guffawed and Annette realised what she'd said, blushing furiously.

"Good one, Annette. It's normally me that says things like that."

Davy glanced at Craig and saw his signal to hurry on and

cover Annette's embarrassment.

"OK. Rogan only w…worked there for a year then she left, had the baby and w…went back to college to complete her post-grad training. She married Conor Rogan when the boy was three years old."

"Nice work, Davy. That gives us a connection between at least two of our victims. Take a look at anything they worked on together. Anything else?"

"Yes. Victoria Linton. When s…she worked in commercial law she had clients in the retail s…sector, consulting firms and insurance brokers; I'll get the full list to you by close of play."

"Excellent. Keep ploughing through our victims' pasts. If there's a connection between two of them, there's something that connects all four."

Craig turned to Annette and nodded her on. She took her notebook from her handbag then set the bag on the floor and started to report. There were some constants in the universe: the sun, the stars and Annette's handbag. It never left her side. It was like a black leather comfort blanket. Liam often wondered what she kept in there but it was more than his life was worth to ask. He'd made the mistake of looking in his granny's bag once when he'd been ten year's old and he hadn't been able to sit down for days. His reminiscence was interrupted by Annette's report.

"I went to a small broker's firm this morning in Rosemary Street. They specialise in precious metals and stones."

Nicky interjected. "Did they show you any gold? I love gold."

"No, unfortunately not. I was hoping for a diamond or two at least but they don't actually keep any valuables there. All they had was boring spreadsheets."

Annette flicked through the pages of her notebook until she reached one near the back. She made a mental note that it was time for a new pad.

"OK. The platinum market is very healthy. Average values

161

over 2013 were between 1500 and 2000 dollars per oz. Twenty years ago the range was four to five hundred, which was worth a lot back then."

"So anyone investing in the 1990s would have made money."

"Yes. And if they hadn't cashed in their shares they'd be making even more now."

The group was quiet for a moment while they all imagined what it would be like to be rich. All except Craig; his mind was still on the case. People were rarely unhappy because they made money. The only example he could think of would be if sudden wealth had destroyed their lives, like some of the bizarre stories of Lottery winners that Sunday tabloids loved to report. But they were rare. It was far more common that people's lives were destroyed by going bust. Annette was still reporting.

"I think that someone either made or lost a fortune on platinum."

Liam snorted. "Lost, more likely."

Craig nodded. "That's my thinking. OK, let's speculate a bit here. The average man in the street wouldn't have traded stocks and shares back in the nineties. They'd have relied on a broker to do it for them. Correct?"

"Aye. But even then trading stocks would have been the luxury of the rich, boss."

"Agreed. So either this was someone rich who lost a fortune on the stock exchange by investing in platinum…"

Annette shook her head. "No, platinum made a profit in the nineties. Anyone who invested in it couldn't have lost."

"OK, or…this is someone who lost money because their money should have been invested in platinum but for some reason it wasn't."

Annette leaned forward eagerly. "Like if a broker was dodgy."

Davy's soft voice cut in. "Or it w…was a badly invested pension fund."

All eyes turned to Davy and he smiled, gratified by their attention.

"OK. If you're w…wealthy and have money to invest in the nineties, you go to a broker. But w…what if you're an average person? Who invests your money for you?"

"Your bank, maybe?"

Davy nodded at Jake. "And?"

Liam leaned in, warming to the subject. He'd be eligible for his pension soon and it was a subject close to his heart. "A pension adviser."

"Yes. A pension adviser. Brokers and pension advisers often get blanket permission to invest as they s…see fit, without asking the pension holder every time. W…What if they invested a pension fund badly, say by taking the fund out of the platinum market instead of leaving it there? And their customers made a loss?"

Craig interrupted. "What if they lost someone's whole pension fund or life savings? It would affect not only them but their family. Our perp is too young for it to have been their fund, but what if it was their parent's and they saw the damage it did?"

"They'd blame the advisors, boss. I know I bloody well would."

Jake leaned forward eagerly. "It happened once, didn't it? The 1929 banking crash."

"That was a slightly different situation, Jake, but yes, a lot of people lost their fortunes through it. People killed themsel…"

Halfway through saying it Craig knew that they were on the right track. Someone had lost their fortune and it had resulted in a suicide. Whoever it was who'd killed themselves, their adolescent child had suffered and it had twisted them so badly that they were intent on making people pay now.

The room was quiet for a moment apart from the sound of computers whirring and faint chatter from another team far across the floor. This was their motive all right, but did it actually bring them any closer to catching their perp? Craig gathered his thoughts. He wasn't quite ready to share John's bombshell with the group so he turned to Jake and nodded him on.

"Game forums, Jake."

Jake handed out the sheets that Liam and Davy had seen earlier and worked through his logic until he held the final page listing the five screen names of the Northern Irish gamers in his hand.

"I've called the internet providers but it's like talking to a brick wall, so Liam's been trying for warrants."

Craig turned to Liam.

"Aye. I've just been down to the court, trying to get them signed, but Judge Patterson was playing hard to get."

Craig frowned. "What's his problem?"

"Apart from a charisma bypass you mean?"

Craig smiled, acknowledging that Liam was right. The elderly judge never had possessed much joie de vivre.

"He hates us for banging Dawson up. The old boys' network is alive and well and down at Laganside Courts."

Liam was referring to James Dawson, the youngest judge in Northern Ireland. They'd put him away the summer before for his part in a people trafficking and murder ring.

Craig shrugged. "Tough. They're happy enough to lock up corrupt cops, so they have to take their own medicine. Go to Judge Standish, he'll sign them for you."

Liam shook his head. "On holiday."

"Damn. Where?"

"Donegal. Up in Rathmullan. He has a house there."

Craig thought for a minute. With a shooter on the loose he needed Liam's firearms experience close by; he couldn't afford him taking a five hour round trip to the Republic. He turned to Jake.

"Jake, as you're leading this strand of work, find out exactly where Judge Standish is and then go there and get the warrants signed. If you apologise for disturbing him on holiday he'll be fine."

Jake nodded sharply and Liam could see that he wasn't best pleased to be away from the action for a whole day. Too bad. He'd traipsed all over the country and done what he was told when he was a kid, it would do Jake no harm to do the same. It might teach him to learn to walk before he tried to sprint up the ranks. Craig continued.

"John saw his shooter, although he won't be well enough to make a formal I.D. for a while." He paused, waiting for the barrage of questions to start. They didn't and Craig smiled. They knew him well enough to know that there was more. "It was a woman."

A gasp ran through the group and they started muttering amongst themselves. Craig halted the babble with a glance.

"It doesn't eliminate anyone on Jake's list because they all use screen names, so it won't help us much until we get behind those, but it's interesting."

"And unexpected, sir. Although God knows we've encountered enough female killers not to be shocked."

"It still surprises me too, Annette. More so this time in some ways. Jessica Adams and Mai Liu used poison and knives, but guns are usually a man's weapon."

Craig was referring to the female protagonists in two murder cases they'd dealt with in the previous eighteen months.

Liam guffawed. "Not a bit of wonder they stick to knives, have you seen women's scores on the firing range?"

Annette bristled and Craig could see a full scale row about to start, so he leapt in.

"Don't generalise, Liam, and Annette, don't overreact. Back to John. He says the woman was auburn with freckles. Her hair looked natural but it might have been dyed. Slim and tall, about five-feet-ten. Late twenties, early thirties." He saw the smile twitching at Nicky's lips and got the crack in before they did. "And no, it wasn't D.I. McNulty before anyone cracks that joke."

"How'd the Doc see so much, boss? He must have only had a

split second."

"God knows, but I'm sure John will explain when he's better. Probably something to do with perception or physics, or something like that." Craig could see Davy about to launch into a scientific explanation and he halted him mid-breath. "When the case is over, Davy, you and John can draw it on a graph for us, but for now let's just carry on."

Craig scanned their faces and stopped at Annette. She was staring at the floor, deep in thought.

"Annette? Have you thought of something?"

She nodded and scanned the group with a puzzled look on her face. "Am I the only one who remembers that it was a man who called us issuing threats? Now we have a female shooter. Are we looking for a couple?"

Craig nodded. "Maybe. It's certainly a possibility. For now let's just concentrate on what we have. OK. We have a tall, red-haired woman. The age range seems correct, late twenties to early-thirties, making her a teenager around the millennium which is the correct time frame for Jake's game. The gothic keys we found link to the game, and the platinum that they're made of may link to financial loss and suicide. That means that the answer to this is somewhere in the information that Jake and Davy are trying to find."

He sipped his coffee and made a face, glancing pitifully at Nicky. She went to make a fresh pot while Craig allocated the work.

"Davy, keep searching on the four numbers we found and the connections between our victims. Annette and Liam, pay Conor Rogan and Nelson Warner's wife another visit, and find out why neither of them mentioned Diana Rogan's son being Nelson Warner's. Follow up on Warner's mistress as well. I want to know why Warner was alone in the love-shack mid-week if she was normally supposed to be there. Davy, chase up anything you can on the bullet and gun and once Jake gets back from Donegal get your heads together on the chat-room. I want real names and addresses by tomorrow please, not virtual ones."

He stood up and headed for his office. "Right, you all know what you're doing. I need to go and clear my head. And remember that they only missed John by accident, so you're all still at risk. Watch your backs."

***

Jenna Graham smiled to herself. The last one was going to be easy. Far easier than he should be for a man who spent all day successfully persuading people to listen to his advice. How much do you earn, Mr Bell? And how much commission is added on top? Just so you can bamboozle ordinary Joes with their life's savings clasped metaphorically on their laps, into handing them to you across your desk. Do you show them graphs and charts, and tables that they can't possibly understand? Then move them swiftly past the small print at the bottom of the page, until they reach the dotted line?

Do you hand them a lovely bespoke pen to sign with, conveying their importance and your gravitas? And then whip the page away so fast that they never think to ask about the cooling-off phase or an independent opinion; simply leave your office smiling, believing that they're safe in your future choices? Investments can up down as well as up, Mr Bell, and in your hands fifty-fifty would be an overly optimistic guess.

Adrian Bell was a small, small man, in every way that counted. His suits might have been marked 'extra-large' but his manners were mean and his way of treating people was even meaner. Framed certificates bearing testament to his business degrees hung emblazoned on his walls, but only money occupied his mind and he spent his days calculating how to acquire more. If a few people got hurt in the process, so what? They'd been warned. Investments can go down, remember that.

Few if any of his disgruntled clients would take legal redress and even fewer would reach the courts, defeated by the expensive lawyers paid for by his insurance company. Bell had it all worked out, every possible option costed and covered to keep him out of jail. Every cost outlined except the human one, but that wasn't his problem, was it? In big finance it was every man and woman for themselves.

Jenna stared up at Adrian Bell's second-floor office window from the doorway across Rosemary Street, her eyes flickering between the window and street level as she waited for the delivery that would change Bell's life. She smiled at the approaching postman and he smiled back, the sight of a beautiful redhead gazing at him making his day. Jenna wound a long auburn curl playfully around her finger and watched him grin as he imagined the feel of her hair against his chest, then she broke his gaze and opened her handbag, pretending to be engrossed with the contents inside.

The postman shrugged and turned towards the building, holding a white padded envelope in his hand. Up you go, Mr Postie, take it to the second floor and then reappear without your charge. One minute later he did, just in time to see Jenna turn and walk off down Wine Cellar Entry. She'd seen everything that she needed to. The parcel had reached its goal. Now all she had to do was wait and then she could score off the final name on her list.

***

1 p.m.

"Davy, have you checked out the links between Linton and McCafferty yet?"

Davy glanced up from the page he was frowning at and frowned at Craig instead. "Yes. S...So far there are none."

He turned back to his page just as Craig spoke again. "And Linton and Diana Rogan?"

This time Davy answered without looking up. "None."

Nicky could hear the exasperated tone in Davy's voice half-way across the floor. She jumped to her feet, marched over to his horseshoe of computers and grabbed him by the ear.

"Ow! What was that for?"

"It was for sounding like you were bored when the Superintendent asked you questions. Show some respect."

Craig watched Nicky, thinking that her eleven-year-old son, Jonny, would grow up with impeccable manners or his mother would die trying. A small blush lit Davy's cheeks then spread upwards to the roots of his hair. He wriggled free and glanced at Craig apologetically.

"S...Sorry, chief. I didn't mean to be rude, It's just..."He frowned again and gestured at the page of numbers in front of him. "I'm getting annoyed with myself because I can't crack this code."

Craig grabbed a chair and sat down, grinning at Nicky. "I don't suppose..."

"I'll bring a coffee over."

She cast a warning look at Davy and headed for the percolator. Craig extended his hand and Davy handed him the troublesome page. It held the four sets of numbers they'd gathered from the keys. Davy sighed.

"I've had The Met's code team w...working on them as well. We've tried every s...sequence we can think of separately and with the numbers together, and none of them fit. The computer's having no joy either. I hate to admit defeat but..."

Craig squinted at the paper, trying to see the individual numbers as cues that had prompted their victims to suicide. Each victim must have understood their number's significance, and they must have been scared stupid or they would never have killed themselves. The numbers had to hold some sort of message, how else would they have known what was expected of them and why else would they have done it?

Were they dates? If they were they weren't dates that looked anything like the modern calendar. Was that in itself a clue?

"Davy, have you run these through any other possible calendars?"

Nicky approached with a tray of fresh coffees and Craig took one gratefully.

"You mean like the Babylonian calendar or the ancient S… Scandinavian one?"

Craig nodded, not knowing the differences but quite certain that Davy did. "Any that you can think of."

Davy nodded, setting his hair flying. He grabbed an elastic band from the desk and tied it back roughly, still talking. "I checked all that a couple of days ago. Calendars, s… substitution codes, latitude and longitudes, you name it. Nothing fits. That's w…why I'm getting annoyed."

Craig sipped his coffee for a moment then thought out loud. "What if the numbers mean nothing? They're just random sequences left there to confuse anyone who looked? "

Davy shook his head.

"They have to mean s…something or why else w…would they have killed themselves? If all that was on the memory stick was the file holding the s…suicide note they were expected to copy and the numbers, then the numbers must have been w… what prompted their s…suicides. But would you kill yourself because of some numbers? 'Cos I know I wouldn't. Not unless I understood w…what they meant."

Nicky's husky voice cut across the floor. "What if something else was on the sticks as well?"

Craig beckoned her across. "Keep going, Nicky."

She perched on the edge of Davy's desk. "Well, what if there was something written on each USB that was personal to the recipient? Something that told them exactly why they were being targeted and what would happen if they didn't kill themselves. And then it wiped itself, leaving no trace, like in spy movies?"

Craig turned quickly to Davy. "Is that possible, Davy? Could there have been another file on each of the USBs, with a virus implanted to destroy the file once it had been read?"

Davy's mouth dropped open. "God, I'm so s…stupid. Of course." He leapt up and hugged Nicky then turned and hammered furiously at his keyboard. After several seconds of typing Craig and Nicky realised that Davy had left their world and probably wouldn't return to it for hours, so they wandered back to Nicky's desk.

"What made you think of that, Nicky?"

Nicky screwed up her small face in a way he could imagine her doing when she was a child.

"When we were kids we used to write secret messages to each other on paper using lemon juice. Pretending we were spies. The words only showed up if you held the paper over the heat. So I thought what if they'd done the same in reverse? Using some sort of computer virus to make the words disappear after they'd been read."

Craig scratched his head. If it was true then it meant that the numbers alone weren't the reason for the suicides, but they still meant something. He was about to ask Davy a question when Jake came bounding through the double-doors with a grin on his face.

Nicky asked the question first. "I thought you were in Donegal?"

Jake walked over to join them, casting a questioning look at the flurry of activity at Davy's desk.

"It turns out Judge Standish had gone to Enniskillen instead. He has a boat down there."

Craig glanced at the clock and gave Jake a wry look, knowing that he must burned rubber all the way there and back.

"You must have driven like a bat out of hell."

Jake blushed, hoping that he hadn't been caught by any speed cameras. That would take some explaining.

"Well, you're here now. Get some lunch and then ask the providers to unlock the chat-room names, please. You'll have to start that on your own. Davy's busy with other things just now.

171

He might have made a break-through on the USBs."

Craig turned towards his office and beckoned Nicky to follow, leaving Jake feeling jealous of Davy yet again. Once inside the high-windowed room Craig motioned Nicky to take a seat.

"Coffee?"

"No thanks, sir. I don't know how you drink so much of the stuff. It makes my jaw ache."

Craig sat down, facing her across the desk. "That was a good catch on the USB."

Nicky grinned, feeling pleased with herself. "Thanks. I get these flashes of brilliance sometimes."

"More often than half of us."

Craig tapped the outside of his mug thoughtfully and Nicky knew he was working up to something.

"What's on your mind? Something about the team?"

He smiled slowly and said nothing, encouraging her to speculate.

"OK. Let me see. It's not Liam or Annette and it's not Davy, apart from the fact that he's a cheeky wee pup these days." She grinned. "Do you remember how shy he was when he first joined us? I thought he couldn't speak for weeks, because he never said a word."

Craig smiled like a proud parent. "Our little boy's growing up."

They laughed together for a moment and then Craig's smiled dropped. Nicky nodded.

"It's Jake, isn't it? You think he's a risk taker."

Craig started to nod but stopped halfway. "Yes and no. Calculated risks are part of the job. We'd get nowhere without them." He stared into space, remembering. "I did things at The Met that would curl your hair."

"You'd have saved me a fortune on hairdressers then."

He sighed heavily. "It's not sensible, calculated risks that I mind. It's bloody reckless ones."

"Like doing one hundred miles per hour down the A4 just so he could get back and keep up."

"Yes. Like that. I saw his face when I said he was going to Donegal. He wasn't happy."

She smiled knowingly. "You sent him deliberately. We could easily have got local uniform to get the warrants signed."

"I needed to see if what I suspected about him was right." He sighed. "He's overly ambitious, Nick and he's started to compete with everyone on the team, especially Davy and Annette."

"He probably thinks the rest of you are too high to reach."

Craig tutted and shook his head. "Davy could flatten him intellectually, except that he's too nice to ever show it, and Annette's far more experienced in life."

Nicky smiled. "Young bucks, fighting for position. It's always been the same, sir. If you harness it, it might be useful."

"Not if it causes friction or Jake gets someone killed in the process, it won't."

***

Liam shook tomato sauce onto his chips then put more inside his bacon roll and took a huge bite. Annette stared at the red stain spreading across his chin and pushed a napkin into his face before the sauce dropped onto his shirt.

"Here, what…?"

Liam pulled the napkin away and saw the red smudge, adding two and two together. "Oh, aye. Thanks. I'd have had to go home and change."

"I was thinking of Danni trying to get that stain off a white shirt, not you."

Liam grinned. "Ah, now. You love me really."

Annette stifled a smile and they ate lunch in silence for a moment. When they reached the coffee stage she started to summarise. "OK, we've done Conor Rogan again. We can do Warner's wife and girlfriend now and get back in time for the briefing. What did you make of Rogan saying it never even occurred to him to tell us about his step-son?"

Liam sniffed and gazed into space. "I think it's fair enough actually. If he's known the boy since he was a tiddler he probably thinks of him as his biological son. And why would you tell some nosey copper something that they hadn't specifically asked? It probably never occurred to him to say 'oh, by the way, the eight-year-old boy's not mine. The woman I loved, who just killed herself, shagged someone else before we met and he's my son's real father'."

Annette's eyes widened in shock.

"You see, you agree. You wouldn't have told us either, would you?"

"I'm not shocked at that. I'm shocked because you've just yelled the word 'shagged' across a small café!"

Liam scanned the surprised faces of the other diners and saw her point.

"Aye, well. Anyway, you get my gist."

Annette nodded. "I think you're right. He thinks of the boy as his child so it didn't occur to him to tell us. I just wonder what Rogan's legal rights are now that the boy's mother is dead. Unless he adopted him he's not the boy's legal father, Warner is."

Liam guffawed then horrified the others diners again with his next comment. "He's dead too so it all works out well."

Annette winced and tried hard not to laugh.

"OK. We're going to see Warner's wife next, so for God's sake try to be tactful, Liam. Don't mention the boy and please don't mention the mistress."

"She already knows about the mistress and she doesn't give a monkey's. Probably glad of the chance of a bit of sleep; Warner sounded like he was permanently on heat. Do we have a name for the mistress yet?"

"Isabella McDonald."

"Let me guess. She's in her twenties or thirties and she

worked for Warner in some job."

Annette frowned at the printout in her hand, wondering how he knew. "Did you get a copy of this as well?"

Liam tapped his nose like a conspirator. "Nope. It's logic, that's all. First, she'd have to have worked with him, because men are lazy buggers and if they're going to be unfaithful it's usually with someone handy. Doctors and nurses, bosses and secretaries…"

He paused for a moment and Annette knew that he was trying to imagine Craig and Nicky together. They shook their heads simultaneously. "Nope… Anyway second, he was a broker, so she was probably either his secretary or a junior broker, hence the age range. Simple deduction."

"Q.E.D."

"What?"

"Quod Erat Demonstrandum. It's Latin. It stands for 'quite easily done' as well."

Liam screwed up his face, remembering his Latin from when he'd been an altar boy. He'd had enough of it then.

"Aye, whatever."

They rose and exited quickly, leaving a trail of napkins, sauce and shocked diners in their wake. An hour later they'd re-interviewed Erica Warner and confirmed yet again that there were no tears being shed for her hubby. She knew nothing more than she'd told Liam on his last visit. Her husband had a second family living twenty miles away and the latest in a long line of mistresses ensconced in his Belfast Pied à Terre. She knew that Diana Rogan had held the job of mistress at one time but she'd heard nothing about an eight-year-old son, although her bored expression when Annette mentioned the boy said that she wasn't even slightly surprised.

After ten minutes they left and started walking back to the car. Annette sighed heavily as they reached it. "You realise we'll have to interview the second wife in Antrim as well?"

Liam grinned. "Is she the second wife or the second mistress?

Here, if you're looking for people who wanted Warner dead I imagine he had more than most, and all of them female."

He guffawed loudly and Annette was grateful that this time there was no-one around to offend. Something occurred to her.

"Has anyone met up with Victoria Linton's boyfriend, Julian Mooney yet?"

Liam thought for a moment then shook his head. "Good thinking, Batman. I wonder if he's back from the South yet. I know Jake talked to her parents." He paused and Annette wondered what was coming next. "What do you make of him?"

"Who? Batman or Jake?"

Liam squinted at her warningly.

"You want to know what I think of Jake? Why?"

Liam sighed exaggeratedly. "Because I just do. You're good at all that people stuff."

Annette preened herself for a moment then hurried on as his squint deepened.

"He's nice but very ambitious."

"Aye, too ambitious."

"If you already thought that then why ask me?"

"I wanted to see if it was just a man's view. He's a good lad and he was excellent on the Carragher case, but he's jockeying for position all the time and it's starting to wear me out. I'm thinking of having a word."

Annette shook her head firmly. "Don't you dare, Liam Cullen. That's the Super's place, not yours. Speak to the boss and let him deal with it."

Liam screwed up his face. He didn't like giving people problems to deal with when he could sort them out himself. Annette glared at him as he checked under the car for booby-traps before they climbed in.

"Liam, leave Jake alone."

Liam said nothing, merely turned over the engine and Annette knew that she'd better speak to Craig before Liam stirred up a hornet's nest in the team.

Chapter Fourteen

3 p.m.

It didn't take long for Adrian Bell to leave his office. He scurried towards Bridge Street making for where his car was parked. Jenna didn't bother to follow. Why would she when she already knew where he was rushing to? Adrian Bell was going home. It was where everyone ran when they were frightened or alone, as if the sound of a Yale locking or a bolt being pulled across could ward off all the dangers of the world. Jenna wished that had been true for her, but the only comfort she'd ever got was from playing her game.

She hadn't touched her computer today, certain that by now Craig's men would be in the on-line fora, squeezing past the screen names to the real people behind. They'd find her eventually, but it would take them longer than the time they had left. Bell was the last one on her list then she was out of here and on to a better life across the pond.

Jenna was already at Adrian Bell's home when he arrived, sitting across the street watching and waiting until his family left. It was what they all did, got rid of their loved ones, once they'd read the USB's contents and realised that there was nowhere else to run.

She wondered idly how Bell would end it. So far she'd had hanging, drowning, pills and gas. A gunshot would be nice, or perhaps poison, although that was almost the same as pills. Jenna shrugged, uncaring. She didn't mind how they shuffled off their mortal coil, just as long as they all did. Each day they kept on breathing made a mockery of everything that she'd been through.

***

Isabella McDonald made Liam smile. He'd smiled when she'd opened the front door at Nelson Warner's luxurious apartment, and he'd smiled as they followed her down the carpeted hallway into the lounge. In fact he was smiling so much that Annette had to elbow him in the side before it turned into a leer.

Annette could see what he was smiling at. McDonald looked like a blow-up doll. They'd interviewed several mistresses over the years and they'd ranged from tall, dark and elegant solicitors through the pretty, to the dowdy and downright shy, but none so far had matched the comic-book image of the brassy blonde. Isabella McDonald had restored their faith in stereotypes.

She'd undulated her ample curves down the hallway in front of them and pouted fetchingly through ruby lips, fixing the bulk of her attention on Liam. Annette didn't care who McDonald pouted at so long as she answered their questions, and it would give her ammunition for teasing Liam when they returned to the ranch. As McDonald folded her legs elegantly beneath her on a plush velvet couch, Annette compared her pneumatic softness to the brittle irascibility of Erica Warner. It was like comparing an angora sweater with a hair shirt. She knew which she would prefer to come home to if she was a man.

"Ms McDonald."

Isabella turned her false-eyelashed eyes in Annette's direction, giving her a faint and vaguely pitying smile. What did she see, Annette wondered? A frumpy woman of middle years working hard in a world full of men, while she simply had to lie back and think of the House of Fraser to get everything she wished?

"Yes?"

McDonald's accent was from an indeterminate location but definitely working class. Annette comforted herself with a moment of snobbery before proceeding.

"Can you tell us your movements last week, please?"

Isabella screwed up her perfect nose, as if trying to recall. She failed and reached for a small rhinestoned diary then recited her activities of the week before.

"Monday, hairdressers, Tuesday, lunch with Cherie; she's my BFF. Wednesday, spa treatment, Thursday, tanning session…"

It was such a whirlwind of activity that Annette didn't know where to start.

"Did you see Mr Warner on those days?"

"Of course. Nelson lives here with me." She realised that he didn't anymore and gave a little sob, turning to Liam for comfort. "Not any more. Poor Nelson."

Poor Nelson indeed if she'd managed to attend her tanning session on Thursday unperturbed by his death the evening before. It didn't hint at a meaningful relationship. Annette returned to her point.

"Did you see Mr Warner on Wednesday, the evening he died?"

Another sob emerged but Annette stared it down. McDonald sniffed at the cruelty of the world then spoke slowly to Annette as if she was speaking to a child. "I wasn't here on Wednesday, was I? I was in Newcastle, at the spa in The Slieve Donard with my friend Zaz." She sniffed again, more haughtily this time. "You can check with the hotel."

"I will. Thank you." Annette glanced at Liam to see if he wanted to pick up on anything. His leer said that he did, but it wasn't the questioning. Annette continued. "Can you outline your movements on Thursday for me please?"

"Well, we were at the hotel till lunchtime then we came back to Belfast and had a tanning session before we came home."

"Your friend Zaz came home with you?" Annette swallowed hard, trying not to laugh at the name. She wondered who Zaz's

179

version of Nelson Warner was.

"Yes, Zaz always stays over on Thursday nights. We have a dance class. Wednesday and Thursday are my nights to do things without Nelson."

She launched into another sob, probably at the thought of how her next spa session would be paid for now that her meal ticket was dead. Annette closed her notebook; Nelson Warner had known his mistress wouldn't be home on Wednesday night and he'd deliberately chosen then to kill himself. The Dolly Parton wannabee sitting opposite was off the hook.

Annette stood up decisively waiting for Liam to do the same, but Liam didn't move. His eyes were fixed so firmly on Isabella McDonald's ample breasts that Annette thought he'd been hypnotised. She reached for his arm and dragged him to his feet, exiting the flat so fast that Liam barely managed a backwards glance.

"Here, what was that for? I hadn't finished questioning her."

"You never started! Honestly Liam, next time I see Danni, I'm telling her what you're like at work."

"She already knows. That's how we met."

Annette gawped at him and yanked open the car door. "You never told me that."

"It never came up. Danni was a witness at a road traffic collision and I took her statement and asked her out the next day."

Annette laughed. "That's abuse of police privilege."

"In a job where the only people you meet are either dead or perps, it's the only way you're ever going to get a date!"

***

Craig was sitting in the I.C.U. watching John's machines bleep when Natalie wandered in.

"Hi, Marc. How's his lordship?"

She saw the oxygen mask over John's mouth and a look of

panic covered her face.

"What happened? Why does he need oxygen?"

John grinned through his oxygen mask and pulled it off, gasping slightly. "Don't panic, Nat. The physio was pummelling my chest for half an hour and it left me out of breath. I asked Marc to put it on for me."

Craig smiled. Natalie was like a mother hen around John. Worse. A mother hen with a medical degree – a lethal combination. He rose to give her his chair and after five more minutes he turned to go. John waved him back.

"Marc. How far have you got with the case?"

Craig made a face then filled them in on the mystery of the numbers and the online game. John's eyes lit up and Natalie shook her head.

"Before you ask, no John, you can't work on it from here. You nearly died yesterday."

"I'm going to die of boredom if I don't have something to think about. Besides, I'm getting better. The sister said they're moving me down to a ward after dinner."

Natalie sprang to her feet with a look of indignation on her face. "I'll see about that."

As soon as she left, John beckoned Craig to sit down again.

"Are you really moving to a ward this soon?"

"Yes. I told you I was Superman. Now, before she comes back, tell me more about this game and then bring me in something to play it on."

***

The C.C.U. 4 p.m.

"OK. Let's start. I want to get through this as quickly as we can. Liam and Annette, what have you got?"

Annette jumped in before Liam opened his mouth. "Erica Warner, Nelson Warner's wife, knew nothing about the Rogan

181

boy, but she didn't seem surprised. We're going to see Warner's other wife tomorrow."

"Other wife?"

"Well, whatever you want to call the woman in Antrim who heads up his other family." She smiled at Liam with a gleam in her eye. "We went to Warner's apartment at St John's Harbour and met the mistress, Isabella McDonald. Wednesday was her regular evening out with friends, so she wasn't there when Warner died."

Craig interrupted. "So Warner chose that night to kill himself, knowing that she wouldn't be there."

"Yes. She was at a spa in Newcastle. I'll check it out but I think she was telling the truth. She didn't look as if she had the brains to lie."

Liam cut in. "Here. That's not on. Just because she was gifted in other directions doesn't mean that she was thick."

"She looked like a blow-up doll, Liam!" Annette turned to Nicky for female understanding. "Honestly, she was like a playboy bunny, all blonde hair and…"

Craig laughed and raised a hand, quieting her. "We get the picture, Annette, including how Liam was probably struck dumb during the interview."

He glanced at Liam for confirmation but he was too busy squinting at Annette to reply.

"OK, so Ms McDonald's probably off our list but check her alibi anyway. And rule out the other wife tomorrow please. OK, Jake?"

Craig's tone of voice changed fractionally as he said Jake's name. It was so slight that only Nicky and Annette picked it up. They exchanged a look that said Jake was going to get a lecture from Craig soon that he wouldn't like. Better from him than Liam. Craig would be kind with it, whereas Liam would just give Jake a boot up the ass.

Jake missed the undertone completely and started to report. "We've got the names and addresses of everyone who played the game twenty years ago, so I'm following those up, but there are no females in the list. The same with the lists from ten years ago and nowadays."

Liam interrupted. "Maybe the account was opened in a parent's name, if they were just a kid when they started playing?"

Jake nodded eagerly. "That's what I thought, but I'll find out for sure when I check them out." He screwed up his face, puzzled. "When we get to the current players it's basically the same ones with the few new ones I told you about before."

Davy asked the question first. "But?"

"But one of the players from here hasn't been online today and they haven't missed a day in years. In fact they're usually online several times a day."

Davy interjected. "That could mean anything. Holidays, illness, even death. Maybe they're busy at w...work or they're bored with it."

Jake's voice took on an irritated tone. "I'd already thought of all that. I was hoping for something new from you since you're supposed to be so bloody brilliant!"

There was complete silence in the group as people stared at either Davy or Jake, their faces wearing very different expressions. As the atmosphere thickened Jake realised what he'd said and a look of panic crossed his face. He stared pleadingly at Annette for support, but she shook her head. Craig glanced at Davy. He'd dropped his face and was hiding behind his hair, looking just like the shy young man who'd joined the team two years before. When Craig spoke his voice was cold.

"See me in my office after the briefing, Jake." Jake went to speak but Craig cut him off. "Not another word, Sergeant McLean." He turned to Davy and said his name in a gentler tone. "Davy, would you carry on please."

Davy started to report, keeping his head down so that his hair was hiding his face. "I've been r...running the numbers

183

through every programme w…we have and w…we, the boss and I, came to the conclusion that they m…might be nothing to do with the individual v…victims."

Craig listened as Davy's stutter worsened to include letters that were normally fine. He wanted to hit Jake there and then but instead he willed Davy on.

"Then w…we thought, how did they k…know to kill themselves? I m…mean, w…what gave them the reasons to k… kill themselves? That's w…when we decided that there m… must have been another f…file on the USBs. N…Nicky had the idea."

Liam stepped in kindly, ignoring Jake's reddening face. "So you're saying that each of the USB's contained a file that gave them the reason to kill themselves but those files have disappeared?"

Davy nodded vigorously and pushed his hair back from his face. He was flushed but looking a bit happier than when Jake spoke. "Yes. I think the n…numbers we found w…will turn out to be a case or account number." He turned to Craig. "I've f…found out what the d…disappearing files on the USBs w… were, chief. They were P…PDFs. I found a file echo on each memory s…stick in that f…format. There was a p… programme on the USBs that was s…set to destroy any PDF files that w…were opened, as soon as they were closed down again."

Craig grinned. "Davy you're brilliant! That means each USB contained two things. A Word file containing the number that we now think might be part of a longer number, and a copy of the suicide note that they had to copy out in their own handwriting. And a PDF file, instructing them to kill themselves and presumably telling them exactly what would happen if they didn't, plus instructions for everything. They opened the PDFs and read them, then once they went to close them down the PDF was wiped leaving no trail." Craig slumped back in his seat and raked his hair. "My God, that's clever."

Davy leaned forward eagerly, more confident now. "Yes, and it w…would take someone very s…skilled at I.T. to do it."

"Like someone who'd been into computers since they were in their teens."

Liam whistled and rubbed his chin. "Even if one of the Vics had brought their USB to the cops they couldn't have proved the PDF ever existed once it had been read and closed down. And no-one would ever have taken the trouble to look this deep." He looked thoughtful for a moment. "But what did they have in their lives that they would kill themselves to conceal, boss? Our searches haven't turned up anything major so far."

Craig shook his head. "It could have been different for each of them and we might never find out what the reasons were. My money's still on their families being threatened, at least for people like Diana Rogan. People like McCafferty and Warner might have had other skeletons in their closets."

Annette cut in "But what would have convinced them that the threat to their families was genuine?"

Craig shook his head. "The only way I would believe someone would carry out a threat to kill would be if there was proof that they'd already done it before…"

His voice tailed away and he stared at Liam as the realisation hit them both. Their killer had killed before and got away with it and they'd provided evidence of that murder to their four victims in the PDFs. Evidence that the victims could easily have checked. He turned to Davy and Jake.

"Both of you: first thing tomorrow I want the search history from all our victims' computers. If that PDF contained proof that our killer had murdered before then the likeliest source of verification would have been on a website they'd provided a link to in the PDF. Find it for me. Davy, you have the lead on this."

Davy shook his head and Craig stared at him quizzically.

"It didn't n…need to be a w…weblink chief. I think t…that w…would be too clumsy for s…someone this skilled in IT. All

they h…had to do was embed a v…video file in the PDFs s…
showing the murder and information on it. It w…would have
been destroyed along with the f…files."

Craig said nothing for a moment. His gut said that Davy was
right; they might never get their perp for the earlier murder,
whoever they'd killed, and searching for it now could waste
valuable time. They would have to work with what they had at
the moment. He glanced at the clock. Ten past five; time to go
home.

"OK. Excellent work all of you. You all know what you're
doing tomorrow. I'm seeing the Chief Constable to bring him
up to speed so I won't be in until eleven."

Craig turned on his heel, signalling Jake to follow. He closed
his office door firmly behind them as the others filtered off the
floor. Liam deliberately dragged his heels and so did Annette.
She'd thought that Liam was being too hard on Jake earlier, but
after the way he'd just spoken to Davy she wanted to hear him
get what he deserved. They could have been in the car-park ten
floors below and still heard it.

It was clear from Jake's shadow against Craig's office door
that the stripping down was happening on their feet. Craig's
words were crystal clear and his voice was hard and cold.

"You arrogant, rude, insulting… who the hell do you think
you are?"

"But…"

"Be quiet! I'll tell you when you're allowed to speak. You
were invited to join this team six months ago because you were
bright and good at your work. You still are, but since your
probationary period ended and you've had some security here
you've shown a side of you that's very unattractive, Sergeant
McLean. You've been competitive with your team mates,
arrogant and high-handed and taken unnecessary risks. And for
what? To look better? To progress faster up the ranks?"

Jake stared at the floor with his jaw set and Craig's voice grew
louder. Annette winced and Liam grinned. Good man. Craig

was reasonable and easy-going to a fault, but when it was really necessary he'd kick someone right in the balls. Craig's next words were a shout.

"Look at me when I'm talking to you, Sergeant!"

Jake lifted his eyes and what he saw in Craig's shocked him. It was a fury that he'd never seen before and he wondered how hard Craig normally had to fight to conceal it.

Craig's voice grew harder by the word. "I write the personal reports on all of you and if you think you can progress in the force without good reports, you're very mistaken. Do you think that back-biting, point scoring and being rude to your team mates, or driving like a bat out of hell to Enniskillen and back just to get a warrant quickly, impresses me? Because if you do then you're mistaken."

Jake remained stubbornly silent and Craig could feel the urge to punch him grow. He turned quickly and sat down behind his desk, leaving Jake on his feet.

"You have a great deal of potential, Sergeant, but if you want to remain on my team there are a few things you need to learn in a hurry. This is more than a team. Behind all the banter people here actually like each other, and they trust each other out on the street. Jockeying for position and trying to compete with other people will get you absolutely nowhere. It doesn't impress me, everyone can see it and I want it to stop. Now! Do you understand?"

Jake's face glowed red and he muttered something under his breath.

"What? I didn't hear that." Craig repeated the question exaggeratedly. "Do…you…understand?"

"Yes, sir."

"Good. Now I want you to go home and think hard about whether you really want to be on my team under these conditions. If you do then tomorrow morning you will apologise to Davy in front of everyone, including me. If you do that then this incident will not be written down and it will be forgotten, but if you don't then I'll replace you within a week. Take it or leave it."

Jake bit his lip hard, so as not to say the words he really wanted to. "Yes, sir. I'm sorry, sir."

"Good, now you're dismissed, Sergeant. Go home."

Liam and Annette hid quickly behind Annette's cubicle partition, holding their breath. When they heard Jake's footsteps enter the lift they emerged and walked straight into Craig's room. He shook his head, half-smiling.

"You just couldn't resist listening, could you?"

Liam sniffed and drew himself up to his full height. "I think you went easy on him, myself. He deserved a good smack."

"And I need an assault charge like a hole in the head. What do you think, Annette?"

Annette nodded. "I think you got it about right, sir, although I could have killed him when he upset Davy. His stutter got far worse."

Craig nodded sadly. "I know. I'll drop round to see him on my way home. There's no excuse for what Jake said, but I suppose he doesn't know how shy Davy was when he joined us."

"Personally, I don't give a monkey's if he stays. There's a good candidate in drugs who wants to come over."

"Sergeant?"

"No, a constable. Wee girl called Delia Anderson. Karl Rimmins rates her highly."

"If she's a constable we might take her anyway. I'd like another junior on the team and another female officer could be a real asset. What do you think, Annette?"

Annette nodded eagerly. The squad was a bit of a boy's club and she felt isolated at times.

"OK, that's settled then. Speak to Karl and Delia after the case is over and let me know what you think. Then I'll take a look at the budget."

Liam tutted exaggeratedly. "It's always about the money isn't it?" His face broke into a grin. "Speaking of money, I think you owe us both a drink."

***

Friday, 7 a.m.

Being woken up by a knock on the door was the last thing that Craig needed, especially not by one that sounded like the tank corps was responsible. He woke at the first thud and was out of bed and at the front door by the third, just in case thud number four was a metal enforcer knocking it down.

"Who's there?"

The neighbours halfway down the hall could have heard the irritation in his tone, but it was completely lost on Liam.

"Just me, boss. Open up."

Craig yanked the door open with a stream of expletives on his lips, only to realise from Liam's amused stare that he was completely naked.

"Well, well. Now I can see why you're so popular with the ladies. Get some clothes on. There's been another one."

Liam kept on talking as Craig headed for the shower. With anyone else that would have been where the conversation ended, drowned out by running water, but not with Liam. His voice was loud enough to cut through walls when he wanted it to and he employed it to full effect now.

"House up on the Belmont Road. Male in his forties, shot himself once in the head. I hope the gun helps with the I.D. 'cos his face certainly won't. It happened about half-past-five this morning and if he's the bloke who owns the house then his name was Adrian Bell."

Craig yelled back, spluttering the words out to avoid swallowing shampoo. "Did he leave a note?"

"Aye. Same as the others."

"What did he do for a living?"

Liam shot a sceptical look towards the bathroom and

189

switched the kettle on to boil. "God, give me a chance. I haven't had breakfast yet. It's all right for you, you got an extra hour's kip."

Just as he said it Craig appeared at the kitchen door wrapped in a towel. He grabbed a piece of toast just as it popped up from the toaster.

"Aye, help yourself to my breakfast, why don't you?"

Craig gawped, amused. "It's my bread! Anyway there's plenty more in the fridge. Do you fancy a decent coffee?"

"We don't have time if we're to get to the scene then into the office for nine o'clock."

"We don't have to do anything. I'm the boss, remember."

Craig grinned and turned towards the percolator, leaving Liam to marvel at the muscle definition on his back. His body was as sculpted as if he spent hours in the gym, except Liam knew that was impossible.

"Here. Do you have a weights machine hidden in your office somewhere I haven't noticed?"

"What?"

"The muscles. Where'd you get them?"

Craig glanced down at his torso vaguely, as if he hadn't noticed it before. He shrugged. "It must have been all those years of sport. I played rugby in London until six years ago, now I play five-a-side when I get a chance. Which is almost never."

He pressed the percolator on and headed for the bedroom. "You sort out breakfast while I get dressed, then you can talk me through the case."

Thirty minutes later they were standing in the kitchen of a modern detached house, staring down at their victim. The place was a mess. The man had shot himself in the head at point-blank range while he was seated in the room's small breakfast alcove. Brain matter and blood were smeared down the wall, congealing over children's crayoned drawings and a shopping list suspended on a magnetic notice board. Liam had told the

C.S.I.s to leave the body in-situ until they got there, so they had to pick their way through yards of tape and smears of black fingerprint dust to reach their man.

Craig could see what Liam meant about it being hard to I.D. the victim. Whatever Adrian Bell had been he hadn't been a very good shot. Most suicides would have shot themselves straight through the temple, leaving a single neat hole surrounded by burn marks. Gunpowder residue on their hand and the position of the gun would have sealed the verdict – suicide by gunshot. Adrian Bell, if that's who the mess in front of them turned out to be, hadn't been so obliging. He'd shot upwards from above his right ear so that the bullet had torn a path through his parietal and frontal bones then blown off the top of his skull. Hence the wall decoration. Only a powerful weapon could have done that and the gun on the floor was certainly that. It was a Mauser C96; a cannon amongst handguns. But where the hell had Bell got it from?

The head C.S.I. had been watching them in silence. He answered Craig's unspoken question.

"The box was upstairs. Looks antique. World War Two or round about."

"The Mauser was popular then. Someone in Bell's family must have held onto it. Any sign of forced entry?"

"None."

"Liam, where were his wife and children when this happened?"

"How'd you know there are any?"

Craig gestured at the drawings on the notice board and Liam made a face at the mess on the wall. He was glad that Annette wasn't there. Gory scenes weren't up there on her list of favourite things with raindrops on roses.

"Don't know where they were, but I'll find out. Can we move him now?"

Craig nodded. The sooner the body got to the lab the sooner John could give them more information. The thought was out before Craig could stop it and he didn't know whether to smile or frown. He settled on a smile, confident that John was on the mend.

"Ask Mike Augustus if he'll take the case. If he says yes then get Marlene Carey back to protect him. Warn him of the risks, Liam."

"Will do. I'll head to the lab now and meet you back at the squad. What time are we briefing?"

"Not until eleven. I've a meeting with the Chief Constable at nine-thirty."

Craig glanced at his watch and startled. "Hell, I'd better get going or I'll be late." He headed for the door then turned back. "Liam, if you get to the office before me confirm the I.D." Then he thought of something. "The key!" He spun back to the C.S.I. "Did any of your team find anything that looked like a large, gothic looking key? Or a USB?"

Liam smiled and reached into his pocket, withdrawing an evidence bag. "Calm down. I got it earlier. I'll get Des to print it at the lab then get the numbers across to Davy."

Craig exhaled sharply. "OK, good. Right, I'll see you later. And Liam…"

"What now?"

Craig shot him a warning look. "Go easy on Jake."

Liam's face was the picture of innocence. "Me? As if I'd do anything else."

***

Jenna Graham watched the cars come and go and the mortuary van arrive at ten o'clock, to carry the last man on her list to the cold dissection table he deserved. Adrian Bell deserved it doubly for refusing to go quietly like the rest.

Jenna often wondered whether her lack of feeling showed something missing in her psyche, but she could remember another, earlier time when she'd felt everything and it had hurt far too much. She'd wondered if her reactions had been normal then. Was it normal to feel so much pain that you wanted to scream and cry and tear down walls, and be prepared to do anything for some peace? And then suddenly, without a sign that it would end, to burn out and feel nothing at all?

She'd felt nothing from that day to this. It was as if someone had pressed her mind's 'escape' button and she'd entered a space where nothing felt real. Perhaps a fuse in her brain had blown, never to be replaced. Whatever it was she thanked God for it, if there was such a being. It had left her free of pain, free to live, with her mind totally clear to think and plan. Now her plan had been completed and she was finally free.

***

"My God, you certainly do get them, Marc."

Craig gave Chief Constable Sean Flanagan a rueful smile.

Flanagan continued cheerfully. "All my other teams get normal killings, with the odd strange one here and there. Domestic violence, death by dangerous driving, normal stuff. But you…"

"We get an episode of 'Criminal Minds' every other month."

Flanagan raised a questioning eyebrow as he poured the coffee. "What's Criminal Minds when it's at home?"

Craig laughed, thinking of John. He loved American cop shows and he knew he'd be catching up on all of them now.

"An American TV series set in the Behavioural Analysis Unit at the FBI. It's based on a real team. John loves it."

"Ah, yes…I've been keeping track on Dr Winter. He's on a ward now, so that's excellent news."

"Certainly is, sir."

Craig sipped his coffee and glanced at the man across the desk. Flanagan was six-feet-five of amiable teddy-bear, except when he was pushed so far that he needed to growl. Then he did and his temper could rip people apart. It was a management style Craig could relate to.

"Right then, update me, Marc. And don't spare the gory details."

In the next twenty minutes Craig outlined their five victims' profiles and methods of death, and his suspicions about the computer game. He rounded up with the missing PDFs and the possible earlier murder by their perp. When he'd finished Flanagan gave a low whistle prompting his curious P.A. Donna to peep through his half-glass office door.

"So you think that whatever coerced each of them to kill themselves was written in the PDF files?"

"It must have been, there's no trace of anything else. And the pressure point was probably different for each of them. The clever part of it is that without the PDF all we have is a suicide note copied out in their own hand and a random six-digit number."

Craig swallowed, wondering whether he should bother to say what he was thinking after Jake's bad behaviour the day before. He chose yes. Jake would either have learned his lesson or he'd be off the squad in a week, today would tell, but that didn't detract from his past good work.

"If Sergeant McLean hadn't recognised the key's design in the first place we would never have got this far."

"Ah yes. Jake isn't it? How's he doing?"

"A bit rough around the edges, but OK. He's a bright boy. It's an asset having two younger members on the team. None of the rest of us play computer games, that's for sure."

Flanagan laughed. "If Liam Cullen can't kick it, throw it or bang into it, it isn't a game in his book. I remember playing GAA football with him back in the day. My God he was strong."

"Still is. He nearly put my door in this morning."

Flanagan grinned and drained his cup, setting it down in a way that signalled the meeting was almost at an end. He clasped his hands on the desk.

"What do you need from me?"

Craig had known the question was coming and he was well prepared. "We need to step up the close protection on everyone involved in the case. I don't want another incident like John's."

"Done."

"I need tracking on all of our phones: home, work and mobile. And enhanced computer support for Davy Walsh, plus dedicated use of someone to support him for a few days."

"OK, and?"

Craig shook his head. "Nothing else yet, sir, but I think things are coming to a head. When they do we may need armed support."

Flanagan nodded. Either their killer was going to disappear suddenly because their work was done, or Craig's team would get to them before they did. His money was on the latter and that meant it could get nasty.

"Right. Just keep me up to date with everything and good luck. I want whoever did this locked away before there are any more deaths of any sort."

Chapter Fifteen

Jenna Graham stared at the phone, willing herself not to be stupid. They were all dead now and Craig had no idea who she was. All she had to do was get on a plane and she was home free. She lifted the photograph from the table and gazed at it for minutes, tracing the couple's outline with a long finger and trying to recall their voices. Her father's, so deep and strong, echoing through the house when he sang. She remembered his baritone soaring towards the crescendo in The Toreador song, or 'Votre Toast' from Bizet's Carmen, as she now knew it was called. Her childish ears hadn't understood its beauty and instead she'd tried to block out the sound, squealing. "Stop, Daddy, stop. Too loud." She'd give anything to hear him sing it now.

He'd swung her high in his arms and laughed, showing large white teeth, while her mother had bustled around chiding them to sit down for their meal. She strained to hear their voices nowadays, they faded with each year but they were still audible enough to make her tears flow, just as they were doing now. Sorrow and hate were the only feelings she had left and even the sorrow was numbed.

Jenna smiled down at the picture, remembering her mother's dark curls and her father's greying pate, then she fingered her own red hair, a legacy of her paternal grandmother just like her blue eyes. She glanced at her new passport, waiting to be used. Only one more day before she caught her flight. She thought for a moment longer then made her decision and headed for the door. Once she was in position she would call Craig and start the chase. What a day it was going to be.

***

The C.C.U. 11 a.m.

"OK, gather round please."

Craig scanned the open-plan office as he grabbed a chair. No Jake. He'd given him a choice and it seemed that Jake's ego had made him take the easy way out. He thought of his words to the Chief Constable. He'd meant them; Jake had a lot of potential but if he didn't want to develop it in the murder squad then there was nothing he could do.

Craig had all but written Jake's final report in his mind when he came bounding onto the floor carrying a white box. Liam recognised what it was and his ire from the previous day was instantly gone. He loped across the room and peered down at the box, waiting for Jake to open the lid. Jake gabbled nervously, desperate for approval.

"I hope these are from the right bakery. It was the only one I could think of nearby."

He lifted the white cardboard lid reverentially, revealing a plethora of cream cakes inside, their number reduced by one as soon as Liam reached in.

"Help yourselves everyone, but before you do I've got something I'd like to say." He swallowed hard and even Nicky's anger softened as she saw a blush tint his ears.

"If you'll excuse my language, I behaved like a complete dick-head yesterday and I'm very sorry." He turned to face Davy whose expression gave nothing away.

"I'd especially like to apologise to you, Davy. I was rude and childish and my only defence, although honestly there isn't one, is that I really want to do well on the squad. I was trying to prove myself so hard that it made me compete with all of you, but particularly Davy." He turned to Annette. "And you,

197

Annette."

He fell silent then he caught the look in Craig's eye telling him that he hadn't finished yet. Craig willed him on, trying hard not to smile until he'd finished. Jake restarted, falteringly, staring at the floor.

"I…y…you've all been so welcoming and kind that it's made me want to excel, but I forgot that this was a team and I started trying to score points at other people's expense. It was wrong." He glanced up pleadingly, almost afraid to read their expressions. "I hope you'll give me another chance. And…and have a cake."

On the word cake Liam interrupted. "That's all grand and stuff, but there are cakes to be eaten so shut up lad and get out of my way." With that he reached into the box and grabbed a second pastry as a chorus of "leave some for everyone else" and "thanks Jake" echoed across the room. Only Davy said nothing.

Jake put two cakes on a plate and carried them over to Davy's desk, trying to catch his eye. It was a challenge through Davy's hair.

"Davy. I'm sorry. I'm a prat."

Davy glanced up shyly and smiled. "Yes, you are." He reached his hand towards the plate then stopped in mid-air. "W…Which one do you w…want?"

Jake smiled. "I like cream horns."

Davy grabbed the only cream horn and bit off a chunk. Craig laughed out loud as he did it, knowing he was telling Jake that his behaviour wasn't that easy to forget. Jake smiled too and lifted the other cake.

"You're a k…knob, Jake."

Jake nodded, agreeing. The scene was disturbed by the phone ringing in Craig's office. He gestured them all to be quiet and motioned Nicky to let the phone ring out. Only their perp could have bypassed everything to call straight to his office phone and they would ring again. He was right. After thirty seconds the sound restarted and Craig walked slowly into his office, beckoning everyone to follow.

"Superintendent Craig."

A man's voice came through and Craig listened hard, but not to the words.

"You didn't listen, Craig. You hunted me and now I'm going to hunt you back. I've finished with the others so it's between us two now. I may have missed with the pathologist but I won't miss with you. Enjoy your last day alive."

The line went dead and Craig motioned Nicky to phone downstairs. She came back a moment later shaking her head.

"Re-routed again, through Rome this time."

It was too much of a coincidence. Rome was where Craig's mother came from.

"OK, I'm obviously next on the list or my folks are. Nicky, tighten the security on my parent's home and call my sister at work and tell her I'll be there in thirty minutes to collect her. I'll take her to my folk's place until this is all over. Davy, did we get it on tape?"

Davy rushed to his computer and typed. A moment later he nodded.

"OK. Then humour me and run it through the programme I asked linguistics to send you this morning."

Davy typed furiously for a moment then beckoned them all to be quiet. He played the words Craig had just heard and then altered the tape incrementally, stripping away the artificial components until he reached a different voice. A woman's. They listened hard as Davy played it three times, then Craig gestured for him to stop.

"Thanks, Davy. OK, opinions anyone?"

Liam spoke first. "There's no partnership, only one perp. Female pretending to be male."

"Yes. They used voice altering software."

Jake spoke tentatively, gazing around to see if anyone minded.

"Young… I think. Early thirties at the latest."

"You're right, lad. And it's a Belfast accent, but posh Belfast. Malone or Cherry Valley somewhere."

Craig nodded. "Davy, there was something in the background. Can you enhance it?"

Davy muted the voice and drew up the background sound as everyone looked on.

Annette gazed at the computer screen. "Our Jordan would love that programme. He's into making short films."

Davy answered without looking up, engrossed in his task. "I'll s…see if I can get him a copy."

After a few seconds Davy sat back triumphantly and pressed play. They listened as the unmistakable sound of church bells rang out. Craig glanced at the clock. It was five past eleven. The bells had rung on the hour.

"Play it again and we'll count the bells."

Eleven. He was right. Their perp was calling from somewhere close to a church.

"OK. I want you all on this for the next hour. Ring every church in Belfast until you find out which one just rang the eleven o'clock bells and then get a sample of the sounds to Davy."

"But that means we'll have to get them to ring their bells, boss."

Craig shook his head. "Most church bells are recordings, Liam. They only use bell-ringers for special occasions. They can probably e-mail the samples through. Davy and Liam, try the churches around Queens, the Malone and Stranmillis. Annette and Jake, you do the ones on the east side of the city."

He headed for the door. "I'm going to my folks to explain why they're on lock-down before my mother rings here giving you all grief."

***

Mirella Craig was so excited to see her son and daughter

appear for lunch that it wasn't until after the Lasagne and Tiramisu that it occurred to her to ask why they were there. Craig's father, on the other hand, had been staring at Craig intermittently since he'd arrived an hour earlier, bearing flowers for his mother and trailing his truculent younger sister in his wake. As Tom Craig started to form the question his son saw it coming and answered before it reached the air.

"I'm sorry everyone, but I've had to put you under close protection."

Lucia already knew and she folded her arms firmly and glared, first at Craig and then at her father.

"I have plans for tonight, Marc. We're all going out for Theresa's birthday."

"Sorry, Luce. She'll have to celebrate without you. I wouldn't be asking this of you if it wasn't important."

Mirella set down a coffee at her husband's elbow and scanned the faces at the table with a puzzled expression. "What you talk about?" She squinted at her husband and then at Craig, suddenly noticing the undercurrent between them.

"Tom Craig! Why you look at Marco like that? He is my good boy. What is happening here?"

Craig senior smiled and grabbed his wife by the waist, pulling her onto his knee, much to Craig's amusement. Lucia rolled her eyes. Richard had annoyed her on the phone the night before and she was completely off romance.

"What is happening here is that your son is basically telling us that we're prisoners in our own house."

Lucia interrupted grumpily. "I'm not even in my own house!"

She turned to Craig and scowled. "I'm not staying here, Marc. I had enough of the Take That décor of my bedroom last November to last me for ten years." She folded her arms more tightly. "Besides, you haven't given us any explanation." She turned to her father for support, releasing one hand to point accusingly at her brother. "He just turned up at my work and

201

made me leave, in front of everyone! I'll be lucky if I keep my job, with all this carry-on."

Tom Craig arched an eyebrow sceptically at his daughter's hyperbole and then turned to Craig with a mute request for information. Craig sighed, not knowing how much to tell them. If he told them that he was under threat of death and so by proxy they were too, his mother would run round the kitchen screaming that the end was nigh. If he told them about his team having been armed and under close protection for days and that John was lying in the I.C.U. seven miles up the road, it would get even worse. She would start praying and promising God unfeasible amounts of money for the church if they were all kept safe. So Craig lied.

It was a plausible lie, one that his mother would believe and Lucia would think twice about questioning. Only his worldly father would hear the truth behind his words and he would go along with his son's version of the world to protect them all. Craig composed his face into a suitably official expression.

"OK. The squad has had a call from Dissidents threatening the families of everyone in the team. So, to be on the safe side we're putting everyone under close protection for a few days. Until we get these Muppets under control."

"Dissident who? Loyalists or republicans?"

Craig hadn't anticipated Lucia's question, so he grabbed for the first word in her list. "Loyalists."

She gawped at him. "Don't tell me they've started up again as well? Good grief."

Whether they had or hadn't was lost as Lucia and Mirella descended into a diatribe about the random elements on both sides of Northern Ireland intent on dragging them all back to the past. Tom Craig gave his son a nod that said 'nicely done' and they returned happily to their lunch, while Craig wondered exactly who the next target was going to be.

***

Jenna Graham watched Craig arrive at his parent's Holywood house with a young woman in tow, then leave an hour later on his own. She scanned the un-marked police car in the driveway and the second one at the back on the house, knowing that the plain-clothed officers inside would be armed to the teeth.

Let them protect Craig's family; she wished that someone had protected hers. Besides, the odds were against her ever reaching them alive with eight men in her way, and she wasn't suicidal. She smiled at the irony in her thoughts and started up the car, trailing Craig down Holywood's narrow High Street and back onto the M3 motorway, taking up position a comfortable three car lengths behind. It was Marc Craig she was after, not his family, just as he was after her. They would just have to see who reached their quarry first.

***

"If Adrian B...Bell was the last victim then this must be the full c...code. Des has just phoned the last six digits t... through."

Craig squinted down at the paper Davy was holding, trying to make sense of the line of numbers. It was far too long for a National Insurance number and the wrong format for passport or driving licence. Besides, that would have been too simple for a killer this sharp. Davy read his mind.

"W...We're running it now. It's too long for lots of s... standard formats, like g...government I.D.s."

Liam chipped in. "What about court case numbers, hospital numbers, bank codes and that sort of thing?"

Davy shook his long dark hair. "Nope. Again, w...wrong length and format." He sighed. "I'm trying insurance policy and pension numbers and the rest. The Met's code-crackers are on it as w...well. We'll just have to hope that one of us catches a break soon."

Craig nodded and grabbed a chair. "OK, thanks, Davy.

Right. Church bells anyone?"

Annette nodded. "We got all the recordings from the areas you mentioned and the closest sound was a small church in Holywood on Downshire Road. I gave it to Davy a minute ago."

Craig's eyes widened. He knew exactly where the church was. He could picture it in his mind: small and made of white stone. The killer had phoned from outside a church less than a mile from his parent's house! She'd routed the call through Rome knowing that it would set Craig running to protect them, exposing himself in the process. She could have killed him as he'd driven through Holywood if she'd wanted to.

Craig kicked himself for playing straight into her hands. He turned to the group wearing a grim expression.

"We have a very clever killer. She knew that we would trace her call to Rome and that would set me running to protect Lucia and my folks. The church is en-route to their house so she could easily have killed me as I drove past, or got to them before me."

Jake went to ask a question. He stopped himself, uncertain what his position was in the team. Craig saw his hesitation and waved him on.

"What happened is history, Jake. Ask your question."

"Well, it's… it's just, if she wants you specifically then she could easily have killed you on your way to your parents or on your way back today. She showed us that she was one step ahead when she made the call and set you running." He realised what he'd said and tried to back-track. "No offence, sir. I mean, perhaps she didn't expect us to make the connection with Rome so quickly. And she probably won't expect us to work out where she called from."

His voice tailed off and a deep-red blush took its place. Craig smiled and shook his head.

"No, you're right, Jake. She knew we would trace the call to Rome and she knew I would go running to Holywood.

Whether she expected us to work out her position from the church bells I'm not sure. But she's definitely clever. She could have killed me today if she'd wanted to, but somehow I don't think that would have been enough of a game for her. She's playing with me."

Liam's voice boomed across the room. "Us, she's playing with us, boss."

Craig shook his head. "It's me or my family she's hunting now, Liam. With John she was trying to stop the forensic investigation progressing so fast. But she knows we're getting close to her now and this has got personal. She wants me or someone close to me dead."

Liam shook his head and repeated himself firmly. "Us. She may not be after us, but if she hunts you then she has to hunt all of us, because you're not going to be alone until we catch her."

Annette nodded and Craig waved them both down, smiling. "That's kind, but you can't follow me around."

Annette nodded again, with a determined look on her face. "Yes we can. And we will until we get this bitch under lock and key."

Craig raised his eyebrows at her choice of words then laughed at the image of him being flanked by body guards for the rest of his life.

"OK. We still have people to interview. Did anyone interview Nelson Warner's family in Antrim? And what about Victoria Linton's boyfriend?" He scanned their blank faces. "OK, then get on it please. Davy's on top of the number codes and Jake's working up the chat-room names. I'm heading over to the lab to see if Mike has got anything for us on Adrian Bell."

Liam shook his head firmly. "No you're not, boss. Sorry. If you leave here then at least one of us has to be with you and Annette and I have interviews to do. I'll get close protection to bring Mike here when he's finished Bell's post-mortem." He stood up and loomed over Craig, folding his arms. "You're under house arrest until further notice. One half-dead mate is quite enough."

Craig sprang to his feet. "I'm in charge here, Liam and I say that I'm going." The slow movement to their feet of the others said that Liam wasn't the only opposition Craig had. After a moment's tense stand-off Craig shrugged, admitting defeat, but only for a couple of hours.

"OK. I'll humour you for a few hours and stay here. Go and do the interviews then bring Mike back with you. We'll brief again at five o'clock. But I warn you Liam, you're not taking over my life. We're going to catch this woman before she kills anyone else, and if me acting as bait is how we have to do it then you're not going to get in my way."

Chapter Sixteen

St Mary's Hospital.

John yawned and went to stretch his arms then the hole in his back reminded him that it wasn't such a good idea. He gazed around his small side-room, finally starting to take notice of his surroundings. The last few days in I.C.U. had been a series of beeps and lights, with people tiptoeing around his bed trying not to disturb him, except that their muttered words and accidental clumsiness had disturbed him more than if they'd shouted in his ear. Whoever said hospitals were restful places had obviously never tried to sleep in one.

He was glad to be out of intensive care. There were only so many muted tones and sad expressions that a man could take, without wanting to yell out, "I'm not dead yet!" The colourful curtains and flat screen TV in his side-room were much more to his taste. He'd just reached over for the remote control to see what the 'Loose Women' had to say, purely in the name of anthropological research of course, when Natalie burst into the room.

"God, I'm going to kill that I.C.U. sister. I thought you were dead!"

John winced and closed his eyes, in a way that he hoped signified a need for peace. Natalie ignored him and continued with her rant.

"I walked into I.C.U. and there was a road traffic victim in your bed, with his legs up in pulleys! I thought you'd died and they'd taken you to the mortuary."

John pictured the traffic victim being subjected to the full weight of Natalie's ire. Poor sod.

"Then that sister, you know, the bolshie one who thinks she runs the place."

John interjected. "She does run the place."

"The doctors run the place. She's only the Maître D. Anyway, then she charges over and tells me off for making noise! Me? Noisy? Am I ever noisy?"

She didn't wait for his answer, which was just as well. She also ignored the armed policeman who opened the door checking out the noise. He closed it quickly again when he saw Natalie mid-rant.

"And then she tells me that you weren't actually dead, but transferred down here. I was furious."

Anyone hearing Natalie's words would have concluded that she was furious he wasn't dead. John wondered whether she realised what she'd just said then decided to save it to tease her with another day. He smiled, pleased by her concern, but he stopped smiling when she started to eat the chocolates Craig had bought for him.

John gawped as Natalie chomped her way through all his favourites while she read his hospital notes, just as he would have done. When she lifted the top layer of the chocolates to search for more of her favourites underneath John decided enough was enough. He closed his eyes in mock pain and moaned. It did the trick. Natalie rushed to his side.

"John, are you OK?"

He gave what he hoped looked like a brave smile and raised a weak hand, waving her to a seat. He needed to be brought up to date with what was happening in the outside world and if pity was the only way to get information then pity it would have to be.

"How's Marc getting on with the case?"

Natalie popped a Turkish delight into her mouth and started to speak and for a moment John pictured her six-feet–six tall and in drag; she could be Liam's younger sister! He shook the image away and listened as she talked.

"Mike Augustus phoned me. There's been another suicide that really wasn't. The man shot—" She stopped abruptly mid-sentence realising what she'd just said and changed tack. "Anyway, I think they're making progress. You know Marc, if anyone can solve it he can." Her face brightened. "Guess what? He and Katy had coffee."

John was still focused on the suicide. He made a note to ask Mike to pay him a visit but thought better of telling Natalie. Instead he feigned interest in Craig's love life.

"When?"

"The other morning. She came up to the I.C.U. and they bumped into each other and went for coffee."

"And?"

"And what? She likes him and he likes her but whether they'll do anything about it God only knows. Those two are worse than teenagers."

She put the chocolates to one side and folded her hands decisively in her lap, signalling maturity. The smear of orange fondant on her chin didn't look quite so mature. John decided not to tell her about it. Craig wasn't the only teenager around.

***

It had been a long time since Liam had spent a whole day interviewing with Annette. Their newly elevated ranks and Jake joining the team had meant they were more often paired with him, as part of his training. But they fell back into their rhythm without missing a step. Liam blunt and sceptical, Annette being the interviewee's best friend, often gleaning far more information than his forceful approach. They were sarky cop and sweet cop without needing to be coached and Annette said as much as they were driving away from the Antrim home of Nelson Warner's second family.

"That felt like old times, didn't it? You offending her and me picking up the pieces."

Liam guffawed. "Aye. Now all we need is the boss to charm them and we'd have the plot of a Mills and Boon."

Annette smiled at the truth of his words. "Do you think he knows he's doing it?"

Liam spotted a gap in the traffic and slipped in easily, ignoring the glare of the driver behind.

"What? Old smoothie Craig? Nah. He hasn't a clue. He just talks to them like he usually does and they fall at his feet." He laughed again. "Imagine him when he was young. Strolling off the rugby pitch, thinking about the game and completely missing the girls hurling themselves on the ground."

"I bet Dr Winter caught them instead."

They descended into a moment's banter about Craig and John when they were young, then the words faded away and they drove on in amiable silence. Liam broke it first.

"What did you make of Pamela Anderson back there?"

Annette laughed so hard that she couldn't speak, picturing the buxom blonde that they'd just left. Warner's second wife had been the spitting image of Isabella McDonald, his official mistress. In a strange way it was reassuring that Warner had had a type; at least he'd been faithful to something.

When Annette finally caught her breath she volunteered. "I think he picked identical models so that he'd feel at home. A simple man."

"Aye. I don't think she had anything to do with his death either. She seemed pretty cut-up."

"So would I if I'd just lost my meal ticket."

Liam tutted. "That's harsh, girl. Maybe she really loved him."

Annette snorted. "She loved something but I doubt it was Warner's sparkling personality."

Liam accelerated onto the M2 motorway as he answered. "Aye, stockbrokers aren't renowned for that, are they? OK. Strike her off the list then. Who's next?"

"We need to go to Diana Rogan's office one last time and I want to drop into Victoria Linton's office as well. Her secretary might know something more."

"Fair enough; they're both in the centre of town. You know what that means of course?"

Annette glanced up quickly from her notes, sensing that Liam was up to mischief. "What?"

"We can drop into The Apartment for coffee. I haven't had a decent latte for years."

***

Craig was pacing his office like a caged wolf and the pounding of his footsteps on the thin office carpet was driving Nicky mad. Finally she'd had enough and she banged hard on his door, yanking it open before he could say 'come in'. Craig stopped mid pace, startled by Nicky's appearance, in more than one way; he couldn't believe he hadn't noticed it earlier. Nicky's dramatic entrance was magnified by the silver streak she'd dyed overnight into her newly blackened hair. With her knee-length leather boots she looked like Morticia Adams, or something from the Rocky Horror Picture Show.

Nicky stood in the doorway in silence, so Craig shrugged and resumed his pacing. Her quiet "Sir" made him halt again. The warning tone in her voice would have stopped him even if her expression hadn't.

"Yes, Nicky?"

"Are you going to pace until Liam and Annette get back?"

Craig stared down at his feet, realising that she was right. He was pacing and he hadn't even noticed. He'd always thought of what he did when he was working out a case as more of a thoughtful stroll, a la Sherlock Holmes. The problem was that he normally did it when John was there to make suggestions. It didn't work half as well when he was on his own.

"I was thinking of it."

211

"Fine."

Nicky turned on her heel and left the office. Craig followed, wondering what her "fine" had meant. He soon found out. She packed her things into her handbag and headed for the floor's double-doors.

"I'm taking some owed time; I'll be back in an hour. If you need me desperately you can get me on the phone."

With a flash of black hair she was out the door. Craig stared after her, wondering what he'd done to annoy her so much. Davy shouted out the answer.

"You w…were pacing, chief. It makes her s…scream."

Craig turned to face him. "She never told me… Can you hear it through the door?"

Davy nodded. "Every thud. No-one else minds, but it drives Nicky mad."

Craig went to pace the open-plan floor then realised what he was doing and laughed. He wandered over to Davy's desk.

"It's Liam's fault for putting me under house arrest." He leaned over Davy's shoulder. "How are you getting on with the numbers?"

"Nothing yet, but I think Jake's had s…some joy on the chat-rooms."

Jake heard his name and joined them with a sheet of paper in his hand. Craig grabbed two chairs and beckoned him to sit.

"Davy says you've had a result on the chat-rooms?"

Jake frowned and then nodded hesitantly. "Yes and no. Remember I took the list of players from twenty and ten years ago and made a short-list of anyone who was on both, anywhere in the world? Then I removed any outside Northern Ireland and that left us with five?"

Craig nodded. "Using the logic that a teenager back then wouldn't have had the know-how to re-route themselves through another country."

"Correct. OK, so that left me with five players here. That's where it's got tricky. Once I'd got the real name and addresses behind the screen names I was going to remove all the men's names, now that we know our perp is female. But they're all male. There are no women."

Craig swore loudly. They'd hit a dead end. "Where does that leave us?"

Jake hesitated and his expression said that what he was going to say next was a leap. Craig nodded him on.

"Well... then I thought. What if our perp hadn't always been female?"

Craig's mouth dropped open, seeing immediately where Jake was heading. Clever lad. What if their player had been a teenage boy who'd since had a sex-change to become a woman? Their female shooter had once been a man.

"Transgender?"

Jake nodded. "It's possible. I've seen some very good sex-changes and Dr Winter only caught a glimpse of his assailant. He could have missed it."

Craig hesitated to agree. John was very sharp. Sharp enough to have registered the woman's eye and hair colour. Unless the sex-change was flawless he wouldn't have confused their sex. But they needed more proof than his faith in John. He turned to Davy.

"Davy, the voice trace. Can you play it back, please?"

Davy hit a switch and they listened as the female voice filled the space around them. The voice was low for a woman and slightly husky, but beyond that it was impossible to tell. It could have been altered by hormones or their perp could still have been born female.

Craig shook his head. "Davy, get linguistics onto it urgently, will you? Tell them what we're looking for." He turned back to Jake. "OK, leaving the transgender option aside for a moment, let's suppose that this is someone who was born female, in which case any female players from Northern Ireland twenty and ten years ago would have been on our present day shortlist of five, which they aren't because there weren't any. Or we're wrong and this is a woman from Northern Ireland who wasn't playing all those years ago and who has only started playing in the past few years, and is clever enough to re-route to anywhere around the world. In which case any woman playing anywhere nowadays gets added to our list."

Jake pulled a face. "Sorry, sir. Again it's yes and no. We know we have no women on our Northern Ireland shortlist nowadays, as you've said, and yes, a woman playing here could divert play as you've said to make it look like she'd playing from outside Northern Ireland. If they were bright enough, and we know our killer is. But our theory has always been based on this trauma starting when our killer was a teenager and that fits with the key, so who is this woman who has suddenly started playing an out-of-date computer game as an adult, and why this game? There are thousands of new games out there to choose from, so why choose 'Justification', a game from twenty years ago, if you're just starting to play nowadays?"

Craig nodded. Jake was right, any woman who'd started computer gaming in the past few years would have made a more modern choice. Jake continued.

"If they're transgender male to female now then twenty years ago they would have been too young to have had gender reassignment surgery. But if they had it ten years ago or more they'd have started to identify as female in everyday life then."

Craig nodded slowly. "And the fact that they chose not to change their identity as female online could mean that they've been thinking about this killing spree for years. So the suspect list in the real population becomes males living in Northern Ireland twenty years ago, males and females ten years ago and females nowadays. That should catch every possibility. But in the online population, it still comes down to our list of five male names."

Davy smiled at the way Craig's brain worked, searching for the flaw in his argument. There wasn't one. Craig crossed to Nicky's desk and poured himself a coffee, still thinking. He was dragged back to reality by a triumphant yell and the sight of Davy punching the air.

"Yes! Jake was right! She's transgender. Linguistics has given the chances of this being the voice of a male to female sex-change as ninety percent."

Craig's mouth fell open. It had been a long shot but it had paid off. "Why did Linguistics miss it before?"

Davy shook his head. "Not looking for it, probably. To be honest, chief, if w…we hadn't looked for it I would never have noticed from the tape, w…would you?"

Craig shook his head. "No. Never. I just thought she had a husky voice." He grinned. "Well done, Jake."

Jake blushed. "Thanks, sir. I've met a few transgender males and females at Sarajevo, so it wasn't such a leap for me."

Sarajevo was a popular gay club in the centre of Belfast.

"OK. Good. So let's have a look at that list again now that we know. So our perp had a male to female transition but they're on Jake's list of five screen names as a man."

They stared at the list in silence for a moment before Craig spoke.

"OK… so in 1994 seven males in Northern Ireland were in the chat-rooms dedicated to the game. If John and linguistics have got the age right at early thirties then our perp would have been a boy anywhere from his early to mid-teens then. Obviously with liberal parents who let him play the game! Ten years later we're looking at either males or females in their early twenties but still no girls. We've lost a player, that's a list of six people in 2004. And now we have just five players from Northern Ireland."

He scanned the lists. "Right, let's just examine the first two lists. There were seven names in '94 then six ten years later, all male. People came and went over that period but we have two names that match on that list, both from Northern Ireland; Harry Lamb and James Mulhearn. They're both still on the 2014 list. Jake, do you have addresses for them?"

Jake rushed back to his screen to check. "Yes, but only one kept the same address for the whole twenty years. Harry Lamb."

"Right, Davy. Check the family at that address."

Davy typed for a second and then started to read. "Harry Lamb and his family. Parents George and S…Susan, sister Kate. They still live there. Harry is recorded as having married and moved to Enniskillen in 2008; he obviously forgot to change his address online."

'Forgot' was giving him the benefit of a huge doubt in Craig's mind.

"His driving licence p…photo is coming up now."

The image of a slim Chinese man appeared on the screen and Craig shook his head. It wasn't their perp. It was easier to change sex than ethnicity.

"OK, good. That rules him out. That just leaves James Mulhearn. What have we got on him?"

Jake and Davy typed away for a moment then Davy spoke. "James Mulhearn thirty years old. Lived on the Malone Road w…with his parents, Mary and Patrick Mulhearn until 1997 when he was thirteen, then nothing. The last record of him w… was in 2004 when he got his driving licence. He was twenty then. He gave his childhood address on it even though the house was demolished in 1999. His picture's coming through now."

Craig walked to the printer and tugged the hot page free impatiently. He stared hard at the image in front of him then shook his head, not because the answer was no, but because he didn't know what the answer was. James Mulhearn was definitely a man and not a bad looking one. He was slight and fine-featured with straight hair and a beard that could have been brown or auburn depending on the light. Hair was easily grown and curled and beards could be shaved off, but they could still only speculate that the man in the photo might be a woman now.

Craig handed the picture around and turned back to the

lists. Jake's voice broke through his thoughts.

"James Mulhearn hasn't been playing online for the past two days, boss."

Craig nodded. "Like I said there could be all sorts of reasons for that."

"Or it could fit with someone who wanted to keep a low profile because they were busy doing other things, like killing."

Craig sipped at his coffee thoughtfully. "I think you're right, Jake. It's too much coincidence that your hunch about transgender was backed up by linguistics. We're on the right track. We're looking for a teenage boy who played this computer game and became a woman at some point in the past twenty years." He gestured at the photograph of James Mulhearn. "I think Mulhearn's our perp." He turned to Davy. "Davy, just to be certain, get me the photograph of every woman playing anywhere nowadays."

"It'll take a w...while. Some of them might be foreign nationals. I'll have to s...speak to the countries they play from."

"Or routed through. OK, do whatever you have to do. We need John to see their photos and rule them out."

Jake glanced warily at Craig. "Actually, sir, I'm pretty sure we're on the right track with James Mulhearn and I'd like permission to start following that up."

Craig nodded. "OK, go ahead. Davy, John's on a ward now so he's well enough to do a sketch for us. Get the artist over there ASAP then run the sketch through face recognition and see if the main markers match James Mulhearn's driving licence photo. Meanwhile, Jake, find me everything there is out there about James Mulhearn, past and present. If you need any strings pulled just let me know."

Just then Nicky entered through the glass double-doors, with her protection officer in tow, looking less than amused. Nicky was carrying a bag from a popular clothes store. She stared pointedly at Craig's feet as she approached.

"Stopped pacing then? Or has he been driving you boys mad

as well?"

Craig smiled at her cheek and then at the bag. "Don't tell me… I drove you to retail therapy."

"You did, so you can explain my credit card bill to Gary when it arrives."

***

Diana Rogan had been well liked. The mood in her office was subdued when Annette and Liam arrived, even though no-one could possibly have known they were coming. It was even more subdued when they left. Everyone from Rogan's secretary and boss to the tea lady had a kind word to say about her, and everyone testified to how much she'd loved her husband and kids. As pleasant office companions went Diana Rogan seemed to have ranked high in the charts. But cautious questioning revealed that none of them knew that her son wasn't Conor Rogan's, so that said something about how little people ever really knew about anyone else.

Victoria Linton didn't rate quite so highly for popularity. Annette smiled encouragingly at the secretary in front of them, assuring her that anything she said would remain confidential. Natasha Nunes took Annette at her word.

"Linton was a bitch. A Class A, nine carat, hard-faced, money grubbing bitch, and I'm not surprised that someone killed her."

Liam burst out laughing and Annette shot him a disapproving look. This was a victim they were talking about, after all. She arched an eyebrow and stared at Nunes again.

"It's obvious that you didn't like Ms Linton, but could you be more specific as to why?"

Nunes folded her arms across her thin frame and warmed to her subject. "She shouted at everyone and expected us all to work our asses off for her without even a thank you." She sniffed. "She never even bought us a gift at Christmas like Mr

Roche did. He's a gentleman, but Linton was just in it for the money."

Liam lurched forward suddenly. "Did you want her dead, then?"

Nunes jerked backwards then stuttered. "N…No, I didn't want her dead! I was leaving anyway."

"To go where?"

"To take a new job; working closer to home."

"Are you still leaving?"

"No. Mr Roche has asked me to stay on. But…"

Annette smiled to herself watching the girl being wrong-footed by Liam's quick-fire approach.

"But what? But you bumped her off so you didn't have to leave?"

The girl stared at him, stunned for a moment by the suggestion, then she re-folded her arms and grinned. "Yeh, that's right. I wanted to stay here so much that I bumped her off. As if!"

Her sarcasm irritated Liam and he rose to his full height. "Right then, that sounded like a confession to me. Come along Ms Nunes. Read her rights, Inspector."

Natasha Nunes' eyes widened and she spun to face Annette, who was trying hard not to laugh.

"I didn't kill her, but there were plenty who wanted to. She'd made a lot of enemies though the years."

Liam sat down again and leaned forward with an intense look on his face. "Like who?"

"W…Well, I'd have to look through the files, but she had a few who rang up regularly, calling her everything. I wasn't allowed to put their calls through."

Annette nodded. Victoria Linton was a prosecutor. That wouldn't make her popular with the criminal classes.

"Criminals that she'd put away?"

Annette was surprised when Nunes shook her head. "Not all of them. She was a commercial lawyer before she turned to prosecution and she lost a lot of people compensation through the years."

It was what they'd already suspected.

"What sort of companies did she defend?"

"All sorts. Insurance companies, pension companies, banks, anyone who could get sued really."

Liam interrupted. "Why did she give it up?"

Nunes shook her head. "She didn't confide in me."

"Would Mr Roche know?"

The young woman shook her head again. "I don't think so. He only became her partner last year. She was solo before that." She thought for a moment. "You might try Mr Lover, Lover."

Annette smiled at the reference to the old song by Shaggy. "Her boyfriend?"

"Julian Mooney. I spoke to him on the phone a few times. Not my sort, but he seemed nice enough. Too nice for her."

"Why not your sort?"

"Too arty for me. I think he's an architect or something like that."

They really needed to interview Mooney.

"Do you have a list of the callers who you weren't to put through?"

Nunes printed off a list of about ten names and Annette sighed, knowing that they'd have to eliminate each one. She rose to her feet and extended her hand to shake, gripping the girl's and smiling. Nunes withdrew her hand swiftly before Liam offered to do the same and watched gratefully as they walked out the door. Then she stared at the list on her screen trying to work out which one of them had done the world a favour by bumping off her boss.

Chapter Seventeen

3.30 p.m.

Jenna swore at the tall C.C.U. building in frustration. It wasn't for an audience; Pilot Street was deserted. The days when it was a bustling thoroughfare between the water's edge and the rest of Sailortown, leading to food, alcohol and a warm woman were long since gone. Its cobbles had been shattered many years before by a developer's jackhammer and St Joseph's, the listed church that had served the area's occupants and visitors since 1878, was boarded up and silent.

She remembered the campaign to save the little 'Chapel on the Quays', as the church had always been known. Catholics and Protestants had stood side by side every Sunday morning, trying to save it from the wrecking ball. They'd managed to save the building but now it stood boarded-up and unexplored, waiting for its protectors to restore its interior and open it again for the world to view. The church watched over the narrow dockland streets like a holy sentinel, as if it was biding its time, waiting for its rafters to ring again with voices raised in prayer.

Jenna imagined the silent chapel disapproving of everything about her life, from the games she played to the abomination its clergy would think her body had become. She shrugged, not caring. If there was a God then it was responsible for her creation, male and female. No use disapproving of me now, Supreme Being, whatever you call yourself, or trying to lay the blame at society's door. I'm your child after all. She laughed, knowing that no-one would hear her and wonder who the madwoman was, laughing alone in the street. Then she turned her attention back to the C.C.U. and waited for her prey.

***

Craig had had enough of being under house arrest. He wanted to visit John and it was a Friday evening so he had to leave the office by seven anyway. Attendance at his mother's Friday night dinner was a three-line-whip and she overcooked her pasta for no-one. He glanced at his watch, calculating that he could get to the hospital and back in under an hour, before Liam and Annette returned for the briefing at five o' clock.

He walked to the door of his office and wrenched it open, watching as Nicky and Jake sprang into high alert. It wasn't his elevated rank that did it, this wasn't the military after all, it was the fact that they'd been tasked by Liam to stop him leaving and they were taking their job to heart.

Nicky squinted at him menacingly. "Where do you think you're going... sir?" The appellation was an afterthought that came reluctantly after the pause. Craig knew what was running through her mind during the two second gap. You couldn't call your prisoner 'sir', even if he was your boss. And that's what Craig was after all, a prisoner. Under house arrest for his own good.

"I was thinking of having a sandwich in the canteen, if that's OK with you?"

Nicky screwed up her face as if she was mapping out his possible escape routes from the seventh floor. There were too many for comfort.

"I can get one for you."

Craig shook his head. "I want to eat it there and read the paper. I need a break."

He caught Davy's grin out of the side of his eye. He wasn't sitting to attention like the others, but then he doubted Davy knew what the stance even looked like. He was a rebel, an artist, and his only possible partner in crime.

"I'll be back for the briefing at five o'clock. But if it makes you feel any better, Davy can come with me to make sure that I don't escape."

Nicky thought for another minute, searching for the catch then she gave Craig a reluctant nod. He was up to something, she had no doubt about that, but she couldn't work out exactly what. Craig nodded to Davy and he loped across the floor, then they started the long walk to freedom towards the lift. When they were out of Nicky's earshot the young analyst turned to Craig.

"W...We're not going to the canteen, are we?"

"Nope."

"We're going to s...see Dr Winter, aren't we?"

"Correct."

Davy rubbed his hands gleefully, feeling like a spy on a secret mission. They entered the lift and Craig pressed for the basement garage then Davy spoke again.

"Just one thing, chief. W...What about my protection guy? If he's finds out that I've gone he'll go berserk."

Craig startled. He'd forgotten about the C.P.Os! He thought fast.

"He's in reception, because that's the way you normally leave. He won't know we've got out through the basement. Give it twenty minutes then ring Nicky and pretend we're still in the canteen and ask if she'd like anything brought back. That should throw her off the scent. By the time she realises we've gone we'll be back."

They reached the garage and Craig gunned the engine of his ancient car. They swept out smoothly onto Pilot Street, completely missing the tall figure standing in Short Street as they drove past.

Jenna smiled as the car whizzed past her. Not because she had any intention of following, she guessed that Craig would be back soon enough. It was mid-afternoon and he had someone in the car; there'd be more work to do before he would head home for the night. No, Jenna smiled because she knew what it meant. Craig was a risk taker; he'd left his office without an armed guard and that meant he was careless and she would get to him soon. She liked people who took risks, as long as they were only with their own lives.

***

Sydenham.

Liam and Annette had one last person to interview before they collected Mike Augustus from the lab and headed back to the ranch for five o'clock. Annette scanned the list on her knee as Liam drove expertly towards Julian Mooney's address. Natasha Nunes had been right. Mooney was an arty sort, but he wasn't an architect, he was into interior design. Annette had always wondered what interior designers did, until she saw the warmth created by the décor in the Merchant Hotel and the cool stylistic elegance of the MAC. That's what interior designers did. They took an empty room and made it feel like something more.

She glanced up from her list and pointed ahead. "It's the second on the right."

Liam ignored her. Back seat drivers. He knew Belfast like the back of his hand and Annette was from Maghera! He wondered why people said 'the back of your hand'? Why not 'your own face'? After all, you spent a lot more time staring at yourself in the mirror than you did looking down at your limbs. His thoughts changed swiftly as he noticed the name of the street they were in. 'Marine Street.' This was it.

Liam parked the car and clambered out, scanning the street cautiously. It was narrow and run-down, like the whole area was. It didn't look like somewhere a barrister's boyfriend would live. The semi-detached house at number 25 was as shabby as the street it was in, and they walked slowly up its untidy path to an unremarkable front door. Annette was disappointed, she'd prepared herself to be wowed by the house, thinking that a designer would live somewhere swish.

They knocked several times but no-one answered so Liam walked across the garden towards the rear of the house.

"I'll look round the back. You keep knocking."

But back and front doors yielded the same result. There was no-one at home. Liam peered through the kitchen windows, looking for some clues to Julian Mooney's life. The room was sparse and cold looking, the only sign of life a newspaper spread across the table top. Annette wandered round to join him, just as he was pushing a window hard.

"Liam, stop that! Mooney isn't a suspect."

Liam frowned. Something felt very wrong. Julian Mooney was supposed to be a designer, the partner of a wealthy woman, yet he lived on a run-down street in a poor area and his shabby décor definitely wasn't an attempt at Bohemian chic. The hairs on the back of Liam's neck sprang up and he motioned Annette back to the car. As they drove off to collect Mike Augustus he scanned the street a final time for threats, certain that their perp had been there.

***

"God, I'm bored. Tell me what's happening with the case."

Craig shook his head. If Natalie found him talking to John about work he'd be a dead man. Davy gazed curiously around the hospital side-room then lifted the remote control, managing to find several TV channels that John had missed. One of them was FOX International which showed the best crime series on the box.

"Stop! Freeze it there, Davy and check what's on tonight, will you?"

Davy flicked up the index and John beamed. Episodes of his favourite cop shows were being played back to back.

"I can die happy now."

Craig winced. "I'd rather you didn't die at all, thanks."

He paused for a second, calculating how much he could get John involved with work before Natalie came after him with an axe. John had seen who'd shot him, and they would ask any witness to give a description, so a sketch should be safe enough ground.

"John, if I get the artist to visit you tomorrow can you do a sketch of the woman who shot you?"

John was still staring at the screen as the opening credits of 'The Wire' started to play. He answered Craig vaguely. "Yeh, sure, whatever you want."

"What time is Natalie likely to visit?"

"In and out all day." He motioned to Davy. "Davy, can you turn that up."

"I'd like the artist to avoid her if possible. You know Natalie when she's having a rant."

John's gaze was fixed straight ahead and he reached out his hand for the remote control. "Yes, very wise. Good."

They'd lost him to the joys of Baltimore's finest and Craig recognised defeat. He motioned Davy towards the door and they left John to solve some of America's heinous crimes.

***

The C.C.U. 5 p.m.

"OK. We'll go round for updates then open it up for discussion. Welcome, Mike, thanks for coming."

Mike Augustus smiled and gazed excitedly round the squad-room, like a man who didn't get out enough.

"Liam, you and Annette start us off."

Craig motioned them on, ignoring Nicky's glare. She'd caught him and Davy as they'd re-entered the floor and wagged a finger in Craig's face.

"You weren't in the canteen. I checked!"

Craig had tried for indignation but it was ruined by Davy's loud laugh.

"We were… for a while."

"And where were you then? Eh?" The wagging intensified. "If I find out that you left this building without protection and took this vulnerable boy into danger…"

The 'vulnerable boy' laughed so hard that Craig wanted to smack him one, but instead he smiled calmly. He calculated that Nicky would have taken the lift to the canteen and took his best shot.

"We went to the canteen and then walked back up the stairs. You must have missed us."

Nicky squinted at Craig's innocent face, suddenly uncertain of her ground. She'd taken the lift both ways, so she could easily have missed them between floors and Davy's protection officer said they definitely hadn't left through reception. The only way to prove her case was to speak to the gate officer in the garage. She'd been about to go down to the basement when Liam and Annette had arrived.

Liam started to report from memory as Annette checked what he said against her notebook. She gave up halfway when he didn't put a foot wrong. Liam ran through their visits to Warner's second family in Antrim and Diana Rogan's office in one minute, basically filing them under 'nothing interesting to report'. When he reached Victoria Linton's P.A he stopped and nodded Annette on.

"It seems that Victoria Linton wasn't well liked, not by her P.A. and not by some of the people she'd dealt with."

"Criminals she'd prosecuted?"

"Not just them, sir. She'd been a defence lawyer for corporate clients before she took up prosecution and she made a few enemies there as well. Her clients were mainly banks, insurance companies and the like."

Craig knew they were in the right ball-park.

"The P.A., Natasha Nunes, had a list of people that she wasn't to put through to Linton if they called."

"Did you get it?"

Annette nodded and tapped a file on her lap. "I'll give it to Davy to cross-check. Then we went to visit the boyfriend, Julian Mooney. Ms Nunes thought he might be an architect. Turns out he was an interior designer but I have to say I wouldn't fancy him designing my house."

"Why not?"

Liam jumped in. "'Cos his own place was a shambles. Neglected house in a rough road and if what we saw was interior design then I'll stick with my own taste."

Davy's timing was perfect. "Neanderthal chic?"

Craig smiled at his droll delivery and Mike Augustus laughed out loud; they never had this much fun at the lab.

Liam drew himself upright in his chair. "Here now, I'll have you know…"

Craig waved them both down, laughing. "I'm sure your taste is impeccable, Liam. Annette, tell us what you saw at Mooney's house."

Annette shrugged. "To be honest Liam's already said it all. There was no-one in so we had a quick look through the kitchen window and it was worse than most student flats. Chilly looking, sparse and dull. If Mooney's an interior designer he's not a very good one, unless the rest of the house is better. To be honest it looked more like a flop pad than a home."

The group fell silent for a moment while Craig thought. "OK… Davy, check out Mooney please. We know he exists because the neighbour, James Wallace, met him. You two, go back to Linton's development and speak to Wallace again. Davy will give you Mooney's photo."

"W…Well actually…"

Craig turned towards Davy, he'd moved back to his computer and was typing something in. After a moment he nodded and returned to his seat.

"I just wanted to recheck something. I s...searched Julian Mooney on the computer when I did everyone else after Victoria Linton's death and nothing came up on him. I parked it because he was only a partner of the victim and she was only one of several suicides, s...so he didn't seem that important, but I've just run him again and there's nothing."

Craig frowned. "Nothing? Driving licence, passport, work history?"

Davy shook his long hair. "Nada. He's the invisible man."

"How is that possible?"

"W...Well, if he doesn't drive or travel, it's very possible he doesn't have any passport or driving licence pictures available. And if he's a freelance designer it might be a lot of cash in hand work."

Liam lurched forward. "Aha! We can get him on tax evasion, then."

Craig looked at him sceptically. "Well one, why would we want to 'get him'? He's a victim's partner. And two, tax evasion only applies if we can prove Mooney actually earned some money."

"He's a bad one, boss. I knew it when we were at the house. It was a mess."

Annette snorted. "Bad taste isn't a crime, Liam, if it was..." She stared pointedly at his cartoon patterned socks.

Craig pulled them back to the meeting. "OK, so Julian Mooney's odd and Liam's gut is telling him that he's something else as well. I tend to agree, so let's dig a bit deeper." He turned towards Mike Augustus, who looked completely bemused. "Mike, could you update us on Adrian Bell, please."

Augustus looked disappointed that the banter had stopped but he smiled and removed a set of hand-outs from a folder that he'd brought. Craig watched him as he handed them out. Augustus was younger than John and him and as chubby as they were both slim. He had a thick thatch of mousey brown hair and a permanently child-like expression, despite the horrific things he saw all day, and he spoke so quietly that Craig always strained to hear. Craig pre-empted it now by requesting that Augustus speak up.

"Ah, yes. I know I mumble. I'll do my best to be heard. OK, in your hand-outs you'll see the results on Bell from both pathology and forensics. Des did the forensics report. Right, on page one is the post-mortem report. It shows that your victim was definitely Adrian Bell: he was identified from dental records. He was a healthy forty-seven-year-old male with no serious systemic illness. He was diabetic but it was well controlled. Death was instant and due to a single gunshot wound to the head. There was gunshot residue on his right hand that indicated he'd shot himself and prints that we're running now. The bullet was a 9 by 19 millimetre Parabellum, full metal jacket, exactly the same as the one that hit John. Bell's was fired from the Mauser C96 that was found at his scene…"

Liam leaned forward to interrupt and Augustus raised a hand to still him.

"Before you ask, no, the markings don't match for John. Same type of bullet but your killer used a different gun. Bell's bullet entered the skull at an angle above his right ear, pierced the parietal bone and travelled upwards at an angle of about forty-five degrees to emerge through the top of the frontal bone and lodge in the wall. Mr Bell left a note which Des said was identical to several others you've seen in this case. It was written in Bell's own hand, as verified by other samples of handwriting found in the house. A USB in a key-shaped casing was found near the suicide scene, again as with earlier victims."

Craig signalled to interrupt. "Were any other prints found in the room?"

Augustus nodded. "Quite a few. Mr Bell had a family so that was to be expected. Oh yes, the blood splatter and brain matter distribution were consistent with his head wound."

On the words 'brain matter' Nicky blanched.

"All in all, the scene was identical to the others that John

P.M.ed, with only one possible difference."

The words were said so casually that Craig almost missed them. Augustus was about to start his next sentence when Craig motioned him to halt.

"One difference?"

"Possibly, yes. There's a suggestion that there may have been physical coercion at the time of Mr Bell's death."

Craig leaned forward urgently. "What?"

Augustus nodded. "We can't be certain but the pattern of the handwriting may indicate that the pen was being forced along.

"By another hand? You mean someone held Bell's hand while he wrote the note?"

Augustus' normally open face became cautious. "May have held. We have no definite proof yet. The handwriting expert only came back with this at three o'clock. They have to do a lot more tests."

Craig's mind raced. If their killer had had to pressure Bell to kill himself then they might have been in a hurry to finish him off. It was a big risk. All of the other deaths had been at arm's length; their perp had deliberately kept themselves remote, outlining their victims' instructions and why they should kill themselves in instantly wiped PDFs.

Something must have signalled Adrian Bell's refusal and made the killer visit the scene to help him along. Was it just haste? Were they eager to complete this murder and then disappear? Or was a compulsion making them careless, and if so had it made them careless in other ways? Craig's next question surprised them all.

"Mike, have you checked if all the prints on the gun and pen belonged to Bell?"

Augustus' eyes widened and he instantly went to say 'what for?' He stopped himself before the words emerged and smiled.

"You clever sod, Marc."

Nicky arched an eyebrow at the way he addressed Craig but Craig merely grinned.

"What do you think? Is it possible?"

"It's very possible. Leave it with me. I'll go back to the lab and check it now."

Augustus rose quickly and was across the floor before the rest of them could ask why he was leaving. They asked Craig instead.

"What's so clever, boss?"

Craig smiled. "Well, I don't know whether it was clever or I'm just warped, but I suddenly thought that if the killer had forced Bell to write his suicide note, why risk it? The only answer I could come up with was that they were in a hurry to complete the task, perhaps because Bell was the last and they wanted to get away. Or because this is a compulsion with them now, so everything had to be right. It had to look as if Bell had committed suicide."

Liam smiled as he saw where Craig was going next and why Augustus had rushed away. "You think if our perp held Bell's hand while he wrote the note..."

"He might also have held it when he shot himself."

Jake interjected. "But what good is that, sir? Wouldn't they have worn gloves?"

"Maybe, or maybe not. Compulsion can make people careless. If they didn't wear gloves there could be trace evidence on Bell's hand, on the pen he used, or even, if we're very lucky, somewhere on the gun."

"It's worth a punt anyway."

Craig nodded. Yes, it was worth a punt, but he wasn't sure that would solve their case. "OK, good. That leaves us with Jake and Davy's findings. Jake, can you start with the chat-rooms and then hand over to Davy."

While Jake and Davy presented in tandem, the others' jaws dropped, as their female killer morphed into a transgendered male. They'd even managed to come up with a possible name. James Mulhearn.

"W...We've got a bit stuck there, chief. I'm waiting for info to come through on Mulhearn but it's the weekend now."

Craig had another thought and kicked himself for not thinking of it earlier. "Davy, sex-change operations aren't that common, even nowadays. Can you find out where they're usually performed?"

Davy smiled smugly. "Already did. In the UK the main gender reassignment unit is at Charing Cross Hospital, overseas it's done mostly in Holland and the Far East."

"Good. Send James Mulhearn's photograph to all of them, please, and outline why we need it I.D.ed."

Liam interrupted in a subdued tone.

"You'll hit a medical brick wall, boss. Doctors won't give out patient information at the best of times, but it'll be ten times worse in a sensitive area like this."

Annette gazed at him in wonder. Liam recognising that something was sensitive was miracle enough, but resisting the urge to make jokes about it was a first. He knew someone transgendered, she was sure of it. She squinted at Liam, trying to imagine him as a woman; it was unlikely, he would have been the ugliest woman ever born. She asked the question.

"Who do you know who has been through the operation, Liam?"

Liam spluttered. "I don't! Me? No way."

Annette wasn't backing down. "Yes you do. You're being far too sensitive for you not to."

Liam relented, nodding. "Aye well, yes I do. My first partner on the beat quit the force and no-one knew why. I met up with him five years later and he'd had it done." He grinned admiringly. "He made a good-looking girl too. Fair play to him, that's what I say. He's married now as well."

Craig cut in. "Where did he have it done, Liam?"

"Charing Cross. It's not just the main place in the UK, apparently it's the largest centre in Europe, or it was twenty years back." He turned to Davy. "You should try there first, lad, but I still don't rate your chances of breaking through the

Hippocratic Oath."

Jake rubbed his chin thoughtfully. "I think Liam's right, sir. We can try to I.D. Mulhearn through the hospitals of course, but while we're doing that perhaps the LGBT scene here might be willing to help as well. After all, if there's a transgender killer on the loose they won't be happy, and they may offer to help us."

Craig nodded. "OK. Jake, you look into that with Annette. Davy will do the hospitals and pursue the code. By the way, John's agreed to do a sketch of his shooter for us, so Nicky, can you get the sketch artist over to the hospital tomorrow morning, please."

Nicky looked at him suspiciously. It was on the tip of her tongue to ask Craig precisely when John had agreed, when she realised that he could have phoned him.

"OK, we'll have John's sketch of the woman and James Mulhearn's image to face-match. Jake and Annette will ask around the LGBT community, and I'll take Julian Mooney. If necessary I'll get a warrant for his house. We'll brief tomorrow at twelve."

Craig glanced quickly at his watch. It was six o'clock on a Friday night and they had homes to go to, so he called the meeting to a close. As he was walking back to his office Liam tapped him on the shoulder.

"What are your plans for tonight, boss?"

"Why? Are you asking me on a date?"

"Nah, you're not my type. But if you think you're going anywhere without an armed guard now you've another think coming. Marlene's busy watching Mike Augustus so you'll have to make do with me."

Craig shook his head firmly. "You're going home to your wife and kids, Liam. Get me a close protection officer, the one who guarded that Minister, Joe Watson, if he's free. I think his name was Ian Sinclair. Mind you, it didn't do John much good. And if it's any of your business I'm heading to my folks. My mum will be tearing her hair out with all those armed guards around by now."

An hour later Craig was in Holywood being proved entirely wrong. Lucia was tearing her hair out at the restriction to her social life but Mirella was as happy as a clam, preparing dinner for seven – the Craig clan and three close protection officers who had never tasted food so good.

Chapter Eighteen

Saturday, 11 a.m.

Saturday came too quickly for Jenna Graham. Her flight to Heathrow was due to leave just after three p.m. and she wanted to be on it, but getting Craig alone to kill him was proving a challenge; she should have just shot him when he'd driven past her in Holywood the day before. He'd been surrounded by family and armed guards since then, one of them had even sat outside his apartment all night. But bodyguards weren't the problem. After all, she'd got to the pathologist when he'd had one. The problem was that Craig lived in an apartment block with a sheer river drop on one side and only one entrance on the other. It was going to be a challenge to kill him there.

She yawned widely and then checked herself. It was almost OK for a man to open his mouth wide but no woman would yawn like that. She tutted, frustrated at the slip; after all these years as a woman it was still the mannerisms that caught her out. She'd been fortunate that she'd been a slightly built man, some people might even have called her a wimp. Her fine features and small hands and feet had proved useful when she'd changed sex. Even her five-feet-ten height wasn't out of the ordinary for a woman nowadays. Once she'd started the hormone treatment things had slipped nicely into place, with none of the large jawed, huge handed stereotypes of masculinity to spoil her gender change. Nine years earlier, after two years of hormones and living as a woman, she'd finally had all signs of her masculine past surgically removed and emerged as a

236

woman. Better than that, with her long legs and fine bone structure she'd emerged as a beautiful one and men had fallen at her feet.

Jenna poured herself more coffee and smiled at how shallow men were, how stimulated by beauty and influenced by sex. She hadn't thought anything of it when she'd been one. Normality always went unremarked. But now it gave her power over them everywhere she went. How fortunate that it was men that she'd always craved. Her sex change had changed her from a homosexual man into a heterosexual woman, except that she'd always known she wasn't gay, just trapped in the wrong body for twenty years.

She gazed around the house's pale-grey living room as she drained her cup. She'd never bothered to decorate the place because it had always had a temporary feel. She would leave soon and whoever lived there after her could stamp their life all over it, it had served its purpose in hers. She strolled into the back room to fill the last of her cases then she slammed the lid closed and set it neatly beside the others by the door. She could make her three o'clock flight or hunt down Marc Craig; it wasn't an easy choice but she had to make it soon.

***

Annette rang the buzzer at Sarajevo's side door, not holding out much hope of an answer. It was eleven o'clock on a Saturday morning and the club had been open until two a.m.; no-one would even be up yet, never mind at work. She tapped her foot repeatedly as Jake stared at a window above them, willing someone to appear. After five minutes of repeating the exercise they admitted defeat and Annette turned back towards the car.

"Everyone's at home in bed. They'd probably been clubbing half the night."

Jake shrugged; probably. He's done it himself often enough.

He smiled, remembering the night he'd met Aaron in the club. He'd just split-up with a guy he'd been seeing for a few months and been at a loose end, when Aaron's wide grin had caught his eye across the dance floor and that was that. They'd been together for almost ten years now and they were very happy, so whoever said you never met a keeper in nightclubs was definitely wrong. Something occurred to him as Annette was starting the car.

"There's a place that everyone goes to for Saturday brunch, we might find a few people there."

"Where is it?"

"A café in Botanic Avenue. It's called Buzz." He glanced at his watch. "If we hurry we might still catch them."

Annette nodded and pulled swiftly into the busy Saturday traffic cutting towards the river then on up the Ormeau Road. Five minutes later they were walking into a small, bright café whose menu of fruit juices and bagels made her mouth water. A mixed group in one corner turned as they entered, and Annette guessed that their Saturday morning suits had labelled them as police. She was wrong; the group had turned out of recognition. As they approached, a young man with a mane of thick black hair met them halfway and shook Jake's hand energetically.

"Jake man, I haven't seen you for ages. How's married life?"

Jake smiled. "Yeh, it's good."

"You and Aaron must have been together for eight years now. Yeh?"

"Ten, but who's counting?"

Jake laughed then indicated Annette. "This is Joe. We were at Queen's together."

The young man stared at Annette curiously for a moment then extended his hand. "Are you Jake's mum?"

Annette laughed. She almost could have been chronologically. Jake intervened quickly in case she took offence.

238

"Joe, this is Inspector McElroy. We're on duty and I wondered if you and the crowd could help us with something?"

The young man took a step back, suddenly suspicious. It was a response they saw often but something told Annette that it wouldn't last long; there was something open about the man. Joe thought for a moment then shrugged assent.

"As long as you aren't after any of us."

He led the way to the table and explained why they were there. Annette was surprised when another man sprang to his feet and offered her a seat. She beamed at him, wishing that her own son Jordan had such beautiful manners. Jake was speaking quickly.

"OK, this is confidential and I'm asking you to keep it within this group please."

He paused, waiting for them all to nod. Some did it more reluctantly than others but finally they all had.

"Right. We have a series of crimes, I can't go into any detail about what they are, but we have reason to believe that a trans woman may be involved. We'll have a sketch of her by this afternoon but for now the only description we have is tall, with long red hair and blue eyes. Does that ring a bell with anyone?"

Annette had been watching their faces as Jake gave their perp's description and she could hear peels of bells playing inside at least two heads. One of the men glanced down quickly at the table and Annette knew he wouldn't give them a name, but a slight girl near Jake nodded vigorously.

"That sounds like Jenna."

Jake turned towards her. "Jenna? Do you have a second name?"

The girl shook her head. "No-one asks people's second names nowadays, unless they're really old."

Annette smiled, watching Jake's horror as he realised the girl regarded him as ancient. She was still talking.

"She's a trans woman and lesbian as well. That's how I know her; we go to the same all women's gym."

Their perp was lesbian! Annette didn't know why she was surprised, but she was. Jake urged the girl on with a smile.

"Can I ask how long you've known her?"

The girl screwed up her face in thought. "Umm… I think it's nearly two years. That's when I joined the gym, but I think Jenna was there long before that." She leaned forward enthusiastically. "She's in the swimming team and she's brilliant at it."

"Do you know anything else about her? Is she in a relationship for instance? Or do you know where she lives?"

The girl frowned as she concentrated; she looked so young that Annette wanted to pat her on the head. Finally she nodded.

"Yeh, I remember her telling me she was seeing someone with a high-up job. Sorry, I don't know her name. I think Jenna lives somewhere on the east side of town."

Jake cut in. "When does the swimming team meet?"

"Dunno. It'll be up on the notice board. I can give you the gym's number if you want to check."

As she reached into her bag Annette quickly scanned the other faces at the table. Two of the men were chatting to each other about something else and Joe, Jake's friend, was ordering another juice. Only the young man who was gazing at the table looked uncomfortable.

Annette leaned forward and caught his eye. "Hello."

He frowned at her and nodded.

"You recognised the woman's description, didn't you?"

He nodded again curtly. "Yes, but I won't tell you anything about her. She's always been nice to me."

"I understand. But you must understand that we're investigating a serious crime and we're just trying to rule her out or in."

He snorted, unimpressed. "You can do it without my help."

Annette was interrupted by the girl thrusting a napkin into her hand with the gym's number written on top. She pointed to a name underneath. Nadine.

"That's me. Everyone knows me there. But you're wrong if you think Jenna's involved in anything bad; she's really nice."

"I'm sure she is."

But not so nice that she hadn't shot John Winter and blackmailed five other people into suicide. Annette nodded to Jake then she stood up and thanked the group. As they were walking back to the car she glanced at her watch.

"Let's head back to the office for the briefing then I'll check out the gym later on my own. It's probably better if a man doesn't visit a women only place."

***

Craig's trip to Julian Mooney's house was fruitless. A search of the outside yielded nothing; there was only so much information to be gained by staring into an empty kitchen. He needed a search warrant. He drove back to the C.C.U. deep in thought, oblivious to the armed companion by his side. Why would Victoria Linton's partner make himself so scarce after she died, unless he had something to hide? Especially when he'd been friendly to her neighbours beforehand.

Suddenly something occurred to Craig and he checked the time. Then he indicated left onto Oxford Street and headed for the Stranmillis road. Ten minutes later he was knocking on the apartment door of James Wallace, Victoria Linton's neighbour. He listened to the sounds of confusion that heavy-handed knocking usually provoked. Doors slammed somewhere inside the flat and voices murmured, as if murmurs didn't make any sound that could be heard. Finally someone approached the front door with a cautious "Who's there?"

"It's Superintendent Craig. I'd like to speak to Mr Wallace please."

The door creaked open and the young man he'd spoken to four days before was standing in front of him, half-dressed and with a tousled look that Craig saw frequently in the mirror. Wallace smiled sleepily at Craig and waved him into a bright living room.

"Sorry, Mr Craig, late night. Would you like a coffee? I'm having one."

Craig nodded and Wallace disappeared into the kitchen area. Craig gazed around the room as he waited. The decor was warm and comfortable and there were photographs of Wallace and a woman dotted all around. Two minutes later Wallace reappeared with coffee. The woman in the photographs was with him.

"This is Elise, my girlfriend. Do you mind if she joins us? She might know something."

Craig rose and smiled, waiting until she sat down before retaking his seat. He cut quickly to the chase.

"Mr Wallace, you mentioned the other night that Ms Linton had a boyfriend. A Mr Julian Mooney."

Wallace nodded. "Yes. I think he's an architect or something like that."

"When did you meet him?"

Craig glanced at the woman, noticing her bare feet. They'd probably been in bed when he'd knocked and their flushed faces said they hadn't been playing tiddlywinks. He missed Saturday mornings like that.

Elise shook her head. "I never met him, did you, Jimmy?"

Wallace screwed up his face in thought. "Well no, I didn't actually meet him, but I spoke to him once on the phone. Well, when I say spoke to him, I was talking to Vicky, inviting her to join a group of us up at Cutter's Wharf and I heard Julian in the background. But she told me all about him."

Elise nodded. "Me too. She said he was tall with a ponytail, like arty types have, and he did interior design."

Wallace turned to face her. "I thought he was an architect?"

She shook her head firmly. "No, he was definitely an interior designer. Vicky probably told you he was an architect because

242

she thought it would sound better." She turned back to Craig. "She was a bit of a snob, Vicky, and she probably thought a barrister should be dating an architect and not someone barely scraping by, working in freelance interior design."

Craig set down his cup and asked a question that he already knew the answer to. "Did status matter to Ms Linton?"

Elise gawped at him. "Matter? It was her middle name. Victoria Status Linton, actually no, it was Victoria 'don't disappoint Mummy and Daddy' Linton. That's more accurate. Her dad's a high court judge in London you know."

Craig hadn't known.

"Vicky spent her bloody life trying to impress him. Perfect looks, perfect job, so she had to have the perfect boyfriend too, and if he wasn't a lawyer then he'd have to be something else professional."

"And an interior designer wouldn't have been good enough as far as her parents were concerned?"

"Correct."

Wallace interrupted his girlfriend's diatribe and stared at Craig curiously. "Are you saying Julian's done a bunk, Mr Craig?"

Craig said nothing.

"But he's not a suspect in anything, is he? I mean, Vicky killed herself, didn't she?"

Craig nodded. "She did." With that he stood up and extended his hand. Wallace shook it hesitantly and walked Craig to the door.

"I'm sorry we couldn't be of more help, Superintendent." He shook his head sadly. "You never really know anyone, do you? And it's not helped by living in anonymous apartments like this."

Craig thought of his own development half a mile away and nodded. People could lie dead in their apartments and no-one would ever know.

12 p.m.

"OK. John's still working with the sketch artist, so we won't have an image of his attacker until this afternoon. Meanwhile we'll have to work with what we've got. I'll go round everyone in a moment but first I want to update you on what I found out about Julian Mooney from Linton's neighbour, James Wallace."

Craig saw Liam raise his eyebrows in surprise, and Nicky gearing up for a rant. He held up a hand, stilling them. "Before either of you start, I took the C.P.O. with me. OK? And the ones at my folk's house have practically moved in!"

"I bet your mum loves that."

Annette's tone was as sarcastic as Craig's the day before but he corrected her wrong assumption.

"That's exactly what I thought yesterday, but she loves it. They had dinner with us last night and when I left, two of them were playing cards with my dad and Lucia." He laughed. "I think Mum would like to adopt them."

Nicky nodded wisely. "Maternal instinct, it never fades."

Craig winced, knowing that once the guards had gone their absence would demonstrate to Mirella that she had an empty nest and she would start hounding Lucia and him for grandchildren. Ah well, that was next week's problem. He turned his mind back to the case.

"OK. I met with James Wallace this morning. He was the person who first told us about Julian Mooney. His girlfriend Elise was there as well and she was even more helpful."

Liam cut in. "Did they know where Mooney was, then?"

"No. It turns out that they've never actually met him, just heard his voice on the phone. But Victoria Linton talked a lot about him."

"Oh aye, I suppose she sat around swooning about how wonderful he was?"

Craig shook his head and laughed at Liam's two-dimensional view of women. Nicky and Annette's pursed lips showed that they were less amused.

"Linton told Wallace that Mooney was an architect, but the girlfriend said she'd told her he was a freelance designer and said Linton had probably lied to him because she thought an architect sounded better."

Nicky snorted. "She was a snob."

"That was certainly the impression the girlfriend conveyed, but it's understandable when you hear who her father is. Henry Linton, the high-court Judge."

Annette looked puzzled. "Who?"

"Henry Linton. He's in London now, that's how I know of him, but he used to work here and he was notorious. It was probably while you were still in nursing."

Liam whistled. "Old 'Hang-em-High' Henry? God, I remember him in court – he was a real bugger. I bet Linton's childhood was fun with him as a dad."

Craig nodded. "That was the impression I got. She would have been expected to do well at everything, and I imagine that meant having a successful boyfriend as well. Anyway, Julian Mooney. Elise said that Linton described him as tall with a pony tail, and arty."

All eyes turned automatically to Davy. His dark hair had grown so long that it touched his shoulders, and in his black shirt and trousers he looked like he belonged in an art gallery or theatre, not the C.C.U. Craig nodded.

"Like Davy, I suppose."

Liam snorted rudely. "Arty! Him? His idea of art's the same as mine. Print on the wall from Ikea."

Davy became animated. "I am arty! I have a modern s... sculpture in my flat."

Liam came back like lightening. "That's your kettle, son."

Even Davy had to laugh at the remark and the group debated for a moment about modern art versus traditional, until Craig dragged them away from the Surrealists and back to the case.

"OK, so Julian Mooney was arty and essentially unemployed and Victoria Linton was ashamed of him, so she never actually introduced him to anyone. I still want to talk to him. Jake and Liam, I want you to get out there today and find him. He's a loose end and you know how I hate those." He nodded at Annette. "What did you and Jake find out?"

Annette ran swiftly through their morning, handing over to Jake to describe the meeting in the café. She finished off with her plan for that afternoon.

"Our woman is called Jenna and I'm going to the gym where she swims, to see what I can find out."

Craig nodded. "Good idea. Take a copy of John's sketch with you. It should be ready at around two o'clock." He turned to Davy and waved him on.

"OK. Unfortunately w...we're still hitting a dead end matching the numbers to anything, but I'm hopeful that Dr Winter's sketch will give me a face comparator for James Mulhearn and something else to s...search on. Mike got back to me this morning with some new prints and I'm running them now."

Craig interrupted eagerly. "Where were they found?"

"The gun barrel. You w...were right; the killer must have handled it. They must have left the prints there when they gripped the gun, to force Bell to s...shoot himself."

Craig wanted to punch the air. With John's sketch, Annette's lead at the gym and the prints, they were closing in on their woman fast.

"Excellent. Get onto that this afternoon. Between the sketch, the gym lead and your prints we should have a surname very soon to put on an arrest warrant. Good. Everyone get on it and we'll brief again at four."

Craig rose to his feet and Liam interjected, with a hurt tone in his voice. "Here, don't you want to know what I found, then?"

Craig startled, realising that he'd completely forgotten him, quite a feat given his size. He sat down again hastily. "Sorry, Liam, you're so shy and retiring that I forgot about you."

Craig's tone was so contrite that Liam wasn't sure how to respond. It was only when Nicky laughed that he knew he was being sarcastic.

"Oh aye, that's right. Make fun of the old guy. Well, I've found a connection between our victims that the rest of you missed."

Craig leaned in attentively. If Liam said he had something then it was something worth hearing. For a second Liam considered dragging out his moment of glory then he couldn't be bothered and blurted out his findings without any preamble.

"They all worked on the same case."

"What?"

"The same case."

Annette asked the obvious question. "What sort of case? Rogan and Warner were brokers, Linton was a lawyer, McCafferty was a banker and Bell worked in pensions. Where's the connection?"

Liam scanned the ring of puzzled faces and grinned.

"Remember when we talked about the platinum market and got as far as someone losing money, then we hit a brick wall? Well I thought, why kill such a random bunch of people and in such a particular way? So I worked back from that basis. "

"And?"

"And what sort of case involves pensions, stocks and all the rest?"

Craig frowned, trying to work it out, but his brain was fogged-up from tiredness and days spent worrying about John. He shook his head.

Liam smiled smugly. "What if I said to you that a lot of pension funds are invested in stocks and shares?"

"OK, and? We got that far two days ago."

"So, what if I have a private pension adviser and he refers me on to a broker…"

Jake interjected. "Who has a junior broker working with him."

"Yes. OK, so I ask my brokers to invest my pension in some shares for me."

"Like platinum."

Liam nodded. "Like platinum. And then they, being crap at their job, don't invest my pension in platinum but in something else, thinking that they know best."

Davy cut in. "Can they do that? Go directly against a client's instructions?"

"Maybe, lad. That's what we have to find out. Bear with me and you'll see where I'm heading. OK, say the shares that they invested my pension in lost their value, and I lost everything I'd saved up all my life, but they try to wriggle out of it because…"

Craig interjected. "The small print says that the value of shares can go down as well as up."

"Exactly. The stock market is basically gambling, so when stocks go down, tough, you lose. But I'd given them a direct instruction to invest in the platinum and now I've lost everything specifically because they ignored me. What would you do?"

"Sue them."

"And the pension adviser who recommended them in the first place."

Annette's voice rang through the room. "But where does the involvement of a high street banker like McCafferty come in? He was nothing to do with stocks and shares. NIBank doesn't have a merchant banking arm, I checked."

Liam gave her a chastising look and tutted. "Patience, I'm coming to that. OK, so what if I had a family to support and I was getting nowhere through the courts because the pension fund and stockbrokers had closed ranks and hired a slick lawyer to defend them? What would I do then?"

Craig's jaw dropped in realisation. "If you were broke you would ask the high street bank manager for a bridging loan."

"Correct! And if they said no, then my family would be screwed and I might kill myself in despair."

Everyone stared at Liam in amazement. All except Craig; he wasn't amazed because he'd seen Liam's brilliant streak before.

"Of course, it's all speculation at the moment, boss. But it fits, doesn't it?"

Craig nodded, thinking for a moment. Finally he spoke. "OK. Adrian Bell was the private pension advisor who put the client in touch with the brokers: Diana Rogan and Nelson Warner. And platinum shares were involved in this somewhere, hence the material used to make the keys." He turned to Jake. "Jake, did we get any more information on the platinum market?"

Jake jumped. He'd been so engrossed in his chat-room search that he'd almost forgotten the information he'd gathered a few days before.

He nodded. "Yes, I have a whole lot on it, especially who in Northern Ireland was involved in its trade back in the nineties. It won't take me long to pull it together."

"Good. OK, so if Victoria Linton was the defence lawyer for the brokers and pension advisor and she got them off, then the bank manager they asked for a loan must have been Jonathan McCafferty."

Annette interjected. "And he refused the loan so whoever it was went bust." Her voice softened. "And killed themselves, leaving their children alone."

Davy looked sceptical. "Both parents killing themselves, w… wouldn't that be unusual?"

Craig answered him. "Suicide pacts aren't unheard of. But OK, what if Davy's right and it's unlikely that both parents killed themselves? Say only one parent killed themselves, then why was the impact on the child so high that it made them homicidal all these years later?"

Nicky had been sitting quietly, now she spoke. "What if they were already a single parent? And the pension was the only thing they had to rely on?"

Craig turned to face her. "You mean that they might have been an older single parent, say fifty or over? Old enough to be living on their occupational pension. So when they lost the pension they lost their whole income and couldn't deal with life anymore?"

She nodded vigorously, setting her black tresses flying. "Yes. They mightn't have been able to cope. And if you're right and this happened back in the nineties then a mental illness like depression might have gone un-noticed back then. So no-one offered them treatment or spotted that they were suicidal."

Craig raked his hair thoughtfully. "OK, so an older, single parent, relying on their pension, gets bad advice and loses everything. Victoria Linton defends the pension adviser Bell, and the brokerage company that both Warner and Rogan worked for then, and the courts side with them. McCafferty refuses them a loan to help out; the parent becomes suicidal and kills themselves, leaving their child or children alone. If this all happened during our killer's adolescence it could have scarred them badly."

Annette shook her head. "No. Single parent or not. What sort of person kills themselves and leaves their children to cope alone?"

"Someone whose mind is very disturbed, Annette. They might have calculated that the care system would look after the children better than they could; that way they'd at least be fed and housed." Craig shook his head. "Poor sod, whoever they were, they must have felt completely helpless."

"I'd want to kill the bastards who did that to my parents as well, boss."

"I don't think anyone here would disagree, Liam, but wanting to doesn't make murder right."

Craig was about to summarise when Jake motioned to cut in.

"What if it wasn't just because they thought the care system could take care of their children better than they could?"

"What else?"

"What if they were actually worth more dead than alive because they had life insurance? They might have left their kids wealthy. That would explain how the kid could afford the platinum for the keys now."

Davy stared at Jake. He was impressed but he was reluctant to say it after Jake's behaviour earlier in the week. Craig saw his reticence and smiled encouraging until Davy squeezed the words out.

"Good call, Jake."

Jake blushed and nodded, acknowledging what it had cost Davy to say the words. Craig carried on.

"OK, brilliant though all these ideas are, this is all speculation, although my gut tells me that Liam's probably right. Davy, if he is then the code from the keys will turn out to be a pension number, so alter your search on that basis and find me a name. Jake, go back to your platinum information and look for the names of investors in the nineties. Link in with Davy to narrow the search. Annette, pursue your gym lead please; Nicky will send John's sketch to you once we have it. All of you, use the sketch to narrow your searches. Liam, can you come into my office for a minute?"

Everyone shuffled back to their desks and Liam followed Craig into his office. He accepted Craig's offer of coffee gratefully and they drank and stared out of the window in silence for a moment, each deep in their own thoughts.

Finally Craig broke the quiet. "Let's take your theory further, Liam."

"Aye, OK. How?"

"What if the children turned out to be an only child who, because they had no-one else in the world, completely retreated into the game and online forums after his mum or dad died?"

"OK."

"And his name was James Mulhearn."

"Right… the name Jake got from the chat-room?"

"Yes. Then, what if James Mulhearn had a sex-change and became a five-feet-ten woman whose first name is Jenna?"

"Aye. I'm with you."

"She paid for her sex-change with her inheritance, and used some of her money to have the platinum keys cut."

As Craig said the words he crossed to the office door, yanking it open.

"Jake, can you come here for a moment?"

Everyone looked up from their desks, surprised by the unusual sight of Craig yelling across the floor. He usually walked over to their desks and spoke quietly. Something must be up.

Jake hurried into the room.

"Jake, I want you to circulate a picture of the key to any jeweller in Northern Ireland. No, make that the whole of GB. I want the name of who made it and who paid them to do it."

Craig re-entered the office. Liam was smiling as he sat down again.

"You yelled."

"What?"

"Across the floor. You yelled across the floor. You never do that."

Craig wrinkled his forehead, surprised. "Don't I? I must do it more often then. Anyway, if we can't find a manufacturer for the keys then that leaves us with one option, the killer made them themselves."

"They're pretty fancy. It would take talent."

Craig smiled as something else dawned on him. "Artistic talent." As he said the words he was out the door and over to Davy's desk.

"Davy, run a search for people trained to design and make jewellery in our perp's age range. Particularly for anyone trained to work with precious metals. Cross-match it with our known names."

Davy opened his mouth to say "cool" but Craig had already re-entered his office and shut the door. He sat down again and stared at Liam.

"OK, let's say our perp made the keys themselves; they'd have to be trained in design."

Liam saw where he was heading.

"Remind you of anyone?"

"You mean…"

Craig nodded. "Julian Mooney. Victoria Linton's invisible boyfriend. He was a designer." He leaned forward eagerly. "What if James Mulhearn and Julian Mooney are the same man? They have the same initials."

"But Mulhearn had a sex change and Mooney's a man!"

Craig shook his head. "Is he? How do we know? How do we know that Victoria Linton wasn't lesbian and having a relationship with a transgendered woman called Jenna, who she called Julian so that no-one knew she was gay? She was definitely the type to want to keep it quiet if she was. Imagine what Hang-em-High Henry would say about that. 'My perfect daughter the lesbian'. She could never have told him."

"But James Wallace heard a man's voice in the background on the phone." Liam lounged back, giving Craig a triumphant look. "And she wouldn't have had a voice synthesizer with her then."

Craig shrugged. "Women can imitate men's voices. And a transgendered woman would have a much better memory of one to draw on and imitate. Without linguistics analysis to say any different it might have passed muster in the background on the phone."

Liam's jaw dropped. "God, Julian Mooney and Jenna Whatsherface are the same person? I thought my theory was a stretch but you're really reaching now, boss. How the hell do we prove it?"

Craig slumped back and shook his head. "We don't, not until

we catch them. It's just a working theory but it fits with the boy in the chat-room, the woman who attacked John and the arty partner of Victoria Linton that no-one ever saw."

Liam stroked his chin thoughtfully and then stood up. "Hang on for a minute."

It was his turn to yell across the floor but this time no-one was surprised. "Annette. Can you come in here a minute?"

"I'm getting ready to leave for the gym."

Liam stared her out and Annette raised her eyes to heaven, knowing that resistance was futile. She stomped across the floor.

"Would you please not shout like that, Liam? What do you want anyway?"

Liam looked down at her wryly. "Don't you mean, 'what do you want, oh brilliant one?' Even, 'what do you want, sir?' would do."

"OK, oh brilliant one. What do you want?"

"Do you have that list of blocked callers that Natasha Nunes gave us?"

"Yes. Why?"

Liam barrelled on without answering. "Let me have a copy. And take Victoria Linton's picture to the gym with you to see if anyone recognises her."

"But it's a lesbian gym."

"Exactly."

He watched her jaw drop, pleased at his delivery of the bombshell then re-entered Craig's office before Annette had time to say any more.

Craig laughed. "That will start everyone talking."

"Little amuses the innocent. My bet is that this Jenna was calling Vicky Linton's office threatening her long before she decided the best way to reach Linton was through sex. But she wouldn't have used the names Julian or Jenna."

"So she probably called as James Mulhearn and his name will be on Linton's blocked caller list."

Craig drained his coffee and stood up.

Liam looked up curiously. "Is it your turn to yell again?"

"Nope."

Liam squinted at him suspiciously. "Then where do you think you're going?"

"The bathroom, if it's any of your business."

Liam's squint deepened. "Well, leave your car keys with Nicky before you go. I don't trust you after that jaunt to Wallace's this morning. You're under house arrest and I'm sticking to you like glue until Jenna whatever-her-name-is, is under lock and key."

***

Jenna Graham glanced at her watch in irritation and scanned the garage exit from the C.C.U. They were all up there, safe in their tenth floor squad-room and she wasn't trying anything inside a police fortress. No–one could get in there without I.D. She would have been very surprised to know that a woman had managed exactly that, eighteen months before, and that Liam Cullen had almost died as a result.

But Jenna had an added reason for believing she couldn't achieve it; she got noticed everywhere she went. Not because she looked transgendered, her sex change had been so successful that no-one meeting her could have ever told that she'd once been a man. She got noticed because she was five-feet-ten and beautiful. It wasn't a vain boast or a skewed self-opinion. She knew she was because everyone told her so and because men's admiring gazes followed her wherever she went. Women's gazes did as well, but they were much less friendly, unless they were gay.

She smiled, remembering how Victoria Linton had stared at her that evening in the gym, just as she'd planned. Linton was a petite brunette, not bad looking but not her type; she'd never found women sexually attractive. She fancied straight men, just as she'd done when she was trapped in a man's body. The difference was that now she was free to pursue her dreams of marrying one she loved someday. Maybe they'd adopt children or maybe her husband would already have some of his own, but either way she'd never found women sexually attractive and she wasn't about to start now.

Vicky Linton had just been part of her quest, a future victim with a place to hide away until she'd done what it took to finish off her list. She'd always known that Linton wouldn't want the world to known about her lesbianism and that had suited her just fine. She could pretend Jenna was a man and call her Julian or whatever she wanted to, just as long as she provided her with cover while she killed the people on her list.

Jenna stepped back into the doorway of the boarded-up priest's house beside the empty Dockland's church. She wrapped her coat around her, ignoring the curious looks of a man leaving the Docker's Club across the street, and prepared to wait for Marc Craig for as long as it took.

***

"Sir, this just came in from the sketch artist. I've scanned it and sent copies to everyone's phones."

Craig dragged his eyes away from the river and swung his chair round to face the door. Nicky was holding a sheet in her hand. He took it from her, peering hard at it as Nicky scrutinised his face. He looked tired, still handsome but handsome that could do with a long weekend in bed. She turned to leave and Craig halted her with a hand laid gently on her arm. The pleading look on his face almost made her laugh.

"I take it you'd like a coffee?"

"A gallon of it, please, I'm falling asleep. And can you send Liam in again?"

A moment later Liam came bounding through the door with an unfeasible amount of energy.

"Give me some of whatever you're on, Liam. I'm dropping

on my feet."

"Aye well, that's what you get for having best mates who go getting themselves shot."

Craig paused for a second as if assessing if it was OK to laugh at John's plight yet. After a second he decided it was and guffawed. John was out of danger so his shooting would be fair game for jokes and dramatic re-enactment for months to come. He'd join in himself, when Natalie wasn't around.

Liam was just re-living John's dramatic dive to avoid the bullet when Nicky re-entered, carrying a plate of biscuits and a coffee pot. She gave Liam a wry look.

"Please tell me that you weren't just imitating Dr Winter being shot." She shook her head. "No, that would be too tacky even for you." She set down the coffee and turned to leave, pursing her lips. Liam waited until her back was turned and imitated her. Craig poured the coffee then handed Liam the sketch.

"Is that our woman?"

"According to John, yes."

"Bit of a looker, isn't she? I wonder what sort of woman I'd make."

"An overweight one."

"I'm just big-boned!"

Craig laughed off his indignation then his voice took on a serious tone. "She really does look feminine. She won't stand out other than because she's tall and beautiful."

"What do you reckon her next move will be?"

Craig shook his head. "Hard to say. It depends if she's finished her list or if there's someone else on it that we don't know about."

Liam looked sceptical. "Like who? She's killed everyone from the pension advisor to the flipping lawyer who got them off. There's no-one left."

"That we know about." Craig paused for a moment then restarted. "OK, let's say she's finished. What would you do next?"

"Get the hell out of Dodge."

"Agreed. So airports and ferries, north and south, have to be our best bet. Get this sketch to them please. 'Wanted to help with police enquiries'. You know the drill."

Craig paused again and Liam leapt into the gap.

"OK. So what if she hasn't finished? You know who's next."

Craig nodded. "Me."

"Yep. You didn't back off when she asked."

"And I'm not backing off now. Every vulnerable target is under armed guard: John, Mike, my folks. Their house in Holywood is like a fortress, so I'm not worried about them."

Liam interrupted. "Will Lucia toe the line? She's not too fond of having her freedom curtailed."

Craig gave a slow smile. "She'll be fine. She's taken a shine to one of the protection officers."

"What about Richard?"

Craig winced. Richard was Lucia's long-term boyfriend, but Craig wasn't certain how much longer he was going to hold the title. He was a concert pianist with the L.C.O., the prestigious London City Orchestra. The job entailed touring for eight months of the year and leaving Lucia alone. Lucia loved Richard but Craig could tell that she was getting worn down by his absences.

"I think his days are numbered. He's away too much."

Liam rubbed his chin, like a sage. "Aye well, if you leave a looker like Lucia alone for too long you deserve everything you get. OK, so that means it'll be you our perp comes after next but she can't get near you if I lock you down here."

Craig shook his head vehemently. "I'm not spending days locked anywhere with you! No offence, but you wouldn't be my choice of bunkmate."

Liam leaned away from him, blustering. "Here, I wasn't suggesting that. None of that talk now. I'm a married man."

"You think there are no gay married men?"

Liam screwed up his face in confusion and Craig smiled at his sometimes naive view of the world.

"Anyway, that's not what I meant by bunkmate. It could be days before we find her and I can't stay locked in the office until then."

"Can't you stay at your folks?"

Craig thought of his teenage bedroom in Holywood. He hadn't slept there for twenty-five years but his mother had maintained it like a shrine, just like Lucia's with her 'Take That' posters all over the place. His posters had been of Bruce Springsteen but the principle was the same. He shook his head firmly.

"I'm staying at my own flat. There's a sheer drop to the river on one side and only one entrance to the block. It'll be easy to guard and I can look after myself."

Liam folded his arms determinedly. "You can't and you won't, not even with Sinclair as your guard-dog. I'm staying with you. You have a spare room don't you?"

Craig sighed, knowing that there was no way out. He resigned himself to his fate and they planned the next phase of the case.

***

2 p.m.

Annette had never been in a women's only gym, come to think of it she hadn't been in any gym except the police one and it had a pretty butch design. She was pleasantly surprised when they walked through the building's automatic front door to find an airy reception area filled with plants and sculptures, with discrete, soulful music playing in the background. Jake had insisted on coming with her for security and as they walked towards the desk he flashed his badge at the girl behind it, whose tanned good looks could have graced any fashion magazine.

She smiled at both of them in turn. "Can I help you, officers?"

Jake looked at Annette, expecting her to take the lead. She was engrossed in a small waterfall in one corner so he continued.

"Hopefully, yes." He showed the girl John's sketch. "Do you know this woman, or could you point us to someone who does?"

The girl's wide lips curved into a smile. "That's Jenna Graham." The smile dropped quickly and was replaced by a suspicious look. "What do you want her for?"

Graham. They'd learned something already. Annette heard the girl's question and stared straight at her, speaking in an official tone. "That's not a question we're prepared to answer. Please tell us anything you know about Ms Graham."

The girl blushed deep red and reached for the reception phone. "I'll get the duty manager. It's not my place to talk about clients."

A moment later a petite woman in her forties approached them, extending her hand. They shook it in turn then she directed them down a short corridor and into an office. The woman sat down behind the desk and turned to Annette.

"How can help you, officer…?"

"Inspector McElroy and this is Sergeant McLean. Ms…?"

"Louise McDonagh."

The woman's voice was a soft monotone, with an almost hypnotic quality.

"Well, Ms McDonagh, as we told the young lady in reception we're looking for this woman." Annette laid the sketch on the desk. "We know her name is Jenna, Jenna Graham your receptionist said. And we think that she can help us with our enquiries."

McDonagh gazed at the sketch for a moment, her face unreadable, then she fixed Annette with a stare.

"May I ask what sort of enquiries?"

"No, I'm afraid you may not." Annette's tone hardened as she sensed a hostile witness. "Do you know her or not, Ms McDonagh?"

The woman hesitated and glanced at Jake. His gaze matched Annette's for sternness and McDonagh realised that she had no friends in the room. Finally she sighed.

"Yes, I know her. You're correct, her name is Jenna Graham. She's been a member here for several years."

"Doing what?"

"The usual things. Gym, dance classes, socialising. She's a member of the swimming team. A very good swimmer I've heard."

Annette leaned forward, not relaxing her gaze. "Are you saying that you don't know her personally?"

McDonagh stammered out a reply. "N...No, I didn't say that. This is a small gym and we all know each other. I just meant..."

Annette knew exactly what she'd 'just meant'. She'd seen it a million times before. Friends, work colleagues, even family members started to distance themselves from someone once the police appeared. It was as if because someone was wanted for a crime the police would suddenly start examining the lives of everyone who knew them. Annette had wanted to say 'give me a break' more times than she could count. Did they really think cops had nothing better to do than dig randomly into people's lives? They had enough crime to solve without looking for more. Annette maintained her neutral approach despite her annoyance.

"So you do know Ms Graham. Tell us what you know about her, please."

McDonagh glanced frantically at the door behind them as if praying that some rescuer would appear. Her face was a shifting picture of 'what should I say?' and 'what do they know?' Annette was tempted to put her out of her misery and say, 'don't worry, we know that Jenna is transgender so you won't be giving anything away', but she kept her mouth firmly shut and tightened her gaze. Finally Louise McDonagh told them what they already knew.

"Jenna is transgendered; male to female."

Annette nodded and the woman looked relieved.

"You know?"

"Yes. What else can you tell us about her?"

McDonagh relaxed and spoke more freely. "She joined us about eight years ago, I'd have to check the records to be accurate but I don't think it was long after her surgery had been completed." She smiled. "She's a truly beautiful woman; you would never know that she'd been a man."

She saw that Annette wasn't smiling back and hurried on, wondering what sort of crime warranted the attention of two detectives on a Saturday afternoon. It had to be something bad.

"Jenna keeps herself to herself really. Just does her classes and leaves. We have a lot of members like that. She joined the swimming team a while back, which was a bit of a surprise."

Annette leaned in urgently. "Why? Couldn't she swim?"

McDonagh's expression showed that the idea hadn't occurred to her. She shook her head. "God, no. She swims like a fish. I was just surprised because…"

Her voice tailed off and Annette could feel her irritation rise in response. She slapped her palm down on the desk, making Jake twitch. The effect on Louise McDonagh was more satisfactory. Her eyes widened and she started to gabble.

"Well, because, the team is a lesbian team."

Annette screwed up her face in confusion and glanced at Jake. He looked equally puzzled. He spoke for the first time in five minutes.

"I'm sorry, but aren't all the gym's members lesbian?"

Louise McDonagh's eyes widened so far that she reminded Annette of a children's cartoon.

"No they are not! This is a women's gym, not a lesbian one."

As if to establish her own heterosexual credentials she pointed to a photograph on the notice board, that Annette and Jake had missed. "That's my husband and children." She stared indignantly at Jake, her voice hardening. "Where did you get that impression from?"

It was Jake's turn to babble. "Someone we met implied that it was."

"Well then, I suggest you correct their assumptions. We cater for all women, not just one group. We have classes for various religious groups, disabled groups, mothers and toddlers and obviously straight and lesbian members. The fact that some of our lesbian members have decided to form a swimming team is their business."

Annette watched the exchange, wondering why McDonagh was so irate. All she'd managed to do with her indignation was confirm that she was prejudiced. Annette returned to the original point.

"Why are you surprised that Jenna Graham joined the swimming team? Are you saying that she isn't lesbian?"

McDonagh nodded firmly. "She definitely isn't. I know that because she met my son one day and was very taken with him. Couldn't stop talking about how handsome he was. She joined this gym to avoid the bullying she'd encountered at mixed gyms when they found out that she'd once been a man. She came here to be safe and accepted, which she was. But she definitely isn't gay. That's why I was surprised when she joined the lesbian team instead of one of the other swimming teams here."

Annette shook her head, bewildered. She watched as Jake withdrew a photograph of Victoria Linton from his pocket and nodded him on to ask the question that was on both their lips.

"Do you have a Victoria Linton among your members?"

McDonagh thought for a moment as if picturing each member's face then she rose and walked to a filing cabinet in the corner, pulling out the top drawer. After a moment rifling through the files she shook her head.

"No, there's no member of that name. Not now and not for the past five years. We keep the past five years files on top."

Jake handed her Vicky Linton's photograph and they both watched as she smiled.

"Oh, that's Vicky Mooney. Lovely girl. She's on the swim team." She nodded. "She's definitely lesbian."

Craig had been right. Vicky Linton was gay and she'd been hiding it from her work colleagues and family by telling them that she was dating a man, the mysterious Julian Mooney. Linton had even hidden her true name at the gym, taking Mooney's surname instead. If Craig was correct then Jenna Graham had joined the swim team deliberately to meet Linton then lied and said she was lesbian to insinuate herself into Linton's life. It was a lot of trouble to go to just to stalk her prey. Graham must have been obsessed with revenge.

Annette stood up to leave. "Thank you, Ms McDonagh. That's been helpful."

"What did I say that helped?"

Annette ignored the question and continued. "Now, we need the names and addresses of every member of the swimming team." They had to find Jenna Graham. It was going to be a busy couple of days.

Chapter Nineteen

The C.C.U. 4 p.m.

"OK, it's the weekend so I'm going to make this short and sweet. You all have homes to go to and in Liam's case he seems to think that his is my flat!"

All eyes turned to Liam and he nodded grimly. "He's not to be trusted. He nipped out to see Linton's neighbours without letting anyone know."

Jake interjected innocently. "Does he have to? Let anyone know I mean? Isn't he the boss?"

The glares Nicky and Liam gave him put Jake quickly back in his box. Craig smiled at him in a way that said 'I thought I was as well…' then he turned back to the job in hand.

"Right. Let's start with Annette and Jake. Anything interesting at the gym?"

Annette gazed at him and shook her head. Not with a 'no' but with an incredulity that said 'how did you know that Victoria Linton was gay?'

"We found out that Jenna's surname is Graham. I'm sure it will turn out to be false but maybe Graham's a family name."

Liam cut in, laughing. "Or maybe there's another corpse out there called Graham that we know nothing about."

Annette shrugged. "Nothing would surprise me about this case after today. Anyway, Jenna Graham joined the gym eight years ago. By the way, it's a women's gym, not a lesbian one. It seems we got our wires a little crossed."

It was Nicky who interrupted this time. "You mean there are

265

no men allowed at all?"

"None."

Nicky sighed and gazed into the distance with a beatific smile on her face. "No rowdiness, perfume and flowers everywhere. I bet there was even a coffee shop with somewhere for kids to play. Heaven."

Annette smiled in agreement, ignoring the mock-indignant expressions of the men in the team.

"Anyway, it was pretty much as Nicky described it. We met with the duty manager, Louise McDonagh, and after she'd been reminded of her civic duty she cooperated and checked her records. She knew Jenna was transgender and said that she joined the gym to avoid the bullying that she'd experienced elsewhere, but she was surprised when Jenna joined the swimming team."

Liam asked the obvious question. "Couldn't she swim?"

His guffaw was ignored by the rest of the group and Annette carried on.

"I asked that but she could swim brilliantly. McDonagh was surprised because Jenna wasn't gay and that particular team definitely was. Every member was lesbian except for her."

Craig leaned forward eagerly. "Including Victoria Linton by any chance?"

"Yes."

"How did the manager know that Graham wasn't gay?"

"Because she met her son one day and made no bones about how much she fancied him. Another thing: Victoria Linton went under a false name at the gym. McDonagh only recognised her from the picture. She called herself Vicky Mooney. Linton must have had a personality transplant as well, because McDonagh described her as a lovely girl."

Liam snorted. "That's not what her P.A. called her."

Nicky nodded wisely. "P.A.s see the true side of their bosses." She attempted a meaningful glare at Craig then giggled. Craig smiled and turned back to Annette.

"Vicky Mooney…" He shook his head sadly. "The poor girl was living in a dream world where Jenna Graham really loved her, but she still couldn't come out as lesbian to the rest of the world. She even took her alias Julian Mooney's surname."

"Actually I think it was the other way around, sir. Mooney had been Victoria Linton's alias since she'd joined the gym in 2009. I think that when they were cooking up a cover name for Jenna Graham, she became Julian Mooney because it fitted Victoria Linton's existing fantasy."

Liam interrupted. "Aye, whatever. But meantime this Jenna Graham really fancied men?" He shook his head. "All this confusion's giving me a headache."

Jake leapt in. "Just don't start thinking you're gay, for God's sake, Liam. That would really upset evolution."

Liam looked at Jake blankly while the others laughed. By the time he got the joke Craig had moved on.

"OK, so Victoria Linton kept her sexuality secret except for the people she met at the gym. Her neighbours had no idea and I'm damned sure that her father didn't know, although I'm going to ask him a few questions."

Annette gave him a warning look. "You're not giving away her secret, are you? It was her business."

Craig shook his head. "Don't worry; I'll keep the questions neutral. I just want to find out how well Henry Linton knew his daughter and if he ever met Jenna Graham in the guise of Julian Mooney. OK, so Victoria Linton showed a completely different side of her character at work and the gym. At the gym she was vulnerable and pleasant and at work she was a shark. Jenna Graham would have seen Linton's vulnerable side but it still didn't deter her from killing Linton along with all the rest."

Davy had been lounging back in his chair chewing on his nails, now he graced them with his giant brain. "She left Linton to almost the last though, chief. Maybe she w…was in two minds about killing her?"

Liam snorted. "More likely she needed somewhere decent to

stay. You didn't see Mooney's house."

Craig thought for a moment. "You've both made good points, although I'm inclined to think it was lodgings rather than love that motivated Graham to kill Linton near the end. But that raises a question. Uniform went through Julian Mooney's house an hour ago and found nothing that indicated a woman was living there, so where are Jenna Graham's clothes? And if she's planning to skip the country she'll need a passport and money, there was no sign of either of those at the house."

Davy cut in. "If I w...were her I'd carry my passport and money with me everywhere."

"Fair enough. But what about her clothes? Unless she's dragging a suitcase around Belfast she has to keep them somewhere. We've put the house under surveillance just in case she comes back but my guess is that she won't."

Liam made a suggestion. "Couldn't she have put them in a left-luggage locker?"

Jake jumped in. "Or how about at the gym? She must have a locker there."

Craig nodded. They were both valid ideas. "Liam, you check the left-luggage at train stations, airports and ferry terminals. Get the Garda Síochána to check down south. Jake, go back to the gym and take a look. Get a warrant for Graham's locker before you go."

Annette was quiet but Craig could see her mind at work.

"Penny for them, Annette."

Annette hesitated, unsure whether to say what she was thinking or not. "Well… it's just a thought, but if I wanted to hide clothes or suitcases somewhere that they wouldn't be noticed, I'd hide them in plain sight."

Nicky saw where she was going and nodded.

"OK, where, Annette? At the gym?"

"No. I'd hide them amongst Victoria Linton's stuff in her flat. If they were in a relationship Graham probably had a key to Linton's flat. It was searched last week but not since and it's not a crime-scene any more so Graham could easily be staying there now. Besides, even if some of Graham's clothes had been there last week who would have noticed them amongst all Vicky Linton's things? Apart from trouser length and shoes Graham and Linton might have worn the same size. And empty suitcases left at Linton's would have been ignored unless they'd been monogrammed differently. If Jenna Graham has been living there, her things could easily have passed as Victoria Linton's. We should go back now and take another look."

Davy nodded. "She w...would have had a key. I gave Maggie a key a few months after w...we started dating. Most couples have keys to each other's places."

Liam sniffed. "I never gave Danni a key until we got married."

"Before you w...were married people still had drawbridges instead of doors."

"You cheeky..."

Liam was interrupted by Craig's raised hand.

"Annette's right. Forget the lost-luggage search, Liam, you and I will take Linton's apartment. My money's on Jenna Graham staying there until she gets ready to run, if she hasn't already gone that is. It's getting late so let's leave it until tomorrow; I want armed support there as well. Graham's already shot two men. Annette, I'm betting that you have a list of names on the swimming team to interview. You and Jake can take those tomorrow as well." He swung to face Davy. "Davy, give us whatever you've got, then we'll call it a day and brief tomorrow morning at ten."

Davy reached back over his head, lifting a folder from his desk and giving the hand-outs inside to Liam to distribute.

"OK. You each have four s...sheets. The top one has the code from the keys. Although it kills me to admit it, Liam was right."

Liam gave a satisfied grin.

"It was a pension number. A private pension purchased with

the health service pension of a Mrs Mary Mulhearn, a part-time nurse who w…worked at the Maternity, Paediatric and Endocrine Unit on Elmwood Avenue. S…She took her pension as soon as she could, in 1998 when she was fifty years old."

Annette winced. She'd been a nurse before she'd joined the police and she knew that the health service pension, while small, was reliable. Why would anyone have taken it out of a public sector haven and gambled by putting it in a private pension fund? Davy answered her with his next words.

"The pension w…would only have given her three hundred pounds per month and she was a widow with a child, a fourteen-year-old boy called James. Her husband died earlier that year so she was s…struggling alone on the pension and the salary of a part-time nurse of ten thousand pounds per year."

James Mulhearn was her son. Jake's chat-room gamer.

Craig interrupted. "She must have been desperate for money if that was all she earned. By swapping over to a private pension she would have been hoping to generate an additional income and be able to live decently."

Davy shook his dark head and frowned. "I think that was the plan but by 1999 she w…wasn't earning at all. She left w… work because of ill health. Depression. S…So by then her pension was all she had. I think I know what happened but I'll confirm the exact details on Monday w…when there are more people around." He paused and his expression changed to one of sadness. "Mary Mulhearn died on the 14th of May 1999 leaving her s…son James alone at fifteen year's old. He ended up in the care s…system, but Jake was right, he inherited her life insurance money w…when he was eighteen."

"How much, Davy?"

"Half a million pounds. Enough to pay for gender-reassignment surgery and more. By the w…way, the operation must have been done abroad somewhere. There's no record of it anywhere in the UK."

Liam whistled. "Half a million! The mother must have

insured herself up to the eyeballs. Even so, how could the boy have claimed on the insurance if she committed suicide? Surely they wouldn't have paid out? And how could any mother kill herself and leave a young lad alone?"

Annette swung on him. "She was depressed, Liam. Not sad, not just having a bad day, depressed. Have you any idea what that means?"

Liam saw the fury in her eyes and leaned back in his seat. "Whoa. Calm down. I was only saying."

"You're always only saying something."

Craig intervened before a full-scale row broke out. "Rein it in you two. Annette, you obviously have strong feelings about this. Why?"

Annette shook her head. "I had a depressed patient once... he..."

Her voice broke and Craig knew what she'd been going to say. 'He committed suicide.' He nodded and turned back to the group.

"OK, Liam, be a bit more sensitive please. Depression's not something people can control. But you have a point about the suicide. However Mrs Mulhearn died she must have managed to make it look like natural causes for the boy to inherit the insurance money."

Annette spoke quietly. "It's easy enough to make a suicide look natural if you know how, especially back then when forensics weren't as advanced. As a nurse she would have known how to do it."

Craig nodded. However Mary Mulhearn had died she'd convinced the insurance company that it was natural causes, but somehow her teenage son had known the truth and suicide had become his fixation. He nodded Davy on.

"OK. Turn the page and you'll s...see the photo of James Mulhearn from 2004 and beside it Dr W...Winter's image of his shooter, Jenna Graham." He stopped and turned to Craig. "By the way, chief, Mary Mulhearn's maiden name w...was

Graham."

It figured. People never travelled too far when they were looking for aliases.

"You can see that the features are the s...same in both photographs. Mulhearn was thin and fine-featured. That made him an attractive girl. Mulhearn had short auburn hair but the Doc s...said Graham's was long and curly, so the sketch artist put that in."

They stared at the page in silence for a moment. There was no doubt about it. James Mulhearn and Jenna Graham were the same person, but where Mulhearn had been an average looking man, Graham was a stunning looking woman. Craig shot Liam a look that warned him not to crack any jokes.

"Good. Did you produce an image of what Julian Mooney might have looked like?"

"Next page."

When they turned over the page a second set of images appeared. On one side of the page was Jenna Graham just as before, on the other was her as she might have looked like as Julian Mooney. Davy had tied her hair back at the nape of her neck, added glasses and a moustache and created a realistic looking man.

"S...She would probably still remember how a man w... walked and spoke, so she'd have fooled anyone who saw Mooney, even close up I would think."

Craig nodded, still staring at the page. "This is brilliant work, Davy. Liam, get uniform to show these around where Mooney lives and get all three images checked against passport photos, please."

Davy shook his head. "I've already done Mulhearn's checks, there's no passport and nothing at all on him after 2004. I'll leave Mooney's and Graham's checks running tonight w...when I go home. There's one last page in your hand-out."

They'd all missed it. The page contained one paragraph: a citation from the Central Saint Martin's in London. 'James

Mulhearn. BA honours in Jewellery Design 2008.'

Mulhearn had created the keys himself. But where had he bought the platinum? Craig went to ask the question of Davy, but Jake jumped in.

"If you were going to ask about platinum, sir, I'm waiting for a last bit of information on that. I should have it tomorrow."

"Good, thanks, Jake, and thanks again, Davy – excellent work."

He glanced at the clock; it was half-past five. "OK, that's it for today. I need to give Victoria Linton's father a quick call. But for anyone who fancies it, I'm buying drinks and dinner at The James in ten minutes. Everyone's welcome."

Craig was answered by a series of nods and he laughed loudly. He didn't fool himself that they wanted his scintillating company or a free dinner; it was just that none of them trusted him out alone.

***

Jenna watched the group as they walked across Pilot Street then she cut round to Princes Dock Street and followed their progress towards The James Bar. The group's banter and relaxed attitude made her anger soar, but more than that, it told her that they wouldn't be leaving the bar any time soon. Her eyes followed the tallest one as he loped along like a big white ghost, shielding the rest of them with his shadow. The long-haired boy matched his strides and punched him playfully in the arm and Craig's lean frame wasn't far behind. She watched as they flanked Craig expertly, knowing that he was her target. She scrutinised the small team, searching for the weakest link.

Craig's and the big ghost's guns were obvious, their bulk spoiling the line of their suit jackets. The boy carried nothing, but he was well protected by his friends. Another glance said that the woman dressed as if she'd thrown on half her wardrobe was the secretary. She was unarmed but she had fighter stamped all over her, so Jenna cast her to one side. That only left two: the mumsy woman and the blond man. They were both cops, that much was clear from their strides and cautious glances around, but not the sort to carry guns routinely, she would bet her life on that.

Jenna laughed at the irony. She would have to bet her life now; that was the level she'd reached in the game. She fingered the passport in her handbag as the group walked through the bar's door, knowing that she'd missed her flight. Without making a conscious choice to stay she'd already decided. The game was on and it deserved an ending worthy of all she'd been through.

***

Sunday, 10.45 a.m.

Craig wandered out of his office for the third time in ten minutes, wondering where everybody was. The squad-room was empty apart from Davy yawning loudly in front of his computer. Craig shrugged. Last night had been a late one and they all felt rough. His own headache hadn't been helped by his conversation with Henry Linton before they'd left for The James the evening before. Linton had been indignant at the idea that his daughter might have been dating a designer, a man outside the traditional professions! Craig wondered how he would react if he knew the whole truth.

But the truth had been the last thing on the Judge's narrow mind. He'd been more concerned that they finalised the verdict of suicide on his daughter, than getting to the bottom of who killed his child. Murder obviously wasn't classy enough for a QC. By the time Craig had hung up the phone he'd felt sorrier for the little girl Victoria Linton had once been than he had for anyone in a long time.

He'd headed to The James with drowning his sorrows high

on the agenda and by the time they'd left they were all the worse for wear. But any hope that he might have slipped off to the hospital to visit John unnoticed was dashed by Liam's shaking head. Even five pints of beer in, he was a sentinel. Craig remembered Liam's tone as he'd said "where do you think you're going?" when he'd headed for the door. The last time he'd heard that tone was when he'd pissed off his old desk sergeant when he was a probationer.

After that Liam had insisted on accompanying him home, despite Ian Sinclair's combat-ready presence. It was only when he'd made Sinclair swear a blood oath to protect Craig that Liam had wobbled his merry way home. But five pints didn't explain why no-one but he and Davy were here today at almost eleven o'clock, especially when the briefing had been called for ten. Craig's speculations were interrupted by noisy chatter from the lift area, followed by the sight of Liam, Annette and Jake appearing all at once. They looked pleased with themselves and Liam announced why.

"Swim team all interviewed and Linton's and Mooney's homes checked and clear. Wherever our girl is staying now it's not in either of those." He lifted Nicky's half-full percolator and poured some coffee into a mug. "Morning, boss. How's the head?"

Craig smiled, wondering what sort of relationships other Superintendents had with their teams. Were many of them bantered in the same way? He doubted it somehow, remembering his own relationship with Terry Harrison; an armed truce would have been the warmest description for it. But he didn't give a damn what people thought, it was his team, his rules. He'd never stood on rank and he wasn't about to start today.

"Not bad, considering. You lot were at it bright and early. What prompted that?"

"Ah, well now. We reckoned the sooner we caught this Muppet, the sooner was could stop monitoring your movements. So we pursued all avenues of investigation, as the manual says, but we came up with zilch."

Jake nodded. "The whole swimming team said the same thing. Vicky was nice, Jenna was nice and they were close. But no-one had the foggiest where either of them lived."

Craig nodded. "Gym buddies. I wouldn't have a clue about the home arrangements of my five-a-side team. Annette, what do you think?"

Annette was fishing a tea-bag out of her mug. She stopped and considered Craig's question, holding it suspended in mid-air until Jake motioned that it was dripping on Nicky's desk. She binned it hastily and carried her mug across to the group.

"I think…"

She glanced at Craig as if reluctant to say her next words. He nodded her on.

"I think she's stalking you, sir. I think that if she hasn't left the country since Adrian Bell died, given that as far as we can work out he's likely to have been the last on her list, then she's not leaving until she's got you." She turned to Davy. "Davy, has she left?"

Davy gazed at her, half-asleep. He couldn't drink as much as the rest of them.

Liam snorted. "Lightweight! You've the breaking strain of a Kit-Kat, son."

"Just because I'd like my liver to last till I'm a pensioner." He turned his back on Liam and faced Annette. "No s…sign of Jenna Graham or Julian Mooney leaving through any possible exit from the country, North or South."

"OK then, she's not going until she's got the Super."

Craig cut in with a puzzled look on his face. "What makes you so sure that her list is finished, Annette?"

"Reverse order."

He motioned her on.

"I thought about it last night." She gave Liam a haughty look. "While some people were getting drunk. And I realised

276

that the order of killing was in reverse. First of all we had Jonathan McCafferty, then Rogan, Warner and Linton, ending with the person that Mary Mulhearn had contact with first, the pension advisor, Adrian Bell. That means the list is finished."

Craig's eyes widened. Jenna Graham had started with McCafferty, the person who had hurt her mother just before her death, and worked backwards. He saw the flaw in Annette's logic almost immediately.

"Victoria Linton should have been one of the first by that reckoning. Just after McCafferty."

Annette shook her head. "She needed Linton for cover and probably a place to stay, that's why she killed her out of sequence. It should have gone McCafferty, Linton, Rogan, Warner then Bell. Instead she did Linton after Warner but before Bell, because she needed her for cover until she was ready to run."

"Except that she hasn't run, has she?" Craig spun to face Davy. "Davy, are there any future tickets booked in the name of Jenna Graham?"

"Not that I can s...see so far, but I'll keep going. I'll run every name in the case as w...well on the off chance she's adopted one of the others as an alias."

"Good. Although she could simply have generated a new identity. She's good at it."

Craig could tell from Annette's face that she hadn't finished.

"As we said last night, sir. If she's finished her list and she hasn't left then that means she's staying for you. She asked you to back off and you didn't, so I think in her warped mind you've become part of the game."

Everyone nodded. Liam's nod was accompanied by a sombre voice that belonged in a movie trailer.

"You're a dead man, boss."

It sounded so macabre that Craig expected him to follow it up with a cackle. Instead there was silence until Craig broke it.

"Oh, for God's sake lighten up everyone. So, she wants me

dead. Big deal; she won't be the first. Remember that this is someone who had to make people kill themselves, she doesn't like to get her hands dirty."

"Until she shot the Doc."

"Aye, and then helped Adrian Bell on his way."

Craig raised his eyes to heaven. "And she made a mess of both of them! She couldn't even kill John at a distance of six inches. This isn't the SAS we're dealing with; it's one woman with a gun."

"Or a knife, or a bomb."

Craig gave Liam a look that said he wasn't cheering him up. "When you leave the force, Liam, I think the grim reaper needs a hand."

Liam laughed and pretty soon they all joined him, temporarily lifting the pall hanging over the group. But Craig knew his bravado wouldn't save him from a bullet if Jenna Graham was determined to get him, so he'd better make sure that something else did.

***

2 p.m.

"There's not much point in us all hanging about, boss, is there?"

Craig shook his head and turned back to his view. The Lagan looked like he felt, brooding. The waves were dark, mirroring the grey April sky. They moved slowly across the river's choppy surface, spending minutes bouncing up and down at one location, as if they were running on the spot or warming up for a race that lay ahead. They were waiting for something big to happen, just like he was, and in both cases it was going to be a storm.

Craig turned back to Liam, watching as he crossed and uncrossed his long legs trying to get comfortable in the desk chair. Finally he gave up and leaned against the office wall, arms folded, muttering something that Craig couldn't make out.

"What?"

He sighed and stared at Craig warily, as if not sure how his words would come across. "I said I wished Graham would just hurry up and try to kill you."

Anyone who didn't know Liam would have misinterpreted what he meant but Craig just smiled. He wished that she would hurry up, too. Anything was better than this damn waiting. He thrust himself out of the chair and strode past Liam, yanking the door back with a bang. Annette startled and Davy sat up urgently, stretching his neck like a Meerkat to see what was happening.

"Right, I've had this. I'm not waiting for her to hunt me. I'm going to set a trap. Anyone game?"

Liam stormed out of the office. "No bloody way. You'll be a sitting target."

"Well, I'm not living the rest of my life locked down in some office or followed around by a bodyguard. I'll go mad before she reaches me."

Annette chewed the end of her pen thoughtfully, surprising them all with her next words. "How will we do it?"

Liam gawped at her. He expected an ally to talk some sense into Craig, not G.I. Jane gearing up for a fight. Craig walked over to her desk.

"My place, tonight. We stand the protection detail down and wait. I'll be armed and wear a vest, I need someone else who'll do the same, then we wait."

Annette nodded and Liam's jaw dropped. "You're both insane. There's no way you're doing it."

Annette set her jaw. "There's no way you can stop us, Liam; he's the boss. And anyway, I agree. We could be waiting forever for Graham to show herself if she sees the close protection officer. This needs to happen."

"Bollocks it does."

For a moment there was silence as the three forty-somethings faced off, while Davy and Jake stared at them as if they were mad. Liam gave in first, mainly because he couldn't keep his jaw clenched for as long as Craig. He shook his head in disbelief.

"You're mad, the pair of you. Well, I'll tell you this much, if there's a sting going down it's not going down without me."

Jake rose to his feet. "Or me."

Davy gave Jake a sceptical look and shook his head. "If you four want to kill yourselves, just tell me w...where to send the wreathes. I'm having nothing to do with this. You've all lost it."

Craig grinned, feeling alive again. He was taking back control and it felt good.

"OK. Jake, thanks for the offer but three of us is enough. You and Davy should go home and we'll see you tomorrow."

Liam snorted. "You mean, hopefully we'll see you tomorrow, don't you?"

Craig's grin widened. "See what I mean? Grim Reaper."

"Is there anything w...we can do to help, chief?"

"Thanks, Davy, but no. Just tidy up your report and make sure we have a neat case, because if I'm right what happens tonight will generate more paperwork than we can handle."

Craig nodded to Liam and Annette and beckoned them back inside his office, closing the door on the outside world. He outlined his plan and they prepared to set the trap, using him as the bait. It was time to bring things to a head.

Chapter Twenty

St Mary's. 6 p.m.

"Thanks for the visit, Marc. I didn't think I'd see you today. What's happening with the case?"

Craig bit on a grape and handed John the rest, scanning the side-room calmly. "It's nice here, isn't it? Is there much noise at night?"

John arched an eyebrow and stared at his friend. Something was up. He knew Craig wasn't going to tell him so he hazarded a guess.

"You're up to something but you don't want to tell me what, so I'm going to guess and if I get it right you owe me a beer."

Craig waved him on, confident that he would never get it.

"You asked Katy out."

Craig smiled. He'd been tempted certainly, but it hadn't felt right while John was in I.C.U.

"Nope. Not even close."

John pushed his luck.

"Aren't you going to, then? Natalie said you had coffee with her the other day."

Craig laughed. "My God! The three quickest means of communication: telephone, telegraph and tell Natalie." He paused for a moment, feigning disinterest, until curiosity drove him on.

"What did she say?"

John smiled innocently. "Who, Natalie?"

"Stop messing about. You know who I mean."

281

"Oh, you mean what did Katy say about you?" John considered dragging the conversation out just to torment Craig, but he couldn't be bothered. "Apparently she thinks the sun shines out of your ass. No accounting for taste I suppose."

Craig gave an award-winning show of cool. "Really? Or are you just winding me up to see how I react?"

John laughed then winced as his stitches tugged. "OK, you got me. She said she thinks you're nice. But nice is pretty good. The fact that Katy commented at all means something; she's an elegant girl. Anyway, if you weren't thinking about her, then you're up to something to do with the case."

"Perhaps."

"Are you going to tell me?"

"No."

"Because I'm ill, because it's boring, or because you think I might disapprove?"

"One of those, definitely."

John thudded back against his pillow in frustration. Craig drove him mad when he played things close to his chest and he'd done it since they were kids. He'd have made a great spy. Craig broke off another handful of grapes then glanced at his watch and stood up.

"Anything you'd like brought in tomorrow?"

"No."

"Are you going to sulk now?"

"Yes."

Craig smiled down at his friend, glad to see him but knowing that he'd visited more for his own benefit than John's.

"I'll see you tomorrow then."

John lifted the remote control and clicked on the TV, not looking at Craig. "Fine. Bye."

Craig smiled again. When he told John tomorrow what he'd been keeping from him, he would kick himself for being a berk. He only hoped that he'd get the chance to see him try.

***

The C.C.U. 8 p.m..

The squad-room was in darkness except for the light shining through Craig's half-glass office door. He sat flicking through some papers, knowing that if Jenna Graham was watching from the street below, she would see the light coming from his window and know that he was inside. He wanted to stand beside it, looking out over the late evening river, to watch its rise and fall and rainbow of midnight blues. But he had his orders and Liam had stood so close when he'd boomed them out that his ears were still ringing from the sound.

"On. No. Account. Are. You. To. Stand. By. That. Window. Understand? You can stare at the Lagan and think deep Italian thoughts some other time."

Craig smiled as he remembered Liam's set jaw and Annette's solemn nod in the background. They were right of course. His silhouette at the window would give any half-decent sniper the perfect shot. There was no point telling them he was sure that Jenna Graham would miss because she wasn't trained, or that she wouldn't try because she'd developed a taste for death to be up close and personal now. He was sure, but there was no point trying to persuade Liam once he'd got his dander up. So instead he sat obediently at his desk and did paperwork, long enough for any street watcher to be certain that he was there.

Finally he turned over the last page in his pile and gave a satisfied sigh. Nicky would be pleased. He'd cleared two months' worth of court reports in two hours. He glanced at the clock. Eight-thirty; time to move. Liam and Annette would be in position by now, parking several streets away then slipping back through the darkness into the C.C.U.'s car-park ten floors below, to take up cramped residence on his Audi's back seat. He imagined Liam hogging the long back seat of his old car and Annette swearing quietly, hunched in the foot-well on the floor.

Liam's swearing would be twice as loud as hers, with half the cause. The charade had been necessary to convince a watching Jenna Graham that he would be home alone tonight.

Craig strode to his office door and flicked off the fluorescent light, walking out onto the dark open-plan floor. He could just make out the shape of his protection office sitting in the darkness, his bulky arms folded, stretching his suit's fabric to the limits of its tensile strength.

"OK, Ian?"

Ian Sinclair unfolded his arms, revealing a muscular torso beneath his snow-white shirt. Craig had met Sinclair on a case in 2012, when he'd been guarding an errant Stormont Minister. He'd been impressed with him. Sinclair had seen a lot of the world, and a lot of war zones during his time in the army and N.A.T.O., but Craig had never got the feeling that he would rush to pull a trigger if a punch would do the trick instead. Sinclair had been stunned that Craig had remembered him from a case more than a year before, but pleased when he'd requested him for protection duty. He'd been less pleased by what Craig had asked of him earlier that afternoon.

When Craig had beckoned him into his office from his guard post outside the floor's double-doors, Sinclair had been surprised to find Liam and Annette there. He recalled the conversation.

"All right, Officer Sinclair?"

"All right, Chief Inspector. Inspector."

Liam could see Sinclair's brain working overtime, knowing that they were hatching some plan but with no idea what it was. When Craig told him what it was, Sinclair had set his jaw and shaken his head.

"Absolutely not, sir."

"Hear me out."

Craig had waved him to a seat and Annette had poured him a cup of coffee as Craig talked on.

"We need to draw our perp out before she kills any more

innocent people."

Sinclair raised an eyebrow sceptically. "Is that likely? Weren't you saying just yesterday that she'd completed her list?"

Craig knew that he'd been caught out. He smiled.

"Fair enough. The public isn't at risk now, but she definitely has one last name on her list. Me. If you agree to step down as I'm asking, I believe that we can draw her out."

Sinclair had set his jaw even harder. "All the more reason that I won't do as you ask. Sorry to be blunt but if I step down this evening and she takes a shot at you, you'll be dead and my career will go up in smoke."

Liam tapped on his jacket indicating his gun. "Here, are you saying that I can't protect him?"

Before Sinclair could answer yes or no Annette shoved Liam hard. "You're not the only police officer in this room, Liam Cullen. So stop making this about your ego."

Craig said nothing, just watched Ian Sinclair's face as he considered the options. After a moment Craig spoke again, more quietly.

"OK. If the perp sees you it won't stop her trying to get to me, she saw Marlene and she still went for John. So how about you come in the car with me to my place, to let her see you. Then I'm proposing that you let her see me being left alone."

Sinclair lurched forward in his chair, ready to object. Craig raised a hand to still him.

"Hear me out. I want her to enter my flat, for all sorts of reasons. One, because once she's broken into my apartment it becomes unambiguous that she's broken the law; she can't just say that she was passing by. And two, because it's only by her raising her gun that we can say it was attempted murder."

Annette interrupted. "But can't we just get her on breaking and entering and possession of a firearm once she's in your place? That should be enough."

"Enough for what? Burglary? She'd get a rap on the knuckles for a first offence if she has a licence for the gun. "

"But we can match the bullet with the one from Dr Winter."

"If it's the same weapon. And before you say we have prints from Adrian Bell's scene, we don't know for sure that they'll match hers, and it's still circumstantial. Graham could have handled Bell's gun another time, when he was showing it to her for instance. A clever barrister would wriggle her free within days then we'd be right back to square one." Craig shook his head. "No. I want her caught red-handed. It's our only guarantee of putting her away for good."

Sinclair's gawped at Craig. "You really want me to let her try to kill you?"

Craig nodded. "Yes. At the moment all we have is a theoretical case with holes in it like a sieve. We'll close them given time, but that time could see her getting out on bail and free to skip the country. I can't allow that."

"Even though she shot Dr Winter and he can I.D. her."

Craig sighed. "We know that but proving it in court is completely different. All we have is a sketch produced by a man who'd just spent two days in I.C.U. It would be ripped to shreds. That leaves us with theory and conjecture. I need hard proof and this is the only way to get it, as far as I can see. If any of you can think of another I'd be happy to hear it. I could do without getting shot in the back."

"Or the head, boss."

Annette rolled her eyes. "Thanks Liam, none of us had thought of that."

Liam set his jaw determinedly. "Well, if she shoots him in the head it'll be night-night Craig, and you can explain it to his family, not me."

Craig stilled the argument and turned back to Sinclair.

"Graham's been clear about hunting me and I'm pretty sure she's been stalking me for days. She's going to take a shot at me sometime and I'd rather that it was on my terms and in a way we can use it. This is the best idea I can come up with. Will you help?"

Sinclair puffed up his cheeks then blew out the air, thinking. After a moment he nodded. What else could he do but go along with it? The protection team's boss was a Chief Inspector and Craig outranked him. If Craig wanted to set a trap using himself as bait the only person who could counter it was the Chief Constable, and he didn't fancy calling him at home on a Sunday night to intervene.

Craig read his mind. "The C.C. already knows. I ran it past him an hour ago." He tapped a file on the table. "Here's your written cover for what I'm asking you to do." He scanned Annette and Liam's faces. "Yours too. If this goes belly-up I'm not having anyone but me taking the blame."

"And you'll be dead, so they can't sack you."

Annette glared at Liam, but Craig just laughed. Liam's tendency to call a spade a JCB was oddly reassuring at times.

Craig nodded. "As Liam said, I'll be dead." He straightened up. "OK. Shall we do this then?"

That had been three hours earlier and now Craig was standing beside Ian Sinclair in the darkened squad-room saying the same words.

"Right. Shall we do this then?"

Sinclair rose to his feet and nodded and the two men walked in silence to the lift. Craig pressed the button for the car-park, where Liam and Annette were waiting uncomfortably and got ready to play the next level in the game.

***

Katy Stevens wandered into the living room of her apartment towelling her blonde hair dry. She poured herself a glass of wine and walked out onto the balcony, staring at the river. Marc Craig's call an hour before had surprised her, not least by its intensity. He'd sounded like a desperate man.

They'd had a nice chat that day at the hospital, but it had mostly been about John and Natalie, and family things; there'd been no hint of romance in Craig's approach. She chided herself for being selfish; why should there have been? It had been nine o'clock in the morning and his best friend was lying in intensive care. Except that the lack of romance explained her shock when he'd called her that afternoon suggesting that they meet tomorrow evening for a drink. Drinks weren't like coffee. Coffee said day-time, cheerful chats in bright cafés, surrounded by mums and their kids or perhaps, at a push, business men out of their offices on a break. But drinks…

She stared into her glass, eying the ruby liquid whose colour alone suggested warm words and romance. Drinks were different. Drinks said softly-lit bars with long leather seats where people sat side by side. Sweet and tart tastes, meshing on tongues and loosening them, to confide childhood memories and secrets that rarely reached the light of day. Drinks were sipped in evenings that turned inevitably into nights. Nights that suggested places to go on to when the wine bar had closed, with all the new experiences that might bring. Slow, shy dancing and long soft kisses were only two.

Katy blushed warmly at her thoughts and glanced around her empty living room as if someone else might see. No-one did, so she slipped back into her fantasy of what Craig's invitation might mean and let her excitement bury her niggling concern about the urgency in his voice.

***

Jenna Graham watched Craig drive down Pilot Street with his burly companion sitting alongside, scanning their dark surroundings the way his job description outlined. She could make out the man's eyes from her vantage point and their expression was just what she expected from a guard-dog: wariness and suspicion. She smiled to herself in the darkness, curling up her beautiful lips; they'd gone from thin in a man to full in a woman, eagerly enhanced now by gloss and paint.

Strange how perception and proportion altered so many things, but perception hadn't altered her view of right and wrong. As an adult woman or a teenage boy, she'd always known who had to pay for her mother's death.

She watched the car's tail-lights fade as it turned onto Corporation Street then she strolled slowly to her sporty saloon. The guard-dog should be no problem; after all, the female version hadn't stopped her getting to the pathologist. She shuddered. What sort of doctor preferred dead people to live? She'd almost helped John Winter join them, but not quite. This time she wouldn't miss, although getting past a Neanderthal outside Craig's apartment might be a stretch.

Jenna shrugged in the darkness. She'd got to five people in a way that had almost been the perfect crime, this should be easy. Anger flooded through her; it would have been the perfect crime if Craig and his cronies hadn't interfered. Suicides, notes and nothing but a decorative key to give a clue. No-one should ever have worked it out. But Craig had and now he had to be dealt with before she could leave. She patted the new airline ticket in her pocket and glanced at the dashboard clock. Almost nine p.m., plenty of time to finish off Craig and catch the early flight to Heathrow, then on to the Far East where her new life could really begin.

Craig fixed his eyes straight ahead as he drove through every shortcut he knew until he finally reached the apartment complex he called home. Jenna Graham would be at least ten minutes behind them. He'd seen her moving through the shadows beside St Joseph's church as he'd driven down Pilot Street. It would take her two minutes to reach her car and ten more gained by his knowledge of Belfast's streets.

Craig pulled sharply into a free parking slot and Sinclair jumped out the passenger door, blocking sight of Liam and Annette's exit from the street. They slipped into the shadows while Craig and Sinclair strode openly towards the apartment block's front door. As Craig made a show of seating Sinclair inside the street-level entrance, Annette and Liam took the stairs silently to Craig's fourth floor flat.

Craig loitered, talking with Sinclair until a pair of approaching dipped headlights said that the game was about to commence. Craig spoke as loudly as he could without it sounding like a shout.

"Stay here, please. There's no entrance to the apartments other than through this door, so you'll see everyone who comes in."

Sinclair nodded and took his seat facing the car-park, folding his arms and scouring the darkened space with vigilant eyes. As Craig turned towards the stairs Jenna watched him go, formulating her plan. What Craig had said was right; there was no entrance except past the guard. Clever. She corrected herself instantly, clever in one way but stupid in another. If she could get past the Neanderthal then she was home free, with only a flimsy apartment door between her and her prey.

Jenna scrutinised the man sitting by the entrance; he just looked like the usual bulky grunt. Good with a gun but without much between his ears. If she'd known Ian Sinclair's background her blood would have run cold. She scanned the area around his chair. There was no paper by his feet and no sign of a photograph anywhere. If they'd known what she looked like then they would have given him an image to match. Craig wasn't so clever after all. The guard had no way to prove she wasn't a resident.

Jenna shook her head immediately at the idea. No, she couldn't be a resident or she would have had a front door key. Damn! Why hadn't she thought ahead? She could easily have made one. She thought for a moment longer then tugged the front of her jumper down, revealing an inch of her hard-won cleavage. She'd pretend to be a visitor to someone in the block. The thought of posing as Craig's girlfriend made her smile then she dismissed it as a trick too far. The guard would have been told if Craig was expecting visitors. She got out of the car then turned to lift her handbag from the passenger seat, deliberately leaning in to display her bottom, certain that the testosterone-ridden guard wouldn't have missed the view.

She was right. As Jenna locked the car and strolled towards the apartment block she saw the smile in Ian Sinclair's eyes, just not where it was coming from. She slipped her hand inside her bag, gripping her gun's handle just in case, but there was no need to fire a shot. The guard stood to open the door for her as she approached.

Ian Sinclair ran his eyes over the redhead as she walked towards him, pretending to find her attractive just as he'd been briefed to do, but he was shocked by his body's genuine response. Craig had shown him the images before they'd left the squad so that he would recognise her, but the sketch didn't do her justice. The woman walking towards him was stunning and he'd defy any man he knew to say anything else.

Her legs were long and shapely, encased in tight black jeans, and her slim waist lay beneath a pair of high, full breasts. But it was her face that really made him gasp. It was perfect, with a pair of wide cheekbones that framed eyes so blue that he'd have thought they were lenses, if he hadn't seen the same eyes in the photo of James Mulhearn from 2004. Long fire-red hair fell heavily to her shoulders, past soft lips that promised everything but gave nothing away.

Sinclair noted her slim hand resting inside her bag, but he was confident that he could beat her in any draw. He spoke first.

"Good evening, Madam. I'm sorry to ask, but could you tell me your name and which flat you're visiting please?"

Jenna smiled, watching his gaze wash over her body and confident that he didn't know who she was. Her voice surprised him, although it probably shouldn't have done. He'd expected some incongruity, a rougher voice than her body would suggest, but he was wrong. Her voice was low but indisputably female.

"I'm visiting my boyfriend in apartment forty-five. My

name's Jane Garston."

Sinclair smiled inwardly. She'd kept the same initials and chosen a flat as far away from Craig's as she could, on the other side of the block. He nodded.

"Thank you. I'm sorry I had to ask. Bit of a security issue."

Jenna feigned concern then turned to walk towards the lift. She was halted again by Sinclair's voice.

"Sorry, Miss. The lift's out. You'll need to walk."

Jenna shrugged and turned towards the stairs. It would only defer Craig's fate for a moment. Ian Sinclair watched her ascend and heard her heels move onto the second floor then he slipped out his phone and quietly made the call.

**

Liam had been moaning for a solid five minutes, complaining at having to squash his six-feet-six frame into the space beneath Craig's breakfast bar. Annette hissed at him from her position behind the settee.

"Shut up, Liam. She'll be here soon and she's not deaf!"

Liam made a face. "It's all right for a pygmy like you, but I'm a man. I'm breaking my neck here."

Craig broke his silence to hiss. "If you don't shut up I'll break it for you. Annette's right. Be quiet."

Liam made another face then stuck out his tongue at Annette. Craig sighed, knowing exactly what he was doing even though he couldn't see. He reached across to the coffee table and lifted his cup, cursing the body armour beneath his sweatshirt for its bulk. It was hard to get comfortable wearing thirty pounds of body armour and a bloody great gun strapped to your hip. Their grumbles were interrupted by a single beep of Craig's phone and Sinclair's name flashing up. She was on her way.

Craig signalled to Liam and Annette then dimmed the lamp beside him. The only thing that Jenna Graham would see when she entered the apartment was his silhouette against the TV's flickering glow. The poor light would conceal Liam and Annette's presence but give Graham enough visibility to take her shot.

Annette had objected vociferously to the plan.

"Why can't you just sit in the dark? She'd have to find you and we'd grab her before she had time to shoot."

"And what would that give us, if you couldn't see her raise the gun? Breaking and entering and possession of a weapon. We couldn't prove that she'd intended anything but burglary. No. I want her for the full whack."

"Whack being the operative word, sir."

She'd looked at Liam for support but he'd agreed with Craig's suggestion.

"Aye… aye, you're right. OK, boss. The full Monty it is then, but you'd better hope that she's a crappy shot."

Annette snorted. "You'd better hope she has a sense of humour if you're doing the full Monty."

So the plan had been hatched. Craig would give Jenna Graham sufficient target to aim her gun at, and Annette and Liam would stop her firing. That was the plan anyway.

Craig held his breath as Graham's high-heeled footsteps halted outside his apartment door. He tensed as the lock was manipulated, calculating that it would take Graham around twenty seconds to break through. It was only a Yale and they were easy to crack. Craig's hand moved slowly to his Glock and he slipped it onto his knee, ready to shoot. What they'd all reckoned without was a crowd of drunken students in the Stranmillis streets outside.

Just as Craig's front door slipped open, a series of loud cracks erupted in the street below, followed by the sound of glass shattering and a girl's high-pitched scream. It was all the distraction that Jenna Graham needed. She burst into the open-plan living room and took in the scene in a glance, pointing her gun straight at Craig's head. Craig moved just as she took the shot and the bullet caught him square on the right upper arm, knocking his gun out of his hand and onto the floor.

Graham raced across the room towards him, passing the breakfast bar just as Liam stumbled numb-legged from his hiding place. Cramp slowed him down just long enough for Graham to turn and take aim at Liam's chest, pumping two shots into him so fast that he had no time to catch his breath. Liam was thrown back against the breakfast bar and slid unconscious to the floor, as Graham considered whether to finish him off with a head shot or kill the man she'd come to kill. In the time it took her to turn back to Craig, Annette was on her feet and standing between Graham and her prey.

"Armed police. Drop the gun or I'll shoot."

Jenna Graham had no decision to make. Every struggle she'd had since she'd been an orphaned teenage boy had been leading to this moment. Her revenge for her mother's suicide, when she'd finally given up struggling against the people who'd refused to help. Her fight against the male body that she'd been born with, to become the woman she'd known she'd been all her life. And now this woman, who'd probably taken her female body for granted since she'd been born; this woman was standing between her and the thing she wanted, needed to do. No-one did that to her now. No-one.

In the moment it took Jenna Graham to make her choice Annette McElroy was making one of her own. She watched the fire grow in Graham's eyes and her heart sank at what she knew she had to do. Time seemed to lengthen as she watched Graham turn a fraction towards Craig and fix her gun on him, just as Craig stretched a blood-stained left hand towards his own. It was too far for him to reach in time and Annette knew exactly where Graham's gun was aimed. She was going for a head-shot so that Craig would never hunt anyone again.

Annette sent up a prayer and eased her finger slowly against the trigger of her Glock, knowing that she had no choice except shoot to kill. Chest or arm couldn't guarantee that Graham was stopped in time; she was a woman possessed. Behind the fire in Jenna Graham's eyes Annette had read insanity as clear as day.

As Graham fixed her sights on Craig, Annette did the same to her and fired. She couldn't see the bullet but she saw the effect it had. Graham's head jerked back at an angle and blood spewed red across her face as she was propelled sideways across the room. Her gun dropped from her hand just as the door flew open and Ian Sinclair rushed in, gun drawn, to see Jenna Graham lying wide-eyed upon the floor. Annette moved quickly to Liam, shouting orders at Sinclair.

"Check the boss and call an ambulance. They've both been shot."

As Sinclair made the call Craig moved quickly to Liam's side, feeling for his pulse just as Annette ripped open his shirt. The rhythmic throbbing at Liam's neck made Craig fall back against the settee in relief. Annette reached beneath Liam's bulletproof vest to his chest and her fingers returned unstained. She motioned Sinclair to help strip it off so that she could examine him. Two large contusions were forming on the right side of Liam's ribs but Graham's bullets hadn't managed to pierce the skin.

Sinclair pointed to Liam's ancient vest. It had two extra ballistic plates stitched inside it, front and back. Craig laughed as hard as he could, given the hole in his arm.

"Typical Liam. I bet he's had that thing since The Troubles."

Annette snorted. "I'm surprised it still fits him with the size of his paunch. That's probably why he was moaning so much earlier."

Liam groaned and Annette looked anxiously at him.

"Liam, Liam, are you OK?"

He turned his head slowly towards her.

"Keep still. You've been shot in the chest."

Liam croaked some words that they could barely make out then he turned his head so quickly that he fell back against the counter, blacking out again. Annette raised her eyes to heaven and went to examine Craig just as the paramedics arrived. She pointed to Liam.

"Check this one first please. He took two bullets to the chest. There are no penetrating injuries but he has bad bruising and he keeps blacking out. He might have a lung contusion. Superintendent Craig was shot in the right biceps." She peered expertly at Craig's arm. "It looks like a through and through."

Annette rushed across the room and scanned the area around Craig's settee for the bullet. She found it embedded in a wooden book-shelf mounted on the wall. She pulled out her phone to call the C.S.I.s and Craig beckoned her across.

"Get Des to lead on this, Annette. I want this scene airtight."

Craig winced as the paramedic tightened a bandage around his arm, to stem the blood still oozing from his wound. He watched as Annette's eyes were drawn irresistibly to the body on the floor and then filled with tears.

"Look at me, Annette."

Craig's voice was so firm that Annette instantly acquiesced. She hunkered down beside him and kept her eyes fixed on his. When he spoke his voice was even softer than usual and slowed by pain, but his words were clear.

"Thank you, Annette, you saved our lives."

"I…"

Craig silenced her objections with a glance. "If she'd killed me she'd have finished off Liam next. She was insane, Annette. Whatever logic she started her revenge spree with wasn't there tonight. Trust me, she was insane. I saw it in her eyes. No amount of reasoning would have stopped her."

Annette nodded, he was right. She'd seen the insanity as well, that was why she'd had to shoot. But it didn't stop her regretting that she'd had to take a life. Craig beckoned to the paramedic.

"Do you have anything sterile in the van?"

"Dressings and surgical drapes."

"OK, can you cover the body with a drape please, until the C.S.I.s get here."

"We need to take you and the other officer to St Mary's."

Craig nodded and motioned Ian Sinclair across. "Ian, could you stay until uniform and Dr Marsham arrive? I'd like Annette to come with us."

"No problem." Sinclair gazed around Craig's blood-stained living room then down at his carpet. He shook his head. "I tell you what, sir. This is going to need some paint job."

Chapter Twenty-One

Craig was out of the emergency department within four hours, with his forearm stitched and wrapped in a pressure bandage so discrete that even Annette was impressed. Once he had a jacket on, no-one would ever notice it. She imagined that was exactly what Craig was hoping for, particularly when he visited his folks. Even imagining Mirella's rant if she found out that her bambino had been shot was giving her a headache.

Liam hadn't been quite so fortunate. The bullets' impact against his chest wall had fractured several ribs and bruised him badly, so the hospital wanted to keep him in for forty-eight hours, to make sure there was no problem with his lungs. When Craig heard that Liam was going to the ward John was in he laughed. He stood beside the trolley and grinned down at his D.C.I.

"At least it'll make visiting easier."

"Aye, thanks very much, boss. Your sympathy's overwhelming. Thank God I won't have to share a room with the Doc. There are only so many American cop-shows a man can watch."

"Funny you should say that. John's offered..."

Liam's eyes widened then he saw Craig was kidding. He gave Craig an evil smile, intent on getting his own back.

"I bet he doesn't even know we're here. Did you tell him about using yourself as bait? No, you didn't. And I bet you didn't tell your family either."

Annette shook her head. "Liam..."

"I think Mirella has a right to know what her blue-eyed boy's been up to all weekend."

Craig squinted a warning and then gave Liam's chest a prod, watching as he almost leapt off the bed.

"That's assault!"

"It's nothing compared to what I'll do to you if my mum finds out."

"Police brutality, that's what it is."

A nurse ripped back the curtain to see what was causing the noise to be greeted by three innocent faces. When she left, Liam turned to Annette with a lascivious grin.

"Is that the kind of gear you used to wear? Very nice."

"Liam..."

Liam fell silent for a moment and Craig knew what he was thinking. He watched as Liam swallowed hard then gave Annette a serious look.

"You saved our lives, Annette. Thanks."

Annette blushed. Liam never used her name when he was speaking to her. Come to think of it, he never used it full stop; he called her girl and woman, or Cutty if he was in a good mood. He must think he was dying.

Craig echoed Liam's words, adding. "I'm putting you up for a commendation, Annette, as soon as the Ombudsman certifies it as a clean shoot."

Annette gave him an anxious look. "When will that be, sir?"

Craig smiled reassuringly. "Couple of days at most. Des is going to rush the forensics through. Don't worry. It's open and shut."

Something occurred to Liam.

"When did you learn to shoot like that? You couldn't hit a barn door six months ago!"

Annette blushed again. "It was after the Carragher case. Remember when you made that crack about me letting the gun slip out of my hand at the firing range? Well, I've been practicing every week since then. The instructor says I'm quite good now."

"You're more than quite good, Cutty. You're bloody marvellous. You got her right through the temple."

Annette winced and Craig could see the conversation heading somewhere that she didn't want it to go. He pulled the curtain back.

"OK, I think that's enough for tonight. We're all tired. Liam, is Danni coming up?"

"Aye. I suppose she'll give me grief when she does, but I'll just tune out the words."

"OK. I'm going to nip up and see John, then head on to a hotel. My place will be a crime scene for the rest of the night and explaining to my folks why I need a bed would be more grief than it's worth." He turned to Annette. "Are you OK to get home?"

She nodded. "I'm going to keep Liam company until Danni arrives, then one of the squad cars will drop me home."

Craig nodded. "I don't want to see you tomorrow morning. Take a rest. We'll chat in the afternoon when you get in."

Craig smiled, thinking of the risks that they'd taken that day and survived. It made him feel strangely alive and he could see that Liam felt the same. Someday he'd ask him if he'd felt that way during The Troubles when his life was constantly under threat, but not tonight and definitely not in front of Annette.

***

The C.C.U. Monday, 10 a.m.

It hardly seemed worth having a debrief with only three of them there. John and Liam were in hospital and Annette was at home, hopefully still asleep; that only left Jake, Davy and Nicky. Craig beckoned them over anyway and perched on a desk.

Nicky was the first to ask the obvious question. "Where are Liam and Annette?"

Craig stared at her, wondering how to tell her what had happened the night before, without being yelled at for a week. After a moment he shrugged – there was no way to avoid it. He took a deep breath and started. He'd got as far as "so Officer Sinclair agreed to go along with it and then…" when Nicky stopped him with a yell.

"He agreed? He agreed! What sort of protection officer is he, allowing you to put yourself in danger like that? He's reckless, stupid…."

Craig let her rant for a moment and when he saw the steam from her ears fading to a light vapour he restarted.

"It wasn't Sinclair's fault. I OK-ed it with the Chief Constable so he only had two choices: come along and keep an eye on us, or refuse to be involved. He decided to help and it's just as well that he did."

Nicky was un-deterred. "Well, I want to hear what Liam and Annette have to say about all this. With all due respect, sir, you think you're at the OK Corral. Where are they anyway?"

"I'll come to that later. Anyway, we went to my place…"

Five minutes later Craig had covered everything up to the shooting and Davy and Jake were leaning forward eagerly, excitement lighting up their faces.

"W…Weren't you scared? I'd have had a machine-gun pointing at the apartment door."

Craig laughed. "That might have defeated the purpose a bit, Davy."

Their eyes glowed as they imagined the daring escapade. Nicky tutted loudly, breaking the 'boy's own' moment.

"You've too much testosterone, all of you. When is Annette getting in? She'll agree with me, you won't see her getting excited about guns."

Craig winced at how she was going to react when she heard what had actually happened. He reached for his coffee and winced again as he picked it up. Nicky saw his pain immediately.

"You're hurt! What happened? Let me see."

Before Craig could stop her she'd pulled up his right shirt sleeve and was gawping at the large bandage wrapped round his upper arm.

"What sort of cut is that?"

Davy gave her the scientist's answer. "That's a pressure bandage to minimise bleeding. Usually it's for quite bad w… wounds. Like gunshots."

Craig threw him an 'Oh great, thanks' look and shrugged his sleeve down, trying to avoid the near-hysteria in Nicky's eyes.

"Shot! You were shot?" Her voice was approaching High C pitch and Craig knew where she was heading next. "Where's Liam? Where is he? Was he hurt? Did your cowboy tactics get him hurt?"

Craig rose to his feet and gazed down at her, placing his hands kindly on her shoulders. His action said 'calm down' and his smile said 'Liam's fine', not strictly true but Liam wasn't going to die so it would do for now. Before she could ask he told her he'd given Annette the morning off.

He sighed, knowing that there was nothing to do now but describe everything that had happened and then wait for Nicky to explode.

"OK, first of all, everyone is fine. Just a few broken bones and bruises." He scanned the group's faces. "Is everyone OK with that? No-one going to shout at me again?"

Nicky snorted and he carried on.

"Sinclair signalled that Graham was on her way up to the flat so we were expecting her. We were ready. I was out in the open as bait, sitting on the settee, supposedly watching TV in the dark."

"W…What was on?"

Craig squinted at Davy, not sure if he was joking. It was hard to tell sometimes, his delivery was so dry.

"Football. OK, then Graham entered my flat and we got shot in the following order. Me once in the right arm, Liam twice in the chest, then she turned back to me again."

"Liam was shot in the chest! You said it was only bruises and broken bones."

"Calm down, Nicky." Craig's tone of voice made it clear that she really should. "We were all wearing vests. Liam's just got a few broken ribs and bruises, like I said. He was kept in St Mary's but he'll probably be out tomorrow."

She shot him a murderous look but Craig ignored it and carried on. "Graham turned to shoot me again and that's when Annette took her out."

He paused, expecting a torrent of questions, but there was only silence as their mouths dropped open in shock. Jake was the first to recover.

"Annette? Our Annette? Who hates guns and can't shoot?"

Craig smiled. "She's been practicing behind everyone's back for months, and thank God she has." He turned conspiratorially towards the two young men and dropped his voice. "Straight through the right temple. Beautiful shot." He straightened up. "She saved both our lives and I'm putting her in for a commendation."

"I don't believe it! Annette?"

"W…What a shot. She must be really good."

"Annette's the only reason that Liam and I are still alive. Graham was aiming for my head and after she'd killed me I've no doubt she would have finished Liam off. He was flat out on the floor, unconscious."

Jake laughed. "I can just picture it. And his face when he found out that a girl had saved his life."

"He'll never get over the s…shame."

Craig let them banter for a moment, watching Nicky's disgust grow from the side of his eye. Finally she rose to her feet. "You're like children! Liam could have been killed. You could have been killed. You could all have been killed, for God's sake, and you're laughing about it! Unbelievable. When Annette comes in I'll…"

Craig's voice hardened. "You'll say nothing to her, Nicky. Get off your high horse. That's an order." He turned to the two men. "Annette feels dreadful about shooting someone, so I don't want any jokes or backslapping from you two either. Get it all out of the way now." He looked at Nicky. "As for you, Madam, moralise all you like in your own time but don't have a go at Annette. The operation was my idea, sanctioned by the Chief Con. It was the only way to get Jenna Graham before she killed one of us or skipped the country. Yes, it was risky, but it paid off; Graham's been stopped. Unfortunately she died in the process, but that was her choice not Annette's."

His voice softened slightly. "No-one likes guns, Nicky, except on TV, but we had to fight fire with fire and Graham had already almost killed John. Annette did what she had to do and I don't want you giving her any lectures about it. Not even a reproachful glance; she feels bad enough." He looked at each of them in turn. "Is that understood?"

Davy and Jake nodded and finally Nicky did too.

"OK, now thank God Annette had been practicing or this team would be two short today and you'd be looking for a new boss. As it is all we have are loose ends to tidy up and a case report to prepare, so get to it, everyone, please. When Annette arrives we'll go to The James for a late lunch."

With that Craig turned on his heel and re-entered his office, closing the door firmly behind him. Nicky gazed at the others and watched as they returned to their work then she slowly made her way back to her desk and sat there, deep in thought. Thirty minutes later she brewed some fresh coffee and knocked tentatively on Craig's door.

Craig smiled to himself at the timidity of her knock and said, "Come in." He stared out at the river, not seeing anything but Jenna Graham's face. He heard a tray being set down and the clink of mugs and a cafetière being laid out; an upscale from the usual percolator. Finally there was silence and he swung his chair round to see a sheepish looking Nicky standing there. The two cups and biscuits said that she wanted a chat and Craig smiled and waved her to a seat. Before he could say anything she started to speak.

"I'm sorry, sir… for earlier. I was… I was just shocked and…"

"Worried? About Liam?"

She read the kindness in Craig's eyes and unexpectedly crumpled in the chair, starting to sob. "You don't know what it's like for me. Knowing that any day one of you mightn't come back. It's bad enough knowing that you might be killed by some nutcase you meet on a case…" She swallowed her tears. "But then you go putting yourselves deliberately in harm's way."

She sobbed again and Craig stared at her for a moment, aghast. He'd never thought what it must have been like for her. Hearing the details of their cases was bad enough, but constantly waiting to lose someone she worked with every day… it had to be hard, yet he'd never even given it a thought. He was inured to the risks they took every day; it was part of their job. But not for Nicky and Davy; they had to stand by and watch.

Craig felt ashamed that he hadn't realised how she felt and then more ashamed that he hadn't noticed the effect. Finally her sobs subsided and he gave her a hanky to dry her eyes. He came around the desk and perched on the edge beside her.

"I'm sorry, Nicky. I didn't think."

She sniffed hard and glanced up at him. Craig wondered fleetingly whether she'd deliberately painted her eyelids black as a fashion statement or whether it was the effect of them being rubbed. It was probably better not to ask.

"No, you didn't think, sir. None of you do, not even Annette."

Craig swallowed, not wanting to ask the next question but knowing that he should.

"Is it too hard for you to keep working here, Nick?"

Nicky's eyes widened. "What? Are you sacking me?"

Craig gawped at her. "What? No! No, I'm not sacking you, but you said…"

"I said it's hard, not impossible. But if you want me to go…"

Craig started to laugh loudly. So loudly that Nicky leaned back in her chair in surprise, and loud enough that Davy and Jake heard the sound from outside the room and stopped what they were doing to listen for what came next. Craig was laughing at the ridiculousness of the conversation they were having and the situations they found themselves in, but more than that he was laughing in relief that no-one had been killed in the past week. He didn't believe in miracles but if he had done he would have said that came pretty close.

When he'd stopped laughing Craig gazed down at Nicky and shook his head.

"You worry about us and now I'm worried about you worrying about us. I don't want you to leave the squad, and it's OK for you to shout occasionally and blow off steam. God knows we all do it, so why not you? But…" His voice darkened. "These are the risks, Nicky. We don't take them deliberately and they're always calculated, but sometimes people get hurt and you need to get used to that. OK?"

She nodded and said a quiet "OK."

He walked briskly back to his chair and poured them both some coffee. "Good. Now what else have you got lurking on your long list of things for me to do?"

***

8.05 p.m.

Katy Stevens walked into the cocktail bar at The Merchant Hotel and gazed around her. She was late, only five minutes late, but still. She hated being late, it made her nervous, especially when she already was.

The warm bar was quiet, with only a few tables occupied by

groups of girls and older couples who were probably residents in the luxurious hotel. She'd only been there once before for a drink, with Natalie, after she'd been interrogated by Craig at High Street Station the year before. Now she was meeting him there for a drink. The irony didn't miss her and she laughed to herself. The pretty sound caught the attention of the young barman and he moved down the bar towards her to ask if she'd like a drink.

"No thank you, I'm meeting someone." She scanned the tables. "He doesn't seem to be here yet."

"Have you looked inside, Madam?" He gestured towards a glass door that she hadn't noticed. "We have another area in there."

He moved from behind the bar to show her but Katy smiled and nodded him away, then she took a deep breath and walked towards the door. As soon as she walked through it she saw Craig. He was sitting by the window gazing out at the street as if he was a million miles away. She'd expected him to be facing the doorway as policemen often did, to assess any threats as they entered the room. But he didn't seem interested in his surroundings; he was lost in thought.

As Katy approached Craig saw her and rose immediately, smiling. He took in her soft blonde hair and pale blue woollen dress in a glance, noting the way that it clung to every curve and echoed the colour of her eyes. She was beautiful, but more than that, she was delicate and pretty, like some Disney princess drawn for the screen. Craig smiled a second time, amused at himself for letting his romantic Italian side take hold. He gazed down at Katy, noticing how much smaller than him she was. Not tiny like Natalie but much smaller than Julia had been. He liked it; it made him feel protective of her somehow.

In the split second it took the thoughts to race through Craig's mind Katy was having her own. One of them was that his right arm looked bulky, in a way that she'd seen a million times before. She stared at it pointedly. "You've hurt yourself."

He nodded, unsurprised at her doctor's astuteness. His arm was the first thing John had noticed as well when he'd visited him that day, even through his suit.

Craig beckoned her to sit down and ordered them both a drink, then he recounted what had happened to his arm for the third time that day.

***

Forty minutes later Katy knew everything. She'd sipped her wine in silence as Craig recounted the happenings of the previous night and when he stopped she'd said nothing. He stared at her quizzically.

"Don't you want to ask anything, or tell me how stupid I've been?"

Julia had always understood the risks that his job entailed. She was in the police too, after all. But Katy was a civilian and a doctor; he'd expected a lecture about his health at least. Katy stared at him and after a long pause she smiled. It was a soft, shy smile, like a little girl peeping out from behind her mother's skirt. It surprised Craig a little. Katy was a professional woman, calm and good at her job, but when she smiled she looked like a mischievous little girl. It made Craig want to kiss her then and there but he knew that would probably earn him a slap, and after the night he'd had he could do without any more pain. He smiled back automatically, encouraging her to speak. Her words surprised him again.

"Were you being stupid, or were you just doing what you had to do to get a murderer off the street?"

He was taken aback at her logic. Instead of the rant he knew he would get from his mother when the story inevitably came out, Katy had answered in the quiet way that his father would. It pleased him.

"No, I wasn't being stupid. Graham was tailing me and we knew that. She'd already been instrumental in five deaths, possibly six if what we suspected about the PDF's was right, and she'd almost killed John. I could have let her hunt me for months and shoot me when I least expected it, but then God knows who else she might have killed along the way, so it had to be brought to a head."

Katy wanted to reach across and trace Craig's full lips with her finger. He read her mind and edged closer so that their knees almost touched. Almost. It sent a frisson a pleasure through him stronger than he'd felt in years. Katy kept talking in her soft, high voice.

"If the confrontation had to happen sometime then I presume you had to make sure it happened in a way that gave you conclusive evidence."

Craig leaned forward eagerly. "Yes. And by breaking into my place and pointing a weapon she'd left herself no wriggle room."

Katy smiled in amusement. "Was getting shot part of your plan as well?"

Craig laughed ruefully. "No, definitely not. Ideally Liam would have jumped out as she pulled the gun but she was too quick. She shot me then she shot Liam and turned back to kill me, so Annette shot her."

Katy shook her head. "Poor Annette, she must feel dreadful. I can't imagine what it must be like to kill another human being."

"Especially one who had already had such a troubled life."

They sat quietly for a moment then Craig ordered them another drink and changed tack. "That's enough about my job, tell me about you."

"What would you like to know?"

"Actually, everything. But first, I'd like to know if you'd like dinner somewhere after this drink?"

Katy smiled. "That would be lovely. Choose anywhere you like, then I can bore you with the story of my life."

***

Tuesday, 9 a.m.

The squad's double doors slid open and Craig sauntered across the floor. Nicky read his mood immediately and knew exactly what had caused it.

"Good evening, sir?"

"Very good, thanks."

She grinned and he grinned back, saying nothing more. As he entered his office he was stopped in his tracks by a voice booming across the room.

"Here, where are my flowers then? I thought there'd at least be a bouquet for a wounded hero."

Craig swung round to see Liam's long legs propped up on his desk and a grin spreading across his face.

"What are you doing here? You're not due back until next week."

"Ach sure, they discharged me yesterday. Said I was creating too much noise. Me? I ask you! I went home for tea and sympathy and Danni said I was getting in her way, so I thought I might as well be here."

Nicky snorted. "I'm sure Danni said no such thing. Or at least, not until you'd disrupted the place."

Liam nodded. "Aye well, she said that as well."

"And the fact that you might have had to change the baby's nappies if you'd stayed at home had nothing to do with you rushing back to work I bet."

Liam guffawed and scanned the floor looking for Annette. Craig read his mind.

"She's meeting with the Ombudsman this morning to get the shooting signed off. She should be in at ten."

He nodded Liam towards his office and he strode across the floor, winking at Nicky as he passed.

"Cup of coffee would be lovely."

She glanced at him sceptically. "Wouldn't it just. If you said that to Danni I'm not surprised she chased you." She gave a mock sigh. "Go on in and I'll bring it through."

Liam went to add something but Nicky said it first.

"With biscuits."

He took a seat at Craig's desk and they stared out the window without saying a word, both of them soaking in the bright spring morning. Nicky brought in the tray and left again and Craig started talking as he poured them both a mug.

"How's the chest?"

"Grand. How's the arm?"

"Fine."

Liam took a gulp of coffee and gave Craig a thoughtful look. "How's Annie Oakley?"

"Annette's fine, but upset about the death, so stow the nicknames for a few weeks, please. She's not proud that she had to shoot someone."

Liam gawped at him. "What? Would she rather Graham had killed both of us?"

Craig bit into a biscuit. "You know she wouldn't. She's just upset. She was a nurse, Liam. She's used to saving lives, not taking them."

Liam grabbed a custard cream. "Aye, all right. I suppose so." He grinned slowly. "Hell of a shot though. Right through the temple."

Craig nodded. "We should enter her for the annual shooting competition; she'd give the protection teams a run for their money. Except I don't think she ever wants to see another gun."

They lapsed into silence until Liam broke it again. "What else is happening?"

"Court reports mostly. John gets discharged today, so I'm nipping off early to take him home."

"Good stuff." He grinned at Craig knowingly. "But that's not what put that grin on your face this morning."

"What?"

"When you walked into the squad. You were grinning like a Cheshire Cat. Who's the woman?"

Craig blustered out a denial and Liam shook his head.

"Don't kid a kidder. There's a woman around somewhere." He lurched forward to say something, so quickly that he banged his bandaged chest against the desk and swore loudly from the pain. As he recovered he squeezed out the name that he'd been so eager to say.

"McNulty?"

Craig's eyes widened in surprise then he felt immediately guilty. He rarely thought about Julia nowadays and he certainly hadn't been thinking about her when he'd kissed Katy goodbye the night before. He shook his head firmly.

"Then what's her name? Because there's a woman here somewhere or my name's not Liam M. Cullen."

"What does the 'M' stand for?"

Liam blushed. "Don't change the subject. What's her name?"

Craig smiled and turned towards the river, determined to keep his private life private for a little while longer. Liam asked the question again in a dozen different ways but he still got no reply. Finally Craig changed the subject to Constable Delia Anderson and whether she would soon become the newest member of the team.

THE END

Fantastic Books
Great Authors

Meet our authors and discover our exciting range:

- Gripping Thrillers
- Cosy Mysteries
- Romantic Chick-Lit
- Fascinating Historicals
- Exciting Fantasy
- Young Adult and Children's Adventures

Visit us at:
www.crookedcatbooks.com

Join us on facebook:
www.facebook.com/crookedcatpublishing